ONLY THE STRONG

AN AMERICAN NOVEL

ONLY THE STRONG

AN AMERICAN NOVEL

Jabari Asim

BOLDEN

AN AGATE IMPRINT

CHICAGO

Library of Congress Cataloging-in-Publication Data

Only the strong / Jabari Asim.

Summary: "The lives of a reformed hit man, a crusading doctor, a genteel mobster, and a headstrong college student cross in a sweltering Midwestern city in 1970"-- Provided by publisher

ISBN 978-1-932841-94-7 (softcover) -- ISBN 1-932841-94-6 (softcover)

1. City and town life--Middle West--Fiction. 2. African Americans--Fiction. 3. Nineteen seventies--Fiction. 4. Middle West--Fiction. I. Title.

PS3601.S59O55 2015

2014040170

9 8 7 6 5 4 3 2 1

Bolden is an imprint of Agate Publishing. Agate books are available in bulk at discount prices. For more information, go to agatepublishing.com.

For my wife, Liana, in this and all things

Love is divine only and difficult always.
—Toni Morrison, *Paradise*

Let me in, let me in, let me in, let me ease on in.
—Otis Redding, "Open the Door"

LEG-BREAKER

G UTS TOLLIVER HADN'T KILLED A MAN in two years. The night Dr. King went down in Memphis, Guts had steered his sedan through streets aflame and undergone a change of heart. Not a complete conversion, to be sure. He still believed in an eye for an eye and, on occasion, had done his part to make the bargain equal. But he had taken to considering whether killing was always the first, best option.

Not that he had ever killed as many people as some folks in Gateway City had suggested. After more than a few highly public, much-talked-about brawls, his legend had spread. His many years as chief enforcer for Ananias Goode taught Guts that the idea of his fists was as compelling as his fists themselves. For those on the wrong side of his wrath, his thick knuckles were the least of their concerns. According to local legend, Guts had put men to death with everything from a hairpin to a sledgehammer. He was tall, massive, and quick. Big men couldn't out-brawl him and little men couldn't outrun him. But he regarded every opponent with equal respect, and it was that attentiveness—a curious mixture of humility and confidence—that kept him alive. By the time of King's death, Guts had become more of a persuader than a killer.

After the Dreamer was laid to rest, Guts went to his longtime employer and confessed to this shift in his thinking. Ananias Goode had come not only to trust Guts, but also to regard him with genuine affection. And, because his business experience had taught him that a trustworthy man was as valuable as at least five others, Goode maneuvered to keep Guts close. The big man's severance package was a taxi stand complete with 31 cabs, for which Goode served as majority investor and silent partner. In exchange, Guts agreed to handle difficult assignments when they arose.

Guts loved managing the taxi fleet—the give-and-take with the drivers, and even sometimes taking to the road himself, to roll down Delmar or Natural Bridge with the wind at his back and nothing on his mind except his pet obsessions: Pearl Jordan and banana pudding.

Before Pearl had become a regular visitor to his bed, Guts had settled for dreaming of her. Lately that had become unnecessary, when all he had to do was wrap his powerful arm around her petite, sleeping frame.

He was snuggled against her, a bear cuddling a bunny, when his phone rang. He grunted and tried to ignore it.

"Lorenzo."

Guts pulled his pillow over his head.

"Lorenzo. You gonna answer that?"

"Answer what?"

"You know you hear that. Now grab it."

Defeated, Guts removed the pillow and picked up the receiver. "Guts Tolliver, problem solver."

It was Sharps, the man who'd replaced him as Goode's driver and right-hand man. Guts had instinctively disliked him the moment they'd been introduced. Now Sharps was snickering over the phone. "'Problem solver?' That's your new handle? I guess 'leg-breaker' is hard to shake."

"Sharps, you better have a damn good reason for bothering me at home. How do you even have my number?"

"Boss man wants you. Meet us at the Frontier at eight."

"Did he say what it was about?"

Guts heard a click and silence. "That mother—"

Pearl swatted his ample rear. "Lorenzo. At least wait until sunrise before you start cursing."

By the time Guts had shaved his upper lip and showered, Pearl was busy in the kitchen. She was wearing a cream-colored apron with bright yellow daisies on it—and nothing else. Admiring her tight curves, Guts let out a long, low whistle.

"Don't get used to it," Pearl said without turning around.

"I could never get used to something so good. The thrill is new every day."

"Talk that stuff if you want to. You know what I'm talking about. I'm 31 years old and my clock is ticking."

"Baby, let's not start an argument so early in the morning."

"Have it your way. What do you want for breakfast?"

"Six eggs, six pieces of toast."

"I thought you were cutting down."

"That is cutting down."

"Let's make that three eggs and two pieces of toast."

"You're serious?"

"Serious as that heart attack you're trying to have."

Pearl required little coaxing to untie her apron and sit on Guts's lap. Between kisses, she lifted each tasty forkful of breakfast and held it to his waiting lips. "You're too good for me," he told her.

"I know," she said, smiling. "But you'll do."

Guts knew her efforts to rein in his appetite were absolutely correct. Still, he struggled to suppress a hunger pang or two, ignoring his disgruntled stomach's protests as he eased his Plymouth away from his home on Margaretta and steered onto Fair Avenue. He tried to avoid even looking in the direction of Fairgrounds Park, but he couldn't help himself as its green borders loomed to his left. He could almost hear the ducks calling his name.

Sighing, he turned into the park entrance, rolled to a stop at a curb, and got out. He leaned against the side of the car. *Just for a minute*, he thought to himself. He could barely see the edge of the pond. The ducks were out of sight, tucked away in the tall fronds skirting the stone bridge. It was quiet, despite the nearby traffic of

Natural Bridge Boulevard already building up to the predictable frenzy of rush hour. A few of the park regulars were going about their activities, and seeing them gave Guts a brief feeling of comfort. He could describe each without so much as glancing at them: The two gray-haired ladies who carefully tended the Abram Higgins Memorial Garden every morning. The quiet fisherwoman sitting still in her lawn chair, her fishing line nearly invisible as it stretched toward the water. An unsmiling man, clad in exercise clothes and cradling several tennis rackets under his arm, sternly herding his four children toward the courts. The man had read newspaper accounts of Arthur Ashe, a black man, trouncing the field at the US Open, and in the nearly two years since that historic triumph, he had pursued his dream of seeing his children duplicate Ashe's feat.

Guts closed his eyes for just a moment, imagining the ducks. Feeding them, quietly assuring them that he had enough for everyone, then sitting back and watching them eat was the closest thing to prayer that Guts had. He'd never been comfortable with the kind of praying he'd grown up knowing—too much desperate pleading in it for him. He never understood begging for things that, in the end, you had to take care of your damn self. His mother had been a fervent believer in the power of prayer. Once, when Guts was about 10, he was sitting at dinner with his parents, head bowed and hands obediently folded, when he peered through narrowed eyes to find his father winking at him.

Another park regular, Jerome "Crusher" Boudreau, spotted Guts and jogged over to him. He was wearing sweats and a towel rolled around his neck like a scarf. Boudreau had been a contender before a roundhouse to the throat nearly disabled him. Now he spoke in an amiable mumble and ran a TV repair shop. He had a reputation for skipping his bills and Guts was glad that Ananias Goode had never been one of Crusher's creditors. If so, it would have been up to Guts to collect. Although Guts had about 40 pounds on Crusher, the prospect of going up against him gave him pause.

Crusher, shadowboxing, tossed a few slow softies in Guts's direction. Guts made a big show of ducking and feinting.

"I see you still got it," Crusher said, smiling.

"I got something," Guts said, "but I'm not sure what it is."

"Ah, you haven't lost a step. How's everything?"

"I'm not complaining, Crush. Not that it would do any good."

Crusher mopped his brow with his towel. It wasn't blazing hot yet but he had already worked up a good sweat. "I hear that."

Guts watched as Crusher stretched his neck toward his left shoulder, then his right.

"Guts, I know you're strong, but not even you can toss breadcrumbs into the pond from this far away."

Guts laughed. "Not feeding the ducks this morning. If I get too close to the water, sit on a bench, watch the ducks, I won't feel like doing anything else. And I got places to be. So I'm just allowing myself a brief visit."

Crusher nodded. "We all got to do shit that we don't want to do. Got to squeeze the quiet moments in where we can."

"Damn, Crush, nobody told me you were a philosopher."

"I think I read that on a cereal box." Crusher continued to stretch. "I saw your boy the other day."

"My boy?"

"Yeah. Nifty."

Many unfortunate souls who'd crossed Guts had paid for it in blood and pain, but Nifty Carmichael was an exception. Guts had sentenced him to a lifetime of servitude in exchange for the privilege of walking the earth intact. Nifty was a fool and a crook, but he kept an ear to the ground. As long as his information was good, Guts let him keep breathing. Guts wasn't particularly concerned with Nifty. He knew where to find him when he wanted him. He feigned interest out of sheer courtesy. "Yeah, what was he up to?"

"Talking to Sharps."

"Sharps?"

Crusher grinned. "Got your attention, right? Saw them having coffee in Stormy Monday's. Looked like they were having a good ol' time. Figured you should know about it."

Guts tried to keep his contempt for Sharps under wraps, but apparently Crusher had sniffed it out. He wondered how many others had.

It was not quite eight a.m. when Guts pulled up beside Frontier Barbershop. Except for the Bona Fide gas station and Kirkwood Cleaners, all of the other businesses along that stretch of Vandeventer Avenue had yet to open. In minutes there would be a crap game going behind Wilma's Tavern and music blasting out of Pierre Records, something like "Baby I'm For Real" by the Originals or "ABC" by those kids from Gary. But right now it was as peaceful and empty as it ever got. A woman left the cleaners and strode purposefully to her car, her cleaning over her shoulder. Guts tipped his hat to her, then waved at the sign painter Reuben Jones, who was at the gas station getting two dollars' worth of regular for his Rambler wagon, his ladders strapped to its roof. Guts noticed that Sharps had left Goode's New Yorker unlocked. Sloppy.

Barbershops traditionally closed on Mondays, but Rudolph Fisher, the tall, pious proprietor, had opened just for Ananias Goode. According to word on the street, Goode had provided the initial down payment for Fisher two decades before, but Guts had never been able to confirm it. At any rate, Fisher had been Goode's personal barber since way back when. Guts waited while Sharps took his time letting him in.

"Finally," Sharps said. He had features to match his name, and his choice of clothing accented his slender angularity. His hat, hiding a full head of processed hair combed straight back, was—like his tie, suit, and alligator shoes—a dazzling shade of lemon yellow. His sunglasses, worn indoors and out, were dark green. Cologne wafted off of him with every movement. Guts marveled that Goode could ride in the New Yorker with Sharps without passing out.

"It's eight straight up," Guts said. "Now, you can step aside or I can walk over you. Make your choice because Mr. G. is waiting."

Sharps paused as long as he dared. He grinned, revealing teeth as pointed as the rest of him. He stepped aside with a dramatic bow.

Guts ignored him.

"My dear Mr. Tolliver," Goode said. "So glad you could join us." He was dressed in bankers' pinstripes as usual, and the gleam on his custom boots was bright. Goode, though bigger than most men, was not nearly as large as Guts, but his personality and confidence were expansive enough to fill any space. He removed his cigar from his mouth and held it out expectantly. Fisher rushed to remove it to a nearby ashtray.

Guts said good morning to Goode and asked Fisher how he was feeling this fine day.

"Praise the Lord," Fisher replied before draping a smock over Goode and fastening it behind his neck with an efficient flourish. Each day brought another customer announcing his abandonment of the close-cropped "quo vadis" haircut in favor of the long, bushy "natural," but Fisher was adapting and staying afloat. Goode, like Guts, kept his head shaved.

"This is a change," Guts said.

"How so?"

"Fish used to come to your house."

"Sharps talked me into it," Goode said. "Suggested a change of pace."

"The boss needs more sun," Sharps said. He pulled up a chair and straddled it backward. "It's healthy, plus he can keep an eye on things."

Guts stared at Sharps. When he was Goode's driver, he never would have sat with his back to the door. He wouldn't have sat at all.

"He's got people to keep an eye on things for him, and you're supposed to be one of them," Guts said. "Folks are crazy. No need to make them think they have an opportunity."

Sharps smirked. "Who'd be stupid enough to go after Ananias? You talk like he's Al Capone. He's a businessman. You're thinking about guns and gangsters when we're talking about stocks and bonds."

Guts turned and looked at Goode. Never, not once during their long association, had he ever called the boss man "Ananias." But Goode seemed to take no notice of Sharps's brazen informality.

Guts began slowly. "That may be so. Still, I'd think about changing things up. Maybe next time, say, come on a Wednesday, before the start of business hours."

Sharps chuckled. "That's a lot of thinking for a cab driver. What are you, one of them intellectuals?" The word sounded bad falling out of Sharps's mouth. "An egghead in dungarees, hard to imagine."

Guts suddenly felt underdressed. Dungarees and work boots had been his standard uniform for as long as he had worked for Goode. The pair's contrasting styles drew a lot of whispered comments, but no one had ever dared to say anything within his earshot. And Goode had never complained. For a split second Guts pictured himself draped in yards of lemon-yellow fabric.

"A lot of things must be hard for you to imagine."

"An egghead in work boots. What size you wear? Sheeit. Them some big-ass clodhoppers, son. Handy on a farm, maybe. But damn, you in the city."

"I got one of them stuck in a man's ass once."

Sharps looked liked he wanted to spit. But there was no place to do it. "Do tell."

"Yeah. He reminded me of you. A skinny bitch in a shiny suit."

"I got your bitch, fat man."

"Too bad. I don't swing that way."

Goode cleared his throat. By then Fisher had coated his generous jowls with a thick lather of shaving cream. Flashing his pearl-handled straight razor, he expertly drew the blade lightly along Goode's jawline.

"Gentlemen. Your repartee is beneath the dignity of our enterprise."

Sharps frowned. "What?"

"Shut the hell up," Goode said. "You too, Guts. Enough."

Both men immediately stopped talking.

"Sharps."

"Yeah, boss?"

"Go across the street and see if Stone Drugs is open. Grab me a racing form and a *Gateway Citizen*. Guts and me got business."

"But—"

"Go on, now. Run along."

Guts was sure that Sharps's eyes were welling behind his shades. Sharps stood, adjusted his tie, and left.

Guts crossed the room and locked the door. Fisher had seen Guts in action more than once but was still amazed that a man so huge could move with such unlikely speed and grace. Wisely, he kept his amazement to himself.

"You like Rip Crenshaw?" Goode asked.

Guts shrugged. "I'm more of a football guy, but you know that."

"Still, you know who he is."

Guts shrugged. "Yeah. Baseball. The home team can't do much unless he's in the game. And he's missed a few lately."

"That's right, he's on the injured list. I need you to keep him company for a while. Drive him around, show him some friendly places, keep him from hurting himself."

"Why does someone like him need babysitting?"

Fisher spun Goode around to face the large wall mirror. "You used to just go out and do what needed to be done, large or small," Goode said, admiring himself. "Now you ask questions. Why are you all of a sudden so curious?"

It's not me you should be wondering about, Guts thought. He was particularly proud of his ability to mind his own business. During much of the past decade, the boss had disappeared nearly every Wednesday afternoon. After they parked in front of Guts's car, Goode would politely dismiss him, move to the front seat, and drive away. Guts used the spare time to track down debtors reluctant to pay their bills. Never was he tempted to follow Goode, figuring every man had a right to keep some secrets to himself. He had been the soul of discretion. Now his motives were being questioned.

"Not curious. Careful," he said evenly. "The streets are changing. No disrespect, but they're changing faster than you and I are used to moving. I just don't want us to be caught by surprise."

"Hmm. Well, you're probably right. When I was a young man I barged right into situations and then had to fight my way out. Probably could have saved myself some scuffling if I'd gone in with my eyes open."

Guts waited.

"Okay," Goode said, finally. "As you know, Virgil Washburn and I are business associates."

Guts wondered where this was going but his face betrayed nothing. He'd heard that Washburn, owner of the home team, had lately grown tired of his star player.

"Crenshaw's becoming a headache," Goode continued, "a bad attitude with a big salary. What's worse, he's getting into trouble off the field. Picking fights, breaking the law, sticking his dick where it don't belong. But the team needs to keep Crenshaw in fighting shape or else they got no shot at the World Series. They want to get their money's worth before they trade him. Everyone would be better off if he kept his partying on the North Side."

"That's all?"

"That's all."

Guts nodded. "All right. Got his particulars?"

"He's got yours. He'll call you later."

Guts waited until Sharps returned. He smelled him before he saw him. A cloud of perfume whisked under the front door, followed by Sharps's appearance. Guts studied him through the glass before unlocking the door.

Twenty minutes later he was heading down Vandeventer, the street now fully awake. Outside the Tom-Boy grocery, two men loaded the Volkswagen delivery van. Through the open door of the laundromat on Labadie Avenue, a slender young woman juggled dimes as she fed them into the slot of a spinning dryer. School kids hung around McCoy's confectionery, counting down the days until summer and freedom. At Sullivan Avenue, next to the shine parlor where Guts, according to legend, once used a shoelace to silence a loudmouth, the crossing guard shepherded stragglers on their way to Farragut Elementary. Guts could have hung a straight left at Natural Bridge, but he couldn't resist cruising through the park, barely accelerating as he looked around. His morning regulars were all gone except for the fisherwoman, still and regal in her metal lawn chair, her hat pulled down low over her eyes. Across the street from the park, Sam the barbecue man was already manning his grills on the lot of the burned-out SuperMart.

Once inside Gateway Cab, Guts passed through the main room and into the inner office, which he shared with two desks, a quartet of file cabinets, and Trina Ames, Gateway's receptionist and dispatcher. Trina was as beautiful and hardworking as she was sweet, and the drivers often pretended to misunderstand just to hear her sugary voice repeat an address over the radio. As far as Guts was concerned, the most appealing thing about her was her knack for staying out of other people's business.

Guts was not much for long phone conversations. Face to face, he could chew the fat with the best of them, even if he spent every exchange casually taking in everything going on all around him, ever alert to dangers. But the phone? Disembodied voices disturbed him in a way he couldn't quite nail down. So even though he was happy to hear from Pearl—how her day was going, her lunch plans, how she couldn't wait to spoon more fresh-baked banana pudding into his waiting mouth—he was nonetheless relieved later in the day to put down the receiver and step into the main room, where the men of the cabstand had congregated for lunch.

Of the three men present, only one had an actual connection to the stand. Cherry, sporting an Afro less out of style considerations than just natural hirsute exuberance, was the in-house mechanic. Good-natured, sleepy-eyed, and skillful, he was adept at hanging around and shooting the breeze, ears attuned to the bell that rang when a cab pulled onto the lot.

Shadrach, long retired, had made the cabstand his second home. Wearing his customary straw fedora with the gold band, he sat with Cherry at one of the three card tables that served as workplace furniture for the Gateway fleet. The two men attacked a platter of ribs while Oliver paced nearby and read from the paper. Oliver worked at the bowling alley across the street. Nervous, bespectacled, of indeterminate age, he took so many "coffee breaks" that it remained a mystery how he managed to keep himself employed.

Guts crossed the threshold and took everything in with a quick, sweeping glance. The plate-glass window gleamed adjacent to the front door, through which the lot's two gas pumps beckoned.

Across the room, a doorway led to the service bay where cabs could be hoisted and repaired. Behind Cherry and Shadrach another door led to a restroom flanked by a water fountain and an ancient soda machine. On the wall above the fountain was a framed *Ebony* cover photo of Nichelle Nichols. Clad in her skintight *Star Trek* uniform, the curvy communications officer of the starship Enterprise appeared to be climbing from a hatch as she stared into the camera, bright eyes ablaze. Those eyes alone would have possessed the power to command every man's gaze if not for the presence of her fabulous right thigh, deliciously exposed as she mounted a rung. Over her left shoulder a headline announced, "Scientists Discover Secret of Skin Color."

Guts sat where he could keep his eyes on the door. The chair creaked and groaned under his bulk.

"'Urban renewal,'" Oliver was saying. "We know what that is. Nigger removal. See, the reason they haven't built up Franklin Square is because they want to take it back. One day the North Side will be just as white as it was before all you burrheads came up from Dixie."

Listening, Guts remembered the buzz of commerce that once swirled around Franklin Square. The convergence of three streets formed a plaza that attracted strollers, people watchers, and shoppers eager to spend their wages at the mom-and-pop grocery, the record shop, the soul-food joint, and the clothing boutiques. During the hot, tense summers of recent years, the plaza had served as a rallying place for the politically awakened residents of North Gateway. Poets recited odes to the people, drummers pounded congas, self-appointed revolutionaries handed out pamphlets calling for armed rebellion, and would-be orators rang the rooftops with phrases cribbed from Malcolm X and H. Rap Brown.

The buildings all burned in the furious hours following King's death in Memphis. Only a solitary wall remained standing amid the rubble. The men of the Black Swan Sign Shop responded with a mural that had long been in the works, a Wall of Respect saluting heroic strugglers from the past and present. Occasionally, Guts rolled to a stop across from the Wall and admired the stern faces of W.E.B. Du Bois, Sojourner Truth, Elijah Muhammad, and others.

It wasn't much different closer to Guts's home. The SuperMart was still gone. One side of Vandeventer from Labadie to Greer had retained its bombed-out look, even as folks on the other side did their laundry and bought small items from a corner store. From Taylor to Newstead, Easton Boulevard looked like a mouth with many teeth missing. A notary public, a greasy spoon, a drugstore— here and there businesses tottered in relative solitude, miraculous survivors of the fires.

"You don't know that," Shadrach said. "That ain't necessarily the future. We might have a black man in charge. Look at Cleveland. Look at Gary. If it can happen in those cities, it could happen here."

"Naw," Cherry said. "Downtown's what they want. How long they been serving us at that Woolworth's? See how much longer it sticks around, now that colored folks can sit at the counter."

"All my life I wanted to sit at that counter," Shadrach said. "I figured white folks' hotcakes just had to be better. Turns out they didn't taste no different."

Oliver didn't seem to hear. "Mill Creek Valley. Meacham Park. Used to be just us in those neighborhoods. Now you might find us cutting grass or scrubbing toilets, but that's it. When they want to move the black man, they just move him."

"Where'd all them revolutionaries go?" Cherry asked. "What happened to that liberatin' nigger? They shoulda told us about this."

Guts knew the answer to that one. "You talking about Gabe Patterson? He got married," he said.

Shadrach sighed and nodded. "It happens to the best of us."

"Better than going to jail," Guts said. "That's where Patterson seemed to be heading before Rose Reynolds calmed him down."

"Hmm, I'm not sure there's a difference," Shadrach said.

"The Warriors of Freedom they called themselves," Oliver said. "It was a good thing they didn't amount to much. This country has no tolerance for revolutionaries. Look what they did to the Chicago Seven."

Cherry frowned. "Them singing boys? What did they go and do to them?"

Oliver shook his head. "That's the Jackson Five, fool."

"I knew that," Cherry said. "I was just testing y'all."

"Well, the revolutionaries, they had their day in the sun," Oliver continued. "We got us our own congressman now and I bet he'll do a heap more than a bunch of beret-wearing snot-noses running around talking about 'off the pigs.' The streets are not where things get done. The real action is in boardrooms and legislatures. You can't be marching against the Man, that's out. Naw, you got to sit down with him, like the siddity Negroes do."

"Oliver, you ain't never been in nobody's boardroom," Shadrach said, "except maybe to empty the trash. Bet you never marched in the streets neither. Hell, I can't even tell if you ever set foot in that bowling alley that cuts you a check every two weeks."

"You don't have to listen to me," Oliver said. "Ask Guts. He knows what I'm talking about. He rubs elbows with the bigwigs. Take a look at the photo of the week." He waved his copy of the *Gateway Citizen* in Shadrach's direction.

Shadrach grabbed it and began to read. "'Here's local businessman Ananias Goode at a meeting of the board of trustees of Harry Truman Boys Club. To his left is Dr. Artinces Noel, the North Side's leading pediatrician. To his right is Virgil Washburn, principal owner of the home team.'"

Oliver crossed his arms in triumph. "See what I mean? From the looks of things, Mr. G. is tight with Washburn—one of the richest men in the city!" He looked at Guts. "Hope he don't sell us little folks down the river."

Guts shrugged. "Not my business. I ain't into politics. And I don't bite the hand that buys my pork chops."

"Amen," Shadrach said. "Speaking of pork, Cherry, we supposed to be sharing this plate."

The door swung open and a medium-sized man in his early thirties walked in, wearing a safari vest covered with zippered pockets.

"Playfair," Cherry said. "What's happening?"

The man strolled straight to the framed portrait of Nichelle Nichols, bowed slightly before it, and crossed himself.

"Boy, you going to hell," Shadrach said.

"Ain't nothing sinful about worshipping a woman," Playfair said with a smile.

"Specially one with thighs like that," Oliver added.

"She got to be the finest woman on television," Cherry said.

"Nope, that would be Gail Fisher," Oliver said. "If I was Mannix I would never leave the office."

Cherry curled his lip in disagreement. "She too dignified for me."

Oliver chuckled as if he knew a secret. "Not behind closed doors, I bet. I'm telling you, that chick's a sex machine." He turned to Playfair. "What you got in your car today?"

"Anything a brother needs."

Cherry laid a polished rib bone on his plate. "Got any women?"

"Any women I get I keep for myself," Playfair replied. "Now, tropical fish, that's another story."

Shadrach pushed his hat back on his head, exposing his furrowed brow. "Tropical what?"

"You heard right. Freshwater fish. Cichlids, kissing gouramis, neon tetras, and such. Perfect for breeding and a reliable source of comfort, serenity, and companionship. Today I charge half of what I'll charge tomorrow."

"Hmmph," Shadrach snorted. "Only fish worthy of my attention is the kind you fry."

"Amen to that," Cherry said.

"Where'd you get them fish from, anyway?" Oliver asked.

Playfair smiled. "They fell off a boat, of course."

"How do you even fit all that 'merchandise' in your trunk?" Shadrach asked. "How do you keep them fish alive?"

"Packaging and display is a complicated art not easily explained to the average citizen."

Shadrach ran his fingers across the brim of his hat. "I assure you, Playfair, nothin' about me is average."

"I heard one time you pulled a totem pole outta there," Cherry said.

"I can neither confirm nor deny that," Playfair said. "All I can say is a genuine indigenous carving of considerable length can be manipulated into a seemingly incompatible space. It comes down to a matter of volume, leverage, and surface tension."

Guts knew something about that. Once he'd successfully squeezed a six-four man into his trunk. But he'd had to break him a bit to make him fit.

"Damn, Playfair, I'm telling you," said Cherry. "You never should have dropped out of Sumner. You'd be a congressman by now."

Playfair shook his head. "Aw, high school was just holding me back."

Oliver pointed to the lot, where a car was pulling into view. "Play, you got a customer."

Playfair looked out the window and nodded. "Excuse me, gents. This here is what the titans of retail call a big-ticket transaction. Back in a bit."

Guts watched as Playfair first stepped toward the door, then turned and headed toward him, pulled up a chair, and sat.

"Let me pull your coat for a minute," Playfair said.

Guts nodded. "What it is?"

"Just thought you should know that Nifty's smelling himself."

"Nothing new about that."

"Right," Playfair agreed, "except he's spitting shit about you."

"Me?"

"Square business. Say he's tired of you playing him for a punk. He say…ah, forget it." Playfair moved as if he was getting ready to leave.

Guts touched his arm. "No way, Playfair. Don't try to walk off in the middle. Tell me."

Playfair sighed. "He say you've gone soft and everybody knows it. Say you used to be Huey Newton and now you Martin Luther King."

Guts winced. "Some motherfuckers are shallow." He heard Pearl in his head: *Lorenzo, you really shouldn't curse so much.* "What else?"

Playfair eyed him curiously. "Ain't that enough?"

"Yeah," Guts said. "I suppose it is."

Heading home later that evening, Guts turned up the radio to drown out the taxi chatter still rattling around in his head. He chose R&B because his favorite jazz deejay, the Man in the Red Vest, wouldn't be on until midnight—another five hours or so. He hummed along while contemplating a shower and a visit to Pearl's. But first he planned to roll by Nat-Han Steakhouse on Easton for a takeout dinner. The song playing was okay, he guessed, but the composer was clearly no W.C. Handy. He could never imagine the great bandleader settling for such crazy lyrics.

Closing his eyes for just a second, he idly drummed the steering wheel, singing despite himself, "*Thank you falettinme be mice elf agin*." He opened them just in time to see a policemen standing in the middle of Vandeventer, both hands raised. Guts slammed on the brakes, gripping the wheel and willing the Plymouth to a rubber-scorching stop just a few feet from the cop's outstretched palms.

The policeman rushed up to Guts's window, his face red with fury. "You blind or something? Or maybe just stupid as fuck!"

"I'm sorry, officer. I let the radio distract me. Really, my apologies."

"All right already. Take a U-turn and beat it. Road's closed."

"Yes, sir. Was there an accident?" Through his windshield Guts saw the familiar elements of a crime scene: cop cars, flashing lights, yellow tape, a small crowd of onlookers on the neighboring sidewalk. And a cloth-covered corpse sprawled in the middle of the street. One leg poked awkwardly from under the tarp, a sock curling upward from the shoeless foot. Guts's eyes followed the trail of broken glass leading from the body to the shattered window of Frontier Barbershop. *Damn*, he thought. *Rudolph Fisher*.

"More like a murder," the cop said. "Say, don't I know you from somewhere?"

"Not likely, sir. Thank you, I'll be moving on," Guts said.

"Wait. You're sure I've never arrested you before?"

"Me? No, nothing like that."

"Tell you what. Pull over and step out of the car."

"Officer, I hardly think that's necessary."

"Did I ask you to think? Now pull over and get the fuck out of the car."

Guts sighed and prepared to pull over. A gloved hand landed on the patrolman's shoulder.

"I'll take it from here."

The patrolman turned to see the taciturn face of Detective Otis Grimes inches from his own. Mirrored sunglasses sat on Grimes's brown face, hiding his eyes.

"Well, yes, sir. Yes, sir, Detective." The patrolman reluctantly left. Guts shifted the Plymouth into neutral.

"Guts."

"Grimes."

The detective, one of a handful of black investigators on the force, was on Goode's payroll. Guts had never seen any money change hands, but he knew it just the same. Whenever Guts got picked up on a humble or was just plain made to eat shit by redneck cops, Grimes always stepped in to loosen the cuffs. He could be counted on to look the other way while Guts carried out his boss's instructions, and—just as important—to induce his colleagues to do the same. On one memorable evening, Grimes had even teamed up with Guts to hide the body of the detective's own partner, a hotheaded little sadist who'd learned his limits under the heel of Guts's size 14 EEE.

In the two years since that night, neither man had ever mentioned it, and each respected the other's personal space.

"So who's dead back there?"

"You know," Grimes said. He rested his gloved hands on the edge of Guts's window.

"Fish."

"Throat slit, probably with his own pearl-handled razor."

Guts sighed. "I just saw him this morning."

"It gets worse," Grimes said. "You don't want to look below his belt. The sight would make a grown man cry. Or else throw up."

Guts shifted uncomfortably in his seat. "You mean—?"

"Yep. His throat wasn't the only thing they slit."

"Why would anybody want to do that to Fish?"

"Tried to get something out of him. Something worth more than what was in the cash register."

"From Fish? Like what?"

"Information, most likely," Grimes said.

"Anything missing?"

Grimes straightened up. "Nothing but the razor. He carried it everywhere, especially when getting ready to make his night deposit. Fish walked by faith but he was nobody's fool."

Guts threw his car into drive. "Well, I hear anything I'll make sure you know. I don't envy you cleaning this up."

"You should."

"Why?"

"I got the easy job tonight," Grimes replied. "You got the hard one."

"What's that?"

The detective almost smiled. "You have to tell Mr. G."

The men of the Black Swan Sign Shop gathered near their front window. It was early Tuesday morning and the air above the intersection of Marcus and Easton was a combat zone of clashing scents: the death-funk of Royal Packing Company, where pigs were already being turned into pork chops, versus the smoky aroma rising from the chimney of Nat-Han Steakhouse, where steak and eggs were the stars of the morning menu. Next to Nat-Han, a line of hopeful drunks waited for the package liquor store to open for business. Directly across the street from the Black Swan, Guts chatted with Nifty Carmichael, a lean man who ran in place as he talked.

"My bet's for 10 minutes," Bob Cobb offered. Cobb, the elder statesman of the Black Swan, puffed on a pipe as he donned his paint-spattered smock.

George West took a sip of his White Castle coffee and shook his head. The motion caused his big, bushy mustache to vibrate. "Naw, it's past that already," he said. "Besides, 10 minutes ain't hard. Hell, I could get to the river from here in 10 minutes."

Lucius Monday laughed as he hunched over a drafting table he'd fashioned from a discarded door. "Here we go," he said.

West was undeterred. "You know I was the public high school mile champion back in the day."

"How could we forget," Cobb said. "Sumner High hasn't had a champion as beloved as you since then. They retired your uniform number and everything."

"You mean I've told that story before?"

Even Talk Much, who usually wore the same inscrutable expression, managed a smile.

"You're a man of many talents," said Reuben Jones, stirring a few drops of black into a large can of optic white. "Too bad lip reading isn't one of them."

From where the men of the Black Swan stood, Guts looked as if he was asking about Nifty's health. But they knew he was doing nothing of the kind.

"My money's on a half-hour," Reuben said.

"More like 15 minutes," Lucius countered.

"Bet," Reuben said. "Loser buys the beer when we knock off."

"Let's make it Pepsi," Lucius said. "I'm still on the wagon."

"Deal."

Four years back, Guts and Nifty had arrived at their peculiar agreement: Nifty had to run in place whenever he saw Guts. It didn't matter if Guts didn't notice him or was too far away to speak with him. As soon as Nifty got wind of Guts's presence, he had to get those knees pumping. If he ever failed to stay in motion, Guts would kill him. Once, in front of a crowd near Katz Drugs in Pine Lawn, Nifty had paused to scratch his ankle. Guts had hit him on the top of the head with his fist, like a hammer pounding a nail. Nifty had blinked and collapsed. Guts had quickly caught him and laid him gently on the ground. Then he borrowed a bottle of beer from an onlooker and poured it on Nifty, reviving him. Guts had helped him to his feet and Nifty had commenced running in place.

"I missed getting to see my lady," Guts told Nifty. "And I missed hearing the Man in the Red Vest. You know what time he's on now?"

"Midnight to five," Nifty answered between gasps. His stingy-brim hat had slid to the back of his head, revealing the beads of sweat forming in his close-cropped hair.

"That's right," Guts agreed. "He still had a few hours of airtime left when I got home but I was too beat to turn it on. I was worn out from listening to Mr. G. react to the bad news I brought him. But that's the small stuff. The worst part about yesterday was seeing a good man dead in the street. I'm sure you know who I'm talking about."

"Fish," Nifty said, breathing hard.

"So informal," Guts said. "You must have known him well."

Nifty shook his head.

"No? Then it seems you should show him more respect."

"Rudolph Fisher," Nifty said. "Mr. Rudolph Fisher."

"That's better. Some folks deserve to die, Nifty. Some deserve to live. When somebody good dies, people get upset. When somebody who should be dead still walks around taking up space and breathing precious air, well, something doesn't seem right. It pisses me off. It almost pisses me off as much as a no-good piece of shit going around talking sideways at me. You know about that? Some piece of shit spitting nonsense about me going soft?"

"Naw, I ain't heard nothing like that." Nifty's tongue was hanging out.

"Thing is, I can't imagine anybody being that stupid. Gateway City ain't but so big. Word is bound to get back to me."

Nifty had begun the encounter with high-stepping strides. Now his feet were barely leaving the pavement, and his arms flapped weakly, as if he were a bird struggling against the wind.

"You know me, Guts. I keep an ear to the ground. I hear anything about anybody talking behind you, I'll let you know first thing."

"You do that."

Guts slapped Nifty lightly across the jaw. From across the street it looked like an affectionate gesture. "I know I can count on you. And if you hear anything about who got Fish, I should be the first person you tell."

The men of the Black Swan watched as Guts got in his car and started the engine. Nifty dutifully jogged until the Plymouth pulled away from the curb and out of sight.

"Wait for it, wait for it…" Cobb said. "And…now!"

Across the street, Nifty doubled over and vomited into the gutter.

In unison, the sign painters groaned and turned away.

"Nasty sumbitch," West declared.

"How long?" Lucius asked.

"Seventeen minutes exactly," Cobb replied.

"Gotcha," Lucius said.

"All right," Reuben conceded. "Pepsi's on me. I saw Guts keep him going for almost an hour once. He let him off easy today."

"Brother Tolliver, have you come to join us in prayer?"

Few people could ever get the draw on Guts, but somehow Reverend Miles Washington always managed to. The senior pastor of Good Samaritan Methodist Church favored the same kind of suits worn by his best friend, Ananias Goode. Dark, handsome, and apparently ageless, Rev. Washington had a scar running down the side of his neck that did no harm to his beauty. In fact, it accentuated his good looks the same way his pinstripes enhanced the luster of his lapels.

Guts had been lost in thought, tossing crumbs to the ducks from his perch on a bench next to the pond in Fairgrounds Park. He was going over his encounter with Nifty earlier that morning when the minister appeared at his side. To Guts's surprise, Rev. Washington wasn't alone.

"Guts Tolliver, have you met Dr. Noel?"

"I haven't had the pleasure," Guts said, removing his hat and scrambling to his feet. "But I've seen your picture in the *Gateway Citizen*."

"Hello," Dr. Artinces Noel said, extending her hand. She was as small as Guts was large, maybe five feet tall. But she radiated enough dignity to outfit an entire regiment of six-footers. Next to her stood two ladies Guts recognized from his frequent sojourns in the park. Usually the two elderly women were clad in pedal pushers and straw gardening hats. This time their outfits were considerably more formal.

"And these are Mrs. Tichenor and Mrs. Means, co-founders of the Gateway City Horticultural Study Club," Rev. Washington said. Guts shook both their hands.

"We know you," Mrs. Tichenor said. "You feed the ducks almost every day."

"Yes, ma'am, that's right," Guts said. "You have a good memory."

"I could never forget such a big, strong man."

"Blanche," said Mrs. Means. She was a good six inches taller than her friend. "No flirting, especially on such an important occasion."

"And what occasion is that?" Guts asked.

Mrs. Means smiled. "Today we rededicate the Abram Higgins Memorial Garden. You do know who Abram Higgins was?"

"No ma'am, I don't. But I suppose I should?"

"Yes, of course, you should," Mrs. Tichenor said. "Abram Higgins was a brilliant black man, an attorney."

"A real leader of his people," Mrs. Means interjected. "The hospital's named after him."

"Of course," Guts said. "Abram H." Nearly everyone he knew referred to the North Side's only public hospital as Abram H.

"Rev. Washington is the volunteer chaplain there when he's not leading the flock at Good Samaritan," said Mrs. Tichenor. "He has kindly agreed to say a prayer."

"And Dr. Noel will also offer some remarks," Rev. Washington added. "She was chief of pediatrics at the hospital for many years. If you have children, you've probably benefited from her trailblazing work in the field."

The pediatrician stared directly into Guts's eyes. He felt, improbably, that he was looking up at her rather than the other way around. "Have you any children, Mr. Tolliver?" she asked.

"No ma'am, I don't."

"Hmm," said Mrs. Tichenor, "now that's a shame."

Rev. Washington cleared his throat. "Ladies, we really must get going," he said.

Guts bowed and stood with hat in hand until they went off. He saw that a humble tent had been erected at the memorial garden, with folding chairs and a podium. A small audience was gathering as a pair of photographers hovered. Guts marveled at the pinstriped pastor's cool demeanor. His unlined face had shown no sign that one of his oldest friends had been murdered in cold blood the night before.

In contrast, when Ananias Goode had heard the news, he slammed his fist on the table so hard that his glass, half-filled with bourbon, wobbled and nearly fell. He stood in his living room, having just risen from an immense, throne-like chair. Guts stood a few feet away, hat in hand. Lawrence, the live-in nurse, sat on the sofa in front of the fireplace.

"Easy, Mr. G.," Lawrence said.

"I'm all right," Goode responded, his jowls quivering.

"No disrespect, but it ain't you I'm worried about." Lawrence nodded toward a closed door. "Any little disturbance—"

Burly as a linebacker, with muscles rippling beneath his hospital garb, Lawrence smiled despite the gravity of the occasion. His apparent lack of interest in the female sex, along with the rarity of male nurses, had always fueled speculation about his private life. But his obvious strength and skill with his fists kept the gossip at a low volume.

Goode had no problem with Lawrence, having trusted him enough to put him through nursing school. Since graduation he had served faithfully as nurse and protector to Mrs. Goode, who slept in the next room as still as death.

"Fish and I were boys together," Goode said. "We weren't close like Miles and me, but we got along. Miles and me were thick as thieves, just like now."

Guts listened attentively, as if he'd never heard any of it before. Goode had told him many times about adventures he'd shared with the reverend when they were growing up in the Deep South. But the stories were often oddly abbreviated and full of gaps, as if Goode were editing himself as he spoke. As a result, Guts's knowledge of the pair's unlikely friendship was frustratingly incomplete. Like most folks in North Gateway, he'd been tempted to fill in the missing pieces with rumor and unfounded speculations. Erratic fragments of gossip suggested that Goode and Rev. Washington had been involved in something shady down South, forcing them to flee North ahead of (a) a mob of angry Klansmen, (b) a gun-wielding husband, or (c) a rival moonshiner with murder on his mind. Guts suspected that perhaps none of the above was true. Still, the men's bond was undeniable, airtight.

"He came up from Liberty not long after us," Goode continued.

He went to the window, parted the curtains, and peered out into the street. Guts knew that nothing on Lewis Place was holding his attention. He was looking all the way back to Mississippi. "Fish cut hair even then. Cut hair and counted money."

He turned to Lawrence. "It's been about 15 minutes since you last looked in on her. It's probably time, right?"

"Of course," Lawrence said. He opened the door, and Guts briefly heard the rhythmic hum and hiss of machines as Lawrence stepped through and closed it behind him.

"Listen, Guts," Goode said. "You're already handling Crenshaw for me. No need to roll up your sleeves."

"I thought this might be a special case."

"It could turn out to be. In the meantime, I'll enlist the services of our fine metropolitan police force."

Guts knew that meant Detective Grimes.

"And I'll make Sharps earn his perfume money. But you keep your eyes and ears open just the same. Now, I need to call Miles."

Guts nodded. He had been dismissed.

Out of habit, he made a couple of circuits around Lewis Place, checking the alley behind Goode's garage and looking for anything that tripped his inner alarm before pointing the Plymouth toward Margaretta Avenue and his cold, Pearl-less bed. It had been too late to disturb her. After a night of fitful tossing, he had paid his visit to Nifty, then undertook his morning pilgrimage to the park, where Rev. Washington's abrupt appearance brought his communion with the ducks to an unsatisfying halt. Guts sighed and stretched. The day was still young.

In his office that afternoon, his eyelids were growing irresistibly heavy when Playfair bopped in.

"What it is, Big Man?"

Guts rubbed the back of his neck. A good night's sleep would have done him wonders. But he was cheered by Playfair's presence.

"Guts, ain't no way you can convince me that sitting behind a desk for most of the day don't drive you plumb stir crazy. It don't suit you somehow."

"It suits me fine. Never mind all that. What's in the trunk today?"

"Eight-track tapes, baby. You name it, I got it."

"Got any W.C. Handy?"

"'The Thrill Is Gone'? I might have that. I'll take a look for you."

"No, that's B.B. King," Guts corrected, but Playfair had already gone out.

Moments later, he returned and placed a portable eight-track player on Gut's desk. He plugged it in. "Maximum portability," he said. "Eight D batteries and you can take this baby anywhere. Plus it's got an AM radio. I didn't have W.C. Handy, but I found something I think you'll dig." He pressed a button and the Carpenters' "Close to You" began to play. Playfair frowned and stopped the music. "Wrong tape. That one's mine. Here's yours."

The mellow tones of Jerry Butler overcame the machine's tinny little speakers and filled the room.

Only the strong survive...

"The Iceman, huh?"

Playfair nodded. "Figured he was more your style."

"How much is this gadget going to set me back?"

"Come on, Guts, you insult me. This don't cost you nothing."

Playfair turned up the volume and leaned close. "Word is people thought Fish was Goode's banker," he confided. "Thought he was sitting on some heavy loot."

"So it wasn't Fish they were after."

"No, probably it was Goode's money, or some clues about where he keeps it. But you were already thinking that, weren't you?"

"That's more thinking than I'm used to." Guts scratched the side of his nose with his index finger. "How long ago did you hear about this? Word is going around this morning already?"

"Try last night."

"Nifty didn't have anything for me this morning."

Playfair laughed. "Nifty? That fool was too busy partying to pick up any information."

"What do you mean?"

"I mean brother man was kicking up his heels. He's been a regular in the clubs since he ain't scared of you no more. He knows he won't see you because you've been domesticated."

"No wonder he was so tired. Domesticated, huh? That's what people are saying?"

"Don't act surprised. You used to have your own table at the Zodiac. You were at the Riviera so much that people thought your boss owned a piece of it."

"Sounds like you're still hitting the spots yourself."

"You better know it. Your boy Playfair is a regular James Brown. I might like the Carpenters, but I can still get down. Check me out."

He raised his right arm and shook his pelvis. Then he raised his left arm and repeated the motion. "That's the boogaloo, baby." He hunched his shoulders and wiggled forward. "This here's the camel walk."

"Watch it," Guts advised. "Don't trip over your bell-bottoms."

"Want me to show you the funky penguin? All the kids are doing it."

"Do I look like a kid?"

"Well, since you put it that way. If you change your mind…"

"I know where to find you. Play, put the tape player out front. It might get in the way of Trina's dispatching if we keep it in here."

Playfair carried it out and plugged it in while Cherry and Shadrach watched from a nearby table. They were supposedly playing dominoes, but neither man had made a move in a while. Oliver paced and read the paper.

"Can you get the ballgame on that?" Shadrach asked. "The pregame show might be on."

Oliver made a clucking noise. "Why don't we see if we can get the news on there? Why a Negro would rather listen to a ballgame than find out what's going on in the world is a riddle I can't figure," he said. "If Nixon escalated his troop numbers today, would any black man know or care? And that's exactly who Tricky Dick is sending overseas: us."

"Oliver, can't you ever talk about anything positive?" Cherry asked.

"You won't catch me smiling while the world is falling down around me. Wake up tomorrow and a whole city block might be gone. That's how they do it, you know. It's like these dominoes.

First they closed the ballpark. Blew it up, actually. Shook dust, debris, and enough asbestos over the neighborhood to make us all fireproof."

"Washburn said he needed to move his team downtown," Shadrach said. "That's his right. It ain't like we were working in that stadium."

"Didn't cost us nary a job," Cherry added. "Besides, they built us that nice boys club right on the spot."

"Carter Carburetor will be next to close up shop," Oliver predicted.

"It ain't like black men are working up in there either," Shadrach said.

Oliver rolled up his newspaper until it formed a tight tube. He looked like he wanted to whack Shadrach with it. "Mark my words," he said. "It's not about jobs. It's about control. If you've got no say over your food, clothing, shelter, or education, you've got nothing. And don't get me started about health."

Shadrach grunted. "The last thing we want to do is get you started."

"I just call it like I see it," Oliver said. "Carter Carburetor's next, then the hospital."

Everybody laughed. "That's crazy, Oliver," Playfair said. "No way in hell they'll come in here and try to take Abram H."

"Ain't gon' happen," Cherry agreed.

Oliver pressed his argument. "All those patients without insurance or money. It's a drain on the city's finances. You'll see."

"That would leave a lot of hurting people on the street," Playfair said.

"My father died in that hospital," Cherry said.

"Died? Shit, find me a Negro who wasn't born up in there," Oliver said. "Everybody in here, right?"

"Except me," Shadrach said, "but only because it wasn't open yet. I was born at home. Still, can't imagine the North Side without it."

An uncomfortable silence descended until Playfair clapped his hands. "All right, let's turn this player on and see what we got."

"Put it on the ballgame," Shadrach suggested.

Oliver began to cluck again. "Shad, haven't you heard a word I said? Sports are just today's bread and circuses, a sideshow to keep you from thinking about your neighborhood being stolen right from under you, about your young men being sent off to fight and die in godforsaken places."

"The home team's got three of us starting in the field and one of us starting on the mound," Shadrach said. "I'm just being supportive."

"Shad, you're the oldest man in the room," Oliver said.

Shadrach frowned. "What's your point?"

"I'm just saying that you should be able to remember better than anybody just how bad the home team treated Jackie Robinson when he first came through here. They called him names, frightened his wife. Hell, they even sent a black cat out onto the field."

"It's different now," Shadrach said. "Look at Crenshaw. He's the highest-paid player on the team."

"You mean highest paid slave," Oliver said. "That's all they are, slaves. Just ask Curt Flood."

The door swung open and a tall, graceful man strode in. He was dressed in the latest fashions and sported aviator sunglasses and thick muttonchop sideburns. A dull bruise sat high on his cheek. He looked around and smiled. "Afternoon, fellas," he said.

The men of the cabstand just gaped. Finally Cherry found his voice.

"Goddamn," he said. "You're Rip Crenshaw."

The newcomer grinned and flipped off his shades. "That's what folks call me. Here to see my man Guts."

"Of course you are," Shadrach said, getting up and moving toward Guts's door. "Our Guts, always rubbing elbows with the bigwigs. He's right through that door. I'll show you."

Shadrach tapped lightly on the open door. Guts looked up.

"Um, excuse me, Guts," Shadrach said. "Mr. Rip Crenshaw here to see you."

Crenshaw had put his sunglasses back on. He smiled at Shadrach. "Thanks a lot, brother."

Shadrach just lingered and stared.

"Shadrach," Guts said. The old man didn't move. "Shadrach," he said again, more forcefully.

Shadrach answered without taking his eyes off Crenshaw. "Hmm?"

"Leave us."

"Oh, yeah, of course. Sure, no problem, right away." He left and closed the door behind him.

Guts eyed the ballplayer. "I thought you were going to call first," he said.

"I was in the neighborhood," Crenshaw replied. "So I decided to stop by."

Right, Guts thought. He said nothing.

"So," Crenshaw said. "I hear you're stone cold."

"Not hardly," Guts said.

"I hear you've slaughtered men and eaten their hearts for breakfast," the ballplayer said. He smiled. Guts didn't.

"And *I* hear any pitcher with a decent curveball can make you his bitch," Guts responded. "But that don't make it so, right?" He smiled. Crenshaw didn't.

"I'm usually treated with more respect," Crenshaw said.

"Same here," Guts said.

Crenshaw looked at Guts a long while before bursting into good-natured laughter. "You ain't no ass-kisser, are you? Brother, that makes two of us. You all right with me."

He extended a hand across Guts's desk. Guts took it, but replied, "My boss and your boss might be friends, but that don't make us friends."

Crenshaw studied Guts. His face brightened as if he'd discovered something. "It's been a while, hasn't it?"

"A while since what?"

"Since you had some."

"Ah, that's a good one."

"Mr. Goode said you can show me how the North Side rolls."

"I ain't been rolling much lately, but I'll do what I can." *Better get it over with*, Guts thought. "You got time tonight?"

"Naw, big man. We play the Cubs in a couple hours. Then we have a five-game road trip. Mets and Phillies. Don't you read the sports pages?"

"Not until football season."

Crenshaw nodded. "I should have figured you for the gridiron. I'm no stranger to it myself. I rushed for close to 900 yards my sophomore year of high school."

"Why did you choose baseball?"

"It chose me. A $60,000 signing bonus when I was 17. Besides, I was clearly too pretty for the pigskin. How about I look you up in a week or so?"

"All right. So I take it you're off the injured list?"

"Yeah, but I'm sitting out tonight. Hangover."

Guts stared at Crenshaw's bruised cheek. "Heard you took a foul ball to the jaw. Looks like it got you pretty good."

"That's the official story. Between you and me, I got into it with some rednecks in a South County bar. I was kicking ass too, til this joker blindsided me with a pool stick."

"You were way on the wrong side of town."

"Guts, you ever been to South County?"

"Once or twice."

"Then you know they have pussy there, too."

Guts sighed. "You looking for white women, you don't have to go that far. You could have been killed."

Crenshaw winked and flexed a bicep. "You should see the other guys," he said.

The All-Star wasn't able to escape the cabstand without some friendly jawing with the regulars. Not that he had tried very hard to get away, in Guts's opinion. He had hesitated for a moment when Cherry offered him a beer from the tottering old Frigidaire, then politely declined.

"I still got a bit of a buzz from last night," he explained. "And I'm headed to the stadium. You've probably heard that I've already got a strike against me."

Among the many stinks Crenshaw had stirred up, the most pungent involved a widely circulated photo showing him quaffing a brew in the dugout during the middle of a closely fought duel with the hated Cubs. Crenshaw had tried to make light of it, pointing out that the beer he was drinking was one of the team owner's brands. But Virgil Washburn was not amused and neither was Nick Schumacher, the squad's longtime manager. Crenshaw had served a three-game suspension and paid a hefty fine.

Shadrach nearly wept when the slugger offered him a pair of tickets to a future game with seats along the foul line, just a few feet from where Crenshaw patrolled first base. He would be on hand when Crenshaw hit home run number 34, breaking the club record.

Playfair excused himself just long enough to go to his car and return with a baseball card. "You mind signing this for me?"

Crenshaw took the card and whistled. "Man, this is my rookie card from when I broke in with the Phils in 1964. Where'd you get this?"

"From my car," Playfair replied. He gratefully accepted the signed card and slipped it into one of the zippered pockets on his safari vest.

"Your car?"

"Yep. My trunk."

"What else you got in there?"

Oliver, Cherry, Shadrach, and Playfair all answered at once. "Anything a brother needs," they said.

Their cocky boast still resonated when Guts went out to pick up a freshly stenciled taxi at Reuben Jones's garage a few hours later. The radio broadcast of the ballgame played in the background while Reuben and Lucius finished up. Guts mostly listened while the sign painters reacted to the announcers' comments about Crenshaw's unfortunate encounter with a foul ball.

Reuben was incredulous. "A little old foul ball is all it takes to put him down? Sounds like he hasn't been eating his Wheaties."

Lucius laughed. "A man that rich should never have to settle for cold cereal. I know I wouldn't. And neither would you."

Both men were married to outstanding cooks. Lucius's wife, Irene, perhaps best known as the Pie Lady, sold her legendary lemon pies and other delicacies at Stormy Monday's, her popular eatery on Goodfellow Boulevard. Reuben's Pristine knew her way around a kitchen too. Reuben could almost smell the pork chops that he knew were simmering to perfection under Pristine's careful gaze. Later that evening, he would push himself away from her table and head to his basement studio. There he would begin work on the paintings that would make his reputation, a series of portraits inspired by his favorite book, *Notable Negroes*. He and Lucius had not yet become acclaimed fine artists, and the Black Swan sign painters had not yet become the Black Swan Collective, subject of documentaries, dissertations, and traveling exhibitions. At the moment they were just two men completing a job.

Their next job the following day was in Fairgrounds Park, where they joined the rest of the Black Swan crew to hang banners at the entrances announcing Afro Day in the Park, a daylong festival of black culture that would take place in July. On a typical day, they might have crossed paths with Guts for the second time. But while the sign painters hung their handiwork amid the resplendent greenery, Guts stood in Goode's living room, watching Rev. Washington pace and fume. A determined scowl had replaced the cool demeanor he had displayed the day before. He spat his words as if they tasted bad in his mouth, and his scar seemed to pulsate as he spoke.

"Fish was on my deacon board," he said. "I derive no consolation from knowing he's in heaven."

Guts nodded sympathetically. He had noted Fisher's white-gloved presence every Sunday, holding the door open for arriving worshipers. Guts rarely stepped inside the church, but he drove one of its vans, rain or shine. After a brief memorial service at Good Samaritan, Fisher's body was to be shipped back to Mississippi per his wishes.

"You mean you *hope* he's in heaven," Goode said. He was holding a glass of bourbon but had yet to take a sip. "Fish was my friend, a good friend, but he was no angel."

Guts had come by to report that he'd turned up nothing so far. He wasn't sure why he was doing it, since Goode had all but excused him for the time being. He was retired, after all. Sort of.

Goode looked at Guts. "He used to hold cash for me. Sometimes he used to clean it up, too."

Aha, Guts thought.

"But that was a long time ago," Rev. Washington said pointedly. "He had never wanted to do it. He got dragged into it." He glared at Goode. Guts had never seen anyone stare at the man with such open disapproval. On other occasions, Rev. Washington had dared to criticize Goode from the pulpit at Good Samaritan. He obviously had immunity.

Goode said nothing.

Guts broke the silence. "Maybe somebody thought he was still banking for you."

Rev. Washington laughed bitterly. "You think?" He picked up his bourbon and drained it.

After another long silence in which Rev. Washington stared at Goode and Goode stared at the floor, Goode turned to Guts. "You have to excuse us. We're grieving."

Guts nodded and turned to leave.

"Guts," Goode said.

"Yeah, boss?"

"Thanks for coming by."

"No problem," Guts said.

He continued to spend a part of each of the next several days nosing around for answers, but had no luck. He'd nearly forgotten about Rip Crenshaw until the ballplayer caught up with him and they agreed upon a time to meet.

Crenshaw was staying at the Park Plaza. He came out dressed to party. Guts's idea of cleaning up included putting on a crisp plain shirt and clean slacks and a pair of slick Florsheim loafers. Pearl had finished her shift at Aldo's and come over to help him get ready. She bathed him and polished his shoes. She tried and failed to talk him into wearing cufflinks. "But you have such a beautiful collection," she said. She had the box open and was sifting through them.

"Uh-huh," Guts said. "Just put that box back on the closet shelf where you found it." She stuck her tongue out at him and replaced the box.

"You're spoiling me," he had told her as she buttoned his shirt.

"It's not spoiling," she said. "I call it caring for you like you deserve." Against his better judgment, Guts left her at his house. She promised to lock up when she went out to spend the evening with some girlfriends. The security-minded Guts thought it was a bad idea. But it was getting harder and harder for him to tell her no.

Pearl had told him he looked like a movie star, but he felt like a hick from the sticks next to the slugger, who sported a silk shirt unbuttoned to the middle of his chest, bell-bottoms, and platform shoes. And jewelry. Guts couldn't help staring when Crenshaw opened the door and slid into the car.

"What?" Crenshaw asked.

Guts shrugged. "You got more chains than a runaway slave."

Crenshaw shook his head. "The first thing a runaway slave would do is get rid of all his clunky iron. He wouldn't know nothing about this gold I'm wearing. Now enough with the ancient history. Let's party."

"You must have had a good road trip."

Crenshaw pushed his aviator shades down to the edge of his nose and peered at Guts over the top of them. "You really don't read the sports pages, do you? I had three homers and knocked in eight runs."

Their first stop was the Zodiac, an intimate place on North Grand. Guts eased his Plymouth into the lot underneath the Zodiac's oversized sign, which featured multicolored renditions of horoscope symbols painted by Reuben Jones. Apparently the sign was the busiest thing about the lounge that night, because the parking lot was less than half full.

"Maybe we're a bit early" was all Guts could come up with when Crenshaw shot him a questioning look. Inside, the ballplayer grabbed a beer while Guts claimed a stool where he could see the small dance space and the door. Crenshaw leaned back on the bar and surveyed the dimly lit room. "It's a Shame" by the Spinners was playing on the jukebox.

That song gave way to "Love On a Two-Way Street" by the Moments, a sweet ballad with butter-smooth vocals. Crenshaw began to mouth the lyrics and sway to the tune. Across the room, a woman Guts recognized as Gladys, a Zodiac regular, began to do the same. Guts watched as the two began to eyeball each other.

"What's her story?" Crenshaw asked.

"Name's Gladys. That's about all I can tell you."

Crenshaw went over and led her to the dance floor. They moved around a bit and Crenshaw leaned over and whispered in her ear.

Seconds later, they parted. Crenshaw said something softly, prompting a smile from Gladys.

Crenshaw looked at Guts and gestured toward the door. Guts met him at the threshold. "All right," Crenshaw said, "let's see what else the North Side's got."

They walked in silence to the car. Guts started the engine.

"You know much about Gladys?"

"I've seen her around enough to nod at her," Guts replied.

"You ever made a move on her?"

"Naw, not my type."

"What's your type?"

"I like 'em petite. Besides, I've got somebody."

"It's just as well," Crenshaw said. "She's scared of you anyway. Said she saw you take a man's finger off one night at a place called High Wheels. You remember that?"

Guts kept his eyes on the road. "I do. He touched something didn't belong to him."

"Shit. What did you cut his finger with?"

"I didn't cut it. I twisted it off."

"Goddamn! You *are* stone cold."

"It was my job. It's not anymore."

Guts could feel Crenshaw's eyes on him but he refused to turn and acknowledge him. They rode in silence down Grand Boulevard, past the Egg Roll Kitchen, the YMCA, and the Harry Truman Boys Club.

"So what happened in there?" Guts asked. "You dropped Gladys like you found out she had the clap."

"Nothing like that. Like you say, not my type."

"No sex appeal?"

"More like no pussy."

"Come again?"

Crenshaw laughed. "You heard me. The sister is a brother."

"Hell naw."

"Hell, yeah. Trust me. I get out a little more than you do."

"What did you whisper in her ear?"

"I asked her how she dealt with stubble," Crenshaw said. "I didn't see any. I mean, it was dark in there but I looked real hard."

"What'd she—he—say?"

"She said a girl's got to have her secrets."

"Ain't that a bitch," Guts said. After a moment, he asked, "So how come you didn't bust her—his—teeth in?"

"I got no beef with her. Most folks know her deal, I figure. Surprised you didn't."

"Gladys a man? Damn!"

The Spotlight, the second club they visited, was much livelier. About a decade ago, a local black musician turned rock-and-roll star had opened an integrated club at the same location. But he was ahead of his time, and authorities were sickened by the sight of white girls lining up outside a place where black men were drinking and dancing inside. They raided the spot a couple of times on made-up missions, took the rocker's liquor license, and generally harassed him until he had no choice but to shut the place down. Two years later, it reopened as the Spotlight, an all-black joint that frequently hosted live entertainment.

When they entered, the hostess turned up her nose as if she smelled a skunk. Guts greeted her first. "Evening, Marnita."

"Guts. I didn't expect to see you around here."

"Neither did I. But I'm escorting a VIP tonight. I'm hoping you'll be kind enough to give us a good booth."

Marnita turned to Crenshaw. "A VIP? Let's see, do you sing, dance, or hit a ball with a stick?"

Crenshaw turned on the charm. "For a woman as lovely as you, I'm tempted to say all three. But that would be foolish. And I am, I confess, a fool for love."

Marnita lightened up a bit. "If you were here with anyone but Guts, your drinks would be on the house."

"Marnita Taylor," Guts said, "meet Rip Crenshaw. He plays first base for the home team."

"My pleasure," Rip said.

"I'm sure," Marnita said.

She led them to a booth with a good view of the stage.

A young woman joined the combo under the lights. She counted off and they launched into the opening notes of "Rescue Me."

Rip had his eyes on Marnita as she walked away. "What happened? You leave that little filly at the altar or something?"

Guts shook his head. "It never got that far."

"You broke her heart."

"I broke her cousin's back. Sort of."

"Sort of?"

"I was chasing him. On a roof. He jumped. Broke his back, put himself in a wheelchair."

A waiter came and took their orders. Both men ordered beer.

"And Marnita couldn't forgive you."

"Sounds about right."

Guts nursed a second beer while Crenshaw worked the room like a seasoned pro. He danced with three different women for three successive songs, then posed for photos with the singer and others when the band took a break. Guts sipped, watched, and imagined what it would be like to have Pearl with him. She was a nimble dancer and he was almost as light on his feet, despite his bulk. But they confined their dancing to their living rooms. He seldom took her anywhere because he had too many enemies, too many people nursing old grudges. Becoming known as Guts's woman would be like having a target on her back.

Pearl had won his heart with her banana pudding. She was the first woman who could make it like his mother did. She was ambitious, hardworking, and claimed to have no fascination with nightlife. Almost from the moment they met, she showed less interest in cutting the rug than in turning Guts's modest house into a genuine home. Before her, he had only a king-sized bed, a refrigerator, a hi-fi system, and his beloved W.C. Handy records. Before her, he found it easier just to cruise down Washington

Avenue and find someone who didn't want anything besides an agreed-upon payment for services rendered.

They met at Stormy Monday's. Guts was staring at the revolving pie case, trying to decide on a dessert to take home. He had been gazing at a banana pudding when Pearl tugged on his sleeve. "Mine tastes better," she said, looking up at him and flashing a wicked smile. Guts took in all of Pearl's virtues in a single glance—the small, high breasts, the pinched waist, bold rump, and surprisingly generous calves—and could think of only one reply: "I bet it does."

Guts's 35 years on the planet had convinced him that belief in true love was a high-risk proposition. The night King died, Guts had wheeled through riot-torn streets at the behest of Goode, who was helping out a young couple that wanted—needed—to be married on the spot. He had driven Goode's New Yorker, steering around rage-crazed North Siders and dodging flaming debris while Rev. Washington rode shotgun and led the giddy, frightened couple in the backseat through their wedding vows. They were clearly crazy in love—and more than a little crazy too, in Guts's opinion. Nearly every man he knew who took the chance on lifelong love had lost out in the end. Ananias Goode. Mr. Logan. His own father. The groom in the backseat had been Gabe Patterson, the former self-proclaimed revolutionary, whom Cherry had described as "that liberatin' nigger." Patterson once claimed that violent rebellion was not only possible but also necessary. He turned his back on all that, though, when he fell for Rose Reynolds. King's death and Pearl's tenderness had combined to cause similar changes in Guts. However, he had shown no willingness to go as far as Patterson—despite Nifty going around and telling people that Guts had been "domesticated."

"Big Man, you think you can stop daydreaming long enough to meet this sexy mama?"

Guts looked up and saw Crenshaw leaning in close, a young woman at his side. She was pretty but looked suspiciously young.

"This is Summer. Summer, this is Guts."

Guts nodded and tried to smile. He suspected that if you took away the shiny dress, high heels, and the carefully layered face paint, there just might be a child underneath.

"How you doin'?" Her voice was squeaky.

"Imagine," Crenshaw said, "meeting a girl named Summer in the month of June. Talk about good timing."

A drink made Summer even squeakier, and compliant enough to accompany Guts and Crenshaw to a third nightspot. Guts had planned to take Crenshaw to the Riviera, a friendly place he knew well. But Summer convinced the ballplayer to choose the Earthquake instead. Once he got there, she promised, she'd introduce him to some of her friends.

Guts rarely visited the Earthquake because the crowd was younger than he preferred. Also, his presence had been discouraged ever since a man had driven through the front window in an attempt to run him down. They had just entered—the large dance floor was packed and the music painfully loud—when three large bouncers stepped in front of them.

"Evening, Guts," their leader said.

"Gentlemen," Guts said.

"Surprised to see you here."

"Not as surprised as I am to see you stepping in front of me."

The leader appeared to be losing confidence. So he spoke louder to encourage himself. "There's three of us," he said.

"And there's three of us," Crenshaw said. He stepped forward and extended a hand. "Rip Crenshaw, first baseman. I really appreciate the hospitality you're showing me and my good friend Guts Tolliver. It will make fine publicity for your club when I mention it during the story about me in the *Gateway Citizen*."

"Pleased to meet you, Mr. Crenshaw," the lead bouncer said, smiling shyly. "I thought that homer you hit against the Cubs last week was going to fly right out of the park. That ball took off like a rocket."

"It's all in the wrists," Crenshaw said.

"Listen, Mr. Crenshaw, anything you want is on the house."

"'Preciate it. We won't be here long. We're meeting a couple of friends."

Crenshaw and Summer strolled off and melted into the crowd.

"We don't want any trouble, Guts."

"Then why are you still in my face?"

With that, the bouncers departed. Guts scanned the crowd. He thought he spotted a lean brother in a stingy brim doing the camel walk. *Nifty?* He took a step in that direction but became aware of someone watching him. He turned and saw the bartender across the room. The bartender quickly looked down. When he looked up again, Guts was staring straight at him. The bartender threw down his towel and ran. Guts saw him darting through the dancers toward the rear. Quickly but calmly, Guts went out the front door.

He went around to the side of the building, counted silently to himself, then stuck out his arm. The fleeing bartender ran into it with his throat. Before the man's back was flattened fully on the pavement, Guts planted his foot firmly on his chest. Guts reached in the waistband of his pants and pulled out a piece of peppermint candy. He freed it from the cellophane and popped it in his mouth.

"The Lord is my shepherd I shall not want," the man gasped. "He maketh me to lie down in green pastures he leadeth me beside the still waters he restoreth—"

Guts increased his pressure on the man's chest, silencing him. But as soon as Guts let up, the man's fierce praying began again. "He leadeth me in the paths of righteousness for his name's sake yea though I walk—"

Guts removed his foot, grabbed his victim's throat, and yanked him to his feet. He shoved him against the wall.

"Stop praying and start talking. Why'd you run?"

"I'm just 23, sir, working my way through grad school."

"Oh yeah? What are you studying?"

"Economics."

"Economics?"

"Yes, sir. Wealth, financial systems, supply and demand."

"I know what it is. Why'd you run?"

"I was there."

"Come again?"

"When you killed that man. I was there."

"You better start making sense."

"In the shoeshine parlor, when you killed that man with a shoelace. I was 12 years old. I knew I wouldn't ever forget your face. I've never been so scared, before or since. I was with my dad.

I thought you were going to kill us. People said you were going around killing all the witnesses, that you wouldn't rest until we were all dead. I'd almost forgotten but then I saw you tonight and I guess I had a flashback. You're not going to kill me, are you?"

Guts had not killed any of the witnesses from that shine parlor. The very fear of him, strengthened by rumor, had inspired every single one of them to remain silent. That had often been the case. In other instances, Ananias Goode had reliably stepped in to grease the appropriate palms.

Guts relaxed his hold on the young man, then straightened his shirt. "Naw, brother. I don't do that anymore. I'm sorry you had to see that in the shine parlor. But that man had it coming. You don't. Go on back to school and study that economics."

"Thank you," the young man said. His breathing had almost returned to normal. "Thank you." He turned and moved toward the entrance. Guts stayed outside.

He had been seconds from snapping the bartender's neck. Guts blamed it on the bouncers for pissing him off. He went to the parking lot, thinking he might take a spin to calm down and clear his head. Leaning forward to unlock the car, he paused at his reflection in the window. Pearl insisted that she saw a matinee idol when she looked at his face. But he knew that most people saw what the bartender had seen: a bogeyman.

Pearl thought he just needed some friends. People would regard him differently if they got to know him in a comfortable setting. He got along with the men at the cabstand, the sign painters at Black Swan. But calling them friends was a stretch.

"Your closest friend is a 90-year-old man," Pearl had said.

"Mr. Logan? He's 83."

"He's old as Methuselah."

Guts opened the car, started the engine, and turned on the radio. Broadcasting from the KSD studio, the Man in the Red Vest was deep into his shift. As Miles Davis's "Kind of Blue" began, Guts got out and leaned back against the Plymouth.

Two Coltrane ballads and one Ellington medley later, Crenshaw strolled up with three ladies arm-in-arm. He was grinning and more than a little tipsy.

"Ladies, this is Guts Tolliver, man about town. Guts, you've already met Summer, and this here is Spring and Autumn. That ain't their real names, but that's what I'm callin' 'em. Too bad we couldn't get a Winter too. I'm not just an All-Star, baby. I'm a man for all seasons. My good man, could you kindly give us a lift to the Park Plaza? It's time to let it Rip."

Guts's rearview mirror showed only blackness. He had the windows rolled down to dissipate the perfume clouds Crenshaw's "girlfriends" had left behind. The Man in the Red Vest was still going strong on the radio. Certain he wasn't being tailed, Guts turned onto Margaretta. He always entered and left through the back door, and he never failed to park his car in the locked garage behind his home. Still, he customarily drove past the front of his house before calling it a night, just to make sure nothing was amiss. His street was quiet and the houses dark, except for porch lights and the occasional illuminated room. Then he saw something that made him turn off the music and pause quietly in front of his house. The light was on in the living room.

He had instructed Pearl to leave on only the porch light and to be sure to set his alarm. Guts eased off the brake, barely touching the gas until he was a good distance past his house. He turned the corner and drove up the alley. He killed the headlights, pulled in behind his garage, and turned off the engine. The basement door showed no signs of forced entry. Neither did the back door, which he unlocked before stepping carefully into the kitchen. He could hear the Temptations and the Supremes crooning on his hi-fi. Guts slid along the hallway, his back against the wall. Slowly he peeked around the corner…and saw Pearl in all her naked glory. She was standing on a chair, hanging a picture on the wall. She sang along with the record.

"I'm gonna make you love me. Yes I will, yes I will."

"Pearl."

She spun on the chair and nearly lost her balance. Guts stuck out a hand and steadied her.

"Tell me," she said. "How does a man as big as you move without making any noise?"

"Practice. What are you doing?"

Pearl turned and went back to work. "What does it look like I'm doing? Hanging this artwork I bought for my man. Every time I come in here and see these blank walls, it makes me want to cry. Don't worry, I picked out something I knew you would like. See?"

Guts took a step back and saw that she had already mounted two paintings of ducks and had two more to install. The ducks looked nearly as real as the ones in Fairgrounds Park.

"They're Audubon prints. Don't the feathers look like you could just reach out and ruffle them? These are mass-market copies, but I figured if the frames were fancy enough they'd look just as good as the originals. What do you think?"

"They're nice. How did you get in?"

"I left the door unlocked because I knew I was coming back later to surprise you with these. The back door, like you insist. If I didn't know any better I'd think you were ashamed of me."

"You left the door unlocked?"

"It's a good thing I checked you out before we got serious. I'd suspect you had a woman hidden in here somewhere. Sealed up in a secret room or something."

"You left the door unlocked?"

Pearl left the third print hanging crookedly from a nail. She got down off the chair and put her arms around Guts's waist.

"Relax, sugar," she cooed. "Who'd be crazy enough to break into Guts Tolliver's house?"

Guts didn't return the hug. "Most people don't know this is Guts Tolliver's house. I aim to keep it that way."

Pearl dropped her arms. "You really trying to have an attitude about this? Sneaking me in and out through the back, changing the subject when I ask for a key. If anybody should have an attitude, it's me."

"Slow down, Pearl. I told you, it's about your safety."

"I *am* safe. You think I'm fragile because I like pretty things…. You're right, though. Maybe we *should* slow this down."

"That's not what I said."

"But that's what you're thinking."

"Hold on, Pearl."

"Hold on nothing. I'm getting dressed."

She hurried out of the room. Guts sighed and scratched the side of his nose with his index finger.

Pearl emerged, carrying clothes. She sat them on the chair she'd been standing on. She put on her bra, glaring at him while she fiddled with the straps.

"Why do you think I'm decorating your house?" She picked up her panties.

"You said you do these things because you care for me and I deserve it," Guts said.

She shook her head. "It's because I care for *us* and because *we* deserve it."

"I thought you were happy with the way things are. I thought you understood."

"Lorenzo, you treat me like a goddamn secret."

Guts tried a gentle approach. He took her hands in his.

"Baby," he said with a smile, "at least wait until sunrise before you start cursing."

It didn't work. "Lorenzo," she said. "Let go of my drawers."

Pearl put on the rest of her clothes in a furious rush. "You claim to be looking out for me, but you're really looking out for yourself," she said. "You're scared, and not of somebody coming to kill us while we sleep. You're afraid to commit to a real-life, grown-up relationship."

"Baby."

"Stop with the 'baby.' I'm obviously not your baby. Look, you can be a gentleman and drive me home, or you can watch the doorknob hit me. And don't fret. I'm going out the back door."

Guts drove her home in silence. Pearl refused even to look at him, let alone speak.

They arrived at her apartment far too soon. She put her hand on the door handle. "Violence follows you. I get that," she said, looking out the window.

"That's not it," Guts said. He paused. "I *am* violence. Last night, a man almost had a heart attack just looking at me. I saw everything

I've ever done in that man's face." "That's who you were, Lorenzo, not who you are."

"Then, there's Fish—"

"You think Fish got killed just because you went to see him? You weren't the only one there."

"I know. It just got me thinking."

"You been thinking on this a while, from what I can tell."

"Well, I'm thinking on it more. If I care about you like I say I do, why do I put you in danger by being with you?"

Pearl rolled her eyes. "You sound like a dang fool. This is North Gateway."

"Meaning?"

"Meaning I face a little more danger every day as these neighborhoods change. We all do. People talk about Vietnam. They should spend some time north of Delmar. At the supermarket on Easton, a snake came out of the collard greens and bit a woman on the neck. A tree branch fell in the Clark Elementary schoolyard, crushing a little girl. It ain't just crime, Lorenzo. It's death, and it's been hanging around more and more since the fires. Sometimes I feel funny walking from my job to the bus stop, like somebody's watching me. And that's the nice part of town. You can't protect me from every little thing. But loving me means doing the best you can."

"I'm still trying to figure things out."

"After three years together?" Pearl got out and shut the door. She turned and leaned in the window. "It's easier when you pay for it. Isn't it?"

Guts got no sleep. He ate nine eggs and a box of bacon for breakfast. He washed it down with a quart and a half of milk. Hygiene was a half-hearted affair. His head and upper lip, normally shaved, each displayed a thin layer of shadow. His beard, usually kept somewhat in check, was bushier than usual. Bits of food glinted in it here and there and remained firmly nestled as the day progressed. Guts was wondering if the folks at White Castle had given him decaf coffee by mistake when Playfair poked his head in the office.

Guts tried to be perky but couldn't quite pull it off. "What do you say, Play?"

"Nothin' to it but to do it," Playfair replied. He lowered his voice. "Look here, I have to pull your coat again. Remember that leather blazer I let you have for half price?"

"Yeah," Guts said. "I remember you had a trunk full of 'em but only one XXXXL."

"Uh-huh. That baby was so rare it could have been a collector's item. I'm guessing it was custom-ordered by some defensive lineman somewhere."

"Sounds about right," Guts agreed. "It's a little bit roomy even on me. Wait, don't tell me you got hold of another one."

"Naw, nothing like that. It's just that I would know that jacket anywhere on account of it being so unusual. I was rolling down Lexington over there by Kingshighway and I spotted it on a pile under a window. A whole lot of extra-large stuff, if you know what I mean."

Playfair watched as the reality of Guts's situation settled upon him. "Lexington near Kingshighway? Damn!"

Playfair stepped aside as Guts blew past him. The big man raced to his car without so much as a nod at Shadrach and Cherry as they huddled over their dominoes. "What's up with the boss?" Cherry asked.

"My man's business is literally in the streets," Playfair explained. "I think he's on his way to clean it up."

Pearl was tossing the last of Guts's belongings out her apartment window when he roared up in his car. He got out and hollered up at her.

"Pearl! What are you doing?"

"That's the same thing you asked me last night," she shouted back. "And once again I'll say to you, what does it look like I'm doing?"

"Sweetheart, let's not be so public about this."

"I ain't paranoid like you, Lorenzo. Have I ever said anything to you about coming in and out of my house through the back door? About keeping the shades drawn?"

"You know I got good reasons for all that."

"Uh-huh. And I got good reasons for pouring gasoline on your stuff and setting it on fire! That's what I'm going to do next if you don't hurry up and get it from under my window."

"Pearl. I take care of you. I buy your groceries. I help you pay your rent so that you can save up and open that dance studio one day. Isn't that enough?"

"Obviously not, Lorenzo."

"Okay, Pearl, what more do you want?"

"I want to know that you'll carry me through the fire."

"What fire?"

"Sometimes you are so dense. Not a real fire! Through whatever I might have to face."

Pearl slammed her window shut. Guts gathered his things and tossed them in his trunk. *One wrong move and everything's shot to shit*, he thought. *Maybe I overreacted about the unlocked door. No, I had to be straight with her. She thinks she knows these streets but not really. I guess I could have said that better.* He was still second-guessing himself when he got back to the cabstand.

Inside, Trina waved a fistful of phone message receipts. "That ballplayer's been calling and calling," she said.

Guts sighed and dialed up Crenshaw. "Hey, this is Guts," he said.

"Them bitches took my shit!" a voice yelled through the phone.

"Crenshaw, is that you?"

"Damn straight it's me! Find them bitches and get my shit back."

"Slow down. Take a sip of whatever it is you're holding and—"

"How did you know I was holding—never mind. Let me hit this right quick."

Guts heard the sound of a bottle being tilted and slurped.

"That's better."

"Good," Guts said. "Now let's try it again, only slower. All right?"

"All right. Them. Bitches. Took. My. Shit."

"The girls you partied with last night."

"That's right. April, May, and June."

"You mean Summer, Spring, and Autumn."

"That's what I said!"

"Okay. They robbed you?"

"I woke up and my wallet had been cleaned out. My chains are gone. Worst of all, them bitches took my World Series ring. I need you to find 'em, get my ring back."

"Do you know their real names?"

"Um, no. We were partying and…well, there just didn't seem be any need to catch those details. But you can find out. You're a problem solver. Go out and ask around. Break some legs, goddammit."

"You want me to risk my neck for a bankroll and some chains?"

"I thought you ran this town."

Guts scratched his nose. "I never told you that. Besides, it's not like it used to be around here. When King died, people set their own streets on fire. Burned down the biggest grocery in the neighborhood. People will do anything. I used to be able to draw a line and dare a man to cross it. He still might not cross it, but he'll give me lip now."

"Sounds like you scared."

Guts paused. There was that word again. "Naw. Just alert."

"Look, I know it was Goode or Washburn who paid you to take me around. Just add this to the tab. Might even be a bonus in it for you."

"Yeah, what's that?"

"My friendship, baby. I know we clicked. We're like two peas in a pod."

"I could see that your chains weren't cheap, Crenshaw. But they're just trinkets. You can get some more."

"I don't care about the chains. It's the ring. It really means something to me."

Guts could almost swear that Crenshaw's voice faltered. Was he choking up?

"That ring gives me strength," he continued. "They can fine me, suspend me, make me look bad in the papers. But they can't take back that ring. It says I'm a world champion. My name's in the books and they can't take it out. It doesn't belong on any finger but mine."

"Why were you wearing it in the first place? Why don't you keep it in a safe deposit box or something?"

"I wasn't wearing it. I was carrying it in my pocket. I'm telling you man, them bitches went through my stuff. Say, Guts—you ever killed a woman before?"

"Naw, and I don't plan to start."

"Just asking, just asking."

"Tell you what, All-Star. I'll put the word out. But I don't want to promise something I can't follow through on."

"Okay, whatever you can do. 'Preciate it."

Guts hung up and yelled for Playfair.

He entered the office immediately, almost as if he'd been listening outside the door.

"What it is? You heard about my wedding dresses?"

"Come again?"

"Wedding dresses. In my trunk. Bridal veils and trains and whatnot. I can let you have one today for half of what I'll charge tomorrow. One I'm keeping, though. For Nichelle."

Guts waited for an explanation.

"Nichelle Nichols. *Uhura*, baby! I got one she'll look perfect in when we walk down the aisle. But from the look on your face that's not why you called me in here."

"No, although I wish you the best of luck with Uhura. Actually, I'm looking for a ring."

Ananias Goode, like Guts, was no fan of churches. Although Rev. Washington was Goode's best friend and he contributed generously to Good Samaritan, he had absolutely no interest in going inside. Even a memorial service for a man he'd known since childhood wasn't incentive enough to end his decades-long avoidance. So he sat outside the church in his New Yorker while Rev. Washington conducted Fish's homegoing service. Oddly enough, Sharps had asked for and received permission to attend, although he'd hardly known the man. Alone in the backseat, his eyes hidden by dark glasses, Goode lifted his glass of bourbon and raised a silent farewell toast.

Nearby, Guts was outside the church, too, leaning against the side of his Plymouth while Mr. Logan bid Fish goodbye. Mr. Logan had practically raised Guts after his parents died. With his eyes failing, Mr. Logan didn't need to be anywhere near a steering wheel, So Guts took him where he needed to go or made sure someone was available to do it when he couldn't. Mr. Logan's fidelity to Good Samaritan was the reason Guts drove the van every Sunday.

Throughout Goode's rise to prosperity, the word "gangster" had clung like white on rice. For example, Good Samaritan was frequently whispered about as "the gangster's church" because of its pastor's curious friendship with him. By 1970, however, Goode had begun to reinvent himself in earnest. His friend Levander Watts, publisher of the *Citizen*, had helped with timely photographs of Goode engaged in community service. His annual turkey giveaway for Thanksgiving, his dedicated service as a board member of Harry Truman Boys Club, his contributions to the Abram Higgins Memorial Garden in Fairgrounds Park—all received front-page coverage. As a result, over time "the gangster" came to be referred to, with admiration, as "Mr. G."

The new nickname pleased Goode. Underneath the displays of power, the long trail of bloodshed and intimidation, the penchants for bourbon and good cigars, Ananias Goode, like most human beings, harbored a desire to be loved and appreciated.

Few men were as aware of this as Guts Tolliver. He tapped on Goode's window.

"Mr. G., I'm sorry to bother you, especially at a time like this," he said. "I need to ask you a big favor."

Goode rolled down his window. "Guts, always good to see you," he said. "Come on in, let's talk. It will be like old times."

PeeWee Jefferson woke up to giggling. That meant his sister and her stuck-up roommates had rolled another sucker.

He got to his feet and ambled toward the sound, scratching his balls. The three women had open suitcases spread out on the beds. They were throwing in dresses and shoes, talking a mile a minute. PeeWee heard something about Chicago.

"I've always wanted to see the Windy City," he said. "I hear they got some fine females up there."

His sister made a hissing noise. "Shut up, PeeWee. Ain't nobody even talking to you."

"I'm your big brother, girl. Show some respect," he said, eyeing the tangle of chains and jewelry on the night table.

"I'll show you some respect when you find some place to sleep other than my couch. Twenty-five fucking years old and ain't got job the first."

"I want to go to Chicago with y'all."

"You can't, there's a height requirement," one of the women said. More giggling.

"We going to meet some real men and don't need you hanging around," his sister added. "We going to Hawthorne, play the horses and catch some big spenders."

"Who'd y'all roll last night? That looks like real gold."

"What makes you think we rolled somebody?"

"You didn't get this at a prayer meeting." He picked up one of the chains and held it to the light.

"You don't even know what you looking at," his sister said. "Put that shit down."

"I just want to make sure you get the best price for your haul. I can boost it for you."

"Like we need your help. Put that shit down."

"Fine!" PeeWee made a big show of throwing the chain down hard on the table. "Just don't come asking for me later," he said.

He left the room. Grinning, he opened his hand and looked at the ring he'd just swiped. *Well, well, look what we have here.*

A large diamond was mounted on a black stone and surrounded by four smaller diamonds. Raised letters spelled "World Champions" around the outside. A major league team logo decorated one shank. "Crenshaw" was on the other.

When PeeWee realized what he had, he thought he might turn it in and get a big reward. Then he decided that doing so might risk being linked to the crime. He'd sell it to a fence instead. But the ring warmed his hand, felt good in his palm. Holding it, he felt stronger. He felt taller. He slipped it on his biggest finger. The world looked better, too. For the first time in a long time, the day felt full of promise. He took it off and put it back in his pocket. *I'll just hold onto it for a while.*

A few days after Fish's memorial service, Guts paced in the parking lot outside Aldo's, an upscale women's department store in the city's West End. Pearl had started out as a customer greeter, then was promoted to elevator operator, and finally became the store's first black salesclerk. Her post was in intimates, upstairs and far enough away to avoid offending customers uncomfortable with the idea of a Negro handling a cash register.

She came out to the lot, looked up, saw him, and marched right at him.

"You can't be here scaring white women. You trying to get me fired?"

"It's your lunch break, right? I need to talk to you."

"And people in hell are thirsty," Pearl snarled. "I wouldn't give you air if you were stopped up in a jug."

"Come on, Pearl. I just want you to see something."

"It better be a ring."

"A what?"

"You heard me. A diamond ring. I know you got that Playfair running around asking about rings. You scared to go into a diamond shop yourself? If it ain't a ring you want to show me, keep stepping. I want to be a wife, Lorenzo. A real wife, not no dress-and-breath."

"I don't think I ever told you that Mr. G. has a wife."

Pearl paused to let that sink in. "All the pictures I see of that man in the paper, he's always by himself. How come I've never seen her?"

"Few people have."

"She doesn't get out much, does she?"

"Never. She never gets out."

Pearl put her hands on her hips. "Okay, you've got my attention. What do you want from me?"

"I want you to meet her."

Pearl sat with her hands in her lap all the way to Lewis Place. Guts snuck a glance at each red light and stop sign, but all he ever glimpsed was her firmly set jaw. He found it hard to believe that she was the same woman who'd only recently danced naked to the Temptations in his living room. He turned on the radio. Tyrone Davis was asking, "Baby, can I change my mind?" In his husky voice he pleaded for a second chance.

Without looking at Guts, Pearl reached out and turned it off.

When they arrived at Lewis Place, Goode opened the door himself.

"Mr. G., this is Pearl Jordan."

"Ah yes, the lovely Pearl. I've heard so much about you."

"You have?"

"Yes," Goode lied. Above Pearl's head, the men exchanged glances. "I'm pleased to meet you at last."

He led them into the living room. "My wife is resting. I have business elsewhere. Lawrence will show you in."

Lawrence opened the adjoining door to reveal a fully outfitted hospital room. Where every other house on Lewis Place had a dining table and chairs, Goode had installed a large hospital bed and the best life-support equipment available. A transparent canopy was draped over the bed.

Pearl noted the hi-fi speakers mounted near the ceiling in each corner of the room, through which a popular ballad was softly playing.

"Johnny Mathis. Mrs. Goode's favorite singer," Lawrence whispered. "You can get a little closer."

Pearl took a tentative step forward. She had already gotten as close as she wanted to get.

What was left of Lucille Goode curled fetus-like in the center of the bed. Her body, shriveled down to 59 pounds, was a tiny, indistinguishable lump. Only her head was full-sized. It hung limply atop her impossibly frail shoulders, crowned here and there with wisps of hair. A tube ran from her abdomen and into a machine next to the bed. Her eyes were closed and her mouth was open.

"Mrs. Goode," Lawrence said. "Guts is here. And this is his friend, Miss Pearl."

Guts removed his hat. "Nice to see you again, Mrs. Goode," he said.

Both men looked expectantly at Pearl.

"H-hello," she stammered.

After what seemed to Pearl an unbearably long time, Lawrence escorted them out. He took one last peek, shut the door softly, and joined them in the living room.

"We don't know how aware she is, whether she can hear anything," he said. "So we try to keep a conversation going in hopes she can understand."

Keep dreaming, Pearl thought. "What was that thing she was wrapped in?"

"An oxygen tent," Lawrence explained. "It pumps in fresh air to make it easier for her to breathe. It monitors the carbon dioxide she exhales and removes it."

"I see," Pearl said. She waited for them to tell her what had happened to Mrs. Goode. When neither man volunteered, she lost her patience.

"Which one of you is going to tell me how she got like that?"

The men looked at each other.

"It was supposed to be a hit on Mr. G. Mrs. Goode—and their son—got in the way," Guts said.

"Son? I didn't know Mr. Goode had a son."

"He doesn't," Lawrence said. "He did but now he doesn't."

Pearl had to leave. Right away.

"Nice to meet you, Lawrence," she said. She was out the door before he could respond.

Guts hustled out after her.

She turned on him, eyes flashing. "You're trying to scare me, Lorenzo. There must be an easier way to break my heart."

"I ain't trying to hurt you. I just wanted you to see why I think like I do."

"That was *her* destiny," Pearl said. "Not mine. I'm supposed to die with all my wits about me, an old lady in a nice bed surrounded by all my grandchildren. I could have told you that if you asked me. I'm as sure of that as I'm black. But you didn't ask me. Instead you drag me over to your boss's house for some kind of horror show, trying to scare me. Sometimes I think you don't have the sense God gave a grape. I'm catching a cab back to work—and it won't be one of yours."

Later that day, Pearl smiled as she waited on one of her few black customers, an elegant woman who always bought classy silk lingerie.

Outside the store, dusk was gathering. PeeWee Jefferson found his spot on the parking lot amid a clump of shrubbery, just beyond the reach of the streetlights. He had lurked here often, watching as the employees and customers came and went. Now, he was convinced, the time had come to strike.

Pearl rang up the woman's purchases. She was so dignified, so reserved, that Pearl wondered if she actually wore the sexy stuff she bought. Maybe she bought it to support the store's only black salesgirl. Pearl handed the woman her packages. "Thank you," said the customer, flashing a brief smile before resuming her usual cool pose.

"Thank *you*, Dr. Noel," Pearl said. "Have a nice evening."

Dr. Noel headed to the parking lot humming softly. Watching her, PeeWee fingered the ring in his pocket. She was distracted, a fact in his favor. She was also tiny. *Hell, her packages are almost bigger than she is.* Stroking the ring, he prepared to pounce.

A solid chop to his nose sent him sprawling on his back. The blow wasn't intended to knock him out, just disturb him.

PeeWee groaned. "What the —?"

"Here, let me give you a hand."

The hand extended in PeeWee's direction wore a ring almost as distinctive as the one in PeeWee's pocket. It was large, rectangular, and emerald green. PeeWee got to a sitting position and scooted backward. Now he could see he'd been surprised by a tall, slender figure with a scary grin. He wore green rectangular sunglasses, a green suit, and green alligator shoes. His bright yellow tie sported a green tie tack.

PeeWee rubbed his nose. "Who the hell are you?"

"I'm the man you'll one day thank for saving you from being sent up on a humble. Call me Sharps. Listen, son, I know what you're thinking. Only rich bitches go to this store, so that one's pocketbook must be busting with cash. You're right but you're thinking small, small fry."

"The name's PeeWee."

"Uh-huh. Let's take a ride, shall we? I'll drive. Those tore-up sneakers tell me you don't have a car."

"I ain't going nowhere with you."

Sharps chuckled and glanced at his watch. "Kid, if I wanted to hurt you, your pitiful black ass would already be on a slab somewhere, or at the very least rotting in an alley. Let's roll before the bitch gets away."

Moments later, PeeWee sulked in the front seat as Sharps eased his Eldorado onto Kingshighway. He headed west, keeping a few cars between him and Dr. Noel. Finally they sat in the shadows across the street from an impressive mansion overlooking the city's largest park, watching as their quarry brought her packages to her front porch.

"Now you see what I'm getting at," Sharps said. "That bitch has more money than she knows what to do with. There's stuff in there that's worth plenty. Furniture, art. I'm guessing those hardwood floors are dressed up in Persian rugs. And a safe, there's got to be a safe. Enough in there to be shared, kid."

"I get it," PeeWee said, his hand on the door handle. "Let's do it."

"Not so fast," Sharps cautioned. "You're not ready for a job like this. It's not like snatching a purse. You need practice, training. I'm gonna put you with one of my associates. He's got experience and can show you the ropes."

PeeWee puffed out his chest. "I'm used to running my own thing," he said. "What makes you think I'll work for you?"

Sharps laughed. "Because you're tired of being hungry and I know how to make sure a nigger's well fed."

PeeWee sighed. "All right then. But on a trial basis only."

Sharps put the car in drive. "Whatever you want to call it, kid. As long as you remember to do what I say."

Guts was buying sweet potatoes. He chose carefully, and when he had a dozen that met his standards, he paid for them and drove to

Mr. Logan's house on Finney Avenue. The first thing he noticed was that the grass was getting high. He made a mental note to have it mowed. The second thing he noticed was three teenage boys sitting on Mr. Logan's lower front steps, the same steps he had sat on when he was their age. They sat with their legs spread out. Empty bottles sat nearby in the grass. One of the boys ate from a bag of sunflower seeds and spat the shells.

"What it is?" Guts asked as he approached. One of the boys nodded. The second one muttered "Whassup?" The third just spat.

"Y'all some kin to Mr. Logan?"

The boys looked at each other and shrugged. "Who?" one of them asked.

"The man who lives here," Guts replied.

None of the boys replied. They stared beyond Guts as if he wasn't there.

"It's getting late," Guts continued. "Don't y'all have school tomorrow?"

"School's out," the seed-eating boy said. "Been out for a week."

Guts reached in his waistband and pulled out a peppermint. "Tell you what. Mr. Logan needs his rest. Peace and quiet is good for him. Y'all gonna have to take your little party somewhere else. I'm gonna unwrap this candy and put it in my mouth. Y'all got that much time."

The boys sat still while Guts went through the motions. One yawned. The second smiled and muttered, "crazy muthafucka." The third just spat.

"What? Y'all are still here?"

"Fuck you, fat man," the third boy said. He reached for his bag of seeds and found that they were missing. Puzzled, he looked up and saw them being crushed in Guts's fist.

Guts smiled. "Pretty fast for a fat man, right? I can get your throat just as quick."

The boy started to reply but Guts grabbed him by the neck and hoisted him skyward. While the boy kicked and gasped, Guts turned to his friends. "If y'all move your asses, he might still be breathing when I put him back down."

The two boys ran away and the third took off as soon as Guts lowered him to the ground. "Wait," Guts called after him. "Don't you want your seeds?"

Mr. Logan's skin and eyes were as close to the burnished orange-brown of sweet potato flesh that a human complexion can get. Guts half-suspected it was because Mr. Logan had eaten at least one roasted sweet potato every day since he was a small boy. He smiled when Guts came in carrying a bag.

"Ah," he said. "I've already got the oven warmed up." He took out a couple of potatoes and put them in the sink.

"They've been scrubbed," Guts said.

"I know. And I'm going to scrub them again. Thanks for the ride to see Fish off. Alice always cut my hair, but after she passed I started going to Fish. Not that I had much to cut." What little hair he had left congregated above his ears.

He shrugged when Guts asked him about the kids on his steps.

"I don't sit out on the porch as much as I used to."

"Why not? You love the sun."

"Well, it's not the same with all those kids out there. I've had my days of sun. It's their time now." Mr. Logan removed the potatoes from the sink and patted them dry.

"No," Guts said. "It's your time. It's your time and it's your yard. They've only been doing this since school let out, right?"

"Longer than that. I don't think they're the schoolboy types."

"Don't worry," Guts assured him. "I'll take care of them."

"Leave them alone, Lorenzo. They're just kids. No fathers. No helping hand." He rubbed the potatoes with oil and sat them in a baking pan.

"I ain't buying it," Guts said. "There's a boys club right up the street. Gabe Patterson's running it now."

"Too many kids," Mr. Logan said. "Not enough Gabe Pattersons."

"I'm still going to run them off your front."

"I didn't run you off."

"And look how well I turned out."

Mr. Logan put the pan in the oven and set the timer. "What's eating you, Lorenzo?"

"Nothing."

"I see. You know, I think I'm going to have to stop saying 'I see'—with these cataracts, I rely mostly on sound."

"It's Pearl. She's done with me."

"That's no good. How come?"

"I don't know. I won't marry her because I don't want her to have to deal with any payback coming my way from hurting people."

"You've done more than hurt people. You've killed people. I love you, son, you know that. But I've told you before and I'll say it again: Somehow, someway, you're gonna have to pay for what you've done. I'm happy that you're backing away from that kind of thing. But it doesn't make it like the past never happened."

"That's what I'm saying. When the time comes for me to pay, I don't want Pearl around."

"What does she say?"

"She's not worried about it. She said she's going to die an old lady in her bed."

"What does that mean to you?"

"She's trying to let me off the hook. She doesn't want me to feel responsible for protecting her."

Mr. Logan smiled. "We can't even save ourselves in the end. But that's not the point. I'd give everything to be able to have Alice with me, holding my hand as everything around me goes dark. But I'm grateful that I got to have her at all. My memories of her, that's my light. We loved each other as best we could. Maybe that's all Pearl wants."

Mr. Logan got out plates and poured two glasses of Coca-Cola, the strongest thing he drank. He arranged an empty place setting for Alice, a ritual he'd practiced ever since she died four years ago.

Guts broke the silence. "About the things I've done. Most of the time I was just doing my job. A lot of them, if I hadn't gotten to them first, someone else would have. They weren't people to me. They were jobs."

"And the man in the shoeshine parlor? Was he a job?"

Guts sighed. "You know he wasn't."

"You've always had a good heart, Guts. I knew that when I first met you. What I can't figure out is how a good heart ever led to bad deeds. You're gonna have to solve that one for yourself."

When the potatoes were done, Guts pulled them from the oven. After they'd cooled a few minutes, he slit them open and dropped in thick squares of butter. They sat down to the small table where the young Guts had eaten many meals that Alice Logan had prepared, meals that sustained him in his lowest moments. He always felt 13 again when he sat at the Logans' table. Guts picked up his spoon but Mr. Logan grabbed his wrist.

"Lorenzo, I'm going to say something to God before we eat. You don't have to pray, but you do have to listen."

"Yes, sir," Guts said. He bowed his head.

L ORENZO LIFTED THE CUFFLINKS and weighed them carefully in his hand. He turned them, examining them in the light. He put them back in the box, took out another pair, and looked at them just as carefully.

"That's right, son," his father said. "Take your time." Clad in undershirt, shorts, and stocking cap, Chauncey Tolliver sat back in his chair. He licked the edge of his cigarette paper and rolled it into a tight tube. Bobbing his head to the W.C. Handy tune playing softly in the background, he touched a match to the end.

Lorenzo's mother called from the next room. "Chauncey! I know you're not about to light up a cigarette when we're supposed to be getting ready."

"Relax, Lucille." Chauncey winked at his son, who was sprawled out on his belly on the floor. "Lorenzo's picking out some cufflinks for me."

Lucille Tolliver came in, fastening her dress. Her hair was done and her face made up. She stood taller than most men in just her stocking feet. Lorenzo thought she had the most beautiful face in the world.

"The Butlers and Chauffeurs Ball don't come but once a year. But you're sitting there just as easy as you please, like we have one every other week."

Chauncey sat his cigarette in an ashtray and stood up. He was a full head taller than his Amazonian wife. "A shindig ain't a shindig without us," he told her.

Having settled on a winning pair at last, Lorenzo turned over and held the cufflinks up toward his father. He started to speak but saw that his parents were embracing, looking deeply into each other's eyes and swaying to the music as if they were alone in the room.

"Watch yourself, Chauncey," Lucille said, smiling. "Our baby is right there."

"Baby? That boy's 13. Almost a man. Ain't that right, Lorenzo?"

Lorenzo smiled bashfully. He was already six feet tall and two hundred pounds.

That night, Lorenzo woke to the sound of weeping. His father was sitting on the side of his bed. It was still dark, and the dim glow of a streetlight outside his window made a shadowy mask of his father's features.

"Papa?"

"It's me, Lorenzo."

"Papa, what's wrong? What happened?"

Chauncey Tolliver said nothing.

Lorenzo climbed out of bed and turned on the light. His father's bow tie was askew. Dirt and blood soiled his collar and the front of his suit. Lorenzo stared at the stains. "Where's Mama?" he asked.

His father wrung his hands. He closed his eyes, clenched them tight. He opened them and, finding the world unchanged, he began to cry even more. In between racking sobs, he gave his son the bad news.

"On the way back from the ball, we had a flat tire," he began. "I pulled over to fix it. A couple of the lug nuts were stuck, so I was going slower than usual. Your mama needed to stretch her legs."

This time Lorenzo closed his eyes. Unlike his father, he kept them shut.

"A car hit her. She's gone, Lorenzo. Our beautiful Lucille is gone."

The funeral was a Butlers and Chauffeurs Ball in reverse, all of white society's servants again decked out in finery, not to celebrate, but to send one of their own to Glory. It was a dizzying experience for Lorenzo: Sympathetic mourners clasped his hands, others squeezed his shoulders, and still others chanted "God bless" softly into his ear until the voices and faces of his parents' friends and coworkers—the Logans, the Lennixes, the Morrises—all melted together into a confusing, heartbreaking mess.

In the weeks that followed, Chauncey became a child again. He forgot how to feed himself, couldn't tie his shoes properly, and couldn't roll his own cigarettes. Refusing to sleep in the bed he had shared with Lucille, every night he sat in his chair in the front parlor until he nodded off. When Lorenzo propped up his father and buttoned his shirt for him in the morning, Chauncey would drop his chin to his chest and mutter the same mournful refrain: "It should have been me, son. It should have been me." At night, when Lorenzo spooned canned soup (one of the few things he could make) between his father's lips, he said it again: "It should have been me."

Once Lorenzo woke in the middle of the night to the smell of smoke. His father had fallen asleep in the chair with a cigarette lit, nearly setting himself and the apartment ablaze. How he made it to work every day was a mystery beyond Lorenzo's wisdom—but it turned out the mystery was solved when Lorenzo came home from school and found an eviction notice pasted to their door.

He took down the note, resigned to discussing it with his father when he returned from wherever he went when he was pretending to be on the job. But there was no need to wait: Chauncey was already home. Lorenzo discovered him slumped in his chair. It was only when he tried and failed to revive his father that he noticed the foam around his lips and the empty glass and the container of roach powder on the table beside him. Lorenzo put his ear on his father's pulseless chest and marveled that a body could get cold so fast.

Heavyset in life, Chauncey Tolliver was even heavier in death. Still, Lorenzo resolved to lift him from his chair and wash him clean before surrendering him to the outside world. Pressing himself against his father's back, he thrust his hands under Chauncey's armpits and began to drag him slowly backward, toward the bathroom. About halfway down the hall, Chauncey's bulk and Lorenzo's grief became too much. The son collapsed, bringing his father's stiffening body down on top of him. There, in the fading light of afternoon, he wrapped his arms around his father and wept. When he had cried himself out, he slid out from under Chauncey, went to the bathroom and filled a pail. He washed his father in the hall, put a blanket under him and dragged him back to the bed he'd shared with Lucille. He dressed the body in Chauncey's best suit, made sure his bow tie was straight. He packed a bag with a few clothes, kissed his father's clammy brow, and turned toward the exit. Suddenly remembering, he rushed back to his parents' room and rummaged through his father's drawers. Finally he wrapped his fingers around Chauncey's treasured box of cufflinks. Then, after one last gaze back, he stepped out and closed the door.

Twenty-two years later, Guts strode happily into the most comfortable setting he knew. School was out, summer had officially begun, and the pool opened every day at 10. Come nightfall, the softball diamonds of Fairgrounds Park would be hosting Little League contests under the lights. Softball Diamond No. 2, near the intersection of Vandeventer and Natural Bridge, would be the site of a popular men's league led by the Moose Lounge and the Tribesmen. The bleachers would be filled with cheering fans and picnic blankets would be set up near the left-field line, just beyond the reach of foul balls. Coolers of beer would dot the grass. There would be laughter, chatter, women…. But it was still morning and all of that busyness was hours away.

Guts raised his hat to Mrs. Tichenor and Mrs. Means, waved at the family of tennis phenoms unzipping their rackets, and exchanged nods with the lone fisherwoman, only her lips visible beneath the fishing hat pulled down over her eyes. He sat on his usual bench and dug into his bag of breadcrumbs.

"You call those crumbs? Them big chunks you feeding, it's a wonder these ducks aren't fat as hippos."

Guts smiled without turning around. "What's up, Crush?"

"Ya know, I keep on keeping on."

"You and me both."

Crusher Boudreau was wearing his customary workout wear. He pulled his towel from around his neck and vigorously rubbed his scalp. "I hear you're thinking about tying the knot."

"Say what?"

"Don't act surprised. The cat's out the bag. The whole North Side's talking."

"*What?*"

"Relax. Not for real. I'm just pulling your leg. It's the ring talk."

"Oh, yeah. I am looking for a ring, a very valuable one. You heard anything?"

"Nothing specific. But you should ask your boy Playfair."

"I already did. He said the trail is cold."

"Hmm. All right, then. Maybe I heard wrong. Anyway, I'm glad to hear it's not a wedding ring you're looking for."

"You got something against marriage, Crush?"

"I've been married before. I didn't deserve her and she figured that out. I'd do it again. In fact, I got my eye on somebody."

"Who would that be? Wait, is it Nichelle Nichols?"

Crush smiled. "Diana Ross. Someday we'll be together," he sang. Guts laughed.

"That's funny, huh? Tell me, what's Berry Gordy got that I don't?"

"You're asking the wrong person," Guts replied. "Only Diana can tell you that."

Twenty-two years ago, in a tidy little cottage on Finney Avenue, Alice Logan summoned her husband to dinner. Passing through the living room, she paused at the front window. "Phil," she said, "there's someone outside."

Cephus Logan stepped out onto the porch. The figure on the lower steps was immense, with shoulder muscles visible beneath the fabric of his shirt. Though the stranger easily made two of him, Logan approached him without fear. "Hello," he called, and the figure turned. Even in the dusk Logan recognized the facial structure, which perfectly blended the features of Chauncey and Lucille Tolliver, former king and queen of the Butlers and Chauffeurs Ball.

"Young Tolliver, is that you?"

"Lorenzo, sir…. My father's dead."

Where Lorenzo's mother had been towering and stout, Mrs. Logan was runty and slight. Where Lorenzo's father had been massive and powerful, Mr. Logan was short and thin. But he had his own kind of strength. Thick, corded veins ran up and down his forearms.

Where Chauncey and Lucille loved to laugh and dance, the Logans preferred to read and pray. But they were kind people, and, Mr. Logan's weird fondness for sweet potatoes aside, not the types to get under anybody's skin. Lorenzo, who seemed as if he would never stop growing, often felt as if he was living in a doll's house. He learned to duck while passing beneath their doorways. He was silent and awkward during his first year under their roof, but in time he grew accustomed to them, and they to him.

Then one night, shortly after he turned 16, Lorenzo entered the house to the sound of something he had seldom heard: the Logans arguing.

"If you're really still waiting on the police to do something, you're going to be still waiting a long, long time," Mr. Logan was saying. "They think the only good Negro is a dead one."

"I always thought somebody should just do something," Mrs. Logan said. "She was murdered and she was one of my best friends. Lucille didn't deserve to die like that."

"We don't know exactly what happened."

"What more do we need to know?"

Mr. Logan didn't answer. Mrs. Logan looked up and saw her husband staring at bulky Lorenzo, silently filling the doorway.

"My mother died in an accident," he said.

Mr. Logan motioned toward the table. "Sit down, son."

Mrs. Logan dabbed her eyes with a handkerchief. "Excuse me," she said.

Lorenzo stepped aside to enable her to pass. Then he joined Mr. Logan at the table.

"You want some ice water?"

"No. I want to know what happened to my mother. Sir."

Mr. Logan took out his handkerchief and held it under the faucet. He soaked it with cold water, wrung it out, and wiped his forehead. Then he joined Lorenzo at the table. "As you know, your parents worked for a rich white family. Word was, the lady of the house was stuck on your father. Wouldn't leave him alone. Told him he'd better do what she wanted or she'd holler rape. What could your father do? We believe her husband found out. He didn't say anything, just kept making your father sweat. But Chauncey wouldn't break and your mother, well, she didn't have any idea. The night of the ball, a car ran your folks off the road. Another car came by, fired shots. Your mother got hit. Some people leaving the ball say it was white folks in those cars. Some of them even say your daddy's boss was in the second car."

Guts thought of his parents dancing cheek-to-cheek before leaving for the ball. He thought of his father slipping away, day by day, sick from guilt and loneliness. Then he stood up. He looked down at Mr. Logan. "May I be excused?"

Mr. Logan looked as if he wanted to say more. But he just nodded.

Lorenzo went to the little room he'd called home and opened the chest of drawers.

When he came out, Mr. Logan was gazing thoughtfully out the front window. He watched as Lorenzo walked to the front door and put his hand on the knob. Lorenzo turned to him. "Thank you for all you've done for me. Someday I'll pay you back."

"Lorenzo, I planned to tell you the truth someday. Just not so soon."

Three years is not soon, Lorenzo thought. He didn't need to say it out loud because he knew Mr. Logan was as aware of that truth as he was. "Thank you kindly," he said. He didn't wait to say goodbye to Mrs. Logan. He just tipped his cap and went out the door. He walked down Finney Avenue toward the river, carrying a few changes of clothes in a battered satchel and his box of cufflinks in his hand.

Lorenzo had been an indifferent student, reserving what little enthusiasm he had for gym class. On Sumner High's track, he astounded the skinny sprinters by thundering past them in the 100-yard dash. In the cramped gym, he could do chin-ups until the bar appeared to bend under his exertions. But school, like his life up to that point, was done. It was time for something new.

Guts leaned back in his chair and put his feet up on his desk. He could hear from the outer room, beneath the racket of what sounded like a flock of birds, the men of the cabstand giving Playfair a hard time about Uhura. He wondered if they'd laugh if they knew about him and Pearl. He was no dummy, he could wrap his mind around an idea if he gave himself enough time, and yet he always felt that he was operating a step or two behind her, scrambling to catch up. Maybe he really was too dense for her, as she'd recently suggested. Maybe he had as much business being with her as Playfair did with Uhura, or Crusher Boudreau did with Diana Ross.

Playfair tapped on the open door.

"What it is, baby?"

Guts folded his arms behind his head. "Hey, Play. I was hoping *you* could tell *me*."

Playfair shrugged. "Sorry, Guts, like I told you, that ring has gone underground."

"Without a trace."

"Exactly."

Guts took his feet off the desk and replaced them with his meaty fists. "I don't plan to hurt those girls, Play. If you've seen them maybe you told them that. I'm just looking for the ring. You don't even have to tell me their names."

"That's good," Playfair said hastily. "That's outtasight, because if my business associates start thinking they can't trust me, there goes my business. Them girls find out I talked behind 'em, they won't look for me when they come back from Chicago. I don't know what they might be hauling."

"So that's where they are."

"They didn't tell me that. But I heard 'em talking."

The two men looked at each other. "I moved their stuff," Playfair said. "It was just a couple chains, a money clip, and a pocket watch. Like I told you, I didn't see no ring."

"Play, you being straight with me?"

Playfair briefly looked hurt. "Guts, when have I ever been anything but straight with you?"

"You're right," Guts said. "My fault."

"It's cool."

"What is that noise?"

Playfair smiled, back to his usual peppy self. "Parakeets," he said. "Looking for a feathered friend?

Nineteen years ago, Lorenzo wound up half-asleep on a bench in the park outside the train station, his satchel and box beside him. He had a handful of dollars and he thought he might catch a train somewhere, anywhere his meager funds could take him. It was early morning, and the ducks in the pond in front of him were already awake.

Inside the station, Ananias Goode was fresh from a trip to Chicago. He had a small entourage with him: some muscle, a runner, his wife, and his infant son. He waited while his men collected his family's bags. Once outside, Goode ushered his family into the backseat of a waiting car while his men loaded the trunk. He looked up and saw a husky youth sitting in the park across the street and was reminded of his young self. He guessed this man-child was newly arrived from the Deep South, friendless as he once was, looking—hoping—for a chance to get a leg up.

Lorenzo stared at the ducks in the pond, entranced. He was drawn to their stolid serenity, the unruffled but constant attention they paid to the ducklings paddling tentatively across the water's surface.

"Hey!"

Out of the corner of his eye, Lorenzo noticed two swaggering young men approaching fast. They were black, not much older than him, early twenties maybe, and neither could match him in size. But they wore fearless expressions and moved with the knowing confidence of the street. Lorenzo ignored them, keeping his eyes on the ducks.

"Hey!"

The second holler was loud enough to land in the ears of Goode and his men. They all turned toward the sound.

Looking back, Guts often wondered what possessed the two thugs to mess with him in the first place. He looked formidable even sitting down. Perhaps he looked so distracted that they felt bold enough to take a chance.

"You heard me, nigger," the first thug said. "What you got in that bag?"

"Fuck the bag. I want that nice little box right there," the second one said.

Lorenzo looked up and took in his surroundings. There were only the ducks and a group of serious-looking men across the street, standing around a pair of expensive cars.

"Why you looking around?" the first thug asked. "You looking for help?"

For the first time, Lorenzo looked directly at his antagonist. "I'm looking to see who you got backing you up."

"What?"

"Forget it," Lorenzo replied.

The brief exchange provided Thug No. 2 an opportunity to go for the box. Lorenzo turned and slapped at him. The box slipped from the thug's hand, hit the ground, and overturned. Cufflinks scattered in the gravel and rolled into the grass.

Across the street, one of Goode's men flicked his Zippo and leaned in to light his boss's cigar. But Goode stayed his hand. The man followed Goode's line of vision. "Damn," he said.

In the park, Thug No. 2 knelt on the ground, bawling. His arm was bent crazily and he was spitting blood. Thug No. 1 was sprawled on his back, pinned to the ground by a large boot, not yet a size 14 EEE, planted on his chest. Satisfied that his tormentors could no longer bother him, Lorenzo turned his back on them and began to collect his cufflinks, dust them off, and place them back in the box.

"Damn is right," Goode said. "Bring that young man to me."

Minutes later, Lorenzo found himself being interviewed by a very important-looking man. He had on a tailor-made pinstriped suit and leather boots spit-shined to a dazzling gleam. A half-chewed cigar dangled from his mouth.

"Where you from, young'un?"

"Right here."

"That so? I had you pegged for a Southern boy."

"Nope."

"Where you live?"

Lorenzo shrugged. No use giving him too much information.

"You box?"

Lorenzo shook his head.

"Wrestle?"

"Nope."

"That was an impressive demonstration you put on over there. Where'd you learn to do that?"

"Don't know," Lorenzo said. "Never had to do it before."

"You need a job?"

"Depends."

"On what?"

"What I'd have to do and how much it pays."

Goode smiled and gestured to his man. The man leaned in and lit Goode's cigar.

"What's your name?"

"Lorenzo."

"We could use someone like you, Lorenzo. You've got guts."

Nineteen years later, Pearl sat under the dryer at Ardell's Beauty Parlor. Her head stinging from chemicals and her heart heavy with loneliness, she flipped through a *Jet* magazine.

There were seven other women in the shop, four customers and three hairdressers. A transistor radio sat on a shelf, playing Jerry Butler just a little too loud.

The cover headline on the magazine read, "Black Man Battles to Become Mayor of Newark," but Pearl could hardly pay attention. She was so caught up in her troubles with Guts that she imagined she heard his name underneath the music and through the ambient whir of the dryer.

An ad for the Ebony Book Club offered three hot titles: *The Spook Who Sat by the Door* by Sam Greenlee, *Revolutionary Notes* by Julius Lester, and *Die Nigger Die!* by H. Rap Brown—all for $14.85. Pearl turned a few more pages and paused, thinking she'd heard it again.

"Thought she could tame that big man. I could have told her that wasn't gonna happen. You can't tame a killer no more than you can put a bow tie on a gorilla."

Pearl's ears felt warm, and now she knew it wasn't because of the dryer.

Jet's "National Report" predicted unemployment among black men would soon reach 40 percent in many of the nation's large cities, a prospect that the Nixon administration considered "worrisome." Pearl sat the magazine on her lap and waited.

"She thinks she's better than us because she gets to wait on white folks all day. Hell, my mama does that and she's a maid."

Pearl was on her feet before she knew it. She turned to the busybody, a tall, stout woman with a head full of curlers.

"Get in my face and say that."

The woman exchanged glances with a couple of the other women. One giggled. Curlers played deaf. "What did you say?"

"You heard me," Pearl challenged. "Stand your hefty ass up."

In the background Jerry Butler continued on, oblivious.

Only the strong survive
Only the strong survive

Curlers got up, amused. "Why you little sawed-off bitch," she said. "I'll beat—"

A lifetime of exercise and dance lessons had blessed Pearl with exceptional calves. She leaped in the air, throwing herself at her talkative adversary. The momentum crashed the stunned woman backward to the floor. Pearl straddled her chest, grabbed her head, and slammed it against the linoleum tiles. Eerily calm, she placed a thumb over each of the woman's eyes, which were clenched shut in fear.

"I will blind you," Pearl hissed. "Hear me? I will leave your ass in darkness forever."

Curlers sobbed quietly. Pearl rose slowly, looking around at her frightened audience.

"Anybody else got something to say? No? Good."

She stomped out of Ardell's, marched straight to the nearest barbershop, and slammed the door. An hour later, she came out with a spanking new natural: short, perfectly round, and gleaming with Afro Sheen. She was still mad, though, and muttering to herself. "That heifer made me curse," she said.

Back at the cabstand, Rip Crenshaw was holding his audience spellbound with the story of how he busted up Hoyt Wilhelm's no-hitter. "With a knuckleballer," he explained, "you just close your eyes and swing. But I went one better. I pretended I was taking a whack at George Wallace."

Even Oliver, who had been slow to warm to the ballplayer, laughed heartily. Guts joined the group, his conversation with Playfair still lingering in his thoughts. Playfair and his parakeets had already left, but more than a few feathers had been left behind.

"Don't tell me," Guts said. "You were in the neighborhood and decided to drop by."

Crenshaw grinned. "How'd you guess? I had a few hours to kill and I hadn't heard from you. Thought maybe you had some news."

Guts led Crenshaw into his office and closed the door. "The chains? You'll never see them again."

"Figured as much. Don't care."

"And somewhere between Summer, Spring, Autumn, and the fence who boosted the chains, the ring disappeared."

"Son of a bitch. Can't you torture them gals and find out exactly what happened?"

"Naw, I can't do that. Besides, I haven't found them yet. They went out of town looking for bigger parties."

"You mean bigger fools."

"I didn't say that. Isn't this a little early for you to be going exploring? The clubs won't open for a long while. You want to pick up women off the street?"

"Never thought I'd say this," Crenshaw confided, "but I may have had enough of females for a minute. Them gals took advantage of my innocence. When you're as rich and pretty as I am, people don't always have your best interests in mind."

Guts nearly gagged on his peppermint. His coughing so disturbed Crenshaw that the slugger reached out and tapped him carefully on the back until it subsided. "I know," he said in as comforting a tone as he could muster. "It's got me choked up too."

"Let's take a ride," Guts suggested.

"To go look for the ring?"

"No, I told you I'm on that. If it's meant to turn up, it will."

"So what are we riding for?"

"I just want you to see that there's more to the North Side than hoes who steal jewelry. There's a lot of history here. Let me call my friend. He'll be the perfect tour guide."

Crenshaw did a double take. "You have a friend?"

They took off in Guts's Plymouth. When they arrived at the house on Finney, Guts rang the bell.

"It takes him a bit to hear it." He pressed the bell again. "His eyesight's not great either. But he's like family to me. He and his wife took me in when I had no place else to go."

"Your folks kicked you out?"

"My folks died."

The door creaked open and Mr. Logan peeked out.

"Rip Crenshaw, meet Mr. Logan. Without him, I would most certainly be dead."

"For real?" Crenshaw asked. "Well, we 'preciate you keeping him among the living."

"Lorenzo exaggerates," Mr. Logan said, "and please, call me Cephus. Lorenzo's been stuck on 'Mister' for more than 20 years."

Now Mr. Logan was exaggerating. Guts had hardly crossed his path for 15 years and might not ever have reconnected if it weren't for Nifty Poindexter. Nifty would pick a busy street corner, lay down a square of cardboard, and sit on it. He'd tangle his triple-jointed limbs so improbably that he looked completely unable to loosen them, let alone rise up and walk. Rush hours and lunchtime were particularly lucrative for Nifty. Compassionate passersby seldom hesitated to unburden their wallets and purses and stuff his cup to bursting. Nights found Nifty miraculously cured and the life of the party. He'd cut the rug until the wee, wee hours, then be back on his cardboard before the early birds began their commute. He "worked" on Sundays too, the better to take advantage of holy-minded citizens with salvation on their minds.

One Sunday in 1966, Mrs. Logan had just heard Rev. Washington's sermon on the Good Samaritan when she crossed a street to put money in Nifty's cup. She, of course, had no idea he was a fraud. She was equally unaware of the bus careening toward her. Guts showed up for her funeral, regretful over never saying goodbye to her so many years before. Mr. Logan, grief-stricken though he was, made Guts promise not to kill Nifty, so Guts came up with making him run in place instead. The idea was to make Nifty's fitness so well known that no one would ever fall for his fake cripple act again.

After Mr. Logan said a blessing, Guts and Crenshaw sat down to a lunch of roasted sweet potatoes. "I know you're not used to this," Logan said to Crenshaw. "But I don't apologize. We ate a sweet potato every day in the fields. I grew up in Arkansas, working in the hot sun like a mule. Sweet potatoes kept us going."

Crenshaw licked his spoon. "Actually, this is exactly what I'm used to," he said. "I'm from a little place called Wigwam, West Virginia. We swear by sweet potatoes."

"Well," Mr. Logan said. "I see no reason at all why you and I won't get along just fine."

Mr. Logan showed Crenshaw the city's first black high school (the first of its kind west of the Mississippi), its oldest black church, the street where the slave pens used to be located, and the neighborhood where the pioneers of ragtime first tickled the ivories. The last stop on Mr. Logan's history tour was downtown, near the river. He pointed to a great domed building with his cane. "See the Old Courthouse there? It's just spitting distance from where you play first base. That's where one of the earliest court decisions was handed down in slavery days. The judge ruled that people like us weren't people at all. Just property, like pack animals or a chair. Turn right and there's the main post office. Used to be a big tree there before there was a building. A black man was burned to death on the spot."

Crenshaw leaned over and whispered in Guts's ear. "Man, is he like this all the time?"

Guts ignored him. "Mr. Logan, can we go down by the docks now?"

"I'll get close as I can, but I can't go as far as you two. Those cobblestones are too much for my old knees."

Guts and Crenshaw stood on the stones and watched the muddy river slap the bank. Nearby, a pair of barges loaded with cargo inched their way into port. "W.C. Handy slept here," Guts said.

"Who? Slept where?"

"The Father of the Blues. He slept right here on these stones when he landed in town. He was a young man and didn't know nobody."

"You know, that would be interesting to me if we were talking about James Brown or somebody. I'm all for this black history thing but a little of it goes a long way. Y'all got me thinking about a nap."

"One last stop," Mr. Logan said when they climbed the cobblestones and once again stood beside him. "But first we need to pick up somebody who can speak on the place with authority."

They drove to a modest little home on Glasgow Avenue. A man in his late sixties opened the door. "Hey, Cephus, long time," he said with enthusiasm. "Come on in."

"You looking good," Mr. Logan said. "Still in tip-top shape, I see. I brought some young people with me. This is Rip Crenshaw and Lorenzo Tolliver. This here's Stanley J. He's well known in these parts."

Crenshaw struggled to stifle a yawn. "Yeah? What are you known for?" He paused to study a photo on the wall. It was a team portrait of the Gateway City Blues, a one-time Negro League powerhouse. Next to it was a publicity photo of a bowlegged center fielder pretending to circle under a pop fly. Crenshaw lifted his shades and took a closer look. Then he turned toward the bowlegged old man, who was reaching to lift his cap—a baseball cap—off a coat tree.

"'Course, most people don't know me as Stanley J. Most people know me as —" He put on the cap and turned around.

"*Slick Daddy Johnson!*" Rip exclaimed. "Hot *damn!*"

Johnson smiled. "In the flesh," he said. He shook Crenshaw's hand.

"I saw you play," Crenshaw said. "I must have been about eight years old. You played an exhibition in Wigwam. It was you, Cool Papa Bell, Ray Dandridge—"

"And a bunch of other old-timers," Johnson said. "That would have been 1950. I hung up my spikes after that."

Crenshaw reluctantly let go of Johnson's hand.

"They say you could go from home to first in three seconds."

"Sounds about right. Although these days it might take me four and a half. Sylvia, come on in here and meet these young fellas."

A beautiful woman about Johnson's age entered with a smile. "Hello," she said.

"You know Cephus. This here's Lorenzo Tolliver. Doesn't he remind you of Roy Campanella just a little bit? And this is Rip Crenshaw, first baseman for the home team."

"Pleased to meet you both. Hello again, Cephus. Can I get you boys something to drink? Beer? Lemonade?"

"Lemonade," Guts said, and a beat later Crenshaw said, "Beer." Crenshaw looked at Guts. "Lemonade," he conceded.

"I'll get it, honey," Slick Daddy said. "I know your story's about to come on."

"*One Life to Live,*" Mrs. Johnson said. "I hope you gentlemen will excuse me." She departed.

"I love that accent," Mr. Logan said. "It must be a joy to hear her talk."

"It never gets old," Johnson said, "but I do."

Mr. Logan laughed. "You think you're old? Wait until you get to be my age. *That's* old."

"Where is Mrs. Johnson from?" Guts asked.

"Dominican Republic. I met her when I was playing winter ball down there. Knew I'd never be the same if I didn't bring her back with me."

"How long did you play winter ball?" Crenshaw asked.

"Twenty-one years. D.R., Mexico, Cuba—I played in Montreal too. I hit three homers in a game in Cuba, second man to do it."

"Who was first?" Guts asked.

"Cool Papa," Crenshaw said confidently.

"That's right," Johnson agreed.

Mr. Logan raised his eyebrows in surprise.

"What? *Some* kinds of history I get," Crenshaw said. "Twenty-one years, huh?" He whistled.

"We were playing mostly for fun," Johnson said. "Wasn't nobody making a whole lot of money. When I played for Gateway City—shoot, we played one hundred and eighty, two hundred games a year."

"But you couldn't have played all year here. Too cold."

"That's right. We played five months. We had other jobs."

"What did you do?"

"Worked at International Packing House."

He pantomimed swinging a bat at a ball. "See, this is a line drive to left center."

He swung again, shifting slightly. "See, this is a sledgehammer to a cow's head. Made about $30 a week doing that. On the field, I played five games a week and made $90 a month. Wanna see the field?"

They piled in Guts's Plymouth, and 15 minutes later they were standing at the corner of Compton and Market, in front of Gateway Teachers College.

"I don't get it," Crenshaw said.

"This is where our field used to be. Right field line went that way. Left field was over there. Had a trolley barn in it, if you can believe that. Center field sitting in between, that was my kingdom. Seventy-five cents a seat. We'd draw about three thousand, six thousand on Sundays. We had lights before the white leagues did. We played the Detroit Tigers here in 1933, beat 'em two out of three."

"I'm not surprised," Crenshaw said, his voice heavy with reverence. "Now that we play with the white players, we go first class. And the game is easier too, better equipment, a livelier ball. I'm not sure I could've cut it with you guys."

"You could've cut it anytime, anyplace," Johnson assured him. "You're a lock for the All-Star game next month."

"I wish I was as sure as you are. Nobody argues with what I do on the field. But off it? They say I'm a loudmouth, a bad influence. You should have seen *Sports Illustrated* last week. They had a picture of me on the cover. The headline said, 'Is Baseball in Trouble?'"

"I know you like your liquor and your horses, women too, but ain't nothing new about that. You're a choirboy next to Ty Cobb. Hell, he wouldn't even play against us when we whipped the Tigers. He was hateful. Hateful and scared."

"Scared?"

"Yeah. Afraid we'd make him look bad. Next time somebody come around calling you out your name, you tell them you're a man demanding his proper respect. But you also got to respect the game—*our* game. When you play, you not just playing for yourself. You're playing for the rest of us."

"Yes, sir."

Johnson's voice softened. "We had our own World Series, you know. The whites got all the attention but we knew—hell, the world knew—who the real champions were. We had our own Series, our own trophies. You have a ring, don't you, son? You got it on you?"

Crenshaw looked helplessly at Guts, then back at Johnson. "Well, I, see, uh—"

"You probably keep it locked up. I understand."

"The truth is, I lost it."

"Hmm. Well. Listen here, if you get it back, drop in on Slick Daddy and let him have a look."

"Yes, sir, Mr. Johnson," Crenshaw said. "I'll be sure to do that."

They dropped the Negro Leaguer at home and took Crenshaw back to the Park Plaza, just three blocks up the road from where PeeWee was lurking in the shrubbery outside Dr. Noel's apparently unoccupied house. PeeWee rolled the ring around in his hand and stared at the dark windows through a pair of binoculars. It was boring work, but at least he was alone, unlike those days when he had to work with that freaky motherfucker Sharps had paired him with. And he was getting paid, couldn't complain about that. He hadn't felt so good since he ran with the Warriors of Freedom in his revolutionary days. That hadn't turned out too well, with the group disbanding and their leader falling for some bitch. Last PeeWee heard, Gabe Patterson was running the boys club. *What kind of shit was that?* But that was the past. *This is a whole new decade, baby. Between the gig and the ring, everything's all right uptight.*

Guts pulled up in front of Mr. Logan's house. "A long time ago," Mr. Logan said, "I'd sit on the porch in the rocker and you'd sit on the top step. Just taking in the sun, talking about whatever came to mind. You remember?"

"It wasn't that long ago," Guts said. "I think we still know how to do it."

He helped the older man up the porch stairs and settled him into the rocker. Guts sat on the top step and watched shadows made by the afternoon sun glide slowly from house to house.

"I was thinking the other day and I remembered something," Guts said. "You called Mrs. Logan 'Queen B,' but her name was Alice."

"I only called her that at home."

"And she called you Phil. Is Philip your middle name?"

"No. It's short for Philemon. She called me Cephus in public."

"I'm not following."

"B was short for Baucis. Legend says that Baucis and Philemon were an old couple that lived in ancient Greece. Two gods disguised themselves as humans and came to visit this one town. Everybody treated them bad except for the old couple. As a reward, the gods showed their true selves and offered them anything they wanted. They wanted to always be together, even in death. So they made Baucis a linden tree and turned Philemon into an oak. The two trees wrapped their trunks around each other. That's how we wanted to be, always together. So we called ourselves Baucis and Philemon."

They sat in silence a moment. Guts was pretty sure the old man was reading his mind.

"Are you going to give Pearl a call?"

Yep, he was reading his mind. "I've been calling her. She doesn't answer."

A mile and a half to the west, Sharps slowed to a stop in front of Goode's house and climbed from behind the wheel. He went around, opened the rear passenger door, and waited attentively while Goode got out. He then hustled back to the driver's side and opened the door for Goode. He waited until his boss was comfortably seated behind the wheel, then said goodbye. He got into his own car and drove around the block. Turning again onto Lewis Place, Sharps then did what Guts Tolliver had never done in his many years of service to Goode. He followed him.

GUTS AWOKE on Mr. Logan's couch, amused to discover that a blanket had been spread over him while he slept. He looked at his watch. It was a little after three a.m. After making sure all the windows and doors were secure and peeking in on his host to make sure he was still breathing, Guts quietly exited. He paused on the front porch. Finney Avenue was quiet except for a tireless chorus of crickets and the occasional distant moan of a train. Glancing at Mr. Logan's unkempt lawn, he made a mental note to send someone over to mow it—again. The old man could remember the details of a Supreme Court decision from 1857, but couldn't remember to take care of his lawn. *I should live so long*, Guts thought as he got in his car and cranked the engine. But he quickly checked himself. He'd never given much thought to living a long, happy life. The deaths of his parents had taught him that such fantasies were a useless waste of time. He'd seen a lot more deaths since then. Each of them, including Fish's violent, messy end, had confirmed his initial impressions. The best a man could hope for was temporary joy, a brief escape from the daily business of being hurt and hurting others.

Pearl had different ideas. She seemed to think that putting up pretty pictures and buying dishes in matched sets would somehow guarantee that he'd come home every night in one piece. Sometimes, in bed, she would go on about picket fences, candlelit suppers, and bundles of joy while running her lovely hands over his expansive chest. Guts, despite being pleasantly buzzed from Pearl's expert lovemaking, could only respond with vague, noncommittal grunts. At 35, he believed he'd seen and done enough to conclude that rose-colored dreams were for suckers.

Had he met her when he was younger, maybe he could have indulged in her wishful reveries. The only time he'd even flirted with that kind of fantasy had been long ago, when he was 17.

Goode and his gang were at his country farmhouse, a weekend retreat with several acres of greenery and its own lake. Guts was still a novice underling, exposed only to the parts of the operation that required his labor. Weekend work mostly meant standing or sitting around on the porch while Goode and his family relaxed. Mrs. Goode, a thin, nervous woman whose fashionable pearls and furs failed to conceal her consistent unhappiness, often paced impatiently as Goode turned what was meant to be a peaceful hiatus into another skull session in which he plotted with his top lieutenants.

One Saturday, fed up with Goode's failure to take her and little Julius for a long-promised ride—just the three of them—Mrs. Goode decided to pile their son into the Continental and take a turn behind the wheel herself. Goode stood on the porch and watched, gnawing furiously on his cigar as she stomped off. She nearly flooded the engine before roaring away in a spray of gravel. Carmel Green, whose duties included mentoring Guts in the fine art of leg-breaking, turned and looked at Goode, his brow knotted in concern. "Boss, should we go after her?" he asked.

At first Goode said nothing, working the cigar to pulp between his teeth. The car shrunk in the distance, making its way down the path that curved around the lake. "No, she's just blowing off steam. She'll be back."

No sooner had Goode gone inside than the faint sound of peeling rubber carried across the greenery and back to the porch, followed by the sound of a splash. Like Guts, Goode was gifted with extraordinary powers of observation. That's how, even in the midst of one of his life's most horrible moments, he noticed Guts easily outracing the rest of his men after they jerked their cars to a halt and spilled out toward the scene of the accident. That's how he saw several of his crew dive into the lake in pursuit of the rapidly submerging car. That's how, in the same sweeping glance, he saw Guts run past the lake toward the small thicket surrounding the water.

Guts had already concluded that Mrs. Goode and Julius had both been thrown free of the Continental before it careened into the lake. Julius died instantly upon impact. Guts found Mrs. Goode facedown in a puddle, unconscious.

After much deliberation, Goode and his top men determined that the Continental had been tampered with, most likely by the Ike Allen gang. Goode sold the farm, never bought another Continental, and wiped out Ike Allen, his crew, and all of their family members who failed to get in the wind fast enough. Guts's fearlessness and chilling efficiency during the war with Allen won him Goode's favor, along with long-term gainful employment.

As a bonus, Goode treated his crew to a wild night at a large but nondescript house on Washington Avenue. The old mansion's faded glamour matched the weathered allure of the whores who lived and worked inside. Miss Nina, the buxom madam, ordered the girls to line up at the foot of the once-grand staircase. Guts scratched his nose with his index finger and studied them all. Up and down the line he went, each time pausing to stare at the same young thing—obviously the youngest available—a petite beauty with long lashes, an amused expression, and a beauty mark on her left cheek, just above her lip. Like the other girls, she was dressed in next-to-nothing. Unlike the others, she wore a long silken scarf around her neck.

Noticing his young apprentice's fascination, Carmel Green poked him in the side. "What kind of ho wears a scarf around her neck like that?" he asked.

"Good question," Guts said. "I guess I'm going to find out."

In her room, "Lucky" removed all of her clothing except the scarf. She relented when he insisted that she get "all the way naked." The grievous scar across her throat emerged inch by jagged inch as she unwound the scarf. She draped the cloth carefully across the back of a chair. "Now you know how I got my name," she said. "Because I'm lucky to be alive."

Guts stared and said nothing. "Can't let the merchandise look too damaged," she continued. "Of course, by the time I get my clothes off, johns aren't looking at my neck so much. I don't want to talk about it, okay? And if you don't want me anymore, well, it won't be the first time."

Something about the way she said it made Guts want her all the more, and he told her as much. Even in the beguiling presence of a beautiful, naked woman, he noticed that the scarf on the chair was decorated with the names of cities.

She slid into bed beside him. "They're all in North Carolina," she said.

"Hmm?" Guts began to nuzzle between her breasts.

"On the scarf. Those cities are all in North Carolina. Know why?"

"Hmm?"

"Because I'm going to live there someday. I know what you're thinking."

He was taking deep breaths of her, inhaling her scent like a bear nosing honey from a hollow tree. "You're thinking, why would a colored girl want to go back down South? It's because I was born there. And I was happy there."

Guts barely knew what happiness was, had never considered it something to which he was entitled, and certainly hadn't expected to find it in the arms of a Washington Avenue whore. But he did, and soon became a regular at Miss Nina's house. He discovered that he didn't care about Lucky's scar. He didn't care that her beauty mark often shifted from one side of her face to the other, and that she never stopped talking about saving enough money to return to North Carolina. All he cared about was the way the whole world disappeared every time he slid between her thighs. In a moment of weakness, Guts allowed himself to imagine that under very different circumstances, they could be just a couple of crazy kids in love. But of course they couldn't. He was a teenage leg-breaker and she was a teenage hooker.

One night Guts showed up early. Miss Nina told him to come back later, but he insisted on waiting in the foyer. Miss Nina's muscle, a tall, building-sized man known as Nightmare, eyed Guts from his nearby perch on a piano bench. "Young fella, don't make me tell you again," Miss Nina warned.

"I got an appointment," Guts said. He saw Nightmare but didn't acknowledge him.

"Right now, somebody else has an appointment, and his hour ain't up."

"Who is it?" Guts asked loudly. He heard the piano bench creak, as if relieved of a burden.

"That's enough, Sugar. You know better than to raise your voice in here. Nightmare."

The whores' protector took one step forward before both his feet left the ground. He sailed backward and crash-landed on the piano bench. It collapsed into a pile of splinters. Nightmare, who had once been an all-city lineman at Sumner High, struggled to rise. But he couldn't on account of the 14 EEE planted on his chest.

"*Shit*," Miss Nina said. "Not my piano bench! That was an antique. Listen, fool, you get out of here before I call Ananias on your ass."

Guts spoke to Miss Nina but never took his eyes off Nightmare. "Tell Lucky I'm tired of this," he said. "No more sharing."

Miss Nina sucked her teeth. "Girl took your cherry and now you can't pee straight. Hear me good, you pussy-whipped baby. Only high rollers get exclusive accounts. You ain't even got enough to run a tab. Go on, get your pitiful ass out of here."

Banned from the house, Guts spent all his spare time sitting outside Miss Nina's or haunting the spots where working girls were known to congregate. He sent Lucky messages that received no reply. After about a month of enduring the amused contempt of the rest of Goode's crew, he gave up. When word of Guts's failed obsession reached Goode's headquarters on Lewis Place, he called the young man in for a stern lecture. "Don't get caught up with a whore, Guts," he said. "She'll tell you anything as long as you paying her. Besides, she said she was saving up to go back home, right? Maybe she did. Or whoever gave her that scar came back to finish the job."

Over time, Guts's awakened appetite overcame his affection for Lucky. He continued to savor the virtues of what Carmel Green called "paid-for pussy." In between transactions, he'd had brief, fruitless relationships with women who didn't charge for their companionship, like Marnita, the hostess at the Spotlight, and Darlene Moore, a temperamental girl who partied hard on Saturday nights and sang solos at the Church of the Living Rock on Sunday mornings. But mostly he relied on ladies of the night. He liked the convenience of it, the absence of small talk, the eventual comfort found in returning to his own private room, his own spacious bed.

An empty, cold bed that seemed to mock him now that Pearl was gone. He drove past her place and saw that the windows were dark. He drove by again, this time parking in front for a while. With only chirruping crickets for company, he stared at her shuttered blinds. Finally he went home.

After another week of just getting by at work, followed by drinking, overeating, and sleeping late behind drawn shades, Guts stumbled into the sunlight and found the world as he'd left it. Nobody on the street had anything to report about Fish's murder. Similarly, making the elusive Nifty run in place for a half-hour shed no light on the whereabouts of the ring. Guts fiddled with paperwork at the cabstand with his office door open, half-listening to Oliver's latest rant. A newspaper article about new schools being constructed on the North Side had, to no one's surprise, gotten him worked up.

"Seems like you'd be happy," Shadrach said. "You always talking about how they're trying to tear our neighborhoods down and now you're raising a ruckus when they try to build something up."

"Yeah," Cherry chimed in. "You can't have it both ways."

Oliver sighed, took out a handkerchief, and wiped his glasses. "Brothers, brothers, brothers," he said. "Those so-called branch schools they got going up? Those are remedial schools. It says right here all classes will be limited to 15 or 20 students."

"That sounds good," Shadrach said. "My granddaughter goes to Farragut Elementary. They got 41 kids in her class."

"It's the remedial part that doesn't sit right with me," Oliver said. "You trying to tell me we got so many kids struggling in class that they got to build new schools just to hold them all? Next they'll be steering our kids onto the short buses, saying they got all kinds of learning disorders, discipline problems. Who they fooling? They're not preparing our kids for careers. They're preparing them for prison. Prisons are idiot factories."

Shadrach cleared his throat in warning. Oliver, catching the hint, looked up and saw Guts filling the doorway. Both Guts and Cherry had more than a passing familiarity with the penal system. "What the fuck that supposed to mean?" Cherry asked.

"Um, no offense. That's not what I meant."

Cherry didn't want to let it go. "What *did* you mean? Say it slow so that we idiots can figure it out."

"Forget it, Cherry," Guts said. "The man has already apologized."

Before things could get any more awkward, Playfair breezed in.

Grateful for the interruption, Oliver greeted him warmly. "What say, Play?"

Playfair ignored Oliver, strutted straight to the poster of Nichelle Nichols, and performed his usual devotions. "First things first, gents," he said. "Anybody want to talk to me about some Florsheims? Got a whole men's department in my trunk. Guts, I might even have some size 14s."

"Is that right?" Guts asked. He had begun to enjoy feeling sorry for himself, but he couldn't help smiling.

"That's what it is, baby. I can let you have them today for half of what I'll charge tomorrow. Got a minute for me? Let's negotiate." They entered Guts's office, Playfair closing the door behind them.

"No 14s," he said as soon as they had sat down. "But I do have a bit of information. It's sketchy and I ain't totally confident in it but I thought I'd pass it along. You can judge for yourself."

"All right, let's hear it."

"I think Rip Crenshaw's goodtime girls may have gotten locked up in Chicago."

Guts scratched his nose. "That would explain why nobody's seen 'em. What for?"

Playfair shrugged. "Might've been a humble. You know, soliciting or something. Or it could've been something stupid, like trying to roll an undercover cop. I'm not saying that's what happened. Just saying they might be back in a minute or gone for a good while. Could be they got that ring stashed away somewhere and can't get to it just yet."

Guts nodded. "If they do get out, things are likely to be tight for them. They'll be more than ready to unload whatever they got stashed."

"And they're likely to turn to me. Don't worry, I'll come see you first thing."

"Don't wait that long. Call me and I'll come to where you are."

"Right on," Playfair said. He gave Guts a Black Power salute and let himself out.

Guts's phone rang. "Gateway Cab. Tolliver speaking."

"Problem Solver, what it is?"

"Crenshaw? It's been a while. I was just getting used to the peace and quiet."

"Talk tough, brother, that's all right. I know you missed me. Been on the road again. West Coast swing. Dodgers, Giants. Me versus McCovey, battle of the first basemen."

"How'd that turn out?"

"Damn, Guts, you really should check out a newspaper every now and then. We got our asses handed to us. But I did okay. Forget about the sports pages. I'm on the cover of *Jet*, baby. Listen to this. 'Rip Crenshaw's difficulty with major league authorities has our readers wondering: Is baseball bad for blacks?'"

Guts knew about the magazine article. Mr. Logan had shared the details over a lunch of roasted sweet potatoes. The baseball commissioner was up in arms because Crenshaw had paid a visit to a Bay Area breakfast program sponsored by the Black Panther Party. The photos included a shot of Crenshaw with a child on his lap, holding her bowl while she ate cereal.

"I read it," Guts said. "Or, I should say, it was read to me."

"Your lady friend reads to you in bed, huh? I hope she does more than that."

"I'm talking about Mr. Logan. He's one of your biggest fans."

Crenshaw laughed. "I dig Cephus, for real. But isn't he around a hundred years old?"

Guts sighed. "Not quite. What's your point?"

"I thought it might be healthy for you to hang out with a hip young fellow every once in a while."

"That sounds like a good idea. Know any?"

"Ah, that Guts Tolliver sense of humor. Nothing like it. For real, though, I got something for you. A token of my esteem."

"Hmm. Now you got me curious. Want me to stop by the Park Plaza?"

"I'm too tired today, just got in."

"All right, come by Fairgrounds Park in the morning. You know where it is."

"Damn straight. Thanks to you and Cephus, I know where everything on the North Side is. Hell, I could drive one of your cabs."

"Tomorrow around seven thirty," he said. "At the duck pond."

"Why can't I come by your pad? Afraid your lady friend might trade you for an All-Star?"

"You know I can't let you know where I live."

"Why not?"

"Because then I'd have to kill you."

Crenshaw was still laughing when Guts hung up.

The next morning, after a breakfast of nine fried eggs, ham steak, a loaf of bread, a stick of butter, and a pot of coffee at Nat-Han, Guts parked behind a red sports car. The license plate said *MVP*. He got out and leaned against his door. The temperature was already 75 degrees, typical for late June. The recent end of the school year meant the park was busier than usual. Kids roamed the grass, skipped rocks across the pond, played catch, hung around waiting for the pool to open. Guts could see Crusher Boudreau jogging on the far side of the park. At the courts, the tennis family pounded balls into fuzzy submission. The fisherwoman sat stone-still in her chair, minding her rod. At the memorial garden, its two faithful tenders appeared to be giving Crenshaw a lesson in horticulture. The ballplayer was dressed in nondescript clothes and a baseball cap but Guts marked his distinctive, athletic gait. He watched and waited until Crenshaw finished charming the ladies and joined him at the curb.

"How'd you know that car's mine?"

Guts folded his arms across his generous belly. "Wild guess," he said.

Crenshaw chuckled. "A razor blade company gave it to me last year for being top dog at the All-Star game. I finally had it shipped to Gateway."

"Nice. I see you've met Mrs. Means and Mrs. Tichenor."

"Man, did I. They don't follow sports but they both subscribe to *Jet*. They recognized me from the cover."

"They're a couple of sweet old ladies, right?"

"Brother, them broads are hot to trot. The tall one kept looking me up and down like she was picturing me with no clothes on. The short one made a joke about rounding all the bases and sliding into home. You weren't lying when you said the North Side was full of surprises."

"I said that, huh?" Guts rubbed his eyes. Bits of egg and grease glistened in his beard.

"Big man, you need to take better care of yourself," Crenshaw said. "You look tore up from the floor up." He fished his keys from his pocket and unlocked his car.

"Yeah, good to see you too."

The ballplayer opened the passenger-side door and pulled out a baseball bat with a ribbon wrapped around it. He handed it to Guts. "Here. Don't say I never gave you nothing."

Guts examined his present. It was a Louisville Slugger. Crenshaw's signature was branded on the barrel. "This is hefty," Guts said.

"Forty-two ounces. Heaviest in the National League."

"Thanks, man," Guts said. He shook hands with Crenshaw. "No one's ever given me a bat before."

"I bet you've taken a swing a time or two. Just not at a ball."

"Why you being so generous?"

"That conversation with Slick Daddy had me thinking about how I should carry myself. People do shit for me, I act like I'm the one doing them a favor. I could do better about that."

"One conversation with a Negro Leaguer was all it took to make you straighten up?"

"Not really. Next week I'll probably be back to my usual jackass self."

Both men laughed.

Crenshaw turned serious, if only for a moment. "I know you were probably just trying to take my mind off my ring," he said. "But still, you know, it did get me thinking for real. I'm glad you and Mr. Logan did that for me. 'Preciate it."

"Not a problem," Guts said. He unlocked his trunk and put the bat inside. "It helped me take my mind off some things too."

"So, Guts, what do you do when you come out here? Work out? Watch the females?"

"Something better," Guts said with a smile. "Come on, I guess I'll let you in on it. Just let me get my crumbs."

Crenshaw followed Guts to a nearby bench. The ducks, nearly as brown and mottled as the grass surrounding the pond, eased gracefully across the water. They kept the same pace even when the first crumbs appeared. Majestic and sure, they gathered near the bank and dipped their bills.

Guts looked at Crenshaw and grinned. He held out the bag. "You want to toss in a few?"

Crenshaw shook his head. "No, thanks. Really? This is what you do? You sit and feed the ducks?"

"Don't knock it til you've tried it."

Guts and the ducks fell into their natural rhythm. He tossed. They nibbled. The sun glistened on the water.

Crenshaw stood up suddenly. "Man, this is driving me nuts. I'm going to take a walk."

Guts barely acknowledged his departure. The ducks' serene motions, the circles emanating from their soft fluttering, was always mesmerizing. He envied the slow, inevitable certainty of their lives. Being a duck was beautifully simple. You were born a duck, had ducklings, and, no matter how you raised them, they would grow up to be ducks. With people it was different, painfully different. You could be a chauffeur, for example, and your son could grow up to be a leg-breaker. You could welcome an orphaned teenager into your home, take him to church and to the library, and he could grow up to become someone who kills an innocent man with a shoelace.

Guts fed the ducks until he was out of bread. He stood up. Crenshaw was nowhere in sight. Guts turned gradually, sweeping his gaze past the vigilant fisherwoman, past Mrs. Means and Mrs. Tichenor, past Crusher Boudreau, who was now bounding up and down the softball bleachers, until he spotted Crenshaw on a distant ball field playing with two young boys. Guts strolled toward them until he reached the cyclone-fence backstop behind home plate. He recognized the boys as the younger sons of Reuben Jones. Crenshaw stood at the plate with the younger boy, a wispy youngster in a baseball cap. They both gripped the bat while the older boy, curly-haired and dimpled, wound up and delivered the pitch. With Crenshaw's guidance, the smaller boy made solid contact and sent the ball into center field.

"See?" Crenshaw said. "Keep your eye on the ball, not the pitcher. Follow it all the way out of his glove. See it turning, floating toward you in slow motion, big as the world. You're all set, you're just waiting for it. Then boom!

"Now give me five," Crenshaw said, extending his palm. The boy slapped it and Crenshaw turned his palm over. "On the black-hand side." They slapped five again. Crenshaw saw Guts behind the backstop. "Hey, fellas, I'll be right back."

He smiled at Guts through the fencing. The diamond-shaped holes reminded Guts of the lines on the glass windows in the visitor's boxes in prison.

"Hey Guts, want to play some ball?"

"I'll pass. I wouldn't want to upstage an All-Star."

Crenshaw pointed at the boys with his thumb. "These boys play Little League over here. I told them I might come see them one day."

Guts nodded. "I know their father."

"This is how it used to be for me," Crenshaw said. "Just me and my brothers in a field. We had a sawed-off broomstick for a bat and a ball made out of rags. We played until it was too dark to see. No fans, no press, no pressure. Just some boys in a field. That's when I fell in love with the game."

Guts tried to recall a moment when he fell in love with beating people to a pulp. Maybe he'd loved it all along but could never admit it to himself. In contrast, he could clearly recall the first time he knew he was in love with Pearl. It was when he told her he'd been locked up.

Ten years before, police raided an after-hours gambling spot that Guts and Carmel Green had been running. Usually, Goode was tipped beforehand and could get his men away clean. But something had gone wrong, resulting in a snarl-up not even Goode and Grimes could untangle. Guts and Carmel were sent to Joliet for two years. He had Goode's protection, even in jail, and who would have been stupid enough to fuck with Guts Tolliver anyway? His name rang out long before he strolled into the prison yard for the first time. He did his bid like a good soldier and returned to find his spot in the organization waiting for him, along with a small house with the deed in his name, a reward for his loyalty and silence.

"So you've been a prisoner," Pearl said. He had been sitting at her kitchen table eating banana pudding. She was sitting on his lap naked, feeding it to him. "Well, now you're my prisoner. A prisoner of love, baby, and I'm sentencing you to life." She stuck her finger into the meringue and sucked it off.

Guts was relieved, but skeptical. "That's all you have to say?"

"What else is there? I know there are lots of bad men in prison. I also know there are men in there who've never done any harm in their lives. They were in the wrong place at the wrong time, or they were forced to defend themselves, or they were mistaken for somebody else, or they were just plain black. My father was one of those—that's right, my father. I can't tell you which men behind bars are bad and which ones don't belong there. But I can tell that you're a good man, even if you've done some bad things." At first

Guts had thought the glow he felt came from a belly full of good pudding and a lap full of warm woman. Then he realized it was something much more.

"Big Man, you're not even listening," Crenshaw chided.

Guts came back to reality. "Hmm?"

"I was saying that tonight I choose what we do for fun. You can bring your lady friend." Crenshaw turned and jogged back toward the boys.

Watching the athlete approach, the younger boy spoke to his brother. "We're playing ball with Rip Crenshaw. Think anyone will believe us?"

"Nope," his brother said, "not even Mom and Pop."

While Crenshaw played catch, Guts went looking for LaRue Drinkwater. He hadn't had much on his mind lately besides Pearl, but LaRue had managed to squeeze in at inconvenient moments. Guts had concluded that if he was going to think about someone all the time, that someone should be Pearl. Somehow, he had to nudge LaRue aside and create the space he needed.

"LaRue? Ain't you done enough to her?"

"Come on," Guts protested. "It's not like that."

Kevin Hawkins was better known as Hot Link. He sold hot pork sandwiches from a pair of tubs straddling the back wheel of a bicycle he rode all over the North Side. Like Playfair, Hot Link was one of the street-savvy operators who served as eyes and ears for Guts.

"She's about to go to work, never misses it," Hot Link reported. "She catches the bus at Leffingwell and Cass." Guts thanked him and he pedaled away.

Guts had kept his eye on LaRue and her two kids over the years. He'd seen her move from one rundown flat to another, noticed her waiting for buses in the early dawn, looking exhausted as she shuffled to some dead-end job. One blistering day, he saw her appeal unsuccessfully to her able-bodied teenage son before shouldering a heavy sack of dirty clothes down the street to the coin laundry. Later, when Playfair got hold of some washers and dryers, Guts arranged to have a pair of the appliances delivered to the woman's address. And he convinced Gabe Patterson to meet her son and give him a guided tour of the boys club. Periodically, he ordered Nifty to leave sacks of groceries and the occasional bag of cash on her back porch.

Cecil Drinkwater, her husband, had been a loudmouth, an idiot, a drunk. He owed Goode no money and hadn't interfered in the operation in any way; his only mistake had been to tease Guts in public on a day when Guts was off his game. It was the anniversary of his father's death, and Guts was chatting with Roscoe, the shine parlor proprietor. Roscoe had known Chauncey Tolliver since both men were boys.

Already juiced at 11 a.m., Drinkwater had compared Guts to Hayseed the Magnificent, a huge bearded wrestler whose resemblance to Guts could not be denied. Guts interrupted his conversation just long enough to unlace his boot and strangle Drinkwater with the string. Roscoe pleaded with him as he dragged the dying man across the floor, told him the man was only kidding. But it was too late. Guts had broken his code, such as it was. Until then, killing had only been what he did on the job.

Guts parked across the street from the bus stop. He walked over to LaRue. She was small, tired, and looked much older than her years. She leaned against the wall behind her, under the shade of a shuttered drugstore's faded canopy. LaRue was wrapped up tighter than an Arab in the desert, but Guts was still able to see the thick, horrible rash splattered across her fingers and the backs of her hands.

Guts tipped his hat. "Afternoon," he said. LaRue looked straight ahead. "I'm worn out, mister," she said. "You come here to say something or do something, best get it over with."

Guts looked down and saw the knife poking from her sleeve. It was a dull butter knife, couldn't slice toast.

"I knew your husband," he said.

"You mean you killed him."

Guts said nothing.

"You're the one that leaves us things," she continued. "Groceries. Money."

"How come you didn't say anything?" Guts asked. "How come you didn't tell the police?"

"Everybody in there was scared you'd come after them. I wasn't no different. I had two kids to raise."

Guts waited. A lazy-looking mutt ambled out of the alley bordering the bus stop. It crossed the street, lifted its leg, and pissed on Guts's tire. A slight breeze carried the whimsical notes of an ice-cream truck from two blocks away.

"Just so you know," Guts began again, "your husband didn't have a beef with me. I barely knew him. I didn't want you to think—"

"Never thought about you at all, mister. I just thought about my husband. I was mad at myself because I had just been wishing he was dead. And then it happened. I had already taken my wish back. I knew it was wrong. But I was too late."

"I'm sorry," Guts said. "I wish there was something I could—"

"He beat me. He was mean to the kids and he didn't take care of them. He was drunk all the time. I know it didn't make sense to love him. But I did. I did anyway."

She turned to Guts. "You want to do something for me? Try leaving. Stop bothering me." With that, LaRue stepped out from under the awning and peered down the street, as if willing the bus to come.

Guts scratched his nose with his index finger, tried to think of something to say. But there was nothing. He returned to his car and drove off.

Still shy about doing more club-hopping, Crenshaw decided to test his luck at Mound City Downs, the racetrack across the river. He joked that he needed Guts to be his bodyguard and help him take home all the earnings he was sure to win. When they met up that evening, he was again dressed in plain, nondescript clothes, dark glasses, and a cap pulled down low. "Looks like you're hiding," Guts teased.

"I am," Crenshaw replied. "If Washburn finds out I'm over here betting the ponies, he'll start wondering if I bet on baseball. That's how you get banned for life."

Guts wasn't a fan of the races, but he knew his way around. Goode owned a few horses in a stable run by Simon Hughes, the first of two black men licensed to train thoroughbreds in the area. He also shared an owner's box in the clubhouse with Levander Watts, the *Citizen*'s publisher. Guts seldom indulged in gambling. But he often accompanied Goode and was dispatched to the ticket window to handle the boss's bets. He hated walking through the grandstand, watching the desolate losers sift through discarded tickets on the ground, hoping to strike gold—or, at least, get enough for bus fare back across the river to Gateway City.

Because he knew Hughes, Guts was able to park behind the scenes, where the owners, trainers, and stable hands had their own lot. When Hughes gave them a brisk tour of his stable, Crenshaw was as excited as Guts had ever seen him. He had no fear of the horses and they seemed to take to him readily. The one exception was a horse that shrunk away from them as soon as they approached. He whinnied and almost reared up on his hind legs before Hughes soothed him.

"What's wrong with him?" Guts asked.

"He's been drugged," Hughes explained. "He's been skittish ever since and certainly can't run. I can't even get a saddle on him."

"What do you mean drugged?"

"He was our best horse, a three-year-old. Mr. G. owns him. A stakes winner. But somebody injected something in him, all but killed him."

"Shit," Crenshaw said. To Guts's surprise, Crenshaw pulled off his aviators and wiped his eyes. Guts wouldn't have guessed that Crenshaw had a soft spot for animals. "They're doing this because they don't want to see a black man beat them at their own game," Crenshaw said.

"Not that simple," Hughes said. "Whoever's doing it is messing with white men's horses too."

As the night progressed, Crenshaw lost more than he won. But he didn't seem to mind. To Guts, the ballplayer seemed fascinated with everything: the blare of the bugle announcing the start of another race, the jockeys in their bright silks, the dull rumbling that grew greater as the horses rounded the far turn and thundered toward the home stretch. He even seemed to enjoy the awful hot dogs that Guts had no problem resisting.

After just missing the seventh-race quinella, Crenshaw suggested they call it a night. They each bought a cup of beer and strolled back toward the stables. The two men leaned on a fence rail and sipped their suds. Nearby, grooms and stable hands hosed down horses and went about their tasks.

"I always wanted a horse when I was coming up," Crenshaw said. "How about you?"

Guts grunted. "Where would I have put a horse?"

"Okay, I see your point. Lots of room for a horse in Wigwam, though. Plenty of people had 'em, too. The whole town didn't have but one stoplight."

"I didn't even know they had black people in West Virginia until I met you," Guts said.

"We're there all right. Half a dozen families where I'm from. 'Our coloreds,' they called us. They thought we were all related—and my old man did his damnedest to make it so. They didn't treat us too bad. They made jokes about not being able to see us at night, stuff like that. Hell, my high school wouldn't have had nothing like a football or basketball team without their 'coloreds.' Now, you want to know where the crazy crackers are? That would be Arkansas."

"Mr. Logan's from there," Guts said. "What were you doing there?"

"Minor leagues. That's where I played Triple A. They hated me. *Hated*. I played the outfield then. Nigger, coon, monkey, jungle bunny—I heard it all. They threw shit at me all the time, and I was the best player on the team they were supposed to be rooting for. The manager started bringing me in to first base in the late evenings because that's when the fans got really rowdy."

Crenshaw took off his hat and pointed to a spot behind his ear. "Look at that," he said.

Guts looked and saw a rectangular dent in Crenshaw's skull. Purple against his dark brown skin, it looked as if still hurt.

"A battery did that," Crenshaw said. "Caught me when I was paying attention to the pitch, knocked me unconscious. Went down face first and chipped my tooth on a rock. Missed two weeks with a concussion. 1963."

"Son of a bitch," Guts said. He sipped his beer. A horse whinnied in the background. "Me, I always wanted a bike."

"A bike? I'm guessing you had room for that," Crenshaw said.

"Yeah, but my folks never had much after the bills were paid. We talked about it but it never happened. I'm about to tell you something that I've never told anyone else. You got to keep it to yourself."

Crenshaw leaned in. "Scout's honor," he promised.

"I never learned," Guts said softly.

"Never learned what?"

"To ride a bike. I got older and bigger and I just never got around to it. Probably won't."

"Bullshit," Crenshaw declared. "It's never too late, Big Man. It's not too late for me to get a horse and it's not too late for you to get a bike and ride it all over the motherfuckin' place."

"I hear you talking," Guts said.

Crenshaw raised his cup. "Let's drink to it. You in?"

Guts touched his cup to Crenshaw's. "In," he agreed.

The bugle blared, announcing the start of another race. It sounded just as clearly back in the stables.

"Guts, you got any brothers or sisters?"

Guts shook his head. "Nope. It's just me."

"What about grandparents?"

"All dead."

"No family at all?"

"As far as I know."

Crenshaw clapped Guts on the shoulder. "Don't feel bad. You might have a leg up on a lot of folks."

"How you figure?"

"Well, most people don't have a choice when it comes to family. Look at me. I'm number six out of eight. Some of my brothers and sisters would steal my shirt off my back. Others would take theirs off and give it to me. My mama, she worked and worked until the day I could tell her she didn't have to. I got her in a nice house. My daddy, well, he had almost as many kids by another woman not far up the road. He didn't have time for any of us, from what I could see. When word got around about my signing bonus, he showed up sure as shit. Talking about 'son, this' and 'son, that' like I had even half a mind to listen to him. You could say I'm stuck. But you? You get to make your own family. Mr. Logan, he's like your daddy—okay, stepdaddy. Mr. G.? He's the rich uncle who helped you get your start. That lady friend of yours? Well, she can be your wife and carry your babies. If I'm in town, I'll stand up with you at the altar."

"Sounds like you got it all worked out."

"Not a bad plan though, right?"

"I don't have a lady friend anymore." *Damn*, Guts thought. *I'm talking too much. Must be the beer.*

"What? That fast? Damn, what did you do?"

Guts shrugged and stared off into the distance. "Didn't do anything, and I guess that was the problem. This guy named Nifty said I was getting domesticated and I let it get under my skin. Her name's Pearl. She threw all my stuff out of her window."

"Aw, she wasn't so mad," Crenshaw said. "If she had been really pissed she'd have set your shit on fire."

"She was about to."

Crenshaw's eyebrows shot skyward. "Oh."

A twig snapped somewhere behind them. Crenshaw appeared not to notice it. Guts turned around and peered into the shadows. He saw nothing.

"Relax, Big Man," Crenshaw said. "You're not on the job. We're just two friends hanging out."

Guts reluctantly returned to the fence.

"You're lucky," the ballplayer continued. "I run into broads who take my shit. You get with a woman who gives all your shit back."

"That's a good one."

"Except I'm for real. This Pearl. From what you tell me, she's passionate, sexy. She goes all out for what she thinks is important. And what she thinks is important is you. Sounds like she'd do anything for you, and wants you to do the same for her. You're a killer—okay, an ex-killer—and here you are with a woman who'd kill for you. That's intense, Big Man. That's a killer combination. Me, I ain't ready for that yet. But the way you mope around and shit, I suspect you are."

"Damn," Guts said. "That almost made sense."

"Stick around, Junior. You might learn something. People think I'm stupid because I'm pretty." Crenshaw drained his cup and crumpled it loudly.

"Will you stop with the pretty shit? Keep that up and people are going to be looking at you funny."

"Muhammad Ali's always talking about how pretty he is. Nobody looks at him funny."

"That's because Muhammad Ali will whip some ass," Guts said.

A shovel blade, swung properly, will knock the average man senseless or even kill him. But Guts Tolliver wasn't an average man, and an amateur was wielding the shovel. The flat part of the blade thudded against Guts's skull, forcing the beer from his hands. The end result, however, was that he was more angry than stunned. He wheeled on his attacker, lowering himself into a crouch as he spun. Crenshaw had also turned and assumed a similar stance.

They faced two men, white, weather-beaten, early thirties. One held a shovel, the other a pitchfork. "Come quietly," Pitchfork said, and "there won't be no trouble."

"What the fuck?" Crenshaw asked.

"We know who you are," said Shovel. "You're the assholes who've been tampering with these horses."

"I'm about to tamper with *you*," Guts warned.

"Shut up!" Pitchfork ordered. "You don't belong back here. You must be up to something."

"We're minding our own business," Crenshaw said. "You should do the same."

He took a step forward.

"Back off, All-Star," Guts said. "I'll take care of this."

"Listen to your buddy," Pitchfork said. "Before I knock you on your ass."

"You don't want to try that," Crenshaw said. He took off his sunglasses. "See? I'm Rip Crenshaw. First base."

"And I'm Spiro fucking Agnew," Shovel hissed.

Guts had heard enough. His head was throbbing. He was probably going to have to take an aspirin and he didn't like to do that. Aspirin was hard on his stomach.

"Hey," he said, advancing on Pitchfork. He faked a right to his head, inducing Pitchfork to duck and swing his weapon. Guts caught it with two hands, snatched it, and bounced it off the man's temple. He went down quickly. Shovel swung his spade. Guts neatly parried it with the pitchfork and took out his legs. He planted his boot on Shovel's chest. He raised the pitchfork high.

Somewhere he heard a voice. It sounded far away, as if under water. Gradually it became clearer. It was Crenshaw, talking him down. "Come on, Big Man. It's not worth it. It was all a misunderstanding. Come on, let's get out of here. Come on, Big Man. We got plans. You know, bicycles. Horses."

Guts lowered the tool and looked around. Pitchfork was still out. Shovel was rolling around moaning, eyes closed. Tossing the pitchfork to the ground, Guts stepped over Shovel and followed Crenshaw out to the lot.

The ducks were hungrier than usual. They swarmed near the edge of the pond, their webbed feet paddling so fast that the water churned. Guts couldn't toss the crumbs fast enough. In a flurry of flapping wings, the ducks leapt up to snatch them from the air. His bag was empty before he knew it. He stood up, stretched, and took a look around. All of the regulars were absent from the park except for the fisherwoman. From her perch in her aluminum lawn chair, she seemed to watch over everything. The scene struck Guts as a little odd. He was sure of it: something was off. He walked toward her. The breeze drifting off the pond was unusually brisk, turning into gusts strong enough to make him stagger. When he got close to the fisherwoman's chair, the wind blew her hat off and she looked right at him. Guts gasped, shook to his core. The woman had his mother's face.

"Mama," Guts said. "You've been watching me. All this time, watching me."

Lucille's hair swirled about her face. She smiled at Guts. "She's the one," she said.

Guts sat straight up in bed. He stumbled into his bathroom and splashed water on his face. He rooted around for the razor he'd been neglecting and carefully shaved his scalp, neck, and upper lip. Handling scissors with uncommon grace, he trimmed his beard to a considerably less frightening length. He brushed his teeth, showered, toweled himself dry, and put on his usual uniform of dungarees and boots. He set his burglar alarm, walked out his back door, locked it, and walked to his garage. Minutes later, he was at Fairgrounds Park. Ignoring the ducks, he went directly to the fisherwoman's usual spot. She wasn't there.

Guts stared at the ground, looking for the bare patch her chair would have created. The grass all around was green and robust. He scratched his nose with his index finger.

"Just the man I'm looking for."

Crusher Boudreau came jogging over. "Hey, Crush," Guts said, still looking down.

"Hey, baby, don't be so sad. Plenty of fish in the sea," Crusher said.

"Huh?"

"Nothing, brother. I'm just joking with you. But listen, you know that gym at 12th and Park?"

"Have you seen her?"

Crusher stared at Guts. "Seen who?"

"A woman. She sits here every day in a lawn chair, holding a fishing pole."

"She must not be fine," Crush said. "Because if she was fine I would have noticed her."

"Crush, I'm serious," Guts snapped. "She wears a hat down over her face."

"I'm telling you, Guts, I have no idea who you're talking about."

For a minute, Crusher thought Guts was thinking about punching him. Then the angry look disappeared and the confused one returned.

"Hmm," Guts said.

"Guts. About the gym."

"The gym?"

"Yeah, the one at 12th and Park. I still spar there sometimes. A little fellow was jaw-jacking in there last week. A buddy told me about it. Said the half-pint was smelling himself and sucker-punched one of the flyweights. Turns out he was wearing a ring. Maybe a World Series ring."

For the first time, Guts looked straight at him. "You're absolutely sure you've never seen a woman fishing right here? Right on this spot?"

Crusher nodded.

"All right," Guts said. He turned and walked away.

"I guess we'll talk about that ring later," Crusher called after him.

Guts's brief interview with the tennis family was equally fruitless. Mrs. Tichenor and Mrs. Means kept stringing him along as much as they could before conceding that neither of them had seen the woman in question. Ever.

Guts drove to Stormy Monday's. He tipped his hat to Mrs. Monday, who was busy directing a pair of cooks as they manned a sizzling griddle. He headed to the back where Playfair was at a booth, tackling a stack of hotcakes. Guts slid in across from him.

"Guts," Playfair said. "You look like you've seen a ghost. I thought Nat-Han's was your place for breakfast."

"Normally," Guts said, "but I knew I'd find you here."

"You found me all right. What it is?"

"I want to talk about a ring."

Playfair speared a sausage link and lifted it to his mouth. "No news yet, baby. Remember, I told you I'd contact you as soon as anything pops up."

"Not that ring. Another one. Another kind."

Playfair added more syrup to his stack. "What kind exactly? Talk to me, baby."

"Well, an engagement ring."

Playfair grinned. "Hot damn, Guts. Congratulations."

Guts shook his head. "It's early for that, too soon to tell."

"I understand. How soon do you need it?"

"I was kind of hoping I could get one now."

"Right now?"

"Yes, right now."

"As in right this minute."

"That's what I'm saying."

Playfair dabbed at his lips with his napkin. "Shit, why didn't you say so? Come on, let's go visit my trunk."

Back home, Guts shed his dungarees and boots and stepped into a pair of pressed slacks. He buttoned up a dress shirt, laced up his Florsheims. He went to his closet, selected a pair of cufflinks from his box, and put them on. Sucking in his stomach and pushing out his chest, he studied himself in the mirror. "She's the one," he told his reflection. He stepped into his living room, a space he had avoided ever since his split from Pearl. The third Audubon print was still dangling crookedly from a nail. Guts straightened it and set out on foot for Lexington Avenue.

At the cabstand, Oliver was lecturing Shadrach and Cherry while they played dominoes and pretended to pay attention. "No way Nixon's getting a second term," Oliver declared. He strutted back and forth across the room, waving his rolled-up newspaper like a drum major's baton. "The man is a crook. Anybody can see that. Hubert Humphrey? Now there's real leadership material. You mark my words—say, isn't that Guts across the street?"

The three men pressed their faces to the glass to watch Guts, all dressed up and carrying a bouquet of flowers, march down the street like a man in a trance.

Lexington Avenue was crowded. Pearl's neighbors spilled over their porches and onto the surrounding lawns. Girls jumped double-dutch alongside the curb. A trio of teenage boys polished a car to perfection, the radio inside it blaring the Temptations and the Supremes. The scene resembled a block party or a holiday celebration. But it was neither; it was Wednesday. Guts gave a kid a dollar to summon Pearl. She appeared in the doorway and smiled when she saw him. He braced for harsh words as she descended the steps but none came.

"Lorenzo Tolliver," she said. "You clean up good."

"Special occasion," he said.

"That's sweet, really. But my birthday isn't until fall."

Guts dropped to one knee, prompting comments from the porch-sitters. Pearl gasped and pressed her hand to her heart.

"You're the one," Guts said, looking up at her.

"The one what?" Her voice was trembling.

"*The* one," Guts replied. "Pearl, I want you to come to my house. I want you to walk through the front door. I want you to be my wife, not my secret. I want you to stay and never leave."

Pearl started crying. "It's about time, Lorenzo."

"Is that a yes?"

She nodded. "It's a yes. It's a yes, it's a yes, it's a yes."

Guts got to his feet. They kissed. The people across the street applauded. Another neighbor whistled loudly. "Y'all nasty," someone else shouted.

Pearl ignored them all. She looked around. "Where's your car?" she asked.

"No car," Guts said. "I've come to carry you."

Pearl folded her arms over her chest. "Carry me where?"

"Through whatever you might have to face."

She looked at Guts. "You're going to carry me all the way to your house? You know that's two miles."

"I promise a smooth ride," Guts said as he scooped Pearl into his massive arms. "Is that all you're taking? Don't you want to grab some clothes?"

Pearl smiled. "You know better than that," she said.

TENDERNESS

BECAUSE DR. ARTINCES NOEL was driving near Fairgrounds Park, she could easily have seen Guts Tolliver, immense and bearded, striding east on Natural Bridge Boulevard with a woman in his arms and tears shining on his face. She might even have recognized the joyful weeping woman as her favorite salesgirl. But Artinces was distracted by the three women who had popped up without warning in her backseat.

Brown, silent, and clad in ragged sackcloth dresses, two of the women stared intently ahead. The third, unlike her kerchief-wearing companions, was bareheaded with long, black, woolly braids. She rolled down the window and leaned far out, smiling as she reveled in the rushing air.

Artinces had seen the women before but never while awake. During their dreamtime visitations, she had noted their ghostly nature. Floating, opaque, they didn't seem especially out of place in the shape-shifting cosmos of sleep. Until that particular Wednesday, they had not seemed inclined to infiltrate the waking world. They had confined their appearances to the lonely hours when Artinces wanted nothing more than a few extra minutes of precious rest. But suddenly there they were, sitting upright and apparently solid. Artinces felt their presence a split second before she spotted them in her rearview mirror. Still, her synapses hadn't reacted fast enough to shield her from shock. She stomped on the accelerator, roaring straight over a curb before regaining her senses and stepping desperately on the brake. She hit the parking lot of Gateway Cab on two wheels, leaving a trail of rubber as she narrowly missed the gas pumps and thumped emphatically into the back end of Playfair's gleaming maroon Electra 225. His legendary trunk collapsed like a tin can, accordioned into a space about one-fourth its former size.

Aside from a busted headlight and a few dents, her Cadillac was none the worse for wear. She was struggling with her door handle when Playfair, Cherry, Trina, Shadrach, and Oliver came rushing out. Cherry and Shadrach ran to assist her. Playfair stared at the remains of his car.

Trina pulled his sleeve. "Say," she said. "You didn't have any animals in there, did you?"

Playfair shook his head. He looked as if he wanted to cry. "Not today," he replied.

Trina exhaled. "Thank you, Jesus," she said.

With her feet firmly planted on solid ground, Artinces gingerly examined herself. She was wearing white gloves and the kind of hat most black women wore on Sunday. "All in one piece," she said to Shadrach, who looked vaguely familiar to her. "I'm more concerned with my passengers."

Cherry leaned into the open rear window. He turned to Shadrach and shook his head.

Shadrach met the doctor's eyes, his voice soft with concern. "Passengers, ma'am?"

"Yes, the three women."

"There's no one back there, ma'am."

Wrinkling her brow, Artinces moved to check for herself.

Cherry stepped aside to give her room. After watching her stare into the empty backseat, he dared to touch her on the wrist. "Can we call a doctor for you? An ambulance?"

Straightening, Artinces stretched to her full height. "I *am* a doctor, young man, and I'm perfectly fine."

Trina approached her. "You've had a scare," she said. "Would you like to sit down? Have something cold to drink?"

"You're very kind, dear, but no, thank you." Artinces turned to Playfair. "From the look on your face, I gather this is your car."

"Yes, ma'am."

"I'm so sorry about this, Mister—? It was just as she said. I had a scare. I got distracted and here we are. I suppose we should call the police, allow them to fill out a report?"

Playfair leaned forward as if to share a secret. "My name's Playfair, ma'am. If it's all the same to you, I'd rather not get the police involved."

"No?"

Playfair smiled. "I'd appreciate it," he said. "How can I put this? My vehicle contains items of a delicate nature."

"I can't imagine."

Playfair never stopped smiling. "With all due respect, ma'am," he said, "I'm sure you can."

Artinces stared back at Playfair. A headline flashed briefly in her head. *Doctor Sees Ghosts, Crashes Car.*

"Very well," she finally said.

She went back to her car and opened the door. For a moment, the men—and woman—of the cabstand thought she was going to drive away without another word. But she returned with her pocketbook. She opened it, peeled several layers from a fat bankroll, and handed them to Playfair.

He counted the bills with the practiced speed of a bank teller. Then he tried to hand them back. "Ma'am, this is way too much."

Artinces put up her hand. "Not at all. I suppose I'd also prefer we keep this to ourselves. I'd be grateful for your discretion."

Playfair bowed. "Understood," he said. He turned to Cherry. "Doctor, this here is Cherry. He's a genius with bodywork. Cherry, can you help her out?"

Cherry grinned. "I can make it like new," he said.

Artinces smiled at him. "That would be wonderful," she said. She turned to Trina. "Young lady, could you please arrange a cab for me?"

When the taxi arrived at the imposing mansion on the edge of Gateway City's posh West End, the driver hopped out and insisted on escorting Artinces up the serpentine path to her front door. He kept a gentle but firm grip on her elbow, taking careful steps, as if the doctor were made of glass that the slightest breeze would shatter.

"This is completely unnecessary," she had told him soon after he slid from behind the wheel and scooted around to her door. But he just smiled and bowed as if he hadn't heard her. To her amusement, the man was considerably older than her and just a smidgen bigger. He wouldn't take her money.

"I can't do it, ma'am," he said when they finally reached her porch.

"I don't see why you can't."

The man took off his hat. "Reid's my name, ma'am. Wendell Reid. Back in '48, my grandson got sick. Seem like every baby on the block did. Some went to the hospital and didn't come back."

In 1948, a diarrhea epidemic had swept Gateway City. Artinces had stood at the center of that storm and played a pivotal part in helping the city weather it. She had been just three years out of medical school.

"He got better, thanks to you," Reid continued. "I'll always be grateful. My wife's been including you in her prayers every since."

"I'm glad to know it, Mr. Reid. What does your grandson do now?"

"Student teaching at Farragut Elementary. God willing, he'll be certified soon."

Artinces smiled and allowed the man to shake her hand. "That's wonderful, Mr. Reid. Thank you for your kindness."

The driver returned his hat to his snowy head, took a step backward, and bowed once more. He offered her his card. "Any time you need a ride, Dr. Noel," he said, "just ask for me."

Artinces doubted she'd call on his services again, but she kept smiling and accepted the card. Over the course of her 25 years in medicine, she'd been offered an impressive bounty of talents and services. They weren't presented as barters from parents with limited resources. Rather, they were tokens of gratitude for services rendered, as if paying the bill—which most did with honorable timeliness—was hardly enough to express their feelings, their recognition of a rare instance in which their faith had been justly rewarded. Wendell Reid's offer of taxi rides on demand joined a list that included paintings, racing tickets, coupons for free press-and-curls, pies, cakes, houseplants, and refurbished washing machines.

Later, after a thorough self-examination and a warm bath, Artinces relaxed in her bed. It was not quite evening, but she was more exhausted than she expected to be. Curled up under her sumptuous duvet, she considered her options. She had ruled out the stack of medical journals on her nightstand when the phone rang. She was in no mood to talk, but Charlotte was still out, so she picked it up.

"Hello?"

"It's me."

"Hey, Me," Artinces said. She grinned more broadly than she ever did in public.

"I hear you might need a healing. I can be there inside ten minutes."

"You know you can't come over. Don't worry about me. I'm in Charlotte's capable hands."

"If you don't want to see me no more, you can just say so. You don't have to go smashing yourself into buildings just to get out of a date." His voice was playful. She knew it masked genuine concern.

"I missed the building and rear-ended a car. I'm certain I'll be fully functional by this time next week."

"Functional. Does that mean what I think it does?"

Artinces giggled like a naughty schoolgirl. "Limber as ever," she said. "Though I am 50 years old, you know. I can't do everything I did when I was a sweet young thing. But that's not why you called, right? You're concerned for my well-being. My emotional state."

"Stop messing with me, Tenderness. Tell me how you feel."

"I was a little shaken up, that's all. There's not a scratch on me."

"You sure? No sore muscles or anything? Because I could come over and rub you down."

"Rub me down? Is that what they call it where you're from?" Artinces allowed the phone cord to curl around her forearm. She had forgotten she was tired.

"Why, Doctor, what in heaven's name are you suggesting? My intentions are honorable."

"Your intentions are seldom honorable. But that's all right. That's what I like about you."

He laughed. His voice sounded smoky and sweet. She described it that way once and he blamed it on cigars and bourbon. "Bad habits and bad breath," he said. "No," she told him. "Hickory and honey."

"Don't worry," she said into the phone. "I told you, Charlotte's taking care of me."

At that moment, Charlotte Divine stood waiting for her order at Stormy Monday's. North Siders who frequented the place seldom left without at least one helping of its renowned lemon pie. Over time, the menu at Stormy Monday's had expanded along with the restaurant's dimensions. The takeout counter where Charlotte stood had once taken up most of the establishment, but now was just a cozy corner in a place big enough to seat nearly 100, and it often did. Its biggest business came from the after-church crowd, as "Sundays at Monday's" had become a popular event. Awaiting her turkey wings, collards, and smothered potatoes, Charlotte was learning that Wednesdays were nearly as crowded.

Pondering the revolving pie case, she heard laughter rising from a booth and saw the men of the Black Swan, Reuben Jones among them. Charlotte liked Reuben, but she'd avoided him ever since she broke up with Ed, the eldest of his three sons. Their high-school romance had helped her escape the dread and drudgery of her days at the orphanage—for a while. But she had been avoiding just about everyone since coming home, and her thing with Ed seemed a lifetime ago. She weighed the reliable lemon versus the blackberry cobbler, without noticing the gaze of a young man standing nearby. He moved slowly in her direction, reducing the space between them until they were nearly shoulder-to-shoulder.

Stroking the jeweled ring in his pocket, PeeWee stood up straight and launched his rap.

"How you doin'?"

When she declined to answer, he cleared his throat and tried again. Later that night, left to pleasure himself on the sad and saggy cushions of his sister's couch, PeeWee would pause to identify the moment when his approach went wrong. He would decide that failing to put on the ring, to actually slip it on his finger, had been his fatal flaw. Only by wearing the ring could he fully harness its power. It would, he was certain, have made all the difference.

"How you doin'?"

Same result. He decided on a bolder approach.

"Hey, girl, you deaf or something?"

She answered without looking.

"No, I'm sick."

"Sick? What's wrong with you?"

"Sick of snot-nose punk asses like you thinking you can just walk up on me and act like we're friends. I don't know you. I don't want to know you. So step back."

"Wait a minute, Slim. You can't talk to me like that."

Finally she turned toward him. "I just did," she said.

Before PeeWee could figure out what to say next, Irene Monday stepped between them. The Pie Lady handed PeeWee a large paper sack.

"Here you go, sugar," she said. "Two T-Bone specials with hot sauce on the side."

PeeWee struggled to make eye contact with Charlotte but he couldn't get around Irene's imposing figure. She was nearly six feet in her comfortable flats. "Better hurry up," she urged. "I bet your boss can hardly wait to eat."

PeeWee pictured Sharps waiting behind the wheel of his Eldorado, picking his teeth in the rearview mirror. "He ain't my boss," he said. "We're business partners."

"Whatever, sweetie. You'll want to get to this while it's hot."

Reluctantly, PeeWee backed away and eased out the door.

Irene turned to Charlotte. "Was that boy scaring you?"

The question prompted an angry glare that surprised Irene. "No? I thought he might have been bothering you."

"Bothering me, yeah. But not scaring me. And you didn't have to run him off. I could have handled it."

Irene looked down at the diminutive Charlotte. She was dressed like a boy but her womanly aspects were clearly perceptible, despite her slouch. Her cap, pulled down tight over the eyes, couldn't hide the long lashes or the singular, comma-shaped dimple. Eighteen years old and 110 pounds, Irene figured. She didn't look like she could "handle" much, but maybe she was tougher than she appeared.

"I see you in here with books some days. I guess you're trying to stay sharp during your summer off."

The girl softened, but only for an instant. "Something like that," she said.

"You're lucky to have the opportunity," Irene continued. "School, I mean. Dr. Noel's a true Christian to be paying your way."

Charlotte was tired of hearing about how lucky she was. She'd bumped from foster home to foster home for most of her young life. A few months in the good doctor's house and all of a sudden she was supposed to forget all that.

"She's not paying my way," Charlotte said sharply. "I have a scholarship. Do you think my order's ready?"

"I'm sorry. Let me get that for you," Irene said. She turned and headed into the kitchen.

Charlotte found the Pie Lady just too jolly to put up with. *What is she*, Charlotte thought, *45? 50?* At any rate, old enough to know that all that smiling and calling everybody sweetie would amount to nothing. Charlotte had known as much since she was a little dirt dauber in diapers. The Pie Lady's dimples and grins resulted from her famously happy marriage to a local sign painter. Even Charlotte knew that story, as did anyone else who ever spent more than five minutes in Irene's company.

Later that evening, Irene would tell her husband about her encounter with the sullen girl. She'd perch on the edge of the bed while Lucius sat on the floor with his back to her, snug between her voluptuous thighs. Her nightgown would ride up and she'd feel the heat of his shoulders while she scratched his scalp with a hard plastic comb and Ultra Sheen. She'd tell him about all the diners she had cajoled and comforted while he had been at the table he shared with the other men of the Black Swan. He'd lean back and close his eyes, his woman reciting an entertaining litany of names, faces, and memorable conversations, until finally he tired of the talking and the scratching. He'd turn his head and plant a kiss on her inner thigh, mumbling sweet nothings about his perfectly delectable Jelly Roll. He used to call her Pie Lady, the way so many others did, but that seemed too ordinary after a while. He arrived at his personal nickname for her after a night of ecstasy led him to declare that Bessie Smith, bless her soul, was indisputably wrong. The truth, he was certain, was that nobody in town could bake a sweet jelly roll like Irene.

Charlotte watched as Irene returned from the kitchen with her order in hand. Underneath the happy expression lurked worry lines and crow's feet so deeply entrenched that not even a century of joy could completely offset them. Thinking about those lines, Charlotte was sure that the Pie Lady had suffered as much pain and heartache along her way as anybody else. Yet she kept on grinning. As if that would help.

"Listen," Irene said. "I don't know what's ailing you, but my lemon pie certainly can't make it any worse. Here, take a couple slices for you and the doctor. On the house."

Charlotte always drove a little too fast. She was not the kind of girl who took note of landscape and landmarks, the sticky crossroads where memories linger. To her, familiar street corners were like scars, stubborn welts that no amount of liniment or distance could soften. She didn't want to profile or promenade, take note or be noticed. She never paused to catch her reflection in the passing glass or cast a knowing nod at anything that could remind her of how far she'd run and how far she'd yet to go—no, she'd never pull a sleeve or coattail and say to the heart inside it, remember this, remember that, remember when? She needed to get up, get through, roll on, be gone. The buildings and boulevards, the funeral parlors, liquor lounges, pool halls, and storefront churches of North Gateway might as well have been streaks of neon, sparks tossed from flicked cigarettes. Her eye was on the end, the destination beckoning like the day's fading light. A fellow driver pulling up beside her at an intersection would see a girl bobbing her head to silence, eyes squinting and unrelenting, not bothering to breathe until the traffic light stopped screwing around and faded from frustrating red to encouraging green. Before that other driver became aware that the light had changed, Charlotte was already exhaust in his eyes, dust on his windshield, an alluring wisp of sinuous neck and gleaming chocolate remembered in the fevered delirium of a late-night dream. If she drove fast enough and the streets were just the right kind of empty, she could pull up to the Noel residence nearly tipsy with momentum. Only then would she slow down and step unsteadily onto shaky ground, tousled and distracted. She shook it off, willed the merciless earth into stillness and regained her tough-girl guise, the fierce mask of resolve the world knew her by.

Charlotte double-checked to make sure she'd locked the car, a secondhand Chevy Malibu the color of dirty dishwater. Artinces bought it for her after Charlotte got into a fight on a public bus. The dust-up began when Charlotte couldn't help overhearing a young mom complaining about Dr. Noel's advocacy of breastfeeding.

"She gave me a brochure," the girl said, "but I pitched it as soon as I got outside." The girl looked 20, give or take. The baby on her lap sucked mindlessly on a lollipop. Round and sleepy-eyed, to Charlotte's practiced eye he was hardly ready for hard candy. She had half a mind to yank the sucker from his lips and perhaps delay the tooth decay he was certain to suffer. As soon as he got some teeth, that is.

"I wanted to tell that bitch, shit, this ain't your child. You should mind your own business," Young Mom continued.

"I know, girl," one of her cohort said. "Formula just as good."

Charlotte couldn't hold her tongue any longer. "You should have listened to her," she said.

Young Mom swiveled, incredulous. "Heifer, was I talking to you?"

Charlotte stared her down. "Do you know how many babies Dr. Noel has saved? Black babies?"

"My baby ain't hardly black. He light-skinded. Shut the hell up before I whup that ass." Young Mom hoisted her baby, already the color of a Hershey bar, and handed him to her friend. She stood up, ready to brawl.

"No," Charlotte said, removing her earrings and rising to the challenge. "*You* shut up, philistine."

"I look like a Phyllis to you, bitch?"

The girl was tough but Charlotte held her own. She even had the upper by the time the girl's friends dragged her away, bruised and belligerent.

"My man gon' get you," she yelled. "He just got out and he gon' get you! His name Bumpy Decatur! You watch and see!"

Charlotte barely blinked when Artinces later determined that her knuckles required a pair of stitches. But the doctor was mortified. "What were you thinking?" she demanded. "You're about to go to college. You're about to make something of yourself."

"I know," Charlotte said, but Artinces went on as if she hadn't heard her.

"Sometimes you just have to let things go. You just have to let them roll off your back. What were you fighting about anyway? What did she say to you?"

"You're right," Charlotte conceded. "It was stupid."

The two had first met when Charlotte proved herself a reliable and impressive volunteer in the pediatric ward of Abram Higgins Hospital, where Artinces had made her reputation and still reigned as a leading eminence. Late evenings, after rocking babies to sleep at Abram H., Charlotte typically wished Artinces good night, declined her offer of a ride, and headed off alone. In time, Artinces grew close to the girl—well, as close as Charlotte allowed—and found out she lived at the nearby children's home. She had never known her parents, she said, and had been in and out of foster homes for as long as she could remember. Charlotte was in the 10th grade then, with straight As and a strong interest in medicine.

Two years later, when Charlotte proceeded across the stage with diploma in hand, she looked out and saw Artinces standing and applauding in the front row, as proud as any mother. The next day, Artinces invited Charlotte to move into her house.

After the fight on the bus, Artinces marched her new ward right down to the nearest car lot, where they discovered the Malibu. Charlotte barely concealed her deep pleasure at receiving the car, and nodded agreeably when the doctor assured her that the Malibu would not be accompanying her when she went off to school.

Charlotte had turned 18 that summer. She had wondered where she would go after the children's home kicked her out, and had felt forced to contemplate the relative pros and cons of highway underpasses and park benches. Instead, she found herself in an opulent room of her own, fortified by nutritious dinners and sporting a complete wardrobe that she hauled to college in a brand-new set of luggage. Decorating her dorm room with her newly acquired treasures, she gave herself permission to hope.

Now that she was back from school, however, Charlotte was more somber than ever. Artinces was perplexed, her patience challenged by the girl's long silences and fondness for vanishing into thin air. There had been some turmoil on her campus, including a student protest that drew the attention of heavily armed policemen. One student had been killed. Charlotte said she had been in the library at the time, far from the tragedy. Artinces surmised that the clash had troubled or even frightened Charlotte, but her efforts to get the girl to talk about it had so far yielded only shrugs and gloomy mumblings.

Satisfied that the Malibu was secure, Charlotte let herself into the house. She put the doctor's dinner on a tray and carefully carried it up the long, winding staircase. When her knock went unanswered, she opened the bedroom door enough to see her benefactor dozing peacefully. She tiptoed in and set the tray on a table, in case she woke up hungry.

ARTINCES STEPPED OUT OF THE CAB. The heat waves rising from her serpentine path made the front porch seem farther away than usual. She stopped and took a breath. Behind her, the ever-vigilant Wendell Reid, standing alertly next to his taxi, called to her.

"You all right?"

"Yes, I think so, Mr. Reid," she replied, turning around. "I'm fine—"

She squinted through the thickening ribbons of heat. Mr. Reid was no longer present. Instead, it was her father. "Pepper Pot," he said. "My little Pepper Pot."

Artinces felt embarrassed to be standing in front of him holding the two Aldo's shopping bags that had suddenly appeared in her hands. They were full of naughty underthings. She hoped he wouldn't offer to carry them.

"Daddy," she said, "what are you doing here?"

She clutched her bags. What if he found out what was inside? She'd explain that the lingerie was just an indulgence. After spending all day serving as a model of dignity and decorum, she needed to unwind a bit, take the pressure off, and fine silk helped her relax. Just one of her harmless diversions—like sleeping with a married man. But that couldn't be helped, right? She couldn't help herself. Like catching a cold.

"Aren't you happy to see me?" Luther Noel frowned and hooked his thumbs in the shoulder straps of his overalls.

"Of course, Daddy. I just wasn't expecting you, that's all."

Her father looked over her shoulder and gestured with his chin. "Were you expecting them?"

Artinces turned, following his gaze. The three women stood directly in her path, close enough to touch her, as brown and silent as they had been in the backseat of her car. Two of them stared back at her. The third, her dark braids half-unraveled, raised her long-fingered hands and shoved Artinces squarely in the chest. She grabbed the doctor's shoulders and began to shake her.

"You're dreaming," a vaguely familiar voice declared. Artinces exhaled, dimly aware of the pillow beneath her head. As she slowly stirred to consciousness, her relief turned to fear. She was aware of a presence in her room. It had to be the three women. Seizing her again. Shaking her shoulders. She moaned and pulled away.

"Dr. N. Dr. N. It's me, Charlotte."

Artinces opened her eyes. Charlotte held her shoulders, concern on her face.

"You were making so much noise. I came to check on you. Bad dream?"

"I guess so."

"What was it about?"

"I can't recall," Artinces replied, the three women still vivid in her memory. She shook off the covers and sat upright. "What time is it?"

"Late," Charlotte said. "You slept right through the delivery men. They brought you flowers."

"So early?"

"Like I said. It's not early. I'll slice you a grapefruit and make you some tea while you get ready."

"No need, Charlotte. I'll grab something on the road. And just put the flowers in a vase."

Charlotte chuckled. "Umm, I don't think we have enough vases."

Still puzzling over her dream, Artinces had nearly forgotten Charlotte's comment by the time she made it downstairs. Then she saw that nearly every visible surface of the first floor was covered in flowers. Roses, lilies, orchids. Daisies by the dozens. The grand piano was buried beneath a mountain of zinnias. She half-expected to hear the hum of bees as they circled the blossoms. The library next to the parlor was so stuffed with tulips and gladioli that her bookshelves were almost completely hidden. Only a bust of Dr. Charles Drew, secure on its pedestal, peeked above the blooms. In the kitchen, perched on a stool surrounded by more flowers, Charlotte smirked and handed Artinces the accompanying card. "From a Grateful Patient," it read.

"What's the occasion?" Charlotte asked.

"It's just a thank-you."

"Some thanks. You must have saved his life."

Artinces had insisted on discretion. It was just like him to push her boundaries. Every time she believed they'd reached an understanding, an acceptable rhythm, he'd start making trouble. Saying things like he couldn't help himself and neither could she.

She decided against asking Charlotte how she knew the flowers were from a man and not from thankful parents. And of course she couldn't tell Charlotte who that man was. She couldn't tell anybody.

Forced to borrow the Malibu, Artinces dropped Charlotte at Abram H., where she worked as a summer fill-in at the registration desk.

"Don't forget to wait for me," she reminded her as they pulled up to the yellow-brick complex. "I'll come get you. I don't want you picking fights on the streetcar."

"You mean the bus," Charlotte corrected. "The streetcars are all gone."

"Oh yes, that's right," Artinces said. North Siders had conducted a bus boycott just four years ago, more than a decade after Rosa Parks had launched a similar movement farther south. That was just like black folks in Gateway, always slow to come to a boil.

"I used to catch the streetcar all the time. Long time ago. Ride all the way to the South Side," Artinces said.

"The South Side? What's over there? Were you seeing a white boy or something?"

"*What?* No."

Charlotte looked openly skeptical. "Then where did you go?" she asked.

"To the botanical garden. I loved the flowers."

Charlotte smirked again. "Now you got your own botanical garden right in your front room. And the kitchen. And the dining room. And the entry hall."

"You exaggerate, young lady. Beautiful as those flowers are, they're dying already. At the botanical garden, the flowers were alive. The ones I admired are probably still there, still blooming."

Both women were silent for a moment.

Charlotte opened her door. She turned to Artinces.

"You know, Dr. N., a man who gives you all that might expect something in return."

"Oh, really?"

"Yeah, he might want to engage in certain kinds of activities. You have any questions about that, I'll be happy to explain."

"Get out of here, Charlotte. We're both about to be late."

Charlotte flashed a smile. Artinces had forgotten how lovely it was. "Nobody can write you up for being late, Dr. N. You're the boss. See you later."

Half a block from her office on Kingshighway, Artinces turned into the White Castle parking lot. Inside the cramped restaurant, onion-scented mist floated above the heads of the customers. Artinces tried her best to ignore it as she waited to order her coffee.

"Morning, Doctor."

She looked up into the smiling face of Lucius Monday. The sign painter was born and bred in Gateway City, but he had something of the ancient and exotic in his face. His spectacularly bloodshot eyes, the result of years of living inside a bottle, remained a robust shade of crimson despite a half-decade of sobriety. His beard, surely one of the most impressive in town, was a dusty blend of black and white, flanked by scars deeply embedded in his slate-black cheeks. Artinces could easily picture him as a tribal chieftain, running through a rainforest naked except for a loincloth and a bone through his nose. It was wrong, she knew. Plenty of other folks had confessed to similar thoughts about Lucius, but that didn't make her feel any less guilty.

"Hello, Mr. Monday," Artinces said, smiling. "How are you today?"

"Just fine, ma'am." He bowed and tipped his painter's cap.

"I'm surprised to see you here instead of at Stormy's. Don't worry, I won't tell Mrs. Monday."

Lucius laughed. Artinces heard the distant rumble of drums, in spite of herself.

"The rest of the crew is next door," he said, jerking a thumb toward the window. "I'm grabbing everybody some coffee while they stock up."

Artinces saw Reuben Jones and the other men of the Black Swan on the lot of the paint-supply store. Reuben's Rambler station wagon was backed against the loading dock with the tailgate open. He wrote on a clipboard while the others loaded heavy drums of paint into the back.

The painters had been the most honorable of her contractors when she built her new offices five years ago. Other workmen could barely contain their amusement (or was it skepticism?) as Artinces oversaw the demolition of a crumbling clothing store and pursued plans for her own establishment. Reuben and Lucius were exceptions, working hard and never failing to respond with a quick "yes, ma'am." She singled them out for special praise when the *Gateway Citizen* photographer came out to cover her grand opening. Artinces insisted that he get a shot of the enormous mural the men had painted according to her design, a delights-of-the-garden panorama featuring the faces of black children smiling as they emerged like blossoms from an abundance of green leaves.

The acclaimed children's hospital on the city's South Side had received far more attention for its own mural, which had as its centerpiece a lollipop "tree" that dispensed real lollipops when children pressed a button. Artinces had been offended by the very notion of giving out cavity-causing treats to kids the hospital treated. Youngsters who endured her examinations and treatments with admirable poise never received anything as wildly inappropriate as candy. Instead, they were rewarded with pencils, bright-colored erasers, crayons, and other school supplies. Occasionally she even gave out copies of *The Snowy Day*, one of the few children's books she could find with illustrations of dignified black characters.

After a bit of easy banter with Lucius, Artinces hopped in the Malibu and pulled onto her parking lot. Her coffee was still steaming when she walked through her door and nodded at Jennifer, her receptionist. The placard on the front desk, also painted by Black Swan, declared, *Every day is black day.*

"Nine appointments and two walk-ins already," Jennifer called as her boss breezed by.

By lunchtime, Artinces had administered four vaccinations, conducted two well-baby examinations, issued a prescription for a sinus infection, pierced a pair of ears, and given three lectures on the virtues of breastfeeding. She'd see one more patient before having a sandwich at her desk.

The young woman wore tight cornrows that curled neatly against her neck, just below her ears. She held her baby, a toddler, as if she was afraid she'd crush her. The baby had consumed nothing besides water and juice over the past 24 hours. The mother feared the worst, but Artinces could see that the child was in the bloom of health. Clad in a dark purple jumper, little Paulette wore her hair in tight, shiny pigtails divided by sharp parts that revealed a gleaming scalp. Artinces made sure to examine the child carefully, moving as slowly as possible so that the mother could see how thorough the procedure was. "Oh, you're plenty feisty, aren't you? A real handful," she said as she pressed gently on Paulette's stomach. She'd already learned from the mother that Paulette's bowel movements were regular and normal.

"Wanna know something? I used to be a handful too. My daddy used to call me his little Pepper Pot." Artinces turned to the mother, who hadn't breathed since the exam began. "She's fine, Mom," she said. "She's just not hungry. When she decides she wants something, she'll it gobble it down. Trust me, hungry children eat."

The mother exhaled, a long dramatic sigh that brought with it a trickle of tears. "Praise God," she said. "I was so worried."

"It's okay to be worried," Artinces said. "It means you're paying attention."

"Bless you, Doctor. Your kids must be so lucky."

Artinces's reassuring smile briefly faltered, just long enough for Paulette's mother to notice. She frowned.

"Did I say something wrong? You do have kids, don't you?"

"No, in fact I don't."

"I'm sorry."

"No need to be sorry," Artinces said quickly. "Not your fault. Billie will be in to finish up with you. Then talk to Jennifer about Paulette's next check-up."

She left the room, mad at herself. The question was not a new one, after all. Her response hadn't made sense either. "Fault" implied an error, a transgression. She'd never wanted a child of her own—not after Brady. After seasons of great pain, she was at peace with the choices she'd made and the choices that had been made for her. Maybe she was just out of sorts because of the ghosts. Back in her office, she spun around in her chair and looked at the picture on the wall. It showed her standing on the steps of Abram H., a newly anointed intern clad in a modest white dress and a long white lab smock. By her side stood four nurses, similarly dressed.

Taken in 1945, that same photo had accompanied her throughout her career. It had also graced a wall at her first private practice, launched 20 years ago in a rundown office suite above a steakhouse on Easton Avenue. When she moved to Kingshighway 10 years later, the photo was one of the first items she hung in her office, along with her diplomas and a quote from Dr. Rebecca Crumpler, author of one of the earliest medical books published by an African American. "There is no doubt," Crumpler had written, "that thousands of little ones annually die at our very doors, from diseases which could have been prevented, or cut short by timely aid."

Artinces realized she could no longer remember the names of three of the nurses in the photo. She conceded to herself that she'd probably forgotten them on purpose. They had been resentful, she recalled, because she expected them to get off their rear ends and work. She required them to bathe every child every morning before she made rounds. She also made a nurse accompany her on rounds and take notes on her observations.

"You're not gonna save every baby," one of them had the nerve to say. Artinces had stared at her, intensely, for several long minutes until the woman, a good four inches taller, visibly shrank under her gaze. "No," Artinces replied, finally, "we are not going to save every baby. But we are going to try."

Those nurses were gone by 1948, when she became chief resident. All of them except for Billie, who was still with her today. It was Billie's voice that broke through her momentary funk.

She stuck her head in the door.

"There's a man out here wants to see you."

"Another walk-in? What's the trouble with his child?"

"He's by himself. Says he's got something for you. Says his name's Playfair."

"All right, tell him to come in."

"He wants you to come outside."

Artinces stepped briskly through the door, prepared to brush him off. She would be polite and quick, cite her busy schedule. She'd been more than generous with him, after all. What more could he want?

Playfair didn't want a thing. The doctor's unfortunate collision with his Buick had proved to be a merely temporary setback, and business continued to be brisk. The transactions he'd conducted that morning on the lot of the Gateway Cab Co. had been reliably lucrative and he'd come to share a portion of his bountiful trade. In addition, his conversation with Guts had left him in buoyant spirits. When he entered the big man's office, he had known right away that something was different—something besides the gleaming scalp and neatly trimmed beard, and the crisp white shirt that had replaced his well-worn tees.

"Cufflinks," Playfair decided. "That's what's different about you. Check *you* out."

In his chair behind his desk, Guts raised his forearm and studied his sleeve as if he'd never seen it before. Sunlight slid through the window over his shoulder and appeared to dance directly on the gleaming link.

Playfair leaned over and squinted at it before sitting down. "Onyx? Man, you got 'em shining like diamonds. Black diamonds."

"Pearl's doing," Guts said sheepishly. "She rubs them until they sparkle."

"I didn't take you for a cufflinks man."

"They belonged to my father. He liked to dress up."

Playfair stared. Guts had never mentioned family.

The big man shifted in his seat. "I had been saving them for a special occasion," he said. "Mostly, I just kept them in a box. Pearl told me every day's a special occasion."

"I can see she's got you looking at things differently."

Guts nodded. "I suppose."

"That's what happens when you let a woman get ahold of the family jewels."

Guts grunted amiably. "Listen, speaking of jewels."

"Right, right," Playfair said, hunching forward. "I went by Crusher's gym like you asked me to. It's true—PeeWee clocked some glass-jawed sucker while wearing a big ring. He got out of Dodge while the getting was good. Funny, I see him at Stormy Monday's a lot, but he never eats in. Lately, though, he's been scarce."

Guts raised his forearm again, turning it this way and that in the sunlight. "At first I couldn't see why Crenshaw could get so wound up over a ring," he said. "Turns out I'm not so different. I've been carrying around a box of cufflinks since I was a kid. They might not mean much to anybody else, but I can't picture not having them." He looked up at Playfair. "That's how Rip is with that ring. I get it now."

"My guess is PeeWee's still holding on to it."

"I wonder why he hasn't tried to move it?"

"Doing what you used to do, maybe."

"What's that?"

"Saving it for a special occasion."

Playfair was leaning against a shiny Electra 225, his arms folded comfortably across his safari vest. Sunglasses rested atop his head. He jumped when he saw the doctor.

She couldn't help admiring the Buick. It looked brand-new. "How did you manage to get your car fixed so fast?" she asked. "That Mr. Cherry really is a wizard."

Playfair, now standing at attention, smiled patiently. "That he is, ma'am, but he didn't work on this. This here's a different car."

Artinces looked at the gleaming maroon, the shiny chrome. She cast a quizzical glance at her visitor.

"See the top? It's black. The other was white," Playfair explained.

"Oh, yes. Still, how…?"

"I've got resources, ma'am. Connections."

Artinces considered the meaning of that. "Well, and I've got a full schedule, Mr. Playfair. How may I help you?"

"Actually, I came to help *you*. To bring you something." He opened the rear door on the driver's side and carefully retrieved a large object with a light fabric draped over it. He set it on the trunk and slid the covering off, revealing a birdcage with a parrot inside.

"Say hello to Shabazz."

Artinces stared. "A bird?"

"A parrot, African Grey. Mostly I deal in parakeets, but every once in a while something special comes through."

"No thank you, Mr. Playfair. A bird could contaminate my office."

"I thought of that. That's why I asked them to bring you out here. Shabazz is for your house."

"That's very kind of you, but I'm not interested in a pet."

Playfair laughed. "You thought Shabazz was a pet? This here is a guard bird."

"A guard bird?"

"Yes, ma'am."

"I didn't know there was any such thing."

"Oh, yeah, birds respond to training. Allow me to demonstrate." Playfair turned to the bird. "Watch yourself," he said.

The bird said nothing.

"Watch yourself," Playfair repeated.

Dr. Noel coughed softly.

"Just a little shy," Playfair explained, "an affliction someone in your profession might attribute to performance anxiety."

Dr. Noel looked at Playfair as if noticing him for the first time. "Are you an educated man?"

"No, ma'am, I just know how to talk to people. Dropped out of Sumner as soon as I was old enough. Couldn't sit still."

Artinces suppressed a chuckle. *Sounds like Charlotte*, she thought. *The girl flits from the counter to the chair to the window as if her rear end's on fire.* Maybe the bird could be a welcome distraction, something to keep her occupied.

She looked at Playfair. "I close my office at six," she said. "Bring him back then."

Playfair grinned. "Yes, ma'am. I'll bring you up to speed on how to take care of him."

Charlotte wasn't impressed when Artinces told her about the parrot later that evening. She rolled her eyes, sucked her teeth, and refused even to look in the backseat where the bird sat quietly in its covered cage.

"Tell me again who gave it to you?"

"A friend."

"Another friend. First flowers, now birds. What kind of name is Shabazz anyway?"

"I think it's Arabic. Muslim."

"Right, like El-Hajj Malik. Just what we need, the official pet of the Nation of Islam."

Artinces laughed. "What do you have against the Nation? You don't like bean pies?"

"I used to. I would buy them from the man who stands in front of Katz Drugs. They were good. But then I heard about the Pie Lady and that was that. I'm tired of her too, though."

Artinces wasn't fond of Charlotte's complaining, but she wanted to encourage her when she showed a willingness to talk.

"Why's that? She seems nice enough."

"Yeah? Maybe she doesn't get all in your business. When I go in there, it's just question after question. Like I'm not entitled to a private life." Charlotte looked pointedly at Artinces, who kept her eyes on the road. "Everybody's got a private life. Right?" The girl acted like she knew something. But Artinces knew it was just bluster. At least she hoped as much.

The next day, Charlotte's sly insinuation still resonated while Artinces sat through a meeting of the Harry Truman Boys Club board of trustees. There weren't many items on the agenda, and board chair Virgil Washburn handled old and new business with his customary dispatch. The board formally renewed club director Gabe Patterson's contract and thanked him for his exemplary service to the underprivileged youth of North Gateway. Washburn's baseball team was playing a home game and Washburn was eager to get to his owner's box by the seventh-inning stretch. Rip Crenshaw was closing in on the club home-run mark and, barring any more injuries, would surely match it by August.

Gabe Patterson was anxious too. His wife, Rose, was nearly eight months pregnant and he didn't like to leave her by herself for long. Still, he risked pausing to soak up the moment. After shaking hands and accepting congratulations, he stood near the window in Washburn's stately conference room and enjoyed its imposing view of downtown Gateway. A longtime activist, he still had trouble believing he was working from within the halls of power instead of challenging them from the outside. Not very long ago, he was handing out pamphlets and speaking at rallies. Now he was looking out over the entire city, watching the last streaks of sun dip behind the Old Courthouse. Rose was so proud of him. She was always curious about these meetings, full of questions about the black movers and shakers with whom he rubbed elbows, the folks whose faces she saw each week in the *Citizen*. If he had to describe the night's proceedings to her with just one word, though, he'd choose "weird."

His renewal was unanimously approved; not a single person spoke against him. However, tension occasionally flared when Dr. Noel and Ananias Goode seemed to speak against *each other*. In each case, they were essentially saying the same thing, a fact recognized by everyone else in the room. Yet they continued unaware, somehow managing to twist each other's arguments into unrecognizable shapes.

Their hostility, barely contained, made the others uncomfortable. Everyone was relieved when Washburn finally adjourned the meeting. Gabe Patterson shook his head as he watched the gangster and the doctor continue to hassle each other while they all waited for the elevator to the underground garage. They were still arguing when he drove away. In Gabe's rearview mirror, Goode appeared to be sneering while Dr. Noel pinched her lips in disapproval. Her posture suggested that the gangster had body odor or a communicable disease.

Goode paused. Although his eyes were on Artinces, he didn't fail to note Gabe's exit. When he was sure Gabe was gone, he relaxed, letting his sneer change into an affable grin.

After Artinces settled behind the wheel, Goode leaned through the open window. "When will the doctor be in? Because I really need to be *in* the doctor."

"Keep talking dirty and I may have to discipline you."

"Promises, promises."

Placing her hand on the back of his broad neck, she yanked his mouth to hers. Her strength always surprised him.

Goode stepped back to catch his breath. Lipstick traces were smeared around his mouth. "Can I get some more of that?"

Artinces smiled. "Wait til Wednesday," she said. She winked and drove away.

Goode pulled a handkerchief from his pocket and rubbed it across his lips. Pressing it against his nose and breathing deeply, he stared after her, watching her car until its taillights twinkled out of sight.

L
UTHER NOEL WAS A SIMPLE MAN. Warmhearted and plainspoken, he had little interest in finery. Each morning he stepped into one of his two pairs of overalls, the daily wardrobe of every dirt farmer in his part of Kentucky. His boots were scuffed and his knuckles were rough and battered. "I've got no use for shine," he had been fond of saying to Artinces, his only child. "You and your mama are all the sparkle I need."

In his view, it would have been downright foolish to waste his precious pennies on baubles. "Why a diamond's worth more than a turnip is a mystery to me, Pepper Pot," he'd said more than once. "They both come out of the same dirt." The starched white shirt he wore under his overalls to Sunday meeting was his one concession to propriety.

Artinces had considerably more resources, yet she still couldn't help feeling improper whenever she purchased a little something to help discard the tensions of the day. She counted jewelry, lingerie, and rare books among her guilty pleasures.

And, despite her father's resonant voice echoing in her brain, she was especially drawn to dazzlement. Some people and things happened to reflect light in a way that caught her eye. A polished grand piano, gold bracelets, Harry Belafonte. Her attraction to radiance probably accounted for her fearlessness when she first encountered Ananias Goode.

On that day, she had just locked the back door of her office and removed the key when she heard a voice. "Hey, good looking."

She turned and saw a man leaning against the fence, faint rays of sunlight framing his head like a crown. He had an elegant topcoat draped across one shoulder. Underneath it, a beautiful pinstriped suit showed a luminous weave of navy and gray. His hat was angled rakishly over one brow. The man looked immense, dangerous, golden. And he seemed to know it.

"You got what I need," he said. "I'm sure of it."

Artinces was still wearing her lab coat. She slipped her hand into her pocket. "Mister, all I have is a scalpel and I know how to use it."

"I know. That's why I'm here."

"That makes no sense at all. I'm warning you. Take one step and I'll slash you to ribbons."

He smiled. Slowly, he pulled open his suit jacket to reveal a red circle just to the right of his tie.

"How about that?" he said. "Somebody beat you to it."

Artinces spun around so quickly that at first Goode thought she had failed to take notice of his injury. But she was only unlocking her door. She swung it open, then turned and looked expectantly at Goode. The sun was just over his shoulder, forcing her to squint.

"Well? Come on," she urged.

In her examination room, Goode hung his coat and hat carefully on the coatrack before settling onto the exam table. If he was in pain, he didn't show it. Artinces scrubbed her hands at the sink, put on latex gloves and laid out an array of instruments. After helping Goode ease out of his shirt, she went to work.

"Private practice," he murmured. "No partners. I figured you for the kind of boss who ain't satisfied unless you batten all the hatches and empty the register your damn self. I'm of a similar philosophy. I also figured you'd be locking up right about now."

Artinces, focused on treating his wound, said nothing.

"How you like having your own shingle? Different from running the baby ward at Abram H., I bet. What's it been, about 10 years now?"

Artinces stopped, eyebrows raised, and looked into her patient's eyes.

"I read the papers, believe it or not. I remember the picture of your ribbon cutting in the *Gateway Citizen*. Back in 1950, but I remember it. It was a big deal. You're a big shot for such a tiny woman." *Such a fine woman, too*, he thought, but he was saving that.

"Never mind all that," Artinces said. "You've been stabbed."

"Naw, just nicked. Stitches ought to do it."

"You're lucky you weren't killed."

"No luck about it. I just let him nick me so that he'd think he had the advantage. I ain't slim, but I ain't slow either."

"Where he is now, the man who 'nicked' you?"

"You don't need to know that."

"Shouldn't a man like you have protection? Muscle—isn't that what they call it?"

"'A man like me.' What kind of racket do you think I'm in?"

"Racket…that says a lot. Sneaking up to my back door instead of walking through the front door of an emergency room says something too."

"So I'm a back-door man. That ain't a crime."

He waited to see if she caught the joke. He continued when she didn't look up. "My best man's detained at the moment."

"You mean in jail?"

"Why you got me on the witness stand? You're a doctor, not a lawyer."

"I'm doing you an immense favor, mister. The least you could do is tell me a few things. Including your name."

Now it was Goode's turn to arch his eyebrows. "You're serious? You don't know who I am?"

Artinces shook her head.

"Ananias Goode. You've never heard the name?"

"Doesn't ring a bell," she replied. "I wish I could say I'm pleased to meet you, Mr. Goode. But I'd be lying."

He laughed. Artinces would never forget that moment—the first time she heard his laugh. The phrase "how sweet the sound" entered her head. She wasn't the prayerful type, but she knew what sin felt like.

"Be still," she warned, "or you'll make things worse."

Goode obeyed, letting his eyes linger. She had a cute, round little nose and rich, full lips. Her brown eyes were large and fringed with long lashes. They were the kind of eyes you saw on children before their other facial features caught up. At the same time, her unblinking gaze suggested a fiercely determined woman, one disinclined to put up with bullshit. She had an air of superiority about her, something they had in common. He was going to enjoy seducing this tight-assed, siddity female. Damn straight.

"Where you from?"

"Honey Springs."

"Kentucky. Damn, a Southern girl."

She decided to ignore his vulgar tongue. "You've heard of it?"

Goode nodded. "I may have hopped a freight there once."

"Why'd you do that?"

"I thought I was on my way to something better. Ended up here."

"Gateway City's not so bad."

"I guess not, if you're a rich doctor."

"You think you know me."

"I got an idea."

Artinces tugged the last of the sutures through his flesh and knotted it. She looked at him, impassive. He stared back. "You don't. You couldn't possibly know me."

"Not in the biblical sense, so far. But I'm working on it."

Artinces suppressed an impulse to tremble. "You don't strike me as a man who spends much time with Scripture," she said.

"Didn't say I was. But I'd read the Bible with you anytime."

"Liar. Good thing for you I don't own one."

"Do tell. I figured you'd have a big crucifix on your office wall."

Artinces could almost taste his breath. He smelled as if he'd been drinking something sweet and forbidden.

"I do," she said, "but it's for my patients. Helps them feel safe."

"How about you? You ever want to feel safe?"

At that moment, Artinces knew that safety was the last thing she wanted. She wanted to flirt with risk, indulge until she was flush and satisfied. She wanted to run breathless to the edge of a cliff, with no idea what waited below. Looking into the stranger's eyes, she decided to jump.

Neither of them spoke as he closed the gap between them. He was close to kissing her before she abruptly turned away and began to fuss with the supplies in her cabinet. She grabbed a roll of medical tape just like the roll she had already laid out. Gently, she covered his wound with gauze and bandages. "You're patched up now," she said in a voice she recognized from years before, a voice heavy with restrained lust. "You need to be on your way."

He didn't move. Artinces took his hat and set it softly upon his head. She shifted it until it sat at the same rakish angle as before. Goode was still naked to the waist.

"At least let me pay you for saving my life," he said.

"You exaggerate," she said. "Just promise me you're going to stay out of danger."

"Why would I say that, when right now danger is all I'm thinking about?"

Instead of answering, she retreated and faced her supply cabinet. He stared at her delicate back, willing her to spin around and look at him again. When that failed, he got up and, wincing, put on his shirt and suit jacket.

"I have to say," he said, "your bedside manner was much better than I expected."

Artinces remained at the cabinet until she heard the door shut. She went to her chair and sat in in it, gripped its arms, and placed her feet firmly on the floor. She breathed deeply, the first full breaths she'd taken since Goode surprised her behind her building.

For most of her adult life, she'd had a ready answer for anyone who asked her what she wanted most in the world. "To save every child," she'd reply. She wanted to keep every baby not just alive, but healthy, no matter the cost. To the mothers and fathers of the North Side, she was a genius with a stethoscope who'd stop at nothing to rescue their children from whatever ailed them. To public health officials, medical school faculty, and hospital administrators across the city, she was a hard-headed colored woman who wouldn't take no for an answer, an uppity upstart who had apparently forgotten that if she'd been born just a few years earlier she'd be swabbing the halls of Abram H. with a mop, not patrolling its pediatric ward with a clipboard and a six-figure budget.

Whenever something like loneliness or doubt or fatigue tugged at her lab coat, she revived herself with her mantra: *Save every child. Save every child. Save every child.* She rocked herself to sleep at night with that simple, impossible phrase ringing in her brain. And she had done her best, through the long hours and late nights, the battles with bureaucrats, the stalwart standoffs with stubborn epidemics, the wars waged against infections with few weapons at her disposal besides penicillin, ice baths, and cough syrup. She'd had her moments when impatience overwhelmed her, when nothing could subdue her existential torment but a round of shopping followed by wine, the comforting coolness of silk lingerie, and Belafonte's velvet rasp on the hi-fi. But those moments of weakness had been rare and mercifully brief. In the morning she'd shake off her hangover, wash her self-pity down the shower drain, and march unswervingly toward the next round of patients, clueless bean counters, and germs.

She hadn't thought about saving herself for years, despite Billie's warnings that she was just wearing herself out. Billie left every day at precisely six p.m., an unlit cigarette between her lips and her handbag dangling from her wrist just so. "Work ain't everything" was *her* mantra.

The sun's fading glow receded from the windows. Artinces stood, flicked the light switch off, and sat down again. Shadows moved across the walls, covering the sink, the cabinets, the helpful posters about vaccinations and the virtues of breastfeeding. She welcomed the encroaching darkness, thinking it would ease her troubled mind. Instead she felt cornered, pushed and prodded by a profound and unexpected loneliness. She had last cried at age 24, and at age 15 before that. Throughout her career, she had never shed tears, even when patients died in her arms. She was saddened, terribly so, but her eyes stayed dry. She no longer beat herself up when patients took a turn for the worse, failed to respond to treatment, didn't wake up. In time, she recognized that knowing the answer wouldn't return the light to a dead child's eyes. Instead of crying, Artinces just resolved to do all she could, all the time. In the dark, thinking on her loneliness, she remained dry-eyed. She determined to examine her situation as she did all others, with the cool, analytical gaze of an experienced clinician.

It didn't take her long to identify her symptoms as indications of a hunger, a need, that she had convinced herself she'd outgrown. She was 40, not a girl. And this handsome stranger, this Ananias Goode, he had to be even older. They should have been ashamed to huff and puff and flirt the way they had. Well, *he* had flirted. She had managed to conduct herself honorably despite the stirrings she felt. Yes, she'd found him attractive, the most magnetic man she'd met in many long years. But she had successfully hidden it from him. He had no idea. She was sure of it.

When he reappeared in the alley 10 days later, she brought him in to remove his stitches. He was polite and smelled delicious, but this time offered no sly double-talk, inserted no witty flirtations into the gaps of their stilted conversation. He kept his hat on, still angled rakishly. Artinces fought off an urge to remove the hat and place it on her own head. She could tell he was distracted, barely listening as she extracted the sutures and pronounced him healed. When she was done, he all but leaped off her exam table.

Hurriedly buttoning up, he finally looked into her eyes. "I have to go," he said. "I'm sorry. I have to."

"Try not to disturb that wound, even now that the stitches are out," Artinces said, trying to be matter-of-fact. She picked up her instrument tray and carried it to the counter.

"I'm going to make it up to you. You'll see," he promised.

Artinces pretended to study the tray. She didn't want him to see how disappointed she was.

He opened the door and crossed the threshold. Suddenly he stopped and whirled around, almost catching Artinces in the act of staring longingly after him. "I've been thinking of you a lot," he said. "Have you been thinking of me?"

Looking up at him, she swayed on her feet, a schoolgirl waiting to be asked to the dance. "No," she said.

He grinned. "Now who's the liar?" he asked. He tipped his hat and left, closing the door behind him.

Artinces's long leap had yet to bring her to the ground. Since taking that fateful step off her imagined cliff, she had gone from surprise to shame to, finally, determination to act on her growing feelings. All the while, she was still falling. And she intended to land in his arms.

Another week passed before he showed up again, and Artinces had done her homework by then. She found out he was a self-described "independent businessman" who had his hands in a number of concerns—most of them illegal. She was prepared to grill him about all of them.

"Doctor," he said. "We've got to stop meeting like this." He was leaning against a dark blue New Yorker, idly turning his hat in his hands. Again the sun hovered just over his shoulder, casting his face in shadow.

Artinces had been getting ready to lock up. Instead, she smiled and turned, leaving the door ajar. "The pleasure's all yours, I'm sure."

He stepped toward her, flashing a smile. To Artinces, the sun seemed dull in comparison.

She shielded her brow with her hand. "Remember I told you I had a scalpel and I know how to use it?" She slowly removed her hand from the pocket of her lab coat and held up the blade. "I wasn't kidding. See, I can get nasty in a minute."

Goode raised his hands in mock surrender. "Mercy," he said.

Artinces ducked her chin and showed him her naughtiest look. "I feel like you're teasing me," she said. "You think I don't know the first thing about nasty."

Goode stepped past her and pushed the door until it was completely open. He turned to her and bowed. "Why don't you show me what you know?"

She went in. He followed, bending to shut and lock the door. He turned and she leaped at him, wrapping her legs around his waist and slamming him back against the door. She kissed and sucked at his face as if she wanted to devour him. He held her there, nuzzling, licking, and finally sliding with her to the ground. Neither of them spoke again until the deed was done. Side by side on the floor, they clung to each other in the rising dark, a puddle of clothes beneath them. Artinces rose first, wrapping herself in her lab coat and topping off the makeshift ensemble with Goode's hat.

"I have to go," Goode announced. "But I want to see you again."

"I know," Artinces said. She helped him dress in silence, both of them understanding that talk would spoil the mood. Still naked under her lab coat, she stood on tiptoes to lay his hat on his smooth scalp.

Outside, the sun was gone. The moon was rising to take its place. The lunar glow combined with the glare of a streetlight, adorning everything below with a silvery tint. Everything except Goode, as far as Artinces was concerned. She watched him get in his car and start the engine, as golden as the first moment she laid eyes on him.

Heading home to Lewis Place, Goode puzzled over his new lover's aggressive, even combative manner. The ferocity of their coupling had staggered him. Like the men who endured his moods and executed his demands in the streets, the women he slept with instinctively knew to serve and obey. As a man accustomed to deference, he understood that his pleasure was the first priority, and he instructed his partners accordingly.

Goode had never grown recklessly arrogant, like some of his rivals. He had never deluded himself into thinking his North Side swagger compared in any way to the real power wielded by Virgil Washburn and the banking and department-store titans who swapped gossip and brokered deals in the steam rooms of the Downtown Athletic Club. In the time it took to smoke a single expensive cigar, those fat cats moved more product and secured more real estate than the local black chamber of commerce could accomplish in several generations. Goode didn't bow and scrape when his interests overlapped with the white elite, but his instincts told him when to grin amiably and when to say nothing. He greased the right palms, offered the right concessions, formed the right alliances, and showed appropriate gratitude for his share of the crumbs that fell from the fat cats' table.

Long ago, when he'd hopped that freight with Miles Washington, they'd left bloodstained Mississippi at their backs with New York,

Chicago, or maybe Detroit on their minds. But they stopped and
staked a claim in this midsized burg on the banks of the river
with that same bloody name, in the heart of a border state best
known for stubborn mules, lager beer, and the infamous 1820
compromise that kept their kinsmen below the Mason-Dixon
clapped in chains until Emancipation. That rail-yard dust was now
far behind him. Like Miles, Goode was also no stranger to the
complex art of compromise. While Miles taught his parishioners
about the kingdom of Heaven, Goode, ever the dealmaker, set out
to make the North Side his personal realm. He wore the crown
and he wore it with ease. No one could gain access to numbers,
gambling, lending, or liquor without kissing his ring, or his ass,
depending on his mood. He'd done some horrible things, true,
but they were necessary things, and the horror of those acts had
spawned a pervasive and equally necessary fear, a zone of which
surrounded him like a force field and functioned as reliably as Guts
Tolliver. Only a few people on the entire North Side were unaware
of him, and thus didn't adopt the nervous posture with which they
were supposed to greet him. For reasons Goode couldn't fathom,
Artinces Noel was among those few.

She had absolutely no fear of him, he was sure. He decided he
liked that.

For Artinces, the route home was short. She typically zoomed
down Kingshighway before crossing Delmar, the southernmost
border of North Gateway, and entering the West End, her
neighborhood. An upscale and ostensibly liberal community, it
occupied a narrow strip that quickly gave way to the South Side,
an alien, forbidden territory for most of Artinces's patients. Once
past Delmar, Artinces could look out her driver's-side window
and see the expensive restaurants, specialty-food emporiums, and
clothing stores (including Aldo's, her favorite) lining the street. Or
she could look out the passenger window and admire the imposing
ornate gates that protected the city's doctors, professors, and
power brokers from the unwashed hordes struggling just blocks
away. Most evenings, Artinces would take little note of the shifts in
the landscape. Her mind would still be at the office, thinking about
charts and x-rays and the case files stuffed into the tote bag beside

her on the seat. But ever since Goode had driven away and left her wearing just a lab coat and a smile, Artinces rolled through the Gateway streets like a stranger in a magical wonderland. Where others may have seen creeping blight or obnoxious opulence, she saw only vague outlines of dazzling gold. Artinces wore sunglasses to counter the tenacious brightness that still enveloped her as she pulled up to her house on the outer rim of the Protected Zone, across the street from the city's largest park.

Although it was Artinces Noel who locked up the building every night, Billie Pope turned on the lights in the morning. She liked being the first to arrive and the first to leave. That's why she was surprised to find Artinces already on the scene, on her hands and knees in fact, scrubbing the floor of Exam Room No. 3 as if her life depended on it. The doctor didn't even look up when Billie entered the room.

"Ahem," Billie said.

Artinces had on rubber gloves and a scarf around her head. She was wearing jeans. Billie tried to recall if she'd ever seen Artinces in jeans. Or even in pants.

"Oh, hi, Billie," she finally said. "Just sprucing up."

"I can see that. Any particular reason?"

"No, the floor just looked a little—it just seemed to me that it could use a little elbow grease."

Billie studied Artinces, waiting for an explanation. When none was offered, she filled the silence with another question. "Elbow grease?"

"Yep."

"Don't we pay a janitorial service to do that?"

"Indeed we do. I just didn't want to wait."

"They're coming tonight. You couldn't wait until then?"

Billie was technically Artinces's employee, but more than that, she had been her friend for 15 years running, one of the few people able to claim any semblance of closeness to the doctor. The two women could speak freely without fear of hurt feelings or misunderstanding. Yet they respected each other's boundaries.

Billie said nothing when Artinces went a decade and a half without a lover, and Artinces kept her lips sealed when Billie went through her typical half-dozen or more partners per year, none of them men.

But on the day after Artinces and Goode made love on the floor, Billie could not hold her tongue. She watched the doctor zip through her roster of patients with more than her usual zest. "What's gotten into you?" Billie finally asked when Artinces slowed down just long enough to gobble a sandwich at her desk. "Or should I say, who?"

Artinces put down her sandwich and dabbed at the corners of her mouth with a napkin. "Mind your own business, Billie," she replied. "Your imagination's getting the best of you."

When decked out in her uniform and standard white shoes, Billie was a routine beauty. In her civilian garb, though, she looked like a runway model. Tall and slim with high cheekbones and dramatic, almond eyes that suggested a hint of Asian ancestry, she had a casual disdain for male suitors that only magnified her haughty allure. She'd done her damnedest to slide some of that unwanted attention to her intense friend and colleague whose obsession with work was, in Billie's view, plainly unhealthy. For Billie, nursing was a means to an end. She was good at it, to be sure. It was her poise and competence that made her Artinces's most trusted ally during the diarrhea epidemic of 1948. Plus, with people always getting sick and dying, there could never be enough nurses. It beat being chased around a desk by a potbellied middle manager or slaving for tips as a hatcheck girl. Best of all, Billie could live freely without ever considering the monetary reasons for keeping a man around. As for any other reason for putting up with men, well, Billie had no need for that either.

She could easily recognize the symptoms of love sickness. The diagnosis was clear: a mystery man had the doctor's nose open. She'd seen people of all persuasions stumble under the spell of a powerful longing, and she'd certainly fallen victim to it more than once. She'd seen women wander streets in a daze, women who couldn't stop grinning, women who willingly used themselves up in service to the great god of love by all manner of acts, some ordinary, some completely baffling. She'd once known a woman who jumped off a roof to prove her devotion to a man who didn't want her. But she'd never seen a woman respond to desire by scrubbing floors.

The aroma of disinfectant had subsided considerably when Goode and Artinces met again in Exam Room No. 3 a few days later. They spared the floor, choosing instead to do it standing up. Afterward, Artinces inspected the wall that had born the brunt of their exertions and found it none the worse for wear. Two days after that, Billie arrived in the morning with her customary promptness and, following her habit, walked through the building turning on lights. In Exam Room No. 3, she discovered the examination table crumpled and bent beyond hope of repair.

When she reported the damage to Artinces, the doctor seemed unperturbed.

"It was getting old anyway," she said, shifting in her office chair. "Order another one. In the meantime, we'll make do with two exam rooms."

"That's it?"

"Yep," Artinces replied, staring at a chart.

Billie lingered at the threshold, staring at Artinces, who refused to meet her gaze.

The collapse of the exam table had briefly frightened Artinces. One minute they were losing themselves in something wonderful, with Goode stretched out underneath her. Then they were on the floor, having destroyed the table with their vigorous exertions. But she and Goode were both laughing seconds later. "Are you okay?" she asked. She was still straddling him. He had lost his erection in the fall, but she knew he'd get it back. "As okay as I can get, with you wearing me out and all," he replied. "I'm almost 50, you know."

"Really? I figured you for about 19," she said.

They graduated from playing doctor in the exam room and moved on to clandestine couplings at each of the three motels that serviced the entire North Side. Once they'd even done it in his car, down on the cobblestones at the edge of the river. So noisy were they that Goode paused mid-stroke to turn on the radio to drown out their sounds.

Had it been four weeks? Closer to six? *You really do lose track of time*, Artinces noted with amusement. As usual, she sat in her car and waited while Goode checked in at the front desk of the Goodnight Motel. Earlier in their affair, she'd allowed him to talk her into sharing a room at the Park Plaza. It had seemed like a good idea, with its grand hallways and posh suites, a far cry from the humble seediness of a place like the Goodnight. Her giddiness vanished when she found that nearly everyone seemed to recognize her, from the white captains of industry in the lobby to the black men who carried luggage, operated the elevators, and ran the shoeshine stand. "Hello, Doctor Noel." "Good to see you, Doctor Noel." "Can I help you with anything, Doctor Noel?" Each interruption chipped at her dignified facade and made it harder to walk with anything like grace.

Artinces was sweat-soaked and furious when she finally got to the room, where Goode awaited. "What was I thinking?" she raged, pacing frantically. "Hey. Hey," Goode said softly. He had already removed his shoes, jacket, and tie. He took her in his arms. "Let me run you a bath," he offered. The warm suds and his skillful hands finally put her in the mood to do what they'd come there for.

She had vowed never to take such a dangerous chance again, preferring instead to risk the tawdry shadows of the motel parking lot until Goode emerged with a room key. Maybe, under the influence of a glass or two, she might have confessed that she liked it a little bit, the sordidness of their escapades. Like her cramped examination room, something about the Goodnight's pervading seediness set loose her inhibitions. And she always brought her own sheets.

The taste of him lived in her mouth. As a result, everything she ate seemed more delectable. She hadn't yet broken his flavor down into individual components, hadn't yet identified notes of chocolate, bourbon, honey, hickory. She'd only learned to let slices of orange linger on her tongue before she chewed and swallowed, to use her teeth to tear through chicken flesh with exquisite thoroughness and, ever so slowly, to suck the marrow from the bone. Although everything tasted better, it was never as delicious as the real thing. She couldn't help looking forward to the next encounter, when she'd eat him up as if digesting his essence was the only thing that could keep her breathing. She'd get lost in the imagining while eating her lunch, grinding bones to powder beneath her molars, blissfully ignorant of the loud crunching and the oily residue coating her lips. Once she looked up and noticed Billie in the doorway of her office, staring at her as if she'd gone crazy. Artinces blinked rapidly and fussed with her napkin. "I guess what they say is true," Billie said. "That chicken really is finger-licking good."

Their six weeks together hadn't gone without interruptions. She had been to two conferences, made presentations, testified at a public health hearing. He had his own absences, the reasons for which were much less clear. He didn't explain and she didn't ask. Mostly she discouraged talk because talking got in the way of the thing they did best, and also because she enjoyed having her life compartmentalized. Keeping it so made it easier to pretend that she continued to honor promises she had made to herself long ago. Goode wasn't husband material, clearly. Did that matter anymore?

She convinced herself she was too mature to be jealous or possessive. Still, when he dropped a pocket square on a motel room floor, she jumped on it and slipped it into her purse. On nights when she didn't see him, she clutched it like a talisman, wondering where he was, what he was doing, and with whom.

She decided that what she felt for him wasn't love. Could you really love someone without knowing him? They had never even exchanged phone numbers or had a long conversation. He'd just show up, flash that devastating smile, and away they'd go, with him cruising in his New Yorker and her following at a discreet distance. She knew his taste and smell, the touch of his hands. What more information did she need?

As it turned out, there were other salient facts. She was in a shop on Washington Avenue when she learned the truth about him. She had stopped there to buy him a hat. President Kennedy had supposedly made hats unfashionable, but word had not filtered down to the well-dressed men of North Gateway. The popular shop attracted a cross section of local black society. On a typical day, pastors and postal workers, some of them accompanied by their wives, tried on trilbies, fedoras, and homburgs alongside pushers and pimps, some of them accompanied by their whores. Artinces ambled along the aisles, imagining her lover in various styles, when she nearly bumped into a broad-shouldered man. "Pardon me," she said.

The man turned, then smiled. "No, excuse me, Doctor Noel. It's been a while. How have you been?"

Artinces tried and failed to hide her confusion. "I'm sorry," she said, "forgive me."

"Don't remember me, huh? That's okay. My name's Lawrence. I trained at Abram H."

"Of course," Artinces said. Male nurses had been extremely rare at the hospital, especially ones built like football players. "Good to see you, Lawrence. Are you still in the profession?"

"Yes, ma'am. I do private, in-home care."

Artinces had already moved on in her mind. "Oh? And how do you find it?"

Lawrence smiled. "Oh, it's good, real good. One patient, easy to manage. And Mr. Goode pays a fair wage."

Artinces stopped. She frowned, then quickly recovered. "You work for Mr. Goode?"

"Yes, ma'am. Ananias Goode. I figure you've heard of him."

"Is he ill?"

Lawrence laughed. Some men's bellies shook when they laughed. Lawrence's muscles rippled. "Mr. Goode? Aw, I bet he could go 15 with Floyd."

Artinces blinked.

"Floyd Patterson? The heavyweight champ? Anyway, I take care of Mrs. Goode. His wife."

The big nurse probably said something else after that. She must have mumbled a few words and politely excused herself, but Artinces had no memory of it. She just remembered sitting in her kitchen sipping wine while Belafonte crooned condolences from the hi-fi in the living room. How had she gotten home? How long had she been there? She stared at the empty bottle. Then she drained her glass and tossed it against the wall.

She'd already known he was into shady dealings. He hadn't lied about that. But she didn't know about the wife. Artinces was many things; some of those things she was only just discovering about herself. But she wasn't a home wrecker and she was certainly nobody's whore. She told him as much a few days later when he showed up at her back door, before she slapped his face.

That clash was the first of many they waged over the course of the next decade, darkening their on-and-off romance with pitched battles that marred their mutual obsession. Artinces never got over the fact of Goode's marriage, even after he explained—in the barest details—that his wife was comatose. But neither could she get over him, despite the impressive stretches when they tried to pretend the other didn't exist. Goode was her one irresistible vice amid a life of exemplary discipline, forbearance, and virtue.

Goode was equally stung, perhaps even more so. He didn't fully appreciate the depth of his attachment until several weeks after he'd worked his way back into the doctor's good graces by way of her willing thighs. He'd left her in the motel room while he went out to buy her favorite wine. When he returned, she cracked the door open just wide enough for him to see that she was wearing nothing but her usual white gloves and—even though it was Tuesday evening—a Sunday-go-to-meeting hat.

"Where's the rest of your get-up?" Goode asked. "For a minute there I thought you were about to go to Bible study."

Artinces crossed her arms across her breasts and pretended to pout. "Are you making me fun of me?"

"No, darlin," Goode assured her, "I'd never do that."

"Yes you would. You think I'm some prim biddy who doesn't know up from down."

"I don't think that. I know you're country smart, just like me. These city women ain't got nothing on you."

She made a soft clucking sound and grabbed Goode by his necktie. "That's right," she agreed. "Now come on in here. I'm about to spin you like a top."

And spun he was. Three hours later, he stepped out on the street with his tie askew and a stupid grin plastered across his face. He needed three tries to get his key into his lock. Finally he eased behind the wheel, realizing even through his fog that he'd likely be bruised and limping in the morning. Even a full night's sleep, or several of them, did little to lessen the residual ache left by his partner's forceful lovemaking. She went full tilt or not at all.

At a subsequent session, he asked her about it as tactfully as he could while zipping up her dress. "Why you do always have to fight me while you're fucking me?" he asked.

"I don't do that," she said. She walked over and sat at the room's tired vanity table. Looking in the mirror, she fastened her earrings. Lately they'd been staying at the Goodnight well beyond the witching hour, escaping just before dawn.

"What? Fight? Then why the hell do I have all these scratches on me?"

"Not fight. That other word."

"Oh, you mean fuck?"

"Yes. I don't do that. I make love."

"You got a funny way of showing it. I dig what you do to me, don't get me wrong. But damn, woman, sometimes I think you're about to kill me, like you're mad about something."

She brushed her hair. "What would you rather I do?"

"I don't know. Maybe slow down a little bit."

The next time they met, she was clad in lingerie from Aldo's, a pale-blue silk peignoir that she kept on, even when he was fully nude. She kissed him like she had never done it before, letting him drink deeply while she drew the breath from his lungs. Every time he let his hands wander down to her breasts or hips, she gently pulled them up and wrapped them around the back of her neck. She finally led him to the bed and lowered him onto his back. Every kiss she placed on his body was sweet agony, slow, soft, and moist. She covered every inch of him. She discouraged every urgent gesture, every impatient thrust, with a finger to her lips and a delicate "shh." She climbed astride him and even when he was fully inside, she hardly moved at all. It was torture. "Remember," she teased, "you wanted it slow. Tender."

Goode had enjoyed women of every size, every flavor, every color. But he had never had a woman leave him so utterly exhilarated. So intense was his desire, and so completely was it fulfilled, that spilling himself inside her prompted a tear to slide from his eye.

After a respectable interval, he excused himself and went to the bathroom. Grasping the sink with both hands, he stared into the mirror. He'd heard of punk-ass niggers who cried when they had sex, but he thought that was just corner talk. Now here he was, weeping like a bitch. What the fuck?

He was still soul searching, or the closest to introspection he ever got, when she entered the bathroom behind him. The air around him changed and he found he could not speak.

But she could. She wrapped her competent hands around his waist and, with one hand, she dipped lower and tugged him playfully. "Ready for round two?" she asked.

As the months progressed and Goode managed to hold on to his presence of mind while holding on to Artinces, information passed between them in fits and starts. For her part, Artinces regarded dialogue as an inconvenience that only delayed what they were both in need of. For his part, Goode had never encountered a woman who talked so little. The way she entered a motel room and resolutely undressed him occasionally left him feeling—what was it? Yes, used. He, Ananias Goode, felt like a mere sexual object instead of a human being. But she rebuffed his efforts at exchanging confidences of any kind. She made it clear that genuine intimacy was not only improbable, but the very last thing she wanted.

On rare occasions, however, wine combined with afterglow to inspire more playfulness and curiosity in her than usual. Curled up on the sheets she brought from home, she would seem in no hurry to leave. Goode, noticing the change, felt uneasy. He convinced himself to relax. After all, wasn't this what he'd been after?

She turned toward him on one such night. "I want to know more about you," she said.

"No you don't."

"You're right, I don't." She kissed him. "Except tonight I do."

"Hmm?"

Sitting up, she propped her head against the pillows. "I do. I want to know more about you."

"Why?"

"Because you're in my bed."

"This ain't your bed."

"You know what I mean."

"You never wanted to know before. Matter of fact, when you did find out something about me, you slapped me. Before you, the last person who raised his hand to me pulled it back with a finger missing."

Goode swung his legs over the side of the bed, resting his feet on the floor. He reached for the wine bottle on the nightstand and poured himself a glass.

"Is that supposed to scare me?"

"Nope," Goode replied, taking a sip. "Just telling it like it is. Come to think, why *aren't* you scared of me?"

"Everybody's got a weakness," she said, batting her eyelashes as Goode climbed back under the blanket. "I happen to be yours."

She reached under the covers, her fingers roaming confidently. "Go on," she said.

Goode closed his eyes. A sigh escaped. "Hmm?"

"You were telling me about yourself. Go on."

"You know I can't think—can't talk—when you're touching me like that."

Artinces removed her hands and primly placed them atop the blanket. "There," she said in her best schoolmarm voice. "Satisfied?"

"Hardly. Just keep 'em where I can see 'em." Goode cleared his throat. "It must have been about 19—"

Artinces slipped her hands back under the blanket and began to tickle him.

He chuckled helplessly before grabbing her wrists and holding them both in a single fist. He squeezed gently.

"Come on now," he said, "you play too much."

"Ooh," she said. "I feel so helpless."

"Are you done?"

"Yes. Sorry."

"For real?"

"Yes. I'm listening."

"Finally." He released her hands. "I made my first bankroll down on the docks, behind the train station. I threw dice with the dockhands and Pullman porters, took their hard-earned wages. Special dice I brought with me from Liberty."

"They never tried to get their money back?"

Goode drained his glass and poured another. "Oh, yeah. One night, Miles and me were still sleeping on the cobblestones down by the river. Three of them tried to take us. May they rest in peace."

"Really? Are you leveling with me?"

He turned and looked at her. "What do you mean? Did we really kill them or do I really wish they're resting in peace?"

"No. You didn't."

"It's kill or be killed, Tenderness."

"You're a Darwinist, Ananias Goode."

"I don't know about all that. Sometimes it's the thing to do. Scratch any man, there's some killer in him. Women too, you push 'em hard enough."

"You sound so sure."

Goode turned and looked directly at her. "Look at it this way. Would your father die for you?"

"He would and he did."

"Would he kill for you?"

Artinces frowned. "Why must everything be about killing?"

"I didn't make life the way it is. I just deal with it. It takes blood, is all I'm saying."

"To do what?"

"Anything." *Especially when it comes to the likes of Ike Allen,* he thought.

Artinces reached for her empty glass and waved it. Goode filled it for her.

"What about Miles?" she asked. "Rev. Washington?"

"What about him?"

"He helped you. He willingly got blood on his hands."

"Miles can speak for himself, but he'll tell you that faith takes blood too. Jesus didn't die easy, he'll say."

"And you never got in trouble for that? Arrested?"

Goode laughed. She usually liked his laugh. She didn't then.

"They were black. Nobody cared."

"Nobody," she said, her voice rising slightly. "Except for their wives. Girlfriends, mothers, fathers, sisters, brothers. Cousins, nephews, frien—"

"You know what I mean. The people that count didn't care. Now, the people they worked for? They might have missed them for a minute. You know what a white man does when his nigger doesn't show up to slave for him? He tells somebody, 'Find me another nigger as soon as you can.'"

"You know I don't like that word."

"Lots of stuff I don't like too. Like when you judge me. Talk to me in that siddity voice like I'm dirty or stupid. I've bled too, more than once. And I've never moaned about it. When you saw me in the alley that time? Wasn't I smiling like my number hit?"

Artinces recalled him in the doorway. The suit, the rakishly tilted hat, the devastating grin. She closed her eyes and each detail faded away until there were only his teeth. "Siddity?"

"You heard me. Anybody can see how you strain to be all damn dignified with your careful walk and educated talk, your white gloves and church-lady hats. Who do you think you're fooling? Honey Springs is more than skin deep, baby. You can't hide it that easy."

"You're right. I can't hide where I come from because nothing can cover it. Just like nothing can cover you. Not even pinstriped suits and custom boots."

"It's different for me," he protested. "I'm a businessman."

"You're a gangster! Your business is hurting other people. Taking their hard-earned dimes and when they've got nothing left for you to take, you gut them like a fish."

"People have to know that I ain't gentle. That ain't how the world works."

"I know! It takes blood. You've already told me. I'm not going to bleed for you."

"I'm not asking you to. I don't do what I do because I like it. I do it because I'm good at it. People know it. When I'm gone from this world, nobody will say I went down easy."

Artinces smirked. "Like Jesus, right?"

Goode ignored her. "People will remember me. My name's gonna ring out."

She laughed outright. "To whom? 'The people who count?' Or the people you stole from? What about those bodies you put in the river? What about the bones? Someday they might float to the surface with your fingerprints on them."

Goode rolled away from her, already reaching for his pants. He stepped into them and grabbed his shirt, buttoning swiftly, erratically. Propped up on her elbow, Artinces watched him tug on his socks and wrench on his shoes. She wanted him to stay, to fight with her like a husband who knew that after all was said and done they'd still end up side by side, sleeping off their anger.

But Goode was halfway out the door. He stopped and turned around. His gaze was level.

"I didn't go to medical school," he said, "but there's plenty I know. Them bodies I rolled into the river didn't come back and they won't. Because I weighed 'em down just right. See? That's something I know."

He left. They didn't share a bed again for nearly two years.

She immersed herself in her practice, devoting herself to the city's children with such passion that a *Citizen* columnist dubbed her "Saint Noel." Some admirers even mounted a campaign to elect her to the school board, an effort she quickly discouraged. Her mission was to keep children healthy, she declared. Someone else would have to make them wise.

Meanwhile, Goode began cleaning up his image, if not his act. In the fall of 1962, he gave Thanksgiving turkeys to needy families and made sure a photographer from the *Citizen* was on hand to record it on film. When the North Side Home for the Aged needed landscaping, he proudly—and loudly—paid for it all. He spent the next year buying legitimate businesses and making sure he was seen going in and out of them. In addition to his policy and lending "enterprises," his holdings by the fall of 1963 included a taxi company, racehorses, a print shop, an artist-promotion agency, prime real estate, part ownership of a beer distributor, and a piece of the popular Nat-Han Steakhouse. He joined the boards of directors at a few charitable nonprofits. At the reception after a church-sponsored event for the North Side's most generous benefactors, he ran into Artinces. They shook hands in front of the refreshments table.

"Nice to meet you," she said a little too loudly, when the event chairman introduced them. When the chairman moved out of earshot, Artinces smiled more warmly than she intended.

"Looks like you're moving up fast," she said.

He nodded but didn't return the smile. "I've come a long way from making moonshine, but I know my limits."

Bootleg whiskey, Artinces thought. *Didn't know that.* "Wasn't Joe Kennedy a moonshiner?" she asked.

"So they say."

She cradled her wine glass with two hands, as if it were too heavy to hold. "Well, look at his son," she said.

Goode half turned away from her. Studying the last sip of bourbon in his glass, he swirled it before swallowing it down. "Yeah, well, my son's not going to be president."

"You never know. We have black men in Congress now. Maybe Rev. King was right. All you have to do is dream."

"Actually I do know," he said, "because my son's dead." He put his glass on the table. "Nice to meet you, too," he said.

Artinces watched him walk away. *Didn't know that, either.*

A month later, the president was shot, plunging the country into shock. Thanksgiving hardly felt like a holiday at all. Not even Ananias Goode's turkey giveaway, complete with fanfare and performances by local talent he'd personally handpicked, could dispel the aura of gloom. Experience had taught North Siders that whatever misfortune fell on the country at large would land on them with considerably more weight. They had hardly been surprised when, earlier that year, Birmingham police turned fire hoses on black children. That kind of barbarity simply served as continuing evidence in a long and endless trial. But there was something very disturbing about a white man—whose wealth and staggering power only amplified his whiteness—shot down in the street like a common Negro. The Space Age, they feared, would tumble to earth before they even had a chance to lift off.

Like any engaged citizen, Artinces felt bad for the country, but her sadness inevitably reverted to its usual, distinctly personal shape. Having lost her appetite, she decided to forgo lunch in favor of an extended session with *Life* magazine and other periodicals that covered the Kennedy assassination and its aftermath.

Sitting at her desk piled high with files, she fixated on photos of the First Lady. In unsettling detail, they showed Mrs. Kennedy crazy with panic as she scrambled across the trunk of the limousine, entering the ambulance carrying her husband's body from the hospital to the airport, and kneeling at his flower-covered grave with a herd of officials and relatives waiting at a respectful distance behind her. What, Artinces wondered, would it feel like to experience such a soul-shattering loss? She'd known heartbreak a time or two, but, having pursued her calling with missionary focus, she had never entertained the possibility of falling so deeply in love that she couldn't climb out. In keeping with this philosophy, she felt she'd managed to confine her affair with Goode to purely physical concerns, simply a matter of two grown people taking care of each other's needs. Or had it been more than that? Artinces refused to pause long enough to give herself a chance to reflect. The one thing she was certain of was the sensation his absence created. Sighing, she conceded to calling it what it was. Pain.

Artinces's door flew open. She jumped, scattering her magazines. Billie stood over her, hands on hips.

"Um, come in," Artinces said.

Billie ignored her boss's sarcasm. "Do you know what Our Lady of Sorrows is?"

Artinces rubbed her temples. "What?"

"Lady of Sorrows. What is it?"

"It's a church," Artinces replied. "A few blocks from here."

Billie strutted across the room and opened the blinds, flooding the office with light. Artinces groaned and put her hands over her eyes.

"Wrong," Billie said. "It's the staff's nickname for you. You mope around here like a goddamn nun."

"Billie!"

Moving swiftly, Billie snatched up the magazines. "All that melancholy wrapped around you like a fucking lab coat."

"Billie! That's enough." Artinces rocked back in her chair and glared up at her.

Billie's eyes narrowed. "Fire me if you want to," she said, her voice softening. "But you should be thanking me. It's about time everybody stopped tiptoeing around you and told you the truth. For all our sakes, you've got to call that man."

"I could never—"

Billie sat on Artinces's desk. She lifted the phone from its cradle and handed it to her. "Do it. Call him."

Artinces leaned forward and placed her elbows on her desk. She rubbed her palms together. "Do they really call me that? Our Lady of Sorrows?"

"Maybe not. But it got your attention, didn't it?"

The women stared at each other in silence. Billie's lips began to quiver. Artinces made a choking sound, then a giggle escaped. Unable to contain themselves any longer, they broke into full-throated laughter. Soon tears were rolling down Artinces's face.

As their merriment faded, Billie stood up. "You won't be sorry," she said, turning to leave.

"Billie."

"Hmm?"

"You're still the coolest."

Billie smiled. "Cooler than Miles Davis, baby."

In the far corner of the print shop's parking lot, Artinces waited discreetly in her car while the men of the Black Swan gave Goode's storefront a makeover. She watched them expertly apply coats of outdoor paint, exchanging wisecracks as they scrambled up and down their scaffolding. Eventually, Goode's car rolled up with Guts Tolliver behind the wheel. Guts got out and opened the rear door, holding it until his boss emerged. Assessing the sign painters' work, Goode offered his thoughts as Guts stood nearby, his massive arms folded. Then, as if somehow sensing her presence, Goode turned and met her gaze. Almost imperceptibly, he nodded.

Back at her office, the hours moved at a sadistic crawl. When she had finally and guiltily shooed the last patient away, and Billie and the others had headed home, Artinces hurried through Exam Room No. 3 and opened the door leading to the alley.

She had just about given up when he slowed his New Yorker to a stop. He got out and leaned back against it, just as he had when they first got together.

"Come here," she said, but he just stuffed his hands in his pockets. He seemed to be looking at a spot just over her shoulder.

"You're awfully far away," she continued. Again nothing.

Okay. This is some kind of test. She left the safety of her doorway and walked purposefully toward him. She could feel his reliable heat before she closed the distance. Confident now, she reached up and placed her hand behind his neck. She shut her eyes.

But he showed more restraint than she knew he had. "You've always known who and what I was," he said. "I never pretended to be anything else."

"Stop talking," she said. She placed her palm on his chest and began to rub him gently. On tiptoes, she pressed her lips against his neck.

"Get your hands off me."

She continued, unafraid. She knew she could make him crumble. Make him bend.

"Like I told you," he said, "hurting people is what I do best. Maybe it's what I was put here to do."

"Nope," she murmured, kissing him. "It's not what you do best." She kissed him again. "Not even close."

And so they were on again, and stayed that way for another few years. She managed her flourishing practice and began to teach at the city's acclaimed medical school, an institution that hadn't accepted its first black student until two years after she'd graduated from Howard. Goode continued to go legit, easing further out of the underworld and into the land of the straight and narrow.

They had their minor spats here and there, the kind of low-grade tempests that would occasionally erupt between any headstrong pair. But there were only clear skies between them when they made plans to get together in Chicago in the late spring of 1966. Artinces had a conference to attend and Goode had a couple of racehorses he wanted to scout at Hawthorne. She took the train. Goode, defying custom and shrugging off the protests of the ever-vigilant Guts, drove himself. His New Yorker, tuned up by the wizardly Cherry, purred all the way up Highway 70.

In between her slideshows and plenary sessions, Artinces dragged Goode through quiet museums and dusty bookstores. In turn, she tried not to look bored in the grandstand at Hawthorne while he followed the thoroughbreds furlong by furlong, a rolled-up *Racing Form* in one hand and binoculars pressed to his brow with the other. On their third night in the Windy City, both were in a festive mood. In a cluttered bookstore in Old Town, she had stumbled on *A Book of Medical Discourses* by Rebecca Crumpler, whose framed quote had long graced the wall of her office. In 1864, Crumpler had become the first black woman in the country to earn a medical degree. Goode, meanwhile, had found his treasure at the track earlier that day: a promising two-year-old colt worth his investment.

Back at their hotel, Goode scoffed when he saw the book. "That battered thing is what's got you all hot and bothered? I haven't seen a colored person so excited about a book since I got trapped at a revival meeting with a bunch of Bible-thumpers."

He carefully lifted a suit out of the closet and laid it on the bed. Artinces sucked her teeth and rolled her eyes. "You've been to a revival meeting?"

"Yeah, I spent a lot of time with Miles's family. Until I outgrew that sort of thing."

"When was that?"

"When I turned eight." He pulled five neckties from a drawer and fanned them out around the suit.

"Maybe you should have stuck around a little longer, picked up some wisdom," she said. "This battered thing will one day be worth more than that horse you can't shut up about."

He leaned toward her and pecked her on the mouth. "Ha! Shows how much you know about horses," he teased.

She nibbled on his bottom lip before she let it go. "Ha yourself," she said. "Shows how much you know about books."

They went to a supper club in Bronzeville, where they surprised themselves by dancing until they shut the place down. It felt so good, so free, to be their true selves in a public place, to cast their usual cares aside and whirl and sweat and clap and stomp. They kissed a lot and laughed too, especially when a photographer peddling snapshots told them they were the best-looking pair in the place. "Y'all one them couples that's gon' always be together," he said. "Trust me, I got a feeling."

Later, after the bartender yelled last call and they held each other and turned slowly beneath the blue lights, swaying to "I'm So Proud" by the Impressions, the man's successful sales pitch felt like prophecy.

In the hush of the hotel hallway, Artinces hugged her fur stole while Goode fiddled with the lock. He was still dancing, singing "Wee Wee Hours" under his breath. Beads of sweat glistened on his bald scalp. "I understand if you're tired," she said, although she was hoping he wasn't. "All that dancing, well, neither of us was prepared for all that."

"I'm tired for sure," he said, swinging the door open. "Tired of being up against you all night without being able to touch you the way I want."

Artinces squealed when he suddenly swept her up in his arms and carried her across the threshold, reaching back with one foot to push the door shut.

In the morning, she woke up first. She sat quietly in a chair next to the bed and watched Goode snore. It had been a wonderful three days. This is how it is for a woman who sleeps all night with the man who belongs to her. She can choose to be annoyed by his snoring or agitated by the scratchy stubble that pushes up from his cheeks in his sleep. Or she can sit and savor the stillness, just be grateful for the solid weight of his presence, the sound of his breath. *I can be fine with this. It doesn't matter if it can't get any better.*

Or could it? Later that day, she returned to the hotel from her conference, having nearly nodded off during an endless discussion about inoculations. She opened the door with a bubble bath on her mind, only to find Goode standing eagerly in the middle of the room. Grinning proudly, he thrust forward a pair of tickets.

Artinces peeked at them, then whooped. "Harry Belafonte! Cabaret!" She leaped onto him, gripped his waist with her thighs.

Goode couldn't help laughing. "Let go of me, woman," he said. "We got to get ready. We don't want to be them kind of colored people who show up late to everything."

She climbed off of him and began to loosen his belt. "Aw yeah, we're getting ready," she agreed. "But first I have something I want to do. To you."

Something was off, she knew. But she couldn't put a finger on it. Was it something she said or forgot to say? Or was it just because things had simply been going too smoothly?

He felt it too. An ill wind blowing off Lake Michigan and settling in his bones. He fought the urge to shiver as they entered the lobby of the theater after the performance. Belafonte had been magnificent and Artinces, as expected, had been transfixed. But Goode had shifted in his seat throughout the entire show. From time to time he swept his gaze across the space, eyeballing the box seats, the balcony, and the orchestra pit, as if he expected an assassin to rise up and let loose with a machine gun. He sensed a general anger swelling in him, a mindless rage with no purpose and no target, except perhaps himself. Being mad for no reason just made him madder. He was in a lovely place with a happy, beautiful woman on his arm. Soon she would be in his bed. What could go wrong?

"Artinces! Dr. Noel! Say there!"

She paused and turned toward the sound. *Damn,* Goode thought. *Is there any place where niggers don't know her?*

He looked up and saw, rapidly approaching in an impressive pinstriped suit, a barrel-chested man of medium height and multiple chins. The woman beside him looked pleasant but meek.

"Why, Bert, look at you," Artinces said. "Look at both of you, all dolled up."

The man's chins shook when he laughed. "C'mon," he said. "You can't go see Belafonte without appearing as *kempt* as possible. Isn't that right, Sugarplum?"

After the woman and Artinces traded pleasantries and kissed each other's cheeks, the couple gazed expectantly and made no attempt to fill the silence.

Goode was vaguely aware of Artinces touching his elbow. "This is my—this is Ananias Goode."

Her voice sounded slightly higher than usual, breathless. Goode glanced at her and saw himself in her eyes, as he believed she was seeing him. Crude. Unpolished. Unlettered.

"Bertram Dudley. Pleasure," the man said. "This is my wife, Jane."

The man smelled vaguely sour to Goode, like a pickle in pinstripes. Goode's attention wandered amid a recap of Belafonte's best moments and gossip about the medical conference. When it returned, the Dudleys were sharing their vast knowledge of the civil rights movement.

"I do hope Dr. King prevails here," the Pickle was saying. "If he doesn't, the gangs and hoodlums will take over. King looks a little lost every time he sets foot in the big city, like a country boy wearing his daddy's suit. But I do prefer him to that awful Malcolm X."

"God rest his soul," Sugarplum murmured.

But her husband wasn't having it. "You mean good riddance. Either way, after all the fighting, educated folks will be left to straighten everything out. Don't you think so, Goode?"

So I'm not invisible after all, he thought. "I ain't so sure," he replied.

The Pickle barely paused to acknowledge his answer. "They can keep their 'black is beautiful,'" he offered. "'Negro' suits me just fine. Talented Tenth, all that. Once they've broken themselves up trying to fight the Man, they'll need surgeons like me to patch them back together. What's your specialty, Goode? Haven't seen you at the convention. Are you a sawbones too?"

There had been a time when Goode could look at a man for just a second longer than usual—lock him in with his silent, steady gaze—and it would be the same as sending him a mental message. The man would quickly understand that he had tarried too long and would excuse himself without further delay. Goode gave the

Pickle the look but he missed it somehow. So Goode sighed and answered his question. "Something like that," he said.

The Pickle wiggled his bushy brows. "How so?"

"I don't mend bones. I break 'em."

As the Pickle and Sugarplum exchanged embarrassed glances, the chill in Goode's spine gave way to rapidly spreading heat. Everything he'd worked to purge from himself oozed out of his skin like sweat.

"It's like surgery but not so neat," he heard himself say. "And there's no painkillers."

"I don't understand," the Pickle persisted.

Goode stepped in close enough to spit on him. "I fuck up motherfuckers," he explained. "Make 'em wish they was dead."

The Pickle frowned. Sugarplum gasped. Artinces grabbed Goode firmly by the arm.

"Forgive us, Bert, Jane," she said. "It's been a long evening and we've had plenty to drink."

Before the Pickle could relax his brow and before Sugarplum could gather up another breath, Artinces and Goode were on their way down the steps.

Goode tried to make small talk as they drove back to the hotel, but each joke and observation crashed and shattered against Artinces's glacial silence. Finally, she shook her head and sighed. "Those people were my colleagues," she said. "My friends."

"And what am I? You couldn't bring yourself to describe me as your friend, or anything else."

"I was just surprised."

"Not as surprised as I was. I had to check my boots to make sure I hadn't stepped in shit."

"Ananias. Haven't you said enough tonight?"

"Damn straight," he said. "Damn straight."

Inside, Goode tried to steer her toward the bar. She shook him off and headed for the elevators. "One drink," he called after her. "What's the matter? Are you afraid of being seen with me?"

She turned and stared at him. He'd always remember her standing there. Feisty women usually turned him off, but not Artinces, never. She looked defiant and angelic at once, a petulant daddy's girl with one hand holding her clutch purse, the other on her hip.

"It's you that's afraid," she said. She turned again and never looked back.

Hours passed. Goode sat and simmered in silence, sucking bourbon until his legs got heavy and his head dipped dangerously toward the bar. When he got to their room, she was gone.

On the train back from Chicago, Artinces sought comfort in the book she had unearthed in Old Town. Its author, a specialist in diseases of women and children, had worked with the Freedmen's Bureau after the Civil War to provide care to more than 30,000 former slaves in Virginia. Artinces flipped intently through Dr. Crumpler's observations, looking for a consoling turn of phrase that might take her mind off her recent drama. But instead her eyes landed on a passage that appeared to mock her. "It is best for a young woman to accept a suitor who is respectable," Crumpler wrote, "vigorous, industrious, and but a few years her senior, if not of an equal age." Artinces sighed. Crumpler began practicing in 1866, just after the Emancipation Proclamation, and the relationship difficulties that would continue to plague black women a century later were already in full flux. Artinces had so many more privileges than her emancipated sisters had ever known. How was it possible that she had the same problems?

She'd spent much of the sixties with a man who was indeed a few years her senior, and vigorous and industrious to boot. But respectable? Apparently it was going to take more than the acquisition of a few upstanding businesses to smooth his jagged edges.

As far as Artinces was concerned, respectability was not in itself a quality that made a man automatically appealing. But that very attribute propelled her through a series of unfortunate encounters in the years after she left Goode to wallow in that Chicago hotel bar.

When the spring of 1968 announced its early arrival in an eruption of bright blossoms and exuberantly budding trees, she hardly noticed all the color around her. By then she'd suffered through enough joyless pairings to reduce the world to splatters of beige and gray. In her mind, she'd begun to compose a long letter. "Dear Dr. Crumpler," it began. "Did you ever arrive at the conclusion that respectability is perhaps overrated?"

She started dating a dull, dignified deacon. He was the kind of man she could be photographed with in the papers, a man far more likely to thump a Bible in righteous glee than harm another human being.

Her office staff, all but Billie, declared him a keeper. But when he finally bent his tall, angular frame to kiss her, she smelled liniment, slippery elm, and dust. No honey, no hickory. She felt dry as a dead leaf. If their lips touched she would crackle into bits and be swept away by the wind. So she turned away from him, cleared her throat, made an excuse.

Instead of enduring another dinner or concert in the company of men who put her to sleep, she took to spending evenings on her terrace, watching people stroll along the path in the park across the street. If she slipped into a certain frame of mind and squinted her eyes just right, she could almost imagine the path was the same one that led to the little shack where she was raised.

There was no chance at all that Artinces's mother could ever have read *A Book of Medical Discourses*, but somehow she'd managed to follow Dr. Crumpler's relationship advice to the letter. Although Sadie and Luther Noel had a limited education, they were smart and had big hearts. Both of them had no problem with hard work and they were, as church folks liked to say, equally yoked. Between them they could birth a foal, plow a field, slaughter a pig, and turn a croaker sack into a satin dress.

Artinces had her own set of skills, talents that she was sure her mother would be proud of. But Sadie would never have slept with a married man and quite likely would never have condoned it. *Things were different then*, Artinces told herself. Her mother had been with her father from the age of 14 until his death. Artinces had never again known a couple so closely attached. She always chuckled when she heard talk of spouses who finished each other's sentences. "That's nothing," she'd want to say. "My parents had whole conversations between them without opening their mouths. They'd simply exchange a look, one of them would nod, and that would be that: an agreement had been reached."

The widow Sadie Noel lived just long enough to see her girl graduate from medical school. She stopped eating after that, and went back to doing what she had done for years: sitting on her porch and staring out at the path. Artinces knew her mother was waiting for her long-dead husband to walk up that path and extend his hand. Sadie's faith guaranteed an afterlife, a place where she and Luther could reunite and love forever, perhaps without having to work so hard.

One day, three spectral women would pop up in Artinces's backseat and challenge her routine dismissal of what she called "hocus-pocus." Until then, she believed that once a person was dead he stayed dead. There were no clouds and harp-strumming angels. No mountaintops overlooking streets of gold.

In the meantime, she had her own terrace overlooking a park. A park with a path where lovers strolled hand in hand. She was on the terrace the night Martin Luther King was killed in Memphis. She had been staring at the path, thinking of her mother and imagining a man of her own—a man with a hat rakishly angled over one brow, gesturing to her with an outstretched hand.

The announcement came over the radio she'd put on the terrace to keep her company. Fearing trouble in the streets, she went inside and shut her windows. But the Protected Zone held, and her neighborhood remained as quiet as on any other evening. Inside, she marveled that King had lived so long. Four years ago, she'd met him on two separate occasions when he'd presided over successful fundraising rallies in Gateway City. She'd been happy to write a check both times, while her physician's eye couldn't help but notice that he was a good 20 pounds overweight, obviously exhausted, and suffering from high blood pressure. She had suspected that a stroke would get him before any assassin's bullet.

The next morning, she drove tentatively through smoldering streets to find her office miraculously intact. A sign had been posted on the door; when she got close enough to read it, she gasped and pressed her hand to her mouth.

Under the Protection of Ananias Goode.

She gave her staff the day off (she couldn't really expect them to come in under such circumstances) and retreated home. That evening, she sat on her terrace and waited for sunset. To the north, sirens, shouts, and blaring horns erupted in intermittent bursts. To the south, the park seemed to exist on a different planet. All was green and quiet. Fewer people than usual frolicked near the pond or sat in the grass, but otherwise there were no visible signs that anything had changed. Local news programs had reported a police cordon surrounding the West End and lining the border of the South Side; they weren't even letting buses through.

City authorities had made it nearly impossible for ordinary North Siders to darken any territory beyond Delmar Boulevard. Of course, Ananias Goode was not ordinary and had never claimed to be.

When Artinces looked out and saw him appear on the path, she could tell that he was looking right at her. But he didn't reach out his hand. He took his hat off and held it in front of him with both hands, like a humble suitor. Then he took a seat on a nearby bench.

It was almost dusk. Goode sat and watched Artinces approach. Here and there, families and couples tried to make the most of the receding sun. Since their last breakup, Goode had secured a woman for Wednesday, a woman for Thursday, another for Friday. Even when he had them all at once, they failed to add up to Artinces Noel. He didn't say that, however.

What he did say, when at last she sat down beside him, was, "I figured out why you aren't scared of me like other folks. It's because of what you said to me once—that when I'm with you I'm at my best. But it seems like you don't want to see nothing but certain parts. I wish you could see more."

"I can't," Artinces said. "It hurts my eyes."

Goode frowned. "Why would it hurt to look at it me? To really look at me?"

Artinces stared straight ahead. A little boy was playing near them, pulling a plastic duck on a string as it floated on the pond. When his mother took his hand, he began to scream and stomp his feet.

"I don't know," she replied. "Maybe it's the light bouncing off your wedding band."

Goode didn't wear a band but he glanced at his hand anyway. He looked tired, uncertain. "I appreciate the way you spare my feelings."

"Who's talking about *you*? Has it ever occurred to you that I've been thinking about your wife? About *her* feelings?"

Goode stared at her but she avoided eye contact. She was lying. She hadn't been thinking of Mrs. Goode at all. Not once had that exemplary pillar of virtue, the humanitarian whom folks in Gateway called Saint Noel, thought about her lover's wife.

"Well, I think you know that she can't feel anymore, Artinces. Not for a long time," he said softly. "She can't feel, can't see, can't hear, can't think."

"You don't know that."

"But you do. You're a doctor. After all this time? She's not going to wake up, is she?"

Finally she felt strong enough to turn to him. "No," she said. "She isn't. But your ring is on her finger, not mine. It doesn't matter that she can't hold you, can't—she's still your wife."

"That hasn't seemed to bother you in the past."

She shook her head. "It's always bothered me."

"Well, it hasn't always showed. Tenderness, I don't know how to solve this problem. But I can't go on being a stranger to you."

She shifted on the bench, turned her body toward him. "What's my middle name?"

Goode twisted his hat in his hands. She'd never seen him so careless with his clothing. "I don't know," he answered.

"Exactly. You don't even know."

"That's not my fault. You never told me."

"I've hardly told you anything."

"There's things you can say without talking. In bed, you used to tell me everything I needed to know. Everything that matters. I didn't complain. It seemed to be fine with you until Chicago."

"I didn't say a word against you in Chicago."

"You didn't have to. I could see it in your eyes when we ran into Dr. Pickle."

"Who?"

"That doctor. He smelled like pickles. I know you smelled it too."

She smiled. "Formaldehyde. He smelled like formaldehyde."

He waved a hand. "Whatever."

They both laughed before settling into a silence that felt natural and comfortable. For a moment, Artinces had the sensation of being one-half of an old couple sitting on a porch. She wanted to see that, tried hard to see it: sipping lemonade on a veranda with Goode, watching the world unfurl beyond their picket fence. But the image wouldn't hold.

"Lula," she said.

"What?"

"It's Lula. My middle name."

"Lula?"

"Don't wear it out. It's after my grandmother, Lula Mae."

"Well, at least they spared you the Mae."

"Not exactly."

"Dr. Artinces Lula Mae Noel?"

"A mouthful, I know."

Goode put his hat back on. He pressed his full lips together and nodded, nearly choking himself until the impulse to laugh subsided.

Artinces watched and waited. "Now you," she said. "Your turn. Tell me something."

He looked away from her, staring at the pond so intently that she turned to see what he was looking at. There was nothing there. The protesting boy and his mother were gone, along with his floating duck.

"I'm 56 years old and I'm drowning," he said at last. "The years are like water, you know? They keep rising and rising. I feel like I'm running out of air."

"What do you want me to do?"

"Save me. You could do that. You could save me."

Artinces said nothing. She slid her hand across the bench toward his until their fingertips barely touched. They remained like that, side by side, as night fell.

The next day, in a motel called the Riverbend, across the river in a little town that hip folks were starting to call East Boogie, Artinces laid down the law. But first she took Goode to bed.

They panted and sweated, going after each other like two hormone-struck teenagers.

To get there, they'd crossed the bridge and taken the second exit. The long, squat structure was built of blond concrete and garnished with turquoise shutters. Bright and ultra-modern, it was totally out of place amid the bleak splintered wood, crumbling brick, and rusty corrugated aluminum of East Boogie. Its unorthodox brightness totally defeated the purpose of a motel, in Artinces's view. But she might think differently, she conceded, if she were a road-weary traveler, lulled to drowsiness by the highway's dividing line and desperate for a blanket, a pillow, and a warm place to snore.

Once inside the fake-wood-paneled room, decked out in Early Proletarian furniture and daringly adorned with a brilliant orange blanket and a Magic Fingers bed, Artinces delighted in the scandalous squalor of her surroundings. As Goode moaned and muttered and urged, she shouted in perfect counterpoint, wondering all the while how anything so good could ever be bad. Why did it have to be a secret? Why shouldn't she be proud to walk with this man in the bright light of black society, bedecked, beribboned, and arm in arm? She'd take him anywhere, follow him anywhere, stamp his initials on her forehead—whatever it took, just as long as she could do this wonderful thing forever.

But her bad-to-the-bone alter ego faded as soon as her hunger was emphatically and completely satisfied. *Of course you could think such foolish thoughts in the middle of the deed*, she chided herself. In the unforgiving glare of day, going public with their affair seemed patently unreasonable. So she issued her ruling. "This is how it will be," she said.

Goode, silent, was nuzzling her breasts, her belly.

"Once a week," she continued. "Wednesdays. My office closes early on Wednesday. You'll have to get your fill of me."

Goode looked up. He had made his way to her hips. "That's crazy," he protested. "A man can't live like that. I could never do that."

"You'll have to. Or you'll get nothing."

Goode sighed. "Whatever you say, Tenderness." He lowered his lips to her thigh but she reached out and lifted his chin.

"On any other day, we hardly know each other. In fact, we don't even like each other." She looked gravely into his eyes before pulling his face to hers.

According to her edict, they bickered at board meetings and brushed by each other at public events. She learned to curl her lip in disgust when they had no choice but to interact in the presence of others. They were like oil and water, people said.

By the summer of 1970, they were going strong as ever. Goode liked the Riverbend so much that he bought it and decorated a suite to which they had sole access. All the furnishings were purchased to suit Artinces's taste and designed to create the illusion of a bedroom in their imaginary private home. She had to admit he'd done a good job. All they needed was that picket fence.

Later, much later, Billie would ask Artinces why she never noticed an elegant Eldorado trailing her a few cars back as she made her way to Goode one Wednesday, shifting lanes smoothly in tune with her own steering. Why, Billie wanted to know, did she think she could carry on with a notorious gangster without anyone getting curious enough to follow her trail?

Artinces would shrug her shoulders and change the subject. She decided not to tell her that when you are preparing to wrap yourself around the man who, despite everything, fits you perfectly, you might not be aware of the curious stares of others. You might not notice a sharp-featured man picking his teeth in his rearview mirror while idling behind you at a random red light. When the man with the perfect fit will soon be moving in you and you will feel nothing besides the sweet pulse of his thrust, the rhythm of his hips as he holds you while chanting, "Tenderness, Tenderness, Tenderness" over and over, you aren't likely to think of anything else at all.

"**H**ELLO, NORTH SIDE," the Man in the Red Vest bellowed. "Welcome to Afro Day in the Park!"

The quiet corner of Fairgrounds Park where Guts Tolliver spent his favorite mornings had been transformed into a carnival. Banners, hung the previous month by the men of the Black Swan, draped the gates at Kossuth and Fair Avenues. A Tilt-A-Whirl, a Ferris wheel, and a carousel surrounded the Abram Higgins memorial garden. Nearby, the Harry Truman Boys Club sponsored a dunking booth. An elaborate sprinkler set, vast and tentacled, sent prismatic spray in the air. Families relaxed on picnic blankets and enjoyed the shade beneath beach umbrellas along the path on which Crusher Boudreau usually ran his miles. Crusher stood a few yards off the path in his standard workout gear, but he wasn't exercising. He'd been drafted to oversee the Swing the Hammer, Ring the Bell game. On the stone bridge, Reuben Jones and Lucius Monday sat behind easels, offering instant portraits and caricatures for three dollars each.

At Softball Diamond No. 1, a bandstand had been erected in the shallow outfield. The Man in the Red Vest presided there as master of ceremonies, strolling a stage festooned with his radio station's call letters. Teenagers gathered at the foot of the stage to mingle and flirt. From her booth between Stormy Monday's pie stand and the autograph kiosk manned by Rip Crenshaw and the home team's fleet center fielder, Artinces offered free blood-pressure screenings and lead-poisoning tests. Charlotte was supposed to assist her, but hadn't showed up yet. It was just about noon.

The last of the lingering morning mist had all but burned away, leaving behind a shimmering curtain of heat. Artinces watched as, on the far side of the pond, the curtain parted and the three women stepped through. Barefoot, they strolled to the edge of the concrete dock jutting into the water. Two of them shielded their brows with their hands. The other twirled a parasol. Fairgoers moved around them as if they weren't there. Oblivious to the trio, a fisherwoman, her hat pulled down low over her eyes, set out a metal lawn chair and fishing gear on the dock. The women apparently didn't mind or notice but they did seem to be aware of Artinces. They were staring right at her.

The emcee introduced the first of the afternoon's bands, a local quartet of siblings whose modest repertoire was mostly limited to Jackson Five covers. Their opening salvo of "I Want You Back" sounded like a cross between a whistling teakettle and faulty brakes.

"Lord Jesus," Irene Monday exclaimed. She fanned herself with a carryout menu from her restaurant while leaning on the counter of her booth. Her vantage point gave her a clear view of her husband at his easel nearly a hundred yards away. "Bless their hearts, but those children should think of taking up something other than singing."

"Yes," Artinces agreed, "like mime, perhaps."

"It's going to get better though," Irene said. "I hear Rose Patterson might sing a little later, if she's up to it. Her belly's so big she's about to burst."

Artinces had met Rose only recently. She and Gabe were expecting their first child any day. Thinking ahead, the couple had already enlisted her services.

"I've heard she has a wonderful voice," Artinces said.

"Like an angel. Sweet as sugar for all she's been through. Her first husband had the devil in him."

"That's no good," Artinces said.

"You telling me. I've been through it too. Thought I'd lose my mind before Lucius came along and swept me off my feet." Irene smiled at Artinces. "Some folks, though, are just blessed. Like you, I suppose. Smart and successful as you are, I bet you've made it through life with hardly a scratch."

Artinces forced herself to turn toward the pond, determined not to let the three women stare her down. They were gone. Near where they had stood, the fisherwoman bent to pick up something lying on the dock. *The parasol*, Artinces thought. But it was a fishing pole. The heat curtain had evaporated, as if it had never been there. Artinces watched as the woman attached bait to her line. "I've had my share of scratches," she said.

If pressed, she might have found a way to change the subject. Or she might have told Irene that her first "scratch" was more like a kick in the gut. That's what it had felt like when she found her mother facedown in the dirt.

It was 1935. Coming down the road and seeing Sadie Noel spread-eagled on the ground, Artinces had the impression that her mother had fallen from a great height. Blades of grass had bent sharply away from the outline of her still form, as if shuddering at the impact of her landing. Neighbor women knelt near her and made comforting noises, but Sadie remained where she lay until four men pulled her to her feet. Then she let loose with a sound that Artinces had never completely forgotten. Half wail and half roar, it was one of the last audible utterances to rise from her mother's throat. Years later, while Artinces stood at the bedside of dying children, when she had to tell the parents that time was running out, she would occasionally recall Sadie's furious bawling. Sometimes, the stricken parents would howl in similarly desperate fashion and Artinces would find herself hurtling backward through time.

Her mother had hit the ground with a head full of thick, dark, shiny hair. Minutes later, with clods of dirt in her eyebrows and thick dust coating her face, she tottered beneath a thatch of stringy white strands.

Artinces grabbed her mother's sleeve. "What's wrong, Mama?" she asked. "What happened?" Her mother stared right through her, shaking her head. She looked blind.

There had been a dispute between Luther and Mooney Hicks, a white man. Hicks had asked Luther about two cows that had turned up missing. When Luther said he knew nothing about it, Hicks suggested it would be a good idea for Luther to turn over a couple of his own cows, to keep things simple and peaceful-like. When Luther declined as respectfully as he could, Mooney Hicks shot him in the back.

Sadie had been preparing to return a basket of clean laundry to Miss Agnes, a mean-spirited white woman who insisted that only Sadie knew how to wash her drawers just right. When the news reached Sadie, she tossed the basket and toppled straight over. She remained there, still as a stone, while sheets, pillowcases, and women's underthings slowly floated down like snow.

The next day, Artinces collected the laundry that her mother had spilled. She washed it in a big iron pot in the backyard, stirring it in boiling water and washing it with homemade soap before rinsing it all and hanging each item on the line to dry. These were tasks she knew well. Her mother had put her to work on small pieces in a tub at the age of six, shortly after she learned to read. She had begun feeding and weeding at age four. By the time she was 15, there was little she couldn't do around a farm. By 15, she was also certain that she despised everything about agriculture. With her father's blessing, she had begun to dream of a different destiny. His brutal erasure hastened her plans.

Miss Agnes demanded to know why the washing was late, even though she already knew the answer. Word of Luther's death had spread quickly.

"My daddy got killed," Artinces said. Standing attentively on the back porch while Miss Agnes frowned at her from the doorway, she held the heavy basket and waited for permission to set it down or bring it in.

"A shame," Miss Agnes said. "Niggers do get into scrapes. Them jook joints ain't nothing but sin and depravity. I thought Luther knew better."

"It was a white man done it," Artinces said, faster than she wanted to.

Miss Agnes leaned down, grabbed her by the chin, and pulled her close. "You listen to me, Lula Mae. For as long as you live, there's three things you should never do. Never lie, never cheat, never steal," advised the woman who had neglected to pay Sadie for the past four weeks. "God sees everything you do and He knows it as soon as you go wrong. You can count on Him punishing you for it just like He punished your daddy."

Artinces was pretty sure some kind of force lurked in the world, a presence she couldn't explain and often preferred to ignore. It wasn't the loving God her mother would mumble to with increasing fervor each night—a pale, patient old man who would one day reward Sadie's lifelong virtue by raising up Luther like Lazarus and sending him back to her waiting arms. Far from that. Artinces suspected the force was a hunger as old as the universe, a phenomenon that was neither good nor evil but nonetheless fed on human suffering. She had no patience for talk of angels and saviors. But she knew the hunger was real.

She determined to sidestep its tireless jaws as best as she could, immersing herself in study until the day she headed off to college. Her white-haired mother, befuddled and nearly mute, had managed to press into her hands a pitiful stack of dollar bills Luther had carefully stashed for the day his little Pepper Pot would leave for school. It was enough to get her about as far as the train depot—thank goodness for her scholarship.

She'd sworn off the world of cotton and cucumbers, confident she'd she soon be setting foot in a hot field for the last time. Back then, she thought she might eventually settle in Honey Springs after exploring distant shores. But when she came back to bury her mother, she knew she'd been kidding herself. Every family struggling in every shack had suffered some version of her loss. The ground, spongy beneath her feet, was soaked with sorrow. Sadness hummed through the air louder than honeybees. Only by leaving and returning was she able to fully appreciate how pervasive it was. Each tree stump, hollow log, and bend in the road was a reminder of the long gone and the freshly killed, the broken and the missing.

Watching the people of North Gateway promenade and cavort on the green grass of Fairgrounds Park, Artinces allowed herself to briefly savor the joyful spirit of the day. They had fled the same history, known the same ruptures and defeats. But there was something daring and admirable about their willingness to take a chance on joy, even if only for a few sun-splashed hours. Everyone in Honey Springs who took similar risks had invariably paid for it. Upon reflection, Artinces conceded that Goode had been right: it did indeed take blood. She'd actually recognized the truth in his words as soon as he spat them out; perhaps that's why she became so upset. He was right, but she had no plans to tell him so.

Sometimes, PeeWee concluded, you just have to say fuck 'em. Fuck stuck-up females. Fuck fake motherfuckers who think they're better than you. Fuck Sharps too. *Needle-nosed nigger wants me to lay low—I know he's over there about to shit on himself—but fuck him. Let him come get me if he's that worried.*

PeeWee strolled cockily down the main path of the park, straight through the revelers and picnickers, the performers and vendors. He and Sharps were parked across the street on Kossuth Avenue, close enough to keep an eye on things without being seen themselves, when PeeWee announced that he needed to take a leak and hustled off toward the portable toilets before Sharps could react. No doubt he was having a fit, but what the fuck could he do? It was a lovely day and there were plenty of fine bitches stretched out on blankets in the grass. Reasons enough for a close-up investigation. Besides, he could handle himself. Hadn't he proved that when he knocked that sucker out at the gym? No harm would come to him, he was certain. There was a good chance, he figured, that he was invulnerable.

He'd discovered hidden strengths since spending time with the ring. He'd persuaded himself that he hadn't stolen it from his sister; the ring, he now remembered, had found *him*. Clearly they were meant to be together. It wasn't like Crenshaw needed it anyway. A big-bucks superstar like him could always buy more shine. When PeeWee went to his barbershop to get his growing natural shaped and blown out, the home team's slugger was on the grainy black-and-white atop the soda machine, strutting into the batter's box. PeeWee could tell that Crenshaw had all the power he needed. He was tearing up the league, with his sights on the team home-run record. Now, watching the All-Star sign autographs just a few feet away, he was more convinced than ever that Crenshaw could do without the ring. He was charming, confident, adored. For him, things were going along just the way they should. But amid PeeWee's barely tolerable circumstances, something had to give. He had been putting up with some inferior folk of late, but not for much longer. When the dust cleared he'd be the last man standing. And the ring would be on his finger.

He turned away from the home team's booth, idly caressing his treasure as Playfair passed by. PeeWee imagined Sharps in the Eldorado, fuming. Let him. Let him see how hard it is to sit still while other folks are having fun. Sharps had told him to watch and wait and, more insulting, to do it quietly while Sharps pondered his next move. That part, the silent obedience, was especially hard to take. But the ring told him to bide his time. He'd be in charge soon enough. The chump change Sharps doled out was more than he had been scoring on his own, that much he had to admit. It enabled him to keep the lights on during his sister's prolonged, mysterious absence. He didn't even feel lonely anymore, stretched out on her sofa at night with only his slick palms to keep him company. He felt more of a man than he'd ever been before, bigger and more powerful in his fist as he squeezed and rubbed himself to sleep. And when he woke in the night and watched moonlight stream through the window, it seemed as bright as the future he imagined. He had no stable income. No place to call his own. No woman. But that was all right. He had the ring.

"Saints preserve us," Irene Monday said. Feeling plucky, the sibling quartet onstage had abandoned the Jackson Five for the Five

Stairsteps. From their lips, the opening notes of "O-o-h Child" sounded like four asthmatics straining for air.

Artinces was grateful when Playfair appeared and captured her attention. "Afternoon, ladies," he said. "How wonderful to see you both."

"Hello," Artinces said.

"Playfair," Irene said with a wink. "I hardly recognized you without your Buick."

Playfair laughed. "Oh, she's parked right outside the gates. As usual, I've got anything a brother—or sister—needs, at my usual cut-rate prices. I just didn't want to pay for a vending permit. Of course, I have a few nice things in my vest pockets, if anyone's interested. By the way, Doctor, how's Shabazz?"

Irene sat up, intrigued. She'd figured Artinces had a boyfriend tucked away somewhere, a Bob or a Milton, maybe. But a Shabazz? She wondered if he was the bow-tied Muslim who sold bean pies in front of Katz Drugs.

"He's fine, I guess," Artinces replied. "I think Charlotte's falling for him, but she won't admit it."

Irene's eyebrows shot skyward, visible above the cup of soda she held to her lips.

"Well, he's enough for the both of you," Playfair said, "as long as you train him up right."

Irene choked on her soda, dribbling a little on the front of her apron.

Playfair, whose roving eyes missed nothing, pretended not to notice. He settled his eyes on a young woman studying a brochure at a booth run by Ardell's Beauty Salon. "Excuse me, ladies," he said apologetically. "Opportunity knocks."

He hustled over to the woman, whose floral sundress stuck closely to her modest curves. "Afternoon," he said. "I've seen you someplace before," Playfair added before she could reply. He squinted. "Zodiac?"

"That's right. You have a good memory."

"How could I forget a face like yours? They call me Playfair," he said, and tossed her a smile.

"I'm Gladys," she said, returning it.

"It is completely my pleasure to meet you, Gladys. Anybody ever tell you that you look a lot like Nichelle Nichols?"

Irene and Artinces watched as Playfair offered his arm and Gladys, grinning shyly, accepted it. Together they strolled toward the bandstand.

Irene sucked her teeth. "He better watch it," she said. "When a woman that pretty is walking around all by her lonesome, something ain't right. People used to say the same thing about my Lucius. They'd say, 'How can a man that pretty be on his own?'" Artinces stole a look at Lucius, hard at work behind his easel. She thought it would be quite a stretch even to call him ruggedly handsome, with an emphasis on rugged.

"He's too pretty for his own good," Rhonda Treadway pronounced, stirring her milkshake with her straw.

"Nothing against pretty," Kendra Lee chimed in. "But my mama said never trust a musician."

"You all talk like I'm about to marry the man," Artinces protested. "I'm just taking lessons from him, that's all."

Artinces, Rhonda, Kendra, and Kozetta Harris were the only female second-years at Howard University Medical School. In addition to living and studying together, they often met at a soda fountain for milkshakes and gossip.

The topic of discussion was Brady Ross, a local piano teacher. Ross was lean and elegant, with prominent cheekbones and wavy hair that gleamed under a thick layer of pomade. He wore stylish short-sleeve shirts and ribbed silk socks that never failed to catch Artinces's eye when he leaned back and crossed his legs.

"All the same," Kendra shot back. She looked around before cupping her breasts. "A Negro who strokes piano keys will never stroke these."

An article in *The Crisis* magazine about a pioneering woman surgeon mentioned that she'd studied piano to strengthen her fingers. So when Artinces saw Brady's ad in the *Afro-American*, she resolved to take up the instrument. After a while, she found other ways to make her fingers strong, such as using them to trace the outline of Brady's sleek, muscular loins. He lived in a neat bungalow with an upright piano in the front room, a kitchen, a book-crammed bedroom, and little else. She usually waited on his porch while the student whose appointment preceded hers ran through his scales a final time. The student, a handsome man with a warm smile and twinkling eyes, would grin and tip his hat. Brady would welcome her in, and before she knew it he was teaching her many fascinating things about rhythm, melody, counterpoint, and call-and-response. They just had little to do with playing the piano.

In between, she gleaned a few facts. He'd gone to Wilberforce. Toured with a few combos. Claimed to have been narrowly bested by Count Basie in a "cutting contest" when the latter came through town with his big band. He was working on a song cycle based on the poems of Countee Cullen. He taught her selected couplets while pleasuring her in his bed.

"*I whom sun-dabbled streams have washed,*" he'd say, lowering his lips to her breasts, "*whose bare brown thighs have held the sun.*"

While prepping Artinces for her upcoming test in her Nervous Systems class, Kozetta insisted that Brady was not showing all his cards. "I'm telling you, there's more to that bear than his curly hair. He's not in school, so how did he avoid the draft? What's he doing with that nice little house with no family in it?"

"He's taking his time, exploring his music," Artinces said. "He wants to get established as a composer before he makes that kind of commitment."

"Oh, is that what he told you? I bet he's got a wife and kids right under your nose. Buried in that backyard, maybe. I'm telling you, girl, you need to ask him some questions."

"Why? It's not like I'm seeing him."

"Artinces? It's me, Kozetta. From *Harlem*. I can see what you're doing with that man. It isn't just all over your face. It's how you walk and sit too. You're stuck on him."

Artinces merely shook her head and returned to her notes. She wasn't stuck on Brady; she simply had an appetite for his body. As for his personality, she didn't know enough, hadn't seen enough, to form an opinion. All she knew was that she liked the way he smelled when he leaned over her to demonstrate a difficult sequence. She inhaled, he noticed, and that was that. She had been a virgin, which surprised him, but they both quickly got over it.

It was then that Artinces learned how to keep up appearances. She never stayed for more than a couple of hours.

Talkative men didn't appeal to her. She liked a bit of mystery, unlike Kozetta, whose boyfriend Bert Dudley never shut up. Her few conversations with Brady took place while they were side by side on the piano bench, apparently the only place where he was entirely at ease. The men she knew growing up, the boys with whom she'd shared clumsy adolescent grappling, could talk of little besides crops, livestock, and Joe Louis. To Artinces, Brady was jazzy and sophisticated, a free-flowing improviser who also provided a sharp contrast to the men in her med school class, most of whom stubbornly adhered to a predetermined script. He'd open up about poetry, music, and world events, even going so far as predicting a postwar prosperity expansive enough to include Negroes. "I'm like Langston," he'd say, "dreaming me a world." He'd take her hand in his and lead her to his bed.

For her part, allowing Brady his secrets enabled her to keep her own cards close to her vest. Ultimately, that involved less about improvising and more about avoiding a destiny she'd strived so hard to elude. As much as she loved her mother, as much as she was grateful for her uncomplaining sacrifice and her patient tutelage, she could not shake the enduring memory of Sadie stumbling to her feet, white-haired and delirious, helpless as a newborn babe. She would never fall to earth for any man, not even one as wonderful as Luther Noel. So she stuck to her books and kept her distance. No matter how much she grew to crave Brady's scent or marvel at the way he easily spanned an octave with his long, sensitive fingers, their couplings would be just a pleasant diversion. They could never be more than that.

It seemed a plausible philosophy until she got pregnant.

She saw herself stepping off the train at the Honey Springs depot, dragging an overstuffed suitcase and groaning behind a bulging belly. She saw herself trudging up the dirt path to the shanty where she first drew air. Then she woke up sweating.

What she felt for Brady Ross couldn't in any way be twisted into the shape of love. She didn't want to be the wife of an aspiring composer. Still, a life of improvisation was, she conceded, far more stable than any kind of life in Honey Springs.

On the day she planned to tell him, she arrived early. She wanted to see him as others saw him, thinking perhaps that a different perspective might reveal in him some unforeseen quality that suggested genius, longevity, a grander design. An odd compulsion led her to the partially open window, where she stood and watched Brady lean over his student, the man with twinkling eyes. Later she decided she wasn't even surprised when Brady put his hands over the man's hands and kissed him on the side of his head. At the moment, though, she found herself frozen until Brady lowered his lips to the back of the man's slim, handsome neck. "*I whom sun-dabbled streams have washed...*" she heard him say. Artinces threw up in the flowerbed outside the window and promptly left.

She had cried at her father's funeral, and then vowed she would never do so again. She had managed to hold to her promise through myriad minor disappointments. But, as she lay on an iron bed in a dim room far from the sterile corridors of Freedmen's Hospital, across several miles and train tracks, tears flowed in rivulets so thick they blinded her while a disgraced former doctor, reeking of booze and foreboding, scraped at her insides. She remembered a sudden, limitless agony, a brutal tearing that made her mother and father appear in brief, frenetic visions, lightning flashes amid the ambient thunder of pain. She sweated, endured, and tried to think of other things, anything, focusing on the crucifix hanging on the wall overhead. Christ, with his own trials to suffer, hung bound and tortured in the shadows while she stretched and yelled and tugged on the headboard until the bars bent.

She was no longer sure about the details—whether there actually had been a crucifix, or whether it was a discarded army cot instead of an iron bed. But she could still vouch for the pain, the delirious stagger home in the relentless heat, and the shuddering collapse when she crossed the threshold. Waking up in Freedmen's with Kozetta at her side, face damp with despair. Kozetta, who had warned her, "Girl, don't do anything stupid."

The litany of questions, the evidence of infected instruments, the irreversible wreckage of her womb. Those facts had followed her to the present, along with the cold realization that she had fed the Hunger, had offered herself in sacrifice, knowing all the while that it could never be satisfied.

The magic of Irene Monday's pies was undeniable. By early afternoon, her stand had become the most popular concession in the park. The line of patrons had begun to curve, obscuring Artinces's booth. The pie seekers shuffled slightly to accommodate two men as they pushed their way through and approached the doctor.

One, dignified and wearing a straw hat with a gold band, looked to be in his late sixties. The other, tall, lean, and nervous, was of indeterminate age. His unlined face was a deep chocolate color and his mustache was sprinkled with gray. He carried a rolled-up newspaper in one hand.

"Good afternoon, Doctor," he began. "My name's Oliver and this here's Shadrach. I guess you could call him my friend."

"Pleased to meet you both," Artinces said.

"Same here, ma'am," Shadrach said. He looked slightly embarrassed.

"I've been telling him to get himself checked out," Oliver continued. "But you can't drag a mule where he doesn't want to go."

Shadrach snorted and rolled his eyes.

"We saw you over here and he told me he'd be willing to have you check him out," Oliver continued. "I told him that you were a children's doctor. Hard as it is for him to admit it, it's been a loooong time since he's been a child. Childish maybe, but that's a dog of a different stripe."

"You mean a horse of a different color," Shadrach said.

Oliver stared at him in disbelief. "Who's talking, you or me?"

"I am a pediatrician," Artinces said, "but today I'm seeing everybody."

"See, I told you," Shadrach said. "One day you'll listen to me."

"How about you sit down right here, sir," Artinces suggested.

Shadrach complied.

As she wrapped his arm in the blood-pressure sleeve, Artinces took note of his dignity and grace.

"You look familiar to me," she said.

Shadrach looked embarrassed again. "We were on hand when you had your accident, ma'am. At the cabstand."

"Were you? Yes, of course. But I meant some other place, some other time. What do you do for a living, Mr. Shadrach?"

"Just Shadrach will do. I've been retired for a good while."

"And that's a good thing," Oliver cut in. "He's half blind, half deaf and, as you can see, he's not too swift."

"That's Oliver," Shadrach said with a sigh. "I guess you could call him my friend. What was I saying before I was so rudely interrupted? Oh yeah, I used to have a hat shop on Easton."

Artinces smiled. "That's where I've seen you."

Before moving her practice to Kingshighway, she'd kept an office on Easton Avenue, the hub of the black community when she first came to town. She had breakfast nearly every morning at the Nat-Han, and just as often she'd get off the streetcar and see a nattily dressed man, always wearing an up-to-the-minute hat, step out and briskly sweep the walk in front of his establishment. He was regular as clockwork, this man, and for a while, Artinces kept her schedule by minding his. If he ducked out in front of his awning to whisk the night's debris to the curb, she knew she was on time. If his walk was already swept, she needed to get a move on.

Many of her patients shopped up and down Easton and so did she. But she also liked to spend a dollar on a service car and ride downtown to shop at the Stix or Famous department stores or to pay her bills. Scooping up bargains on Dollar Day was another dependable diversion. Usually near the end of the month, the stores moved merchandise that hadn't sold down to their basements and happily handed it over in exchange for a buck, as long as Negro shoppers understood that they couldn't try on clothes on that floor or any other. The Famous store had a restaurant that featured world-acclaimed onion soup. The restaurant was on the second floor, but its tantalizing aroma penetrated every nook and cranny except the perfume counter. Artinces loved the smell of the soup, but never tasted it because Negroes weren't allowed to dine there. You could stand up and eat in the back of Kresge's, but you couldn't sit down. Aldo's had yet to admit black customers, so even someone like Artinces, who had money in her pocketbook, had to take what she could get.

She was already something of a name by then, having established a well-baby clinic at Abram H. that lowered the death rate of premature infants from 80 percent to 20 percent in two years. She all but lived on the premises after taking over as chief resident, proving to be as skillful at bureaucratic tussling as she was at healing. She wrote stinging letters to newspaper editors and legislators and camped out in the offices of unresponsive agency directors, forgoing sleep to secure supplies of bananas and ice cream for her sick children. She increased access to vital fluids for the diarrhea sufferers and Gordon Armstrong incubators for the preemies.

She continued to oversee the pediatrics ward, even after hanging out her own shingle. Parents who had seen her work miracles at Abram H. followed her to the little office on Easton, where she made sure they always felt welcome. North Siders had been resigned to their children receiving care on a catch-as-catch-can basis, totally dependent on the whims of indifferent white pediatricians. Some outright refused to treat black children; others had "black days," during which black youngsters could be admitted (always at peculiar hours) without contaminating the waiting room or white patients with their presence.

Artinces had been so sickened and outraged by the tradition that she made "Every day is black day" a slogan of sorts. She had it painted on a placard, which she placed on the front desk to greet every newcomer. It was on every brochure, including those she'd made available at Afro Day. Shadrach picked one up from her counter after she pronounced his blood pressure well within the normal range. He was a good deal older than Ananias Goode, but something about him seemed similar. There was the rakish angle of his hat, but something else beyond that. He seemed strong, masculine in an old-fashioned way, yet gentle and patient at the same time. The brochure rested lightly in his weathered palm.

Her fondness for rough lovemaking aside, Artinces had grown to appreciate and encourage the gentle side of Goode. She invited him to join the volunteers who came into Abram H. to hold babies who had no one else to comfort them. "You'd be surprised how good it feels," she told him. But he wanted no part of it.

"The last baby I held is long gone," he said. "I ain't held one since." She added his name to the list anyway, and told him so.

"I have a daughter," Shadrach said. "And she has a daughter. They live across the river, but I'm going to tell her to come see you. I'm going to recommend it."

"I appreciate it," Artinces said. Shadrach opened his mouth to say more, but at that moment Rose Patterson stepped to the center of the bandstand. And she opened her mouth too.

"*Oh, happy day*," she sang.

> *Oh, happy day*
> *Oh, happy day*

Shadrach removed his hat and placed it over his heart. Irene Monday had promised that Rose was the real thing, but Artinces was still surprised. She looked over at Irene, who smiled and nodded.

> *When Jesus washed*
> *Oh, when he washed*

Rose reminded Artinces of the women she'd heard growing up, singing in the cotton fields. They sang strongly but without effort, devoting the bulk of their strength to the labors at hand. Rose's voice contained that same grit formed of earth and sweat, but she was more polished, as if she knew the city demanded something different, something redolent of factory floors, rush-hour traffic, church bells, and concrete. Her melodies took Artinces back to pleasurable days, to her father walking with her arm in arm.

> *When Jesus washed*
> *When Jesus washed*
> *He washed my sins away!*

All across the park, Rose's listeners indulged in similar journeys. Children paused in their games of tag and devil-and-the-pitchfork; some of them stood still under the sprinklers. Women on picnic blankets halted their conversations in the middle of sentences and just listened, holding cans of beer and sauce-drenched ribs in midair. Men looked up from their grills and let the burgers sizzle. On the bridge, Lucius stopped his sketching and stared. Next to him, Reuben closed his eyes and continued to draw, letting the music guide his hand.

Artinces believed that Jesus could wash her sins away as much as she believed the world was flat. But while Rose sang, Artinces found herself yearning for absolution, hoping that somewhere, on some glad morning, people could indeed be made new. If she could make herself over, who would she become?

Rose sank from a crescendo to a sigh, and then her knees buckled. Gabe, hovering in the shadows behind her, caught her before she fell. Gently, he lowered her to the ground. The Man in the Red Vest was as quick as he was smooth. He rushed to the mike. "Put your hands together for Rose Patterson," he said. "One more thing: is there a doctor in the park?"

Minutes later, Artinces squatted by Rose's side. "Give them room," the Man in the Red Vest urged the growing crowd. Lucius and Reuben had grabbed an Afro Day banner and stretched it between them, forming a privacy curtain around the scene. Rose was sweating heavily. Artinces could see that her water had broken. Stretched out on her back, Rose rested her head and upper shoulders against Gabe. She bit her lip and moaned. Gabe dabbed her forehead with a handkerchief and leaned forward to whisper in her ear. "It's going to be fine," he said. "You and the baby will both be fine."

Rose smiled in the midst of her pain. Artinces saw the fear and confusion wiped away. She could tell Rose really trusted her man.

"Now, I'm going to have remove your underpants," Artinces said softly. She took a look. The baby was already crowning.

"Dad, you're going to have to help me," she said to Gabe. "She believes in you. Let's make her glad she does."

Leaning against his Eldorado just outside the gates, Sharps had a clear view of the proceedings. Alone among Rose's rapt audience, Sharps had kept a safe emotional distance throughout her performance. He never stopped smirking when she slumped to the stage floor. He waited patiently for PeeWee to return with the two pies he'd filched in the confusion. *All the world's a stage*, Sharps thought, *and it's time for the final act.*

His family had greased the right palms in sweet home Chicago, and twisted a few limbs besides. Armed with a rigged recommendation and fake credentials, he'd come to town and gotten as close to Ananias Goode as anyone ever had, including that fat fool Guts Tolliver. His reports home had included the suspicion that Goode, who was turning into "a melancholy nigger," aimed to disappear after draining the sporting life dry. "I'm no fool," Sharps had reported, "I can see what he's up to. Buying up legit shingles left and right. He has to be laundering loads and loads of cash." He figured the doctor—"the avenging angel in a lab coat," as one newspaper breathlessly described her—was Goode's bank. He'd almost proved it for himself when he followed Goode one Wednesday, but Detective Grimes, that spooky bastard, had stopped him on a humble and prevented him from tailing their two cars across the bridge. Couldn't be nothing else going on, Sharps had concluded later. No way a bitch wound up that tight would fuck a gangster. Not that Goode was much of a gangster anymore, the way he sat around feeling sorry for himself. True, Goode was a general, not a soldier. His job was to give orders and plot strategy while his lieutenants carried out his plans. Julius Caesar was a general, Sharps knew, and that motherfucker got his in the end.

Sharps fetched his gold toothpick from his breast pocket and slid it between his teeth. Shortly after his arrival, he'd sworn on the grave of his cousin Ike Allen that he would avenge his name and make things right. The time was near, he decided. But first he was going to get Goode's money.

PeeWee had returned while Sharps was ruminating. Earlier, using the power of the ring, he'd disabled the doctor's car according to his business partner's instructions. That task accomplished, stealing from the Pie Lady's booth was almost beneath his dignity.

He raised both pies and smiled proudly. "Lemon meringue and sweet potato," he said. "Just like taking candy from a baby." Startled, Sharps nearly choked on his toothpick. When he recovered, he glared at PeeWee. "For the last time," he warned, "if you keep on interrupting me when I'm thinking, I'll slice you from stem to stern. That's a nautical phrase, motherfucker. You know, nautical. Ships and shit."

Inside his house on Lewis Place, Ananias Goode sat and watched his wife. Lawrence had been given the day off so that he could enjoy the festivities in the park. The day was growing old. Goode made no move to turn on a light. The gloom suited his mood. He sat listening to the wheeze and hum of the machines while clutching a pillow on his lap. Occasionally he snuck a glance at the still form in the bed, the limp swirl of wispy strands barely visible beyond the edge of the blanket. Finally he got up, leaving the pillow on his chair, and went to a table in the corner of the room. He picked up the phone sitting on it and dialed a number.

"Miles? It's me. Yeah, I know. Half of the North Side's in the park. I decided to sit it out and apparently so did you. I called you because…I want you to pray for me."

Miles Washington's voice was as sonorous over the phone as it was when issuing thunderous sermons from his pulpit. "I pray for you every day. You know that. Why the special request? Has something happened?"

"No," Goode replied.

"Is something going to happen?"

"Just do that for me," Goode pleaded, his voice nearly soft as a whisper. "Just pray."

He hung up the phone and stared at his hands. He stood like that, unmoving, for several long minutes. Then, sighing, he grabbed the pillow from the chair and stepped toward the bed.

Artinces sat on a park bench staring at the water. Behind her, Park District employees dismantled the booths and began to cart them away. The drama of the afternoon had played to a satisfying climax. Rose's baby boy made his entrance into her reliable hands, with the joyful outcome dutifully recorded by a *Citizen* photographer. Now she sat waiting for the three women to emerge through the curtain of shadows formed by the gathering dusk. They'd return to the dock where she'd seen them earlier, she figured, and once again try to stare her down. She planned to confront them, ask them why they were taunting her and why they wanted her to suffer. She had once considered the possibility that they *were* her, variants of former selves, or phantom images of women she could have been. But she'd come to doubt that: everything about them—their wardrobe, the expressions on their faces—bore the marks of an earlier time. She attacked the mystery as she would any complex case, and her investigations had at last borne fruit: she was now certain she knew who they were. She felt them watching her while she worked on Rose. She'd even cast a hurried glance around the crowd and though it turned up nothing, she knew they'd been there, looking over her shoulder—close enough, perhaps, to touch her, as they had in her dream.

But as evening fell they apparently had other appointments, promises to keep or break. She stood, stretched, rubbed her eyes, and sat back down. Finally she gave up and left the park, taking one last look around as dusk dissolved into the surrounding black.

C HARLOTTE SKIPPED THE FESTIVITIES IN THE PARK, having had enough of celebrations of black pride for a while, maybe forever. Instead, she spent most of the day at the riverfront, listening to Mozart and dreaming of boats. Artinces had recently abducted her favorite jacket, a lightweight men's houndstooth, and personally escorted it to Kirkwood Cleaners. Undaunted, Charlotte rescued a pale-blue seersucker from a veterans' thrift store. She wore it at the riverfront with the sleeves rolled up to the elbow and her linen plaid cap pulled low over her brow. She sat directly on the cobblestones with her knees drawn up to her chin and her arms wrapped around her shins.

Gateway was more of a barge city than a boat city. Charlotte made do with a mud-splattered tug patrolling the muck just off the wharf. Behind it, in the near distance, a paddle steamer decorated to look like Mark Twain's plaything made slow circuits, stopping now and then to discard its cargo of tourists and pick up another group. When it neared the Gateway City shore, the pilot-host's booming voice blared over a tinny PA, interrupting Charlotte's reverie. But it was only a temporary annoyance, one she quickly overwhelmed with the Queen of the Night's piercing aria from *The Magic Flute*. The soprano sang in German, but Dr. Harrison, Charlotte's music appreciation teacher, had provided the class with an English translation.

On the steamer, the tourists, once animated, were now still. Shadowy stick figures, they clutched the rails as the boat wheeled around a final time. *The vengeance of hell boils in my heart,* the Queen declared, her crystalline voice ringing above the cobblestones, *death and despair flame about me!*

Charlotte had been listening to the same song all day on an eight-track player she'd bought from the man known as Playfair. Artinces couldn't hide her puzzlement on the day Charlotte brought it home.

"Why would you buy that? It's probably stolen."

"Probably," Charlotte said in response. The tape player sat on the kitchen table while she made tea. She'd noticed that Artinces was freshly bathed and powdered and a little jumpy, as if she was in a rush to get out of the house. She smelled faintly of flowers.

"How can you be so casual about it?"

"Didn't you casually bring home that bird in the hall? Where do you think it came from?"

"I bought it for you, to keep you company. Anyway—I don't have time to argue with you." Artinces stood in front of a glass-front cabinet and checked her face in the reflection.

"I know," Charlotte said.

"What do you mean, you know?"

"I mean I know you don't have time. It's Wednesday."

Artinces stopped primping. But she didn't turn around. "What about Wednesday?"

Charlotte got up and grabbed the teakettle before it started whistling. "You tell me. You're the one who's always running off."

"You know, there was a time when young people addressed their elders with respect. Anyway, there's nothing wrong with my hi-fi in there."

"Except it's stationary," Charlotte said, remembering Playfair's sales pitch. "With eight D batteries, you can take this baby anywhere. Plus it's got an AM radio."

As it turned out, her exchanges with Artinces, sometimes warm and sometimes cool, left her more than prepared for her first encounters with Dr. Leonora Harrison.

"One might ask about the proper role of music in life," Dr. Harrison had said on the first day of class. "Or one might ask if life without music is even possible." Tall and stylish, Dr. Harrison had imperious features that were completely out of harmony with her joyful approach to her life's work. "In this class, you will learn how to progress beyond mere hearing," she promised. "By semester's end, you will know how to *listen*." Fond of waving a conductor's baton as she played recordings and lectured, Dr. Harrison was just the first of a number of instructors at River Valley A&M who made a lasting impression on Charlotte. They were smart, confident, and dedicated. Willing to urge students past their preconceived limitations, they never concealed their desire to see them succeed.

Charlotte enrolled as a pre-med major in the College of Agricultural and Natural Sciences, one of four colleges serving 3,000 students on the 170-acre campus. Colored Union soldiers had founded River Valley right after the Civil War. Until the turn of the twentieth century, its curriculum focused on farming and trades, a reflection of Booker T. Washington's then-dominant influence. Over time, the faculty members and trustees who favored the W.E.B. Du Bois approach to self-improvement won a hard-fought majority. Their victory eventually led to an expansion beyond River Valley's industrial-education roots and the recruitment of students like Charlotte.

"I will play a song and you will identify it," Dr. Harrison commanded one day. She marched to her desk, lifted the tone arm on her portable record player, and touched the needle to the record.

Propulsive drumbeats filled the room, followed by the eager blare of a clarinet. "'Maple Leaf Rag'!" someone hollered. Charlotte turned and spotted a slim, well-dressed young man whose appearance seemed out of step with the times. A sharp part was razored into the left temple of his short hair, and a thin, impeccable mustache lined his upper lip. His short-sleeve shirt and tie made him look less like a like a super-bad soul brother than a refugee from the Montgomery bus boycott.

"Composed by Scott Joplin, of course," he continued, "but performed in this case by...Sidney Bechet."

"You are correct, Mr. Conway," Dr. Harrison said. "Next time, please do us the courtesy of raising your hand."

"Sorry, Professor," he replied. It was clear that he wasn't apologizing at all. "I lost control of myself."

Four notes into the next song, he interrupted again. "'Für Elise,' Beethoven. How about something challenging, like his Fifth Symphony?" He chuckled, amused with himself.

Dr. Harrison lifted the tone arm from the record. With one hand on the hip of her tailored skirt, she raised her baton and aimed it at the impudent student. "Really, Mr. Conway. I warn you not to push me. Especially on the first day of class."

Conway, whom Charlotte would soon learn was better known as Percy, stuck out his bottom lip in a bold parody of pouting. "Yes, ma'am," he said. Charlotte snuck another glimpse. He looked sharp, almost jittery with intelligence, and he was the color of lightly toasted bread. Percy caught Charlotte looking at him and winked at her. She grinned and looked away.

A saucy clamor of horns introduced the next song, and a bold brassy voice followed them.

> *I can't sleep at night*
> *I can't eat a bite*
> *'Cause the man I love*
> *He don't treat me right...*

"Bessie Smith?" a voice offered.

Dr. Harrison frowned. "Remember, we raise our hands in this class. But you were close. Anybody?" She scanned the neat rows of desks, ignoring Percy's raised hand. He stretched, leaned, and gestured wildly, eliciting giggles from his classmates.

Dr. Harrison sighed. "Mr. Conway."

"The singer would be Mamie Smith. The song would be 'Crazy Blues.'"

"You are correct, Mr. Conway, very good. Now, no more from you. Let someone else have a chance."

"Fine," he said. "My work here is done." He leaned back in his seat and folded his arms.

Dr. Harrison's next selection made Charlotte sit up straight in her chair. A woman's voice, crisp, lilting, and nearly startling in its beauty, leapt from a cushion of fluttering strings. As it rose, Charlotte heard flights of fluty warbling that she could hardly believe came from a woman's throat. Riding on waves of horns, the voice seemed everywhere at once, a covey of songbirds flushed from their grassy enclave and sent soaring into the sky.

> *So bist du meine Tochter nimmermehr.*
> *Verstoßen sei auf ewig,*
> *Verlassen sei auf ewig,*
> *Zertrümmert sei'n auf ewig...*

Charlotte couldn't understand the words but she recognized that hearts and lives were at stake. Orders were being given, oaths sworn. The song ended long before she realized it.

A nudging in her ribs made her jump. It was Percy. "It's okay," he whispered, "you can breathe now."

Dr. Harrison broke down the aria for the class. She explained that the Queen of the Night, much like the blues queens with whom the students were far more familiar, was venting her frustration through song. In this case, her daughter had been on the receiving end. Charlotte had never known a mother's wrath or passion, but had never imagined it could sound like that. She knew it would be impossible to get those notes out of her head. She didn't want to. After the last class of the day, she headed to the campus library and checked out everything it had on Mozart and *The Magic Flute*.

At the checkout counter, she was amused to find Percy's signature confidently scrawled on the checkout slip at the back of each book. Evidently he had a thing for Mozart. On a whim, she left her findings on the counter and returned to the stacks. She grabbed a book at random off the shelf: *Physics and You*. Only a single individual had checked it out: one Percy Conway. She crossed the room and pulled another title. *An Oral History of Appalachia*. Flipping to the checkout slip, she found it again: Percy

Conway. In a far corner, she slid a good half-dozen volumes, each
of them more obscure than the last, and each weighed down by a
thick layer of dust. Percy's signature was in all of them.

Shaking her head, she went back to the counter. The clerk, a
heavy-chested girl wearing Afro puffs, chewed her gum like she
was mad at it. "You're a freshman, huh?"

"Yeah," Charlotte replied. "That obvious?"

The girl smiled. "Well, I saw you playing Percy Patrol."

"Playing what?"

"Percy Patrol. It's fun on a slow night."

"What exactly is it?"

"You go around the library trying to find a book that doesn't
have his name in it. Last year a fraternity sent its pledges on patrol.
It took them until closing time."

"You mean to say he's read every book in here?"

"No, but damn near."

"How do you know he's not just signing his name?"

The clerk finished stamping due dates in Charlotte's books. She
slid the stack toward her. "Have you ever talked to him? Asked him
a question? He remembers everything he sees, maybe everything
he hears."

Charlotte sighed. "Why would anyone want to do that?"

"What makes you think he wants to? Can you imagine carrying
all that around in your head?"

"Poor baby."

"Yeah, be careful. He gets that a lot. If you're looking for him,
he'll be with the Soldiers."

In commemoration of the River Valley founders, a life-size
sculpture of three black Union soldiers stood in a plaza surrounded
by a circle of benches. At one of them, Percy sat with his eyes closed.

Charlotte waited several long moments in hopes he would stir or
open his eyes. No luck. Finally, gathering her wits, she approached.

"Excuse me," she said.

He opened his eyes, saw her, and pretended to be alarmed.
"Uh-oh, here comes Trouble."

"Hardly. Unless you've done something wrong."

"If I had, I sure wouldn't tell you. For all I know, you could be FBI. Or worse: an FBI informant. COINTELPRO, don'tcha know."

"Right, I'm a fed. What are you doing?"

"If you must know, I'm dreaming of boats."

"Boats? Here on the plaza."

"Closest thing to water we got."

"Are you a music major?"

"Nope."

"How do you know all those songs?"

He chuckled. "Two songs and suddenly I know them all."

"Three," Charlotte corrected. "It was three. And you obviously knew more but Dr. Harrison made you quit."

He shrugged. "Talk about a killjoy. Do you mean how do I know all those songs or how do I know so much about so many things?"

"I don't know that you know all that. I'm talking about the songs."

"Then this is one case in which my reputation has failed to precede me. It would take far less time to ask me what I don't know than to ask me how I know what I know."

"Okay, what don't you know?"

"For starters, your name."

Shortly after Artinces had taken Charlotte under her wing, she began to impress upon her young protégée the centrality in medicine of what she called the Hippocratic principle. The essence of it, according to Artinces, was that physicians must do good, and must do no harm. Charlotte found that the principle also served as a useful gauge when evaluating potential boyfriends. For her the bottom line became, *Will this boy do me harm*? The less likely he was to hurt her, she reasoned, the more likely he was to do good. The better the boy, the better his chances. Of the boys who approached her in high school, Ed Jones's deep-rooted, unassailable kindness elevated him above his peers, and she ultimately granted him full access to her charms. She believed she detected similar qualities in Percy Conway.

"I should walk you home, lest you catch the vapors," he said to her that first night, after she'd cornered him at the Soldiers. In his language and mannerisms, she found no hint of the forced swagger that most young men hid behind. In its place, an unabashed gentleness flourished, a willingness to regard the world and himself with a healthy sense of humor. His conversation unfolded in a rough music of complete paragraphs and compact, ornate nuggets as he strolled with her books tucked under his arm. Every breath and motion suggested to her a celebration of the life of the mind.

"You talk funny," she said. "I mean, a little bit."

"I won't tell you how many times I've heard that."

"I like it, though. It's nice."

"I'm glad someone thinks so, especially someone as lovely as you. However, I have to confess an abiding fear of our fair state's statutory laws. Therefore, although my intentions are completely honorable, I must ask, exactly how old are you?"

"I'm 18."

"Aha. Sounds like trouble."

"I may be young and I might even be trouble. But I'm not illegal. I'm not even a vir—"

"*Whoa.* Cease and desist. A few facts at a time, please. That's so much better, don't you think? Speaking for myself, once I know a thing it's stuck with me."

"Okay, then, how old are you?"

"I'm 23."

Charlotte eyed him carefully. "Really?"

"Boyish demeanor aside, don't the gray temples give me away?"

Charlotte laughed. His hair was completely brown. "How come you're so old? Why haven't you graduated?"

"I took a couple years off to take care of a loved one."

As the semester unfolded, they each became what the other needed. For her, a wise guide to the rudiments of college life; for him, an affectionate witness who could listen tirelessly and without judgment. While other coeds had proved themselves unequal to the task, Charlotte found joy in her service. She stood in the windy plaza while he performed monologues for an audience of one. She was certain that his luminous speech made the bronze faces of the Union soldiers glow with enlightenment. She was convinced that everyone, even inanimate objects, could detect Percy's incandescence; she just appreciated it more. His intelligence burned so brightly that he gave off sparks.

That first nighttime stroll went way too quickly for Charlotte. She'd hardly taken a breath between the Soldiers and Taplin Hall, an all-freshman girls' dorm that horny young male students referred to as the Virgin Vault. At a lamppost adjacent to the entrance, he paused and handed over her books.

"What's your major?" he asked.

"Pre-med. And you?"

"Philosophy and religion."

"Why?"

"Why not?"

"Are you trying to find something to believe in?"

"Not exactly," he replied. "I believe that I don't believe. I'm at peace with that. But I am interested to find out what makes others believe. Stepping out on faith, I think they call it."

Charlotte scratched the side of her nose. "So you read a lot of books, the Bible and other books like it, and you think that will tell you? Why not just ask people?"

"The reading's for background. In grad school, I'll do real fieldwork, like Du Bois. When he did *The Philadelphia Negro*, he knocked on dozens of doors. Can you imagine that?"

"Good thing he did that in Philly," Charlotte said with a smile. "If he'd done that in my hometown, somebody would've gone upside his head."

Without warning, Percy swooped in on her, gently cupping her head in his hands. He pressed his lips against hers, then pulled away. "Power to the people!" he said.

"You're crazy," she said, grinning.

He whirled around the lamppost, a brown Gene Kelly revving up for a song. "Ah," he said, "crazy like Mamie Smith."

Students crossing the plaza during the fall semester, swaddled against the cold and exhaling fat plumes of steam, often saw the two of them engaged in passionate discussions, trading arguments as if the fate of the world hung in the balance.

"We don't have the weapons," Percy would say with a sigh. "We don't have the resources, we don't have the *wherewithal*. It takes all that to overcome systematic oppression. And all that talk of revolution doesn't sufficiently address our complicity in our own mistreatment. For Du Bois, this was an unavoidable question: whether or nor the slavery and degradation of Negroes in America has not been unnecessarily prolonged by the submission to evil. We put up with it, in other words."

"So we're all Uncle Toms," Charlotte would offer in return, prompting Percy to shake his head.

"No, no, that's not what I'm saying. I'm saying let's put aside all the bluster about offing whitey and face the fact that our real gift is endurance. It's the only thing we have real confidence in. We pray without ceasing, sister, that slow and steady will one day win the race."

By October, passersby likely would have missed them hunkered down in a dimly lit corner of the chapel, with little beside body heat and rhetoric to keep them warm. Percy would be standing, gesturing dramatically, or pacing with his hands deep in his pockets. Charlotte would be sitting comfortably (as comfortably as possible, that is) on a blanket, wrapped up in her oversize men's coat and wondering when Percy would pause in his delivery and lean in for a kiss.

"Life is solitary, nasty, brutish, and short," he'd exclaim. "Hobbes hit it on the head, didn't he? He was no James Brown but he wasn't half bad."

Charlotte would toss him an exaggerated come-hither look. "Is that how you make a move on a woman? You just keep quoting philosophers? Funny."

"Maybe," he'd say, finally leaning closer. "But you know what's funnier? You keep listening."

Finally, acting on an anonymous tip, the maintenance man got wise to their makeshift camp in the chapel and chased them out. They ran, puffing and giggling until they collapsed at the feet of the Soldiers. They shared shots of cocoa from Percy's battered aluminum thermos. Savoring the heat rising from the thermos cap in her cupped hands, Charlotte asked him why he chose River Valley.

"I'm a legacy, bound by blood. You're looking at the son of a bricklayer who taught his craft right here on this venerable campus.

The Conways have gone from tradesman to aspiring philosopher in a single generation. I'm telling you, the Talented Tenth's got nothing on us."

Charlotte sighed, watching the steam vanish into the frigid air. "That's way more than I can claim," she said.

"Aw, don't be so hard on your people. No doubt you're familiar with the spirit of the age. How does the song go? Oh, yes, 'We shall overcome.' Any and all obstacles, including humble origins. Greek societies, Black and Tans, colored aristocracies—all exposed as corrupt traditions, the blueblood perversions of a bygone age. If straw can be made into bricks, then men and women, no matter how lowly, can be molded into models of purpose and accomplishment. Just don't call us New Negroes."

Charlotte looked at the ground, her jaw clenched. He lowered himself beside her. "I'm sorry," he said. "Sometimes I don't know when to stop." He put his arm around her and waited.

"I don't know my father," she said. "Mother either. Somebody left me on a doorstep."

"Who? How?"

She shook her head. "Your guess is as good as mine. They put me in different foster houses. I refuse to call them homes. Sometimes I was an excuse for a check; sometimes the man of the house had eyes on me. If I fought or ran away, they put me down as a troublemaker. Nobody wants someone like that sharing a room with their *real* children, disturbing their peace. I got too big, too old. Everybody wanted babies. I lived at a children's home until Dr. Noel took me in."

They sat in silence. The cocoa cooled and Charlotte's fingers grew numb inside her gloves.

"Do you ever think about finding them?"

"I used to. Not anymore."

"If you did find them, what would you say?"

"I'd tell them that I wasn't looking for anything, especially love. I'd tell them it's too late for that. I'd just want to know who they were. Why they gave me up."

"I couldn't imagine that."

Charlotte shifted her hips and looked him in the eye. "Imagine what? Not knowing your people?"

"No. Giving you up."

C HARLOTTE DISCOVERED THAT being unable to *imagine* giving her up was not the same as being unable to actually cut her loose. The campus grapevine told her that Percy devoted the fall semester of every year to seducing some starry-eyed freshman with his amazing mind and golden tongue. The speeches he'd given Charlotte, the grapevine said, he had most certainly given before. The ultimate result was always the same. Percy would get in the wind while the smitten girl sobbed all the way to her sophomore year.

Charlotte knew that wasn't the complete picture. Percy delighted in her, but with a genial affection that fell short of devotion. He could take her or leave her, and some days he left her. He'd slink in quietly to Music Appreciation after Dr. Harrison's lecture had already begun, and race out without so much as a glance in Charlotte's direction. She felt him go without turning around, sensed him sprinting feverishly down the hall in a headlong rush to who knows where.

Sorority girls and cheerleaders harrumphed and tittered when she went by. Her sudden solitariness confirmed their initial suspicions: she was an ignorant upstart who didn't know the first thing about romance. Did she really think that marching around in a baggy man's coat with her hair piled up under a cap was the way to go? She was backwards, country, peculiar. And the smartest man on campus had her on a string.

She found comfort and moral support in the company of her roommate, Laurie Jo Pippen. If Charlotte were compelled to describe her new friend in a single word, it would have been *homespun*. An unpretentious education major from Kinloch, Missouri, Laurie Jo wore dresses that her mother had stitched together on the family Singer and that the other girls on campus found laughably out of style. "Somebody should let that poor thing know that this is the seventies," a classmate would whisper. Laurie Jo would turn around and face her critics with a grin. "Talk louder," she'd advise, "'cause Laurie Jo can't hear you." The only time she didn't wear a dress was when she donned cutoffs to race Alphonso Jordan, a loudmouth sophomore from Jefferson City. She beat him by 10 yards and Alphonso hid out for the rest of the semester.

Laurie Jo took matters in hand when she returned to Taplin Hall one Friday afternoon and found Charlotte moping about the room.

"You know what you need? Some home-cooked vittles. Come to Kinloch with me this weekend. You can't beat my mama's biscuits with a stick. She can put ten pounds on you in two days."

"You're sure your family won't mind? It would beat sitting with the Soldiers, watching my nails grow. You guys don't really say 'vittles,' do you?"

"Not really," said Laurie Jo, tossing her overnight bag on top of her bed. "I got that off *The Beverly Hillbillies*."

Laurie Jo was the oldest of three girls. Her father ran a tire and wrecker service. The busybodies on campus figured the Pippen household was a homestead complete with an outhouse, a chicken coop, and a rusted, wheel-less tractor resting on blocks. In reality, it was more like a well-oiled machine. Laurie Jo's parents split the chores at home and at work. While Mr. Pippen hauled errant cars from ditches and patched up steel-belted radials, Mrs. Pippen managed the billing and balanced the books. While Mrs. Pippen fried the chicken and mashed the potatoes, Mr. Pippen swept the floors and washed the clothes. Meanwhile, the girls pitched in with their own tasks, moving through each room with precision and skill. Charlotte helped but mostly watched admiringly as the Pippens kept a steady pace without ever bumping into each other.

She reveled in the harmony enveloping the Pippens' table, almost forgetting her recent difficulties with Percy. The food, the laughter, the easy, warmhearted bantering—it was an orphan's dream, and Charlotte shamelessly lapped it up. She wondered, too, why her own experience had been so starkly opposite, what trick of genetics had made Laurie Jo and not her the daughter of Moses and Jackie Pippen.

Ed had a similar family. Once she'd entered the Jones home with Ed and found his mom sitting on his dad's lap, spooning warm cake into his mouth. The adults paused to offer greetings but quickly returned their attention to each other. Charlotte felt somewhat awed, but Ed, as usual, seemed ashamed. He often behaved as if his family's closeness was bourgeois and "counterrevolutionary," one of his favorite words. Unlike him, Laurie Jo was matter-of-fact about her situation. She knew her family life was special, but the way she moved about her house suggested that she expected nothing less, as if specialness could be a birthright.

After dinner, when the dishes had been put away and the house was quiet, Charlotte and Laurie Jo stayed up late. When Charlotte told her about her own far less fortunate upbringing, Laurie Jo took it in stride like she did everything else. On campus, Laurie Jo was voluptuous and friendly, but men seemed a little afraid of her. She had round cheekbones that glowed when she smiled. She was faster and stronger than many of her male peers but didn't hold it against them. She regarded her lack of a boyfriend with patience instead of frustration. "I have a good thing here at home," she told Charlotte. "It's going to take a real man to make me want to leave."

The next day, Charlotte accompanied Laurie Jo and Mr. Pippen to their woodshed, which he had converted into a firing range. All of the Pippen women had become crack shooters under his tutelage. "I want them to be able to protect themselves," he explained, "in case no one else is around to do it."

He showed Charlotte how to hold and load a pistol. Although the black metal was surprisingly heavy resting on her palm, it felt more reassuring than dangerous. Mr. Pippen helped Charlotte squeeze off a few rounds before Laurie Jo peppered the homemade target with a series of perfectly aimed shots.

"I should have known you can shoot," Charlotte said. "I bet you can hunt too."

"Of course she can," Mr. Pippen said.

"That's right," Laurie Jo agreed. "If you like my homemade dresses, you should see my Christmas coat. I made it myself from squirrels I shot."

Charlotte gasped, imagining the furry thing. "Just kidding," Laurie Jo said. Charlotte sighed, relieved, while Mr. Pippen laughed so hard he nearly split his britches. He walked the girls back to the house before heading off to his shop.

In the kitchen, Laurie Jo and Charlotte made sandwiches from leftovers. "Have you ever had to shoot?" Charlotte asked. "I mean at a human being."

"No," Laurie Jo replied. "But I could if I had to. Next time Tish starts mouthing off at you, tell her that. Tell her I'm looking out."

Instead of a punch line, Tish Grant had almost been an invited guest. But she had forced Laurie Jo to choose between her and Charlotte, and Laurie Jo had been happy to oblige. Tish had spent much of fall semester blithely ignoring her fellow freshmen while strutting under the watchful wing of her indulgent dad, a round-bellied man who appeared to love shiny cufflinks, cigars, and pinky rings as much as he loved his little girl.

"She is one spoiled individual," Laurie Jo had said the first time they gossiped about her. "Her father's so overprotective that no boy will go near her. Tish. What kind of name is that for a colored girl?"

Charlotte grinned. "What kind of name is Laurie Jo?"

Laurie Jo ignored her. "You ever noticed how long she ties up the phone? The line of girls in the hall will be five or six deep and she doesn't even bat an eye. Going 'Daddy, this' and 'Daddy, that' like the old man's made of money. And the way she waltzes through the dining hall? Like she's fine as the queen of Sheba."

Tish was as dark as bittersweet chocolate and looked every bit as delicious. There wasn't a cat in the world that could slink through the jungle with such supple splendor. Some girls who looked like her struggled under their burden of beauty; they trudged tentatively as it pressed its weight on their lovely, fragile shoulders. Not Tish. Sloe-eyed, she wore her pulchritude with pride as she swung her delectable curves through the drooling masses with her mouth slightly parted, color shimmering on her perfect lips.

On those unexpected but oddly welcome occasions when she acknowledged Charlotte and Laurie Jo's existence, Tish proved a candid and attentive companion. Days she passed by Charlotte and Laurie Jo on campus with a nod or a raised eyebrow; nights she was a fount of knowledge and sardonic commentary. She knew how to avoid getting pregnant, how to get sex stains off a car seat, how to make a lover shout your name. Charlotte and Laurie Jo wondered how she could accumulate so much experience under her father's watchful eye. From what they could tell, Tish was double-majoring in sex and shopping. From what Tish could tell, Charlotte was a devoted student of just one subject: Percy Conway. The poor girl's lack of knowledge was going to lead her down a bad road. One night in the study lounge, Tish took it upon herself to enlighten her.

"Percy?" she asked, interrupting Charlotte's monologue, although she knew perfectly well that he was the topic of discussion. "He's just a motor-mouthed schoolboy."

Charlotte hissed. "He's nobody's boy. He's 23." Charlotte had grown fond of telling people that.

Tish sighed and shook her head. "Listen, you virgins, while I educate you."

Charlotte said nothing to refute her. She had spent many sultry nights in Ed Jones's bedroom sweating and writhing while Johnny Hartman and John Coltrane spun seductive rhythms on the nearby stereo. Since then, Percy had shown her the delights of the garden—the wonderfully private, gated campus garden named after George Washington Carver—and introduced her to other sacred rites during their feverish couplings in the chapel. By no means, then, was she was a stranger to what Tish was fond of calling "a good dickin' down." She wasn't ashamed and had certainly exchanged confidences with Laurie Jo. She just didn't want Tish in her business.

"Okay, he's not a boy. He's a male *type*. That's what most of them are around here: male types. They have outside plumbing and fuzz on their balls, but they aren't men. When they lean close to kiss you, you can smell their mama's titty milk on their lips and tongue. They want to suck on you for nourishment because they're still growing. Men, though? They're already fed. That's why I like a man with something around his middle. With a man like that it's only the sweetness he wants and he knows it don't come free. Male types ain't too proud to beg, but men know better than to come up on you with empty pockets. Take a look at this."

Tish leaned forward and showed off the necklace gleaming on her throat.

"Looks like a diamond," Laurie Jo said. "Is that a diamond?"

"Maybe," Tish replied.

Laurie Jo's eyes grew big. "Girl," she said, "what did you have to do to get that?"

Tish purred. "If you knew, you wouldn't be calling me girl."

"What would your father say?" Charlotte asked. All that talk of "male types" had turned her stomach. She wanted to bring Tish down a peg.

But Tish just laughed. "What my father don't know don't hurt him."

Charlotte drifted, thinking again about Ed. Sweet Ed, steadfast, devoted, and already an afterthought. Like Tish's suitors, he always wanted to give her things. When Charlotte told him it was over, he gave her a bracelet that remained on the dresser in her room at Artinces's house, still in its original box. They were going to different schools, the distance was too great, they were better off ending as friends, she said. Ed told her she was breaking his heart, but she knew that deep down he had reached the same conclusion. Since then, she'd never written Ed and he'd never contacted her, except once when she opened a parcel postmarked Cambridge, Massachusetts, and slowly removed a charcoal sketch, matted and framed. It was an 8½-by-11 portrait of her naked. Ed had been fond of sketching her while she stretched out on his bed, smiling and waiting for the moment when he couldn't stand it any longer, when he'd grab hold of her as if he would never let go.

Artinces asked about Ed when she visited for parents' weekend. Charlotte hadn't asked her to come and was more pleased than she expected to be when the doctor called and suggested it. The dining hall served steak, one of the two occasions (the other was homecoming) when it featured something more tasty—and identifiable—than its usual mystery meat. Artinces, though, suggested they skip that momentous fare in favor of a restaurant in town, a place that wasn't particularly fancy but nonetheless too expensive for Charlotte to ever sample on her own. Charlotte had hoped to bring Percy along, but he had made himself scarce. Over pork chops stuffed with bacon and apples, she reminded Artinces that she and Ed had agreed to be just friends.

"And he's gone along with that?"

"So far. He's written me only once and I haven't written him at all."

Artinces looked at Charlotte over the edge of her teacup. "What did his letter say?"

"It wasn't a letter really. It was a drawing he'd made of me."

Artinces said nothing, prompting Charlotte to wonder if the doctor somehow knew that it wasn't just any old drawing. Then, looking at Artinces, she concluded that her thoughts were elsewhere. Although the doctor's behavior was as prim and dignified as ever, she still seemed somehow altered from her stalwart Gateway City persona. She appeared restless, full of an excitement she could barely conceal. Charlotte wanted to tell her about Percy, but when she opened her mouth, something entirely different spilled out.

"Dr. N., have you ever been in love?"

Artinces, who had been merely moving her food around her plate, carefully cut her meat into smaller and smaller slices. Charlotte vaguely suspected that she was in a hurry to get somewhere.

"I had dalliances here and there," Artinces finally said. "But when I was in school I really wanted to concentrate on doing well and making it through."

"But what about when you weren't in school? What about now?"

Artinces set her fork down without lifting any food to her lips. She looked up from her plate. "I had to make difficult decisions, you see. At first I didn't have time—didn't make time—for love. And now…I'm still facing hard choices. Have you had enough, or would you like some dessert too?"

Artinces rarely moved slowly, whipping through hospital corridors with the tail of her lab coat swirling behind her, or marching resolutely to a committee hearing with a reporter at each elbow. She moved even faster, however, after wrapping up dinner with Charlotte. Dropping her baffled protégée off near Taplin Hall, she gave her a quick hug and kiss and zipped off into the night. Charlotte lingered under the streetlamp outside her dorm, sniffing. The doctor had smelled different. Charlotte, unfamiliar with cigars and bourbon, couldn't identify the scents.

When she got to her room, Laurie Jo was reclined on her bed with a *Jet* magazine on her lap. Tish was admiring herself in the mirror.

"Look who's here," Laurie Jo said. "How was your dinner with the doctor?"

"Fine," Charlotte replied. Tish's presence irritated her, although she wasn't sure why.

"Was it just the two of you?"

Charlotte wished that Laurie Jo had waited until they were alone before throwing questions at her. But she plopped down on her bed and answered anyway.

"Just us two. I couldn't find Percy anywhere. Not at the Soldiers, not at his room."

"Hmm," Laurie Jo said. "What do you think he was doing?"

"Probably the nasty," Tish said. "On Sorority Row."

Charlotte stood. "You saw him?"

"Didn't have to. Why do you make a big mystery out of everything?"

"What are you saying?"

Tish continued to study her reflection. "It's not like I'm beating around the bush. If he's a man like you say he is, then he has a man's needs. He wants to do more than talk. Lots of females around here will give him that."

"He can get whatever he needs from me."

"Yeah? Did he tell you that? You're the last one to see that all he needs from you is somebody to clap every time he farts."

"You're just jealous."

Tish finally turned and faced Charlotte. "Jealous? Honey, I don't want your job. I could have it if I wanted it, but I got more pride than that."

"Hush, Tish," Laurie Jo advised, but Tish foolishly kept talking.

"All the senior girls laugh at you," Tish continued. "They say Percy slides around campus dribbling spit and you follow behind, licking it up."

Charlotte slapped Tish. The beauty fell back against the wall hard, but quickly regained her feet. Later, Laurie Jo would describe the slap as resembling the motion behind Satchel Paige's windmill fastball. "First there was the windup," she'd say to anyone who asked, "then there was the pitch," a violent whirlwind of overhead motion. In truth, Laurie Jo, sensing what was coming, had winced and looked away at the moment of impact. Tish, no stranger to a scuffle, admired Charlotte's quickness even as she felt its sting. She pressed her fingers to her cheek and smiled.

"So that's how it is?"

Charlotte nodded. "That's how it is."

Laurie Jo managed to escort Tish out before more blows were thrown. She walked back down the hall looking subdued and remorseful. Once inside the room, she broke into a wide grin. "Girl, you cleaned her clock," she said to Charlotte. "She should have known better than to jump salty with you."

An awkward enmity developed between Charlotte and Tish, one that occasionally erupted into nose-to-nose clashes that Laurie Jo or someone else quickly stepped in to defuse. For most of the year their feud would simply smolder, sustained by hissed insults and mutual eye rolling. Although she kept her chin up and faced Tish without fear, Charlotte struggled with the recognition that her rival had the upper hand. True, Charlotte had enjoyed the visceral pleasure of wiping Tish's nauseating smirk right off her face. But Tish basked in the glory that came from being right. Percy would soon vanish like a ghost, withdrawing from all his classes. His phone would be disconnected, the puritanical Holy Roller who rented him a room off campus would decline to account for his whereabouts, and he wouldn't bother to leave behind so much as a letter or forwarding address for Charlotte.

The morning after the epic slap, however, Charlotte's thoughts were far from Tish Grant. To avoid dining-hall chatter about their fight, she'd slipped out early and taken a long, head-clearing walk to a diner at the edge of the black community. Her plan was to eat breakfast in peace and solitude. But Percy had introduced her to the place. Without him the eggs and toast seemed cold and unappetizing, and the bits and pieces of conversation that she overheard lacked his customary wit. She choked down as much as she could before stepping outside. Across the street from a gas station, she spotted Artinces's car rolling away from the lot. She waited for it to approach, prepared to wave as it passed by. But the car quickly gathered speed and, as it whizzed past her, she saw that Artinces wasn't behind the wheel. Charlotte caught only a rakishly tilted hat, a snatch of jaw, and a cigar clenched between generous lips before the car zoomed out of sight. Charlotte stared after it, imagining Artinces in the passenger seat, leaning affectionately on the shoulder of her mysterious lover.

"Hard choices," Charlotte muttered.

As weeks came and went without any sign of Percy, rumors haunted Charlotte's every step. Speculation included catastrophic illness, a shotgun wedding, and solemnly sworn Sorority Row testimony that Percy had been spotted chopping weeds on a Southern chain gang.

After banging out her last essay of the semester on the state-of-the-art typewriter Artinces had bought for her, Charlotte got up from her desk and tossed herself onto her bed. Her room was quiet. Like many other students, Laurie Jo had already departed for winter break. Outside Charlotte's door, the Taplin hallways were desolate. Charlotte sighed and flopped an arm over her eyes.

She was halfway between sleep and wakefulness when a spray of pebbles rained softly against her window. She got up and looked outside. Percy was in the courtyard below.

"Hey, Beautiful!" he shouted when he saw her. "Let me up before I get arrested for disturbance of the peace."

She opened her window. "Where have you been?"

"Medical leave," he said. "But enough about me. Are you going to let me up there?"

"Why should I?"

"Because if you don't, I'm going to start singing. Then they'll take me to jail. Do I look like a criminal to you?"

He smiled, and she couldn't help smiling back. "There you go," he said.

"My RA will never let you up."

"Please. I tutored her through Differential Calc. She owes me her life."

"I'm tired," she said. "I was about to go to bed."

"Is that an invitation?"

She shook her head. "I'm going to close this window."

"All right then, you give me no choice." He took a dramatic breath. "*Can't turn you loose*," he wailed. "*Let me in, let me in—*"

"Okay! Come up. But quit with the Sam Cooke."

"Actually, this is my Otis Redding. You want to hear my Sam?"

Up close, Percy looked gleeful, wild-eyed, a little frightening. His hair, neatly cropped when school began in August, was now lengthy and barely tamed, and glistening with flakes of snow. His shirt and pants were clean but disheveled, and his thin suit jacket offered little protection against winter. His face had an unsettling sheen. He came in and immediately tried to kiss her on the lips but she gave him her cheek.

"The cold shoulder. Okay, I deserve that. Look, I brought you something."

Charlotte folded her arms across her chest. "Make it good. I expect a man like you to do better than candy or flowers."

"Two things." He reached in an inside pocket and pulled out a cassette. "An eight-track recording of *The Magic Flute*. Pretty good, huh?"

"Pretty good," she agreed. "Thank you." She took the tape and studied the label. She wasn't looking at him when he reached into his jacket a second time.

"And this." Charlotte looked up and saw Percy presenting a gun as if it were an engagement ring. A .38-caliber revolver, it looked much like the one she had held and shot at Laurie Jo's house, except it was older and tarnished instead of shiny.

She pressed her hand to her throat. "Percy, what are you doing with that? I don't want it."

"There's a box of bullets too. I need you to take it."

"Why?"

"Because I trust you. More than I trust myself."

Percy explained that parents' weekend fell on the anniversary of his father's death. It had been too much for him to take, and when the weekend had passed he decided the semester was also too much, so he applied for and received a medical leave. Since then, he'd spent most of the time holed up in his room, "resting and healing."

Charlotte struggled to organize her many questions so that she could ask them one at a time.

"I'm sorry about your father," she said. "How did he die?"

"He killed himself. With this gun."

Charlotte shuddered. She took the gun from Percy's outstretched hand. Remembering Mr. Pippen's training, she checked to make sure it wasn't loaded, then placed it carefully on her dresser.

"Why did he do it?"

"For the same reason I talk all the time. To shut them up."

"Shut who up?"

"The voices. He heard them. I hear them."

Charlotte remembered the first time she encountered Percy at the Soldiers. She had had the feeling that she'd interrupted a conversation. But no one else was around. He had seemed so relieved when she walked up.

"Voices. What do they tell you?"

"That I'm going to die."

Percy lowered himself to the floor, resting his back against the side of Charlotte's bed. The room's harsh light exposed the dark circles under eyes that had gleamed with excitement just moments before.

Charlotte had never heard voices. She had wished for death though, more than once, before deciding that she had been reading too many poems about longing and despair. She sat down beside him. "Don't listen to them," she said.

Percy smiled. "Easy for you to say. What if they're right?"

"We're all going to die, Percy. There's no point in thinking about it all the time. When you told me you took time off to care for a loved one…you were talking about yourself, weren't you?"

Percy nodded. He grabbed her hand without turning to look for it. Charlotte reached out and gently took hold of his chin. She turned his face toward hers. "Why are you telling me this now?"

"I knew you'd be leaving soon. I owed you an explanation."

"Will you be in school next semester?"

"I expect to."

"And what about us?"

"I hope that we'll be friends."

Charlotte let go of his chin. She couldn't help laughing bitterly. "It figures," she said.

"What figures?"

"The whole 'friends' thing. The sorority girls told me you break a young girl's heart every year. Do you try to scare them off with the same story?"

"I've had other girls. But I've never dumped them. I simply tell them the truth. Just like I'm telling you."

"What did they say?"

"What do you think?"

"I'm guessing they were angry. Maybe scared. Like I am."

"I wanted them to stick around," Percy said. "I couldn't blame them when they didn't. But there's a difference this time. I don't want you to stay."

"Why? Because you don't think you can rely on me? Because you think I'll turn tail and run at the first sign of problems?"

Percy shook his head. "Because I care so much more for you."

"Don't bullshit me," Charlotte snapped. "I'll hate you for it."

"I'd rather you hate me than love me."

"Stop! You're talking crazy."

"Only because I am crazy. You're brilliant, Charlotte, more than you know. You're incredibly beautiful. When I first saw you in Music Appreciation, I said to myself, hurry up and impress this girl before someone else does. And you're tough, really tough. If I were just a little bit different than I am, we'd be perfect. But you can't fix me. Nobody can."

Percy stretched out on his back and rested his head against Charlotte. Soon he fell asleep. She got up carefully and turned off the light. A wedge of moonlight glowed through a seam in the drawn curtains, illuminating Percy's still form. She returned to the floor and sat with her knees drawn up, arms wrapped around her shins.

On the riverfront, Mozart hummed in Charlotte's ears. The mud-splattered tug had puttered away. The paddle steamer rested in the near distance alongside the gangplank that tourists walked across to embark on sightseeing tours. Clouds crept across the face of the sun, casting the entire scene in shades of gray. Perhaps an hour of daylight remained. Charlotte turned off the tape player. Shouts and laughter occasionally interrupted the soft slap of the river against the cobblestones, reminding her that the riverfront bars would soon be packed with partygoers, dockworkers, and drunks. She stood, brushed off her pants, and walked to her car.

That first night with Percy, when she sat with him near the Soldiers, he encouraged her to imagine the concrete, bench-ringed plaza as a body of water. "See the light dancing serenely on the surface," he said, "see the rippling currents." His voice was hypnotic, seductive.

"I used to marvel about boats," he said. "I love their beauty, their sublime usefulness. I used to tell myself that one day I'd have a boat of my own, maybe even live on it. I can think of few human inventions so wonderful. Somewhere near the dawn of civilization, an ancestor pushed a hollow log into the sea and climbed inside. And from that simple act, transport became more than walking or wheels, more than moving with the ground always beneath you. It meant steering by the stars, depending on the wind. Seeing new worlds, new people. Sometimes just floating. Floating."

Watching him, listening to him, Charlotte promised herself that she wouldn't fall too easily, that she'd make him work. She'd just gotten to college and she had big plans. How dare he lure her so brazenly, with his imagination and his dreamy language?

"Time passed," he continued, "and we turned wonders into weapons, just like we do everything else. We used them to carry blankets infected with smallpox, dragged people in chains into nightmares they hadn't imagined, loaded their decks with cannonballs and bombs. All of that ugly history began to ruin my visions of serenity. It occurred to me that dreaming of boats might possibly be better than actually having one. So here I sit."

Surprising herself, Charlotte asked him if a slave was better off dreaming of freedom instead of actually being free.

He looked at her a long moment. "Shut my mouth," he said with a smile. "I knew you were trouble."

BEFORE ANANIAS GOODE SHARED his swelling fortune with his best friend Miles Washington, enabling the man of God to build a sparkling new edifice for his flock, Good Samaritan Methodist Church occupied a smaller building on the eastern edge of North Gateway. Back then, neighborhood regulars called it "the children's church," because its front steps were known as a place where an unwanted infant could be safely deposited. That durable tradition likely prompted unknown hands to leave a baby girl, just two weeks old, on those very steps in 1952.

Charlotte had no memory of that, of course, and the adults who'd brought her this far in the world had not encouraged her to dwell on the unfortunate circumstances of her earliest days. She did reflect upon them from time to time, such as when she sat down at the Jones family dinner table during her high school romance with Ed, or when she spent a joyful weekend with Laurie Jo's bustling clan. Mostly, though, she saw no point in trying to hold on to such potentially dispiriting details. There was more value, she discovered, in letting them go. She said as much—wrote it, actually—in the essay that secured her a full scholarship to River Valley A&M.

"Old people talk like it takes years and years of living before you can start talking about memories," she wrote. "But I've lived so much and taken on so many memories that if I could, I would forget just about everything. That's wishful thinking and I don't waste much time with that. Wishing, I mean. For most of my life, thinking's all I've had."

It was her precocious thoughtfulness, or rather the suggestion of such qualities on her infant face, that first caught the attention of Miss Shirley Griffin, the church secretary who discovered the wriggling bundle in a basket on the steps. "Look like she's thinking on something important, don't she?" she said to Rev. Washington as the two of them admired the church's latest foundling. Miss Shirley had already washed and changed the baby girl and fed her from the bottle of formula that had been stuffed alongside her in the basket. She had wrapped her in one of the many blankets that the church kept on hand for precisely such events.

"Well, she definitely has something on her mind," Rev. Washington said, smiling. "Any clues as to how she came to us?"

"No," said Miss Shirley, "except for this." She held up a woman's kerchief. It was a souvenir of sorts, with names of North Carolina cities embroidered on its rayon surface. "She was wrapped in it."

"Hmm," said the reverend, examining the scarf. "That will at least give us a name for her if nothing else."

Miss Shirley frowned. "Raleigh? Caroline?"

Rev. Washington chuckled. "Of course not, Miss Shirley. Charlotte. It has to be Charlotte." He took the infant in his arms. "Welcome to the world, little one," he said. "May God's abundance be yours."

Babies left in Good Samaritan's good graces acquired last names reflecting the godly protection that had ensured their safe arrival. Accordingly, kindergarten teachers at the neighborhood school were seldom surprised to look at their class lists and find a Paradise, Blessing, or Providence tucked among the Smiths, Joneses, and Johnsons. Gazing at little Charlotte's glowing brown face, Rev. Washington decreed that her appearance that morning had been nothing less than Divine.

Those little Paradises and Blessings, so fortunate to land in the cushioning embrace of Miss Shirley or some other capable parishioner, often found that God's protection didn't necessarily extend beyond the church walls. Some of them indeed joined households that weren't yet complete until they arrived, creating families bound and sustained by an all-abiding love. Others, like Charlotte, became rolling stones who passed under many roofs without ever finding a place that could truly be called home.

Throughout her journeys, Charlotte held on to the scarf. She carried it carefully from foster home to foster home. Even on occasions when she ran away, she was mindful of it. When Artinces learned of its significance, she convinced Charlotte to have it framed and mounted on the wall in her bedroom.

Her bedroom! Charlotte had never enjoyed her own space. She appreciated everything Artinces had given her—the car, the clothes, the kindness. She was especially grateful for the room. She had endured many roommates by then, though not long enough to ever form a genuine friendship. At college, Laurie Jo was a terrific roommate, but Charlotte tired even of her sometimes, craving the solitude of her bedroom in Gateway City. Like Charlotte, Laurie Jo could speak fondly of the virtues of privacy. She had shared sleeping quarters with her sisters until adolescence, when her parents mercifully allowed her to claim four walls of her own. But she had alternatives even then, including her parents' spacious back porch, and their yard, big enough to include a swing set and a seesaw. She shuddered when Charlotte told her about waking covered in a bedmate's sweat, piss, or worse, and she smiled appreciatively when Charlotte bragged about the dimensions of her room in Artinces's house. "Is it warm?" she once asked. "Warm?" Charlotte replied. "I bet you could fry bacon on my desk."

Laurie Jo laughed. "It's wonderful to feel safe, isn't it?" Charlotte knew her friend meant well, but her smile vanished just the same. "I could never feel safe," she said. "There's no such thing. Not for me, anyway."

She explained that instead of a strong father who shooed away strangers, she'd had a foster parent who pinched her, squeezed her, and wiggled his tongue at her whenever his wife's back was turned. Instead of a mother who sewed dresses, she had a skinny, nervous woman who never stopped smoking, reeked of beer, and kept little in her refrigerator except a jar of mayonnaise and a tin of sardines. When she got older and lived in the relative security of the children's home, Charlotte was nearly raped behind the old Comet Theatre on Washington Boulevard. A shortcut behind the shuttered cinema turned out to be a mistake when a growling stranger dragged her down from behind.

"I fought back," she told Laurie Jo, "but he was too strong. I thought it was over for me."

"What happened?"

"This man came out of nowhere and saved me."

"Thank God," Laurie Jo said.

"Thank Guts."

"What?"

"Guts. I found out later that his name was Guts."

After Guts Tolliver stomped her assailant to a bloody pulp, all the while urging her to run away without looking back, Charlotte kept to herself even more than usual. She avoided Ed and everyone else, wrestling with a conclusion that was as sickening as it was perhaps inevitable: somehow, it all had to be her fault. The perverted foster fathers, the would-be rapist, they were attracted to her because of something she was doing. Was she giving off a scent? Showing too much flesh? She turned her collar against men's ugliness by trying to make herself unattractive. She decided they would see little of her besides her eyebrows.

She began to wear men's hats and men's jackets big enough to drown in, thinking they would smother whatever signals she was transmitting, throw predators off her trail. She couldn't bring herself to cut her hair, so she wound it into a single long braid that she tucked into the back of her shirt. Her costumes may have turned off a few men and prompted wisecracks from some of the clueless coeds on Sorority Row, but they never fooled the PeeWees of the world, who sniffed after her anyway. Nor did it dissuade Percy, who claimed he was dazzled by her beauty the first time he saw her. As their relationship warmed, he told her that not even a croaker sack could distract from her good looks. "You'd climb out of that sack just like Venus rising out of that shell," he cooed. "One look at you and Botticelli would have dropped his brush."

One thing about being dumped on a doorstep is you lose all your blood connections, not just your mother and father. At first Charlotte hung on every word when Percy shared anecdotes about his grandmothers, especially the one he called Mama Ruth. When he misbehaved as a young boy, she'd make him cut a switch from the weeping willow tree in her front yard. After dozens of such stories, Charlotte's fascination turned to envy and she couldn't wait for him to shut up. Charlotte also resented the pictures of grandmothers published in *Ebony* magazine. Gray haired, honey voiced, probably smelling like sweet potato pie, wire-rimmed glasses dangling from a chain. The closest she ever came to having a grandmother was when she was nine. That year, she was kept by Mrs. Speight, a foster mother who also provided day care for toddlers in her small, neat flat. Unlike many of Charlotte's guardians, Mrs. Speight was a straight shooter with no criminal tendencies. Her one vice, if you could call it that, was watching *Let's Go to the Races* on TV. Perched in her threadbare easy chair with Charlotte sitting at her feet, she dozed off during the Kroger grocery commercials, then sat up suddenly at the blare of the starter's bugle and the racetrack announcer's loud "and they're off!"

Perhaps unsurprisingly, Charlotte's time with Mrs. Speight inspired a brief but intense fascination with horses. Her bookshelves in Artinces's house included *Misty of Chincoteague, King of the Wind*, and other remnants of that obsession. When Mrs. Speight died of a stroke, Charlotte was again left to her own devices. For months afterward, Charlotte rode horses in her dreams. Sometimes she was astride a wild stallion, thundering across an island plain. Other times she was a jockey clad in colorful silks and

Mrs. Speight was the announcer, rousing the crowd to an excited roar as Charlotte urged her horse toward the finish line without ever raising her whip.

Mrs. Speight would have made a great doctor, Charlotte thought as she wheeled her Malibu onto the Abram H. parking lot. It was Mrs. Speight who showed her how to hold a baby, how to burp it and bathe it, how to use the rhythm of her own breath to calm it down.

Sharps ate pie like a pig. All that effort that he put into appearing slick and smooth fell by the wayside as soon as someone slid something sweet under his nose.

Sitting beside him in the Eldorado, idling in the alley behind Artinces Noel's house, PeeWee wished he had discovered Sharps's weak spot earlier. He'd have him eating out of his hand by now instead of scooping cold lemon meringue from the pan and stuffing it into his mouth like a Third World toddler in a starving-orphan commercial. He could barely look at him, and the sound of his munching was equally annoying.

At least the preoccupation with pie encouraged Sharps to ease up on all the lecturing. PeeWee took advantage of Sharps's distraction to take out the ring and enjoy its weight in the palm of his hand. He was so sick of Sharps constantly criticizing him that he had half a mind to just put on the ring and beat the piss out of his needle-nosed ass right there in the alley. But he knew he had to wait. It wouldn't be smart to lose his cool on the edge of their big score. But once they'd pulled it off and divvied up the loot, *pow!* He'd become one with the ring, and the whole North Side—maybe the whole world—would know his power.

A car pulled up behind them and flashed its headlights. After spotting it in the rearview mirror, Sharps put down the pie and wiped his hands delicately on a silk pocket square. He pulled his toothpick from his breast pocket, stuck it in his mouth, and glanced at his watch. "'Bout fuckin' time," he said.

The emergency room was strangely quiet. Passing through, Charlotte took note of a handful of patients, none of whom seemed to be suffering from anything more traumatic than an aching stomach or a sprained ankle. She noted the relative calm with faint surprise, half-expecting to see the entrance clogged with screaming ambulances, rushing paramedics, and frantic people. Despite its notoriously inadequate budget, Abram Higgins was the best in the city when it came to handling gunshot and stab wounds. The staff had become so proficient, the joke went, because North Siders gave them more than enough practice. Charlotte had anticipated seeing a few stragglers from the Afro Day event, revelers whose enthusiasm for beer and excitement had exceeded their capacity for self-control. But as she left the emergency ward and walked the long corridor leading to the well-baby center, all was hushed and as close to serene as a building full of sick and injured people could be.

Signing in, she spoke quietly to the familiar nurses on duty. At first she thought she might read to the babies (another Dr. Noel innovation: regularly scheduled reading sessions during which soft-voiced volunteers introduced the newborns to the world of books), but decided instead to take a seat in front of the glass and simply watch them sleep.

The hallowed peace of the well-baby center always calmed her nerves. When she first came there as a volunteer, she attributed its unruffled character to the personality of its founder and the staff of nurses and young doctors that Dr. Noel had personally trained. She realized now that the ambient tranquility could just as easily have derived from the sacred purpose of the place. She learned about sacred purpose in Introduction to World Cultures, a popular class taught at River Valley by Dr. Bernard Murray.

Charlotte had yet to come up with a word comprehensive enough to describe Dr. Murray without help from other words; at semester's end the leading candidates had been *dapper* and *fastidious*. He delivered his lectures, supplemented by anecdotes of his far-flung wanderings, with the force and drama of fervent sermons as he urged his students to uncover the "numinous connection" that bound everything on earth. His pupils often remarked that his classroom orations put Chaplain Stuckey's pulpit mumblings to shame. Chapel attendance was no longer mandatory, but enough students attended on Sundays to testify that they were ponderous snore-fests. Stuckey, who appeared to be half-asleep himself, made little effort to improve. Indeed, they swore, the only thing longer than his sermons was his nostril hair, which joined his robust mustache in a riotous, barbed tangle above his upper lip. Not so with clean-shaven Dr. Murray. He punctuated his lectures with jokes (occasionally raunchy), animated gestures, and more voices than a ventriloquist. In his version of the fire-and-brimstone cosmos, Illumination was the heavenly, sought-for goal; Ignorance, more punishing than the fiery pits of hell, was inexcusable and to be avoided at the price of one's soul.

Dr. Murray's slides offered visual proof of his epic globetrotting. There he was at the Great Pyramids, his spectacles gleaming, his straw boater resting perfectly on his pomaded head, a pipe clenched between teeth that rivaled Teddy Roosevelt's. There he was outside the Globe Theater in London in his immaculate herringbone three-piece, his bow tie flawlessly knotted.

He was a professed skeptic, an outlook that many of his colleagues saw as detrimental to his character—colleagues whose attachment to what Murray called "conventional belief systems" remained steady even as the rebellious philosophies of the Black Power movement challenged the prayerful civil rights movement. Still, he claimed to have an open mind (an acknowledgement that Charlotte appreciated, since she was still figuring things out) and was often at his most eloquent when describing various religious sites that he had visited. He spoke patiently of civilizations that spent centuries erecting shrines to a distant, bearded god who busied himself with watching over sparrows and counting hairs on human heads while wars devoured children and earthquakes swallowed cities whole. He was even more tolerant of cultures whose gods were half-human, half-animal hybrids and whose scriptures told of permeable boundaries between the living and the dead. Regardless of spiritual practice, he said, in temples and cathedrals he felt a Something that he couldn't describe, a rhythm or power that defied language. The real mystery, he argued, was not in humanity's compulsion to properly describe it; rather, it was in why we felt compelled to describe it in the first place, instead of just letting it be.

Listening to him, Charlotte thought she knew what he meant. She felt that mysterious Something herself whenever she came to see the babies. Sure, they were helpless. They couldn't feed themselves. They couldn't talk. They had to lie in their own waste until someone handled it for them. And yet, at the same time, they were emissaries from a celestial otherworld, the most perfect beings on earth. To harness science and compassion in their service, as Artinces had done, was, to Charlotte, the ultimate incarnation of the Holy. Reveling in it, she had determined to be a healer.

When Charlotte first got to River Valley, she learned that the science part of her calling was heavier duty than she had previously realized. Her high-school teachers had been diligent but they frequently worked with outdated material. She was dismayed to find that her science textbooks had been, on average, about 12 years old.

"Surprise, surprise," Percy said when she whined to him about it. "That's the essence of Negro education: catching up. And you thought 'separate but equal' was all in the past."

Unlike Percy, Charlotte had to knuckle down and actually study. As her Organic Chemistry final loomed, she was forced to acknowledge that she'd neglected her books all spring. She hadn't spent that much time with Percy; he was more off than on at that point. But that didn't stop her from sitting at the Soldiers or taking solitary moonlit strolls under the constellations that he had pointed out to her.

Finally, Laurie Jo pulled her coat. "I'm going to talk to you like I talk to my own sister," she said as they sat in their dorm room. "You're really young. There's a lot of men in this world. Chances are you haven't run into the one for you just yet. The fellows you've known are probably just…dress rehearsals. Right now, your soulmate is somewhere else doing something important to make him become the man you need him to be. He might be in Michigan. Or California. Or Bangladesh."

Charlotte scratched the side of her nose. "Where?"

"I just like saying Bangladesh. Blame it on World Cultures class."

Laurie Jo made her point so persuasively that Charlotte chose to sit out the opening hours of Indestructible Black Consciousness Day and sequester herself in a cubicle at the library. Black pride could wait, Laurie Jo said. Organic Chemistry could not.

Charlotte strolled across the quad at midmorning, Bromo Seltzer bubbling in her stomach and a Lifesaver melting on her tongue. All around her, fraternity brothers and lettermen were busy transforming the dew-drizzled space into party central. They aligned barbecue grills and stoked them with charcoal, and set up a horseshoe pitch and a volleyball net. Sorority sisters and cheerleaders spread colorful blankets on the grass. On the second story of the education building, massive stereo speakers supported the raised windows. A banner with "IBC" emblazoned on it stretched across the front of the redbrick science building.

In previous years, the event had been christened Brotherhood Day. An all-day picnic in celebration of humanity's God-blessed kinship, it began with a psalm and ended with a benediction, all under the paternal guidance of the surrounding town's civic fathers. Charlotte's freshman year marked a change in theme that coincided with a change in student leadership. The student council president, sporting a sky-high natural and wearing a polished bone pendant dangling from a rawhide cord, became the newly anointed chairman of the board. The treasurer remained treasurer. The recording secretary became minister of information. The newly created post of minister of defense had so far remained vacant. In a dramatic gesture of strength, the new council struck down Brotherhood in favor of Indestructible Black Consciousness, launched without benefit of administration approval or funding.

The leaders laughed off rumors that River Valley's president, widely derided as a lackey of the white power structure, planned to intervene. "They think Jackson State's got us scared," the chairman had declared at a rally on the quad. "But it's just made us more determined."

"More determined to have a picnic," Percy said when told about the rally. "So that's what they mean when they talk about speaking truth to power."

The students at Jackson State had been demonstrating against the war, a far more noble cause, in Percy's opinion. Police troopers weren't so impressed. They fired on the assembly, killing two and wounding twelve. Students at River Valley held a candlelight vigil in support, amid a growing sentiment that peaceful gatherings of that sort were beginning to outlive their usefulness. The administration had stood pat, believing that students would soon go home for summer break and return the next fall with cooler heads. Meanwhile, less than two weeks after Jackson State, they were preparing to barbecue.

"Kumbaya," the traditional overture of Brotherhood Day, had been emphatically dismissed. As Charlotte mounted the stairs to the library, Nina Simone was wailing across the quad, threatening to break down and let it all out.

Late afternoon and the stubborn sourness in her mouth roused her from a brief nap. She raised her head from her table and slid her tongue over her crusty teeth. Fishing coins from her purse, she headed to the vending machine in search of a 7UP. She'd nibbled on toast for breakfast and pecked at crackers for lunch, but so far none of her methods had done a thing to reduce the bile insistently brewing in her belly. The sickness stemmed from a late-night encounter outside her dorm room.

She'd stayed in the stacks until closing time before stumbling sleepily to Taplin Hall. Once she reached her room, she let her bag fall loudly at her feet as she reached into her pockets for her key. Sighs and murmurs beckoned. She turned and saw Tish and the round-bellied man devouring each other's mouths. Tish's back was against the wall. The man leaned heavily into her, locked into place by her long, sleek thigh. Tish whispered encouragement as he rubbed his face into her throat, sucked at the hollow between her breasts.

Charlotte snapped forward and threw up, splattering the bottom of her door. The lovers paused and took in Charlotte's mess. Stunned, she returned the stare. The man disengaged from Tish, his pinky ring flashing as he popped his pocket square with a flourish. Charlotte thought he was going to hand it to her but instead he raised it to his own glistening brow. Chuckling softly, he kissed Tish's cheek with surprising delicacy, and walked past Charlotte to the end of the hallway, where he descended the stairs.

Tish smirked at Charlotte while she buttoned her blouse. "What's the matter?" she taunted. "Never seen how grown folks go at it?"

Charlotte glared. Apparently one slap had not been enough. "How could you?"

Tish took her time, getting her key out of her bag before replying. "How could I what?"

"That's sick," Charlotte sputtered. "Something's wrong with you. With both of you."

At last Tish caught her meaning. "Wait. You think because I call him Daddy that he's—you silly little girl. He's not my father. He's my pastor."

Charlotte retched again. Still bent over, she braced herself by placing one hand against her door. She didn't want to straighten up. Didn't want to look at Tish.

"Careful," Tish warned. "You almost got my shoes."

Standing at the machine waiting for her Dixie cup to drop and fill with fizzy liquid, she became conscious of a vague chanting. She figured the frats were stomping the yard as part of the festivities on the quad. But what were they saying? It was only when she got to the window, when she looked out and saw the policemen lined up with their hands on their holsters, that she could finally make out the words, rumbling up from the ground like hints of disaster.

"Jackson State!"

"Jackson State!"

Years later, some who claimed to be among the witnesses or, even more presumptuously, the activists, would swear that hundreds of cops, clad in riot gear and armed to the teeth, lost a bloody battle with an even larger gathering of fearless and fiercely committed students. In reality, less than two dozen semi-concerned officers kept watch over a roughly equal number of students. Acting on orders from the college president, the cops had come to shut the "illegal" picnic down.

The student resisters had removed the IBC banner that had been hanging across the science building. They held it in front of their thin, ragged line as they chanted. Behind them, perhaps 60 students watched and shouted encouragement from the steps of the science building. From her perch in the library lounge, Charlotte could just make out the stern faces on the front line: fraternity leaders, a football player or two, and the chairman of the board.

The chants grew louder. The policemen fidgeted. Out of nowhere, a stone sailed above the heads of the masses and struck an officer on the shoulder. He unsnapped his holster. The crowd chanted louder as a solitary figure ducked under the banner and approached the officers. Charlotte squinted, although it was entirely unnecessary. She knew that walk anywhere.

In her literature class, the teacher had marveled over Robert Burns's poem "To a Louse," in which he wishes that humans had the gift "to see ourselves as others see us." Charlotte hadn't been impressed. She remembered thinking that she already knew how men saw her; their actions throughout her life had made that painfully clear. What was the value in adopting someone else's perspective? In the end, what was to be gained? She insisted on her own point of view because doing otherwise would concede the possibility that she was just a member of the chorus in someone else's play. It would lend credence to the suspicion that she was the spear carrier, the expendable crewman, the scapegoat scribbled into the script to absorb the main character's pain. To take all the punishment and anguish so that the prima ballerina can emerge unscathed, tutu intact, all sparkles and twinkles and pink chiffon. But she was aware, so aware, of what any student in the frightened but unbending mass may have seen when he turned a curious head toward the library window: a small girl lost in clothes too big for her, nearly undone by fear.

The glass was an annoying barrier, a teasing nuisance that illustrated the vast distance between her and the ground, the space she had to travel. She ran like she drove, to hell with it and devil may care, so the three flights of stairs flew by in a burst of adrenaline as she threw herself through the doors and over the grass toward the gathering storm. But there's always someone faster, someone like Laurie Jo. She caught Charlotte in a matter of strides and wrapped her in her arms. She held tight while Charlotte kicked and screamed, a marginal player in the scene unfolding, far from the heat and glare of center stage. The spotlight, where Percy stood and gestured before the now-restless guns.

The photo that would appear two days later in the campus newspaper would provide few clues beyond the elements that everyone knew. The students, the cops. Percy in between them with his arms outstretched.

The crowd's roar dipped to complete, unbelieving silence as Percy and the policeman in charge shook hands. The roar returned, a resurgent bellow of victory, as the cops executed a crisp about-face and walked away. "Percy! Percy!" became the crowd's chant as the students mobbed their new champion. Their enthusiasm carried him to the upstairs reception area in the science building, where students had commandeered chairs, tables, and couches and transformed them into a makeshift lounge. Someone turned on a radio. Downstairs, platters of food and coolers of cold drinks found their way inside. Upstairs, Percy sat on a chair in the middle of it all. Students gathered around to await his word.

"What did you say to them?" the chairman asked, admiration glowing on his eyes.

"I recited some poetry," Percy replied.

"What?" The chairman's disbelief went through the crowd like a wave, sparking murmurs and exclamations in its wake.

"That's right. Music isn't the only art with charms to soothe the savage beast."

Percy stood on his chair and spread his arms as he had done on the quad.

> Ah, love, let us be true
> To one another! for the world, which seems
> To lie before us like a land of dreams,
> So various, so beautiful, so new,
> Hath really neither joy, nor love, nor light,

Nor certitude, nor peace, nor help for pain;
And we are here as on a darkling plain
Swept with confused alarms of struggle and flight,
Where ignorant armies clash by night.

"That's what you said?"

"That's it exactly," Percy said, warming to his audience. He was nervous, shiny, electric. "And the sergeant said, 'I like that. That was beautiful. Did you write that?' I said no, that was Matthew Arnold. 'Dover Beach.' I told him our forefathers shed blood over important things like land and freedom. I said to him, do we really want to shed blood over barbecued ribs? He said 'No, son, I guess not.' Then he told his men to stand down."

The chairman shook his head. It was just crazy enough to be true. "You're shittin' me," he said.

"No, Brother," Percy said, "I shit thee not."

The students erupted in laughter and applause. In the span of a few taut minutes, Percy had gone from the smartest (and perhaps the craziest) man on campus to the bravest.

"Percy," the chairman said above the clamor, "you should be our minister of defense. Our Huey."

"Yeah," Percy agreed. "Because I'm a regular Ralph Bunche, baby. Now that's what I call a mixed metaphor."

In the background, the radio hummed. Downstairs, a pair of frat boys, although exhausted by the day's excitement, were dancing energetically with a couple of cheerleaders when a third brother strutted in. He had been as far from the policemen as humanly possible, but in the story he was already composing for future generations he had moved to the front of the line, close enough to spit on a pig's polished badge.

His brothers shouted in greeting, exchanging knowing nods over the heads of their dance partners. They had gotten into something harder than Pepsi or 7UP.

Upstairs, Charlotte recalled Percy belittling the chairman earlier in the year for equating jazz with revolution. Too simplistic, Percy said. "It's a cliché, self-parody even, to pretend to dig jazz and scream about black consciousness at the same time. To argue that jazz alone is the people's music is like saying that suffering is the only 'real' black experience. If anybody contains multitudes, it's us."

The chairman had glowered at Percy while he ranted. Now, in the radiance of Percy's eccentric genius, he gazed at him like a love-struck fan. Percy blew Charlotte a kiss and she beamed, lightheaded and a little ashamed of herself for being so fretful. This was Percy, wasn't it? At his best, couldn't he do anything? Charlotte caught glimpses of his future in his golden glow: he'd get his PhD (with honors, of course), return to River Valley, and build a world-class philosophy department. In time he'd take over the College of Arts and Letters before ascending to the presidency. After a long and exemplary career and annual recognition as one of *Ebony* magazine's 100 Most Influential Blacks, he'd retire to a life of pastoral splendor. On campus, a statue would go up in his honor, right next to the Soldiers.

Though she adored every syllable that Percy spat (damn that Tish), she knew the events of the day would eventually wear him down. Soon he'd be parched and hoarse. She wanted to be the one to quench his thirst.

She headed downstairs in search of a soda.

"The cops are gone," the frat boys needled their pal. "Good of you to come out from your hiding place."

"Too bad," the newcomer said. "I had something for them."

Charlotte reached the first floor. She turned, looking for the coolers she'd seen lined up earlier. When she found them she marched directly to them, barely noticing the frolicking frat boys and their giggly dates.

One of the dancing men howled like a wolf. "Nigger," he said, "where were you when the shit was going down?"

"I was getting this piece, fool. Not like I carry it around on me. Lock and load, like brother Huey says." The newcomer pulled a pistol from his waistband. The others had seen it before.

"Brother Huey, my ass."

"He means Huey the duck. Dewey and Louie's brother."

"Fuck y'all."

"I think he was hiding under his bed, calling for his mama."

"I think he was on the toilet scared shitless."

Undeterred, the frat boy spun it on his finger, like the hero in a cowboy drama on TV. *Gunsmoke. The Wild, Wild West.*

Charlotte heard their banter like white noise, the static between stations. She ignored the sideshow, eager to return to manic, magic Percy in the center ring. To jazz, Ralph Bunche, and "Dover Beach."

The first cooler was empty. Nothing inside but dissolving ice chips and brittle water.

"Bet you can't do that twice."

"Ha! That's what his girlfriend said."

The frat fool went at it again. The second spin was wobblier than the first. He grabbed at the gun with his other hand.

The second cooler held one can. It was on the bottom, leaning against the far corner. Charlotte bent over and pushed her hand into the icy melt. She plunged her face in after, and for a second she was a diver, leaving the world of heat and hubbub for a cool descent into the welcoming azure. She registered the sound of a shot as a distant underwater event, muffled, mysterious.

She raised her head, the chill lingering on her face like a cold hand against her cheek. She shivered, laughing at her impulse until she turned and saw two of the frat boys staring wonderingly above their heads. She stood and approached them. The one holding the smoking pistol swayed fitfully. The other steadied himself with his hands on his hips. Next to them, the third frat brother stood open-mouthed, an arm around each cheerleader.

Charlotte followed their gaze to the small hole in the ceiling. To the red drop forming as it hung suspended before falling precipitously to the floor. Another drop followed, then a thin, steady stream. In the room above them, somebody screamed.

She hurled herself toward the sound. Upstairs, she split the crowd like an arrow, not stopping until she reached Percy, sprawled on his back in front of his chair. She knelt beside him and took his hand. Although he was motionless, a nervous energy still surrounded him. He looked shiny, electric, unafraid. His eyes were aimed at the ceiling. But he knew it was Charlotte beside him. In the swirling background, she heard crying, prayers, calls for an ambulance.

"Here comes trouble," he said. His words gurgled, like a clogged drain.

"Shh, don't talk."

"You were right," he said. "There's no point in thinking about it all the time."

After the memorial service on campus and the burial in his hometown, Charlotte returned to Gateway City. She tucked her braid under her shirt, pulled her hat down. She took long walks and even longer drives. She swung from adolescent whimsy to downhearted blues, with long silences in between that left Artinces concerned and confused. She turned her collar against the intrusions of horny boys and curious neighbors. She carried books by W.E.B. Du Bois and Alain Locke and stared at the pages in isolated corners of coffee shops and diners. Though the words often wiggled and darted on the page, she kept at it, intent upon doing anything but remembering. *Forget* became the closest thing to a prayer that she ever uttered. Forget. Until she could no longer hear Percy's voice, his laughter. Until she couldn't see his skin the color of lightly toasted bread. Until she was no longer drawn to the water. Until she no longer dreamed of boats. All summer long she had been telling herself she could do it. She'd forgotten worse things.

No, that was a lie. Nothing had been as bad as this.

One of the babies began to stir. Charlotte leaned forward and peered through the glass. It was a girl, clad in the hospital's customary pink. Charlotte was tempted to hold her, to whisper in her ear. "His name was Percy Conway," she wanted to say. "And he wasn't a male type. He was a *man*." She stopped herself. It would be unfair to curse an innocent baby as she had been cursed, to send her down a difficult path without ever knowing why she was burdened, without knowing that someone else's sadness was dogging her steps.

She had to tell someone. Why not Dr. N.? The *whole* story. Tell her that her tale about being at the library during the shooting was only partly true. Tell her she needed a break from school before she broke into pieces. Tell her that walking around pretending to be normal was the hardest—only—work she could do.

She headed for the exit. As she left, she passed a man signing in. He wore a custom tailored suit and a hat rakishly tilted to one side.

"My name's Ananias Goode," he said to the nurse. "I'm on the list."

Despite declaring war against memories, Charlotte felt helplessly drawn to the site of the old church when she pulled up to a stop sign next to its ruins. Little was left of the building except the steps; like the rest of the block, the former Good Samaritan had been reduced to rubble as part of a corporate development campaign. Where there had once stood a church sign welcoming worshippers to Christ, there now stood a placard announcing the imminent construction of Killark Light and Power Co. Only a single streetlamp stood near the sign, conceding everything beyond the steps to the darkness of night. The street, formerly a hub of commerce, was now a one-way road to somewhere better, bordered on one side by cyclone fencing and on the other by the crumbling skeletons of abandoned buildings. Charlotte knew that the stone steps, cracked but still sturdy, had been important to the lives of many other babies besides her.

Charlotte was still looking at the steps when a car smacked violently into her Malibu's rear end. The impact threw her against the steering wheel, forcing air from her lungs. She opened her door and stumbled out to assess the damage. Before she could take two steps, her rear window shattered.

"That's her," someone shouted. "That's the bitch!"

"I said, would you like to hold a baby?"

Goode blinked furiously. He had the foggy aspect of a man emerging from a dream. The nurse waited patiently.

Goode smiled at her. "That's okay, I'll just look at them. It's my first time."

"You sure? Well, why don't you scrub in, just in case."

He grunted in protest but the nurse behaved as if she hadn't heard him. Before he knew it, she had removed his hat and replaced it with a surgical cap. She helped him slip a gown over his suit, turned him toward the sink, and showed him how to scrub. Goode felt like he was an infant himself, the way she guided him with confident, practiced gestures.

He took his post in front of the glass. The first time he had noticed Artinces Noel, she was standing in the very room into which he now peered. She was young, not long out of medical school. But she had looked comfortable with her authority, displaying an ease bolstered by principle and conscience. At the grand opening of the well-baby center, she posed for the *Citizen* photographer with one infant in her arms and four others arrayed on an exam table. When he saw the picture in the paper, Goode couldn't help focusing on the doctor. He liked the arch of her eyebrows, the upright posture and pursed lips suggesting that under no circumstances would she ever fall for the okey-doke. She had the kind of regal, self-assured profile that belonged on a coin.

Artinces had been after him for a while, urging him to visit the babies. "You'd be surprised how good it feels," she said. So there he was, not sure what he was looking for but looking nonetheless.

Earlier that day, Goode had stood at the bedside of his barely breathing wife. Barely breathing, barely there. Through the speakers at the corners of the room, Johnny Mathis demanded to be flown to the moon, a pitiless reminder of how utterly earthbound Goode was.

He was drying out, shrinking, finding new folds in his skin everyday. One day he'd be curled up in a hospital bed too, wearing a diaper and tubes up his nose. He used to think he wanted to go out in a blaze of glory. Now he just wanted to die in his sleep. Why did he feel so much older than he was?

Barely breathing, barely there.

The beep and whir of the machines.

Was she dreaming under there? When she twitched or shuddered, Goode had the idea that she was dreaming of falling, a long, breathless plunge through endless stories. But she never approached the ground. Never woke up sweating, thirsty for air, relieved.

Beep. Whir.

A pillow over her face could end the ache for both of them. He had been a man with muscular, even monstrous appetites. With his gambling, his death-defying criminal escapades, his many mistresses, and his myriad cruelties, he had crushed the life out of her long ago. According to his thinking, the pillow would be less a killing device than an instrument of freedom, a cushion for her to land on after years of descent.

Behind the glass, a baby stirred. The nurse appeared and bent over the cradle. She lifted the infant out and disappeared. Soon she was at his side, holding the blanketed bundle before him.

"How about for a little while?"

"I don't know."

The nurse placed the baby in his hands. He was a beautiful boy, brown and bright-eyed.

"You've held a baby before?"

"I have."

"Then you've got nothing to worry about. It's like riding a bicycle."

Children usually made him jumpy. He avoided them, especially boys. For years, every time he saw one, the boy turned into his Julius, dented and lifeless, still as a stone in the huge hands of Guts Tolliver.

Looking down at the baby, Goode smiled through his nervousness. "You're a big baby boy, aren't you?" he cooed. "A big boy. Yes you are."

To press the pillow down. To nudge her toward the peace that she likely longed for in some miniscule, still-flickering fragment of consciousness. To press the pillow down. Let her go. Set himself free.

In the space between the pillow and the ravaged countenance, amid the beep and whir of the vigilant machines, while Johnny Mathis crooned "Chances Are," insight arrived: this sleeping woman, once his whole world, posed no barrier between him and the elusive, rejuvenating calm that hovered just out of reach. He knew that losing her wouldn't help him find it. Her death would offer him no deliverance.

He wouldn't do it. Couldn't.

Tossing the pillow aside, he fell to his knees and wept, a silent, choking agony that left him windless and drained. Finally, he stood and brushed off his pinstriped trousers.

Maybe he had a heart after all.

The baby began to writhe in his arms, his little face wrinkling in anguish. The first few cries had squeaked from his lips when the nurse reappeared.

"You'd better take him," he said. "I think I scared him."

"Nonsense. He likes you. Just sing to him."

Goode shook his head. "I can't do that."

"I don't believe it."

"What would I sing?"

"Whatever comes to mind. You'll figure it out." She smiled and left him.

Goode took a deep breath. His mind traveled back to Liberty, to the memory of his mother's sweet voice. He was shooting marbles, a small circle drawn in their neatly swept dirt yard. His mother hung laundry a few feet away, pulling clothespins from her apron in pairs and holding them between her lips. The clothespins dangled as she sang. But they never fell.

"*Hush,*" he sang. The baby's movements slowed as his little body relaxed. Eyes wide open, he looked up at Goode. "*Hush,*" Goode sang again. "*Somebody's calling my name. Hush, hush. Somebody's calling my name. Oh my Lord, Oh my Lord what shall I do?*"

A CONFESSION FROM CHARLOTTE might very well have changed her tentative rapprochement with Artinces into something richer and more mutually assuring. They might have huddled at the kitchen table over cups of tea while Charlotte explained her wanderings, the great grief behind her peripatetic moods. Artinces might have shared something about her own past beyond platitudes and up-from-poverty clichés. She might have told the girl that she, too, had wrestled with the consequences of love. Charlotte might have told Artinces that she would never again give away her heart, because when you love somebody, something always happens. Artinces might have held Charlotte when the girl finally broke down. There, Artinces might have said, softly, like a lullaby, it's all right. At least somebody in this house knows how to cry.

But first they had to get home.

At the park, Artinces sat behind the wheel in disbelief as her car's engine repeatedly failed to turn over. She was tempted to slap her head in frustration. It had been a childhood tendency until the day her father caught her wrist in mid-air. She was six, her hair in pigtails with ribbons on the end. "Nope," he cautioned, "your brain's in there. Be kind to it."

So instead of slapping her head she hissed, slowly and loudly like a deflating tire. After a long day of working the booth and waiting in vain for the three women to reappear, she was close to exhausted. She searched in her purse, dipping her fingers blindly until they emerged with a business card. She gathered coins from a zippered pouch and walked across the street to the parking lot of A&U Barbecue, where a pay phone stood under a security light. She pushed a dime in the slot and dialed the number on the card.

"Hello," she said. "Mr. Reid? Wendell Reid? This is Dr. Artinces Noel. I'm fine, thank you. I'm wondering if you might be available to give me a ride?"

When Goode had his country retreat, before the Continental plunged into the lake and ended his flirtation with feudal pursuits, his men sometimes played baseball in a neighboring field. He'd join in occasionally, his suit jacket left behind in the farmhouse, shirtsleeves rolled up to the elbows, suspenders straining against the bulk of his chest. His men knew better than to pitch him high and tight or risk beaning him with a curve. They knew to lob something soft toward the plate and wait for him to wallop it past the deepest man, to greet his home run with requisite cheers and the gravest respect. To shout encouragement as he took his gentlemanly jaunt around the bases, Josh Gibson in custom boots, stogie clenched between those powerful teeth.

White men loved baseball, he'd tell his men after the country breeze cooled their sweat and they cracked open beers under a canopy of maples and oaks. With its fenced-in frontiers and diamonds carved out of cornfields, baseball was the American Dream played out under the lights. You could start out in the batter's box with hope and a stick, steal your way across the heartland in search of a big score, and end up a winner by the time you got home.

But white men would soon hate it, he continued.

They'd soon hate it because, in places, like Kansas City and Indianapolis and Oakland and Birmingham, black men had grabbed hold of the national pastime with their black hands and dragged their jazzy flair from Jim Crow sandlots to Ebbets Field and the Polo Grounds. They circled under pop flies with deceptive ease and turned double plays like wizards of the air. Jackie Robinson was only the beginning; it was a new game now. Soon, only the ball would be white. They'd hate it because they made the game and we're remaking it. They made the country from black sweat, Indian blood, and grand theft. If we can remake their game, we can damn sure remake the country.

Three beers in and Goode would be ballistic, proclaiming his expertise on the art of making and remaking. "Just look at me," he'd declare. "I'm one self-made motherfucker." Hadn't he come from Liberty with little more than the lint in his pocket and a talent for inflicting pain?

His men, stretched out in the grass and tipsy themselves, eyed one other nervously, lest Goode's temper take a fearful turn. If he kept it aimed at white folks, they were safe. If he aimed it inward, they were safe. Sometimes he went down to the lake and raged at his own reflection.

They call baseball the national pastime, he ranted, and they love it sure enough. But the real national pastime is crushing niggers. So crush or be crushed, goddamn.

He might be from Mississippi but his mama didn't raise no fools, he'd say. He knew the rules, he'd say, and if he ever struck out he'd go down swinging.

Back then, everything was an argument to be proved, a score to be settled. But now he was standing in the well-baby center at Abram H., holding a baby in his arms. The infant's fresh innocence was a shock to his system, a balm to his soul, and all he wanted to do was forgive. Forgive his wife for never forgiving him. Forgive Artinces for refusing to save him. (For whom had he ever saved? Not a single soul.) Forgive himself for asking her.

Because he still had business to take care of, Goode's upstart compassion was not expansive enough to include those who had foolishly dared to cross him. Of late, only one misbegotten individual had been so reckless: Sharps.

That thing about keeping your enemies closer? Damn straight.

Thinking about Sharps brought to mind another of Goode's countryside homilies, delivered to his disciples as they sucked down their beers: a skunk can spend all day in a garden, rolling around in the roses, eating them, shitting them, but when the sun goes down his black ass is still gonna stink.

That perfumed chump had been fouling his air for long enough.

Pretending to be stupid had been torture. But he had to bumble along as if clueless until he discovered what the hell Sharps was after. The idiot overestimated himself when he tried to follow his boss one Wednesday. Goode, on his way to meet Artinces at the Riverbend, shook him long enough to place a call to Grimes. The detective caught up with Sharps at the edge of the bridge.

"I work for Goode," Sharps said when Grimes pulled him over.

"Don't know him," Grimes quickly replied.

Sharps lowered his sunglasses and looked directly at him. "It's me, Sharps."

He got silence in return. "I work for Goode. Ananias Goode."

"I'm going to tell you again that I don't know him."

"But I thought—"

"Don't think and drive. It's a dangerous mix."

"What's the problem?"

"Your brake light's out."

"No way. I just had this car tightened up from stem to stern."

Grimes turned and walked to his unmarked cruiser. He came back with a baton, which he swung at Sharps's taillight, shattering it. He returned to Sharps's window. "I got a good look at it," he said. "I'm pretty sure it's out."

He wrote Sharps up and sent him on his way. By then Goode and Artinces were long gone.

Goode had planned to send Guts after Sharps, knowing how much the big man detested him. But then he saw the strangest thing. He'd pulled up at an intersection beside Fairgrounds Park and spotted Guts on the playground, pushing his girlfriend in a swing. Guts looked ecstatic, transformed. His happiness removed years and pounds from him, making him look as young and uncorrupted as the strapping youth Goode had noticed outside the train station so many years before. He liked seeing that young man again. Seeing that joy. So he called Grimes instead.

When Grimes got the call he was doing what he always doing while off duty: sitting on the couch in his front room, staring at the painting on the wall. His wife, Virginia Grace, was upstairs cleaning the bathroom, it sounded like. He could hear her humming as she worked; some defiantly cheerful church song, something that reminded him of *when you're happy and you know it clap your hands*. Her humming was soft and reliable. It didn't ride above the other sounds, the gently controlled splashing and the brisk-brisk of a scrub brush, so much as it accompanied them, melody marching to harmony's dependable beat.

When Grimes was not on call, when he was not rolling eagle-eyed through North Gateway and scooping low-life, double-dealing vermin from its deep black streets, he sat on the couch. He looked at the portrait of Cheryl, his only child. It had been three years since leukemia swooped in and swept her up. Seven weeks from diagnosis until that terrible ceremony, the preacher mumbling bullshit (*bullshit!*) about ashes and dust and God's will, Virginia Grace leaning heavily against him under a black umbrella while the rain poured.

On the job, some colleagues—and some criminals too, if pressed—would describe Grimes as spooky. The more charitable among them might call him intense. For the grieving, unbelieving couple, their dear Cheryl still lived and breathed. Not Cheryl was. Cheryl is. Every day the Grimes set a place at the table for their daughter. They continued to cook the meals she favored. They included her in any conversation suitable for 12-year-old ears. They laughed at tender suggestions from concerned relatives, who murmured that Cheryl was not there with them but in some better place, free of pain and suffering. And Virginia Grace cleaned, forever on the lookout for germs, evil bacteria that could assault their little girl, subject her again to the demonic fury of disease.

They were united in this sustained illusion, Detective and Mrs. Grimes. It bound them as tightly and warmly as the love nurtured across nearly two decades of wedded bliss.

Tall and brown-skinned, Grimes was one of two black detectives in the entire city. While his policing skills were beyond dispute, most observers credited his promotion to his mysterious relationship with Ananias Goode. The men had never been seen together, but informed observers swore that Grimes was Goode's inside man. With the support of a cooperative (and well-compensated) precinct captain, he showed up at opportune times to grease the wheels of law enforcement on Goode's behalf. He did indeed receive "bonus pay" for his extracurricular work, but evidence of it would be hard to find. He was squirreling it away for when he was done protecting and serving. He planned to supplement his pension with enough capital to live in other climes, far from annoying relatives who had limited ideas about life and death.

Weeks after receiving the assignment from Goode, while the reformed gangster held babies in Abram H., Grimes sat on his couch like usual. Hands on knees, he admired Cheryl's portrait. Reuben Jones of the Black Swan Sign Shop had created the painting from a handful of photographs, the only ones they had.

Something else, that Reuben Jones. One hell of an artist he is.

As he got up to work the night shift, Grimes was thinking he needed another portrait of Cheryl. Maybe several. Maybe one for each room in the house.

Sugar. Flour. Bananas. Damn.

Pearl Jordan, soon to be Pearl Tolliver, discovered she was out of vanilla wafers. Strutting into the front room where Guts slept, she nudged him with her foot. Guts opened his eyes and found a foot between his thighs, the big toe flexed suggestively on his crotch. It was perfect, the foot. Slender, brown, exquisitely arched. Nails perfectly polished. He had never noticed women's feet before Pearl. In fact, he hadn't noticed hers until she proved as talented with her toes as she was with her fingers.

She lifted her foot and stroked the front of his pants, all along his inseam.

"I love you from head to toe" had once been just an expression to Guts. He knew better now.

"Hmm?" he said.

"I need you to go to the store."

He had dozed off while listening to the ballgame on the radio. Rip Crenshaw, closing in on his club's home-run record, had flied out in his only turn at bat. Earlier, Guts had stopped through Afro Day and spoken with the slugger while he was on a break from autographing glossy photos of himself.

"Uh-huh," Crenshaw said when Guts walked up to him in the presenters' hospitality tent.

"Uh-huh what?"

Crenshaw laughed. "You know exactly what uh-huh I'm talking about." He leaned close and whispered in Guts's ear. "You've been getting some."

"That's what you think?"

"That's what I know. You've got your swagger back."

Guts shrugged. "I don't know what you're talking about."

"Oh, but *I* do. That's why you took my advice with that Pearl. Be careful, though. Heed the voice of experience. Too much of that good loving can sap your strength."

"Doesn't seem to be hurting you any."

Crenshaw shook his head. "I've sworn off women, remember? That's the lesson I'm supposed to get from losing my ring."

"It's not lost forever," Guts said. "It's just temporarily misplaced."

"No sweat, brother. If it's out there, I know you'll get your hands on it."

"I haven't given up."

"It looks good on you, by the way."

"What's that?"

"Being domesticated. That's what your boy Nifty called it, right? You told me about it that night at the racetrack. He made it sound like you'd come down with a disease. Looks to me like you're in the pink. In the pink every day, I suspect. Did you catch that? Man, I'm one nasty All-Star."

Now Guts shook his head. "You are nasty. We talked a lot that night. I'm surprised you remembered."

Crenshaw tapped his temple. "Steel trap," he said. "You think I'm all reflex and bone structure, right? Let me tell you something. In my head I keep a book on every pitcher I face. Whether he likes to go inside or outside, high or low. Which pitch he'll go to in a jam. I just tell folks it's all in the wrists because I don't want to give away my secrets."

"Forgive me for underestimating you."

"Right on. I got to get back to the autograph booth. Can you believe I got a game tonight?"

"You can handle it."

Crenshaw grinned. "'Preciate the vote of confidence. Say, we get in the World Series, you'll be in the box seat right along the foul line." They shook hands.

Pearl removed her foot, bringing Guts out of his reverie. Aside from the nail polish, her apron, and her engagement ring, she was in her birthday suit.

"Vanilla wafers," she said. "For your pudding. Hurry up now."

Guts groaned. "I was out earlier," he said. "Why didn't you tell me about the cookies then?"

"Just go get them before I put some clothes on."

"Anything else?"

"Yeah, get some milk and eggs."

"Milk, eggs, and vanilla wafers, coming right up."

Guts kissed Pearl and headed toward the door. He stole a glance in the mirror before he left. Crenshaw was right. Being domesticated did look good on him.

Sharps had made them wait until dark before they broke in. Now safely inside, PeeWee scanned Artinces's bookshelves in her downstairs library. He heard Nifty overhead, thumping around like Long John Silver. Instead of a peg leg, the triple-jointed freak had a sword strapped to his waist. The weapon was slightly curved, like a cutlass, and nearly reached his feet. The plan had been to get in and out quickly, and neither Sharps nor PeeWee could see how the sword would help them do that. Nifty had insisted. He had been carrying it everywhere. For protection, he said. In case he needed to "cut a nigger down to size."

Sharps had cursed and sighed. "We don't have time to argue," he finally said. "Let's do this."

PeeWee had never seen so many books outside a public library. He pulled down a well-worn volume and glanced at the title. *A Book of Medical Discourses*. Boring shit, he should have known. When PeeWee had flirted with being a revolutionary, he'd carried around a copy of Eldridge Cleaver's *Soul on Ice*. He'd even cracked it open a couple times. But he'd never gotten past the first paragraph. He was surprised to see it on the shelf in front of him. What's this siddity bitch doing with revolutionary stuff?

When some bright but troubled young men had contacted Artinces about her research on infant nutrition, she actually flew to their Bay Area headquarters and gave them a crash course. They had plans to start a breakfast program. PeeWee had no way of knowing that. Even if he bothered to read the *Gateway Citizen*, he wouldn't have found it there.

Moving to the desk, he found a book spread open. Across two pages, a full-color portrait showed three white men dressed in old-fashioned suits. They stood around a black woman kneeling on a table. She was clad in a ragged sackcloth dress and her hair was wrapped in a red kerchief. Two other black women peered from a behind a curtain stretched across the background. One woman wore a kerchief. The other was bareheaded with long, black, woolly braids. Fascinated, PeeWee sat on a chair and looked closer. The caption read, "J. Marion Sims, Gynecologic Surgeon." The accompanying text described the "excruciating ordeal" of slave women Lucy, Betsy, and Anarcha. Apparently Dr. Sims had purchased the women and experimented on them repeatedly without anesthesia. Ultimately, his work led to improved gynecological and reproductive health for generations of women. The trio suffered, the book said, so that other women might experience the joy of good health and fertility. PeeWee saw that Artinces had scribbled a note in the margin. "There you are," it read.

"Weird shit," he muttered.

Sharps was concealed in the shrubbery when Artinces rode up in Vernon Reid's taxi. He waited quietly while the doctor politely rejected the old man's offer to walk her to her door. He stared, puzzled, as his diminutive prey appeared to have a conversation with herself.

Artinces hesitated. The three women stood resolutely in front of her door, silent and intimidating. The bareheaded one had lost her smile. Artinces took a step forward.

"Lucy. Betsy. Anarcha. See, I know who you are. And I know why you're here. You want to punish me for a mistake I made a long time ago."

The women remained silent, inscrutable, as if their appearance in this world had come at the price of speech.

"I understand that you didn't endure what you did so that women like me can do what I did. It was a long time ago and I won't define my life by the things I've done wrong. And I won't let you do it either." Taking a deep breath, she walked right through them.

When she entered the house, a slight movement—of feathers, it turned out—caught her eye. Leaving the door slightly ajar, she turned and looked at Shabazz. Clearly agitated, he hopped in a circle, thrashing his wings.

"Watch yourself," he said.

Upon hearing the bird, it occurred to Artinces that instead of merely blocking her path, Lucy, Betsy, and Anarcha had actually been trying to keep her out of harm's way, some danger that they had anticipated but to which she was blind. But realization dawned too late.

The glare from the other car's headlights made it hard to see. Charlotte saw two figures advancing on her. Before she could make out their faces, a solid punch to the solar plexus dropped her to her knees. Gasping, she looked up into the leering face of a brown-skinned man, not much older than her, thin, wiry, and quick. Peering from behind him, Young Mom emerged. The girl she'd fought with on the bus.

"Remember me, bitch?" she jeered. "I told you that me and Bumpy was gonna get your ass!" Still on her knees, Charlotte watched Bumpy raise his weapon. It looked like a table leg wrapped in electrical tape. She closed her eyes and flinched but Bumpy was just faking her out. Instead, he swung at her driver's side window, shattering it. Charlotte thought she'd have a chance if she could just get back to her car. Her bag was on the front seat. Inside it was Percy's gun.

She tried to get to her feet, but Bumpy casually planted his foot in her chest. Extending his leg, he pushed her onto her back. Charlotte began to scoot away from him, backward. Another car entered the street and slowed down. Bumpy waved his club at the driver. "Get on away from here," he yelled. "Mind your own goddamn business." The driver took his advice and screeched away.

"Say you sorry," Bumpy ordered. "Tell her you sorry and I just might let you live."

"Kiss my ass," Charlotte replied.

"What did you say?"

"I. Said. Kiss. My. Ass!"

"Aw, this bitch is crazy," Bumpy decided. "I'm gonna enjoy this."

"Bumpy!" Young Mom shouted. "Look out!"

Bumpy looked up, puzzled, as another car, headlights blazing, roared up to within three feet of him and braked to a halt. "Who the fuck is that?" Bumpy said. When he got no answer he advanced on the car, swinging his club. "I said, who the fuck—"

The driver's door swung open and smacked into him, knocking him to the ground.

"Bumpy!" Young Mom yelled again. She ran to him. The driver's door shut.

The door on the passenger side opened. Charlotte got up and ran around. She peeked in and saw the plump, familiar face of Guts Tolliver.

"Hurry up," he demanded. "Get in!"

Charlotte moved toward the seat but remembered her bag. "One second," she said. She retrieved her bag, took the keys out of the ignition, and returned to Guts.

Bumpy was holding his side and groaning. "This ain't over!" Young Mom shouted. "You hear me? This ain't over!"

Bored with the books and dissatisfied with the work assignments— he was nothing more than a glorified lackey, when he really should have been running things—PeeWee slipped his trusty World Series ring from his pocket and held it under the lamp on the desk. He never tired of that, turning the ring slowly as light slid through the jewel and threw blackness everywhere.

Dr. Noel sprung from the shadows near the floor and slashed his Achilles tendon with the scalpel she kept in her lab coat. "Ow! What the fuck?"

He dropped to one knee, enabling her to slice the same tendon behind his other ankle. While he wobbled, she grabbed her bust of Dr. Charles Drew from its pedestal and swung it against his head. PeeWee grunted and slumped to the floor. The ring fell from his hand and rolled into the hallway. Artinces heard furniture moving overhead, the sound of drawers being yanked out and tossed aside.

Sharps entered. He saw PeeWee on the floor, out cold. From behind the desk, Artinces hurled the bust at him. But it was too heavy to sustain much momentum and he easily avoided it. "Well," he said, "the doctor's in the house."

Guts's car was in motion before Charlotte yanked the door shut. He wasn't sure but it was almost as if the girl was angry with him.

"Are you following me?"

Guts shook his head. "Just picking up some vanilla wafers."

"I can take care of myself, you know."

"Yeah," Guts said, "I can see that. Want to tell me where we're going?"

"Just keep driving. I'll tell you when to turn."

They rode in silence for a while.

"You in college or high school?"

"College. I was, anyway."

"Why 'was'?"

"I might not go back. I want some time to think about things."

"To think? What are you, about 19?"

"Almost."

"Eighteen then. What you got to think about? You got your whole life in front of you. Opportunities. Good things."

"You think that? You really think that?"

The girl turned toward him, looking for an argument. He kept his eyes on the road.

Sharps had a wide-open stance, like a bull rider in a rodeo. Artinces threw herself at the opening, hoping to slide through his legs and slash at his testicles as she passed. But Sharps was as quick as he was slick. She got a piece of his thigh as he shifted his feet, inflicting only enough damage to make him mad. Sharps roared. He pressed his hand to his thigh, felt the warm trickle of blood.

"Bitch! If I didn't know any better. I'd think you were trying to kill me. Guess what—you're not the first."

He snatched her up as she tried to run. He punched her in the face and hurled her into a bookcase. Pain sizzled from her tailbone to her skull like oil poured into a hot skillet. An avalanche of books tumbled on her as she blinked, trying to focus. Twin images of Sharps swayed before her. Both of them were bellowing.

Following Charlotte's directions, Guts headed west on Delmar. The tiresome landmarks flashed as they rolled. Package Liquor. Chinese Food. Church.

The girl seemed calmer now, reflective. Despite her boyish disguise, Guts recognized her as the girl he'd saved behind the Comet Theatre. He'd seen her again at the grand opening of the Harry Truman Boys Club not long after. But not since then.

"What were you doing when you were my age?"

Guts thought a minute. "Nothing good, I can tell you that. Besides learning about love."

"What about it?"

"How hard it is to get over it. She was beautiful. And nice to me. Made me feel like right beside her was my place to be in this world."

"What happened?"

Guts glanced at the girl. She was pretty when she wasn't scowling. More landmarks flickered in the side-view mirror. Colt 45. Fried Rice. Jesus.

"It didn't work out," he said.

Summoning what was left of her waning strength, Artinces struggled to a sitting position. Breathing hard, she rested her back gingerly against the bookshelf. Her tongue felt thick and her mouth was full of blood.

Sharps leaned close to her face. He was done yelling. "Bitch, what all you got in here? You got Goode's shit? Where the stock certificates? Where the diamonds?"

She laughed. The man was making no sense at all. She spat a tooth into the palm of her hand. "Makes no difference," she said. "Diamonds, turnips, they come from the same dirt."

Sharps stared at her. Before he could reply, they both heard a car pulling up outside. "Shut up," he instructed. "Don't say a word." Muttering curses, he grabbed her by the hair and dragged her into the next room.

Outside the Noel mansion, Guts raised his eyebrows.

"You live *here*?"

"Dr. Noel lives here. I just take up space."

Guts insisted on walking Charlotte to the door. He sensed a wisecrack about to bubble forth from her lips. She surprised him by swallowing it. Instead, she accepted his offer. They got out of the car. She looked even younger out in the open, more vulnerable. At the porch, Guts noticed that the door wasn't completely closed.

There was also a pungent, familiar scent that set his nerves on edge. What was it Goode used to say? Something about a skunk.

He turned to the girl. "What's your name?"

"What?"

"Tell me your name."

"It's Charlotte. Why?"

"Charlotte, I want you to go wait in my car."

"Why?" She was sullen again.

"I need you to trust me. Have I let you down so far?"

"No," she replied. "No, you haven't." She almost smiled, revealing a comma-shaped dimple on one side of her face. It reminded Guts of something, but he couldn't put his finger on it.

"Okay then. I need you to go back to the car and stay there. Don't come out until I let you know it's safe."

Charlotte nodded. She jogged back to the Plymouth.

Slowly, Guts pushed the door open. On the floor in the middle of the hallway, a tiny object glittered on the marble floor. It was a ring. A World Series ring. What the hell was it doing here?

Bingo, he thought. He reached down and pocketed the ring. A streak of blood led him to the library, where he saw PeeWee stretched out on the ground. Books were strewn everywhere. A curtain was torn and one bookshelf was toppled completely over. A sculpture of a man's head sat on the floor in chunks.

PeeWee sat up and mumbled something about three women. Guts punched him and sent him back to sleep. Guts heard sounds of movement overhead, heavy breathing, something being dragged.

He stealthily climbed the long, winding staircase, arriving on the second floor without a sound. The torn-up interior of the master bedroom reminded him of the streets of North Gateway after the riots. The mattress had been slit and flipped over. The bureau and chifforobe were in splinters. Earrings, underwear, and necklaces hung from the ceiling fan. Any space not blanketed with discarded items of clothing was covered by papers, some still in neat stacks and others shuffled and tossed like playing cards. In the center of the room with his back to the door, calmly studying what looked like bank documents, stood Nifty Carmichael.

Guts began to creep toward him.

"Figured you'd be here," Nifty said.

Guts stopped.

"What? You surprised? Sharps ain't the only nigger that stinks. Except he smells like rotten flowers. You? You smell like blood."

Guts listened, mind racing. Something was different about Nifty. Besides the fact that he wasn't running in place.

"We been connected, me and you. Ever since that old bitch stepped in front of that bus trying to give me a quarter."

Whatever it was that was different about Nifty made Guts hesitant, unsure. Nifty usually shook helplessly in Guts's presence, teeth chattering, like a nudist at the North Pole. Sometimes he even wet his pants. Where was that Nifty and what had this impostor done with him?

"I don't just watch the streets, Guts. I watch you, too. I been studying you for years, waiting for you to get careless. Lo and behold, it finally happened. Love does that to you, right? Steady pussy makes a man weak. I seen you keeping company with that bitch that works at Aldo's. That's one fine bitch, finer than you're used to. I knew she'd have you limping soon enough. Knew I'd catch you one day, dragging a leg behind you and grinning like a fool."

Guts took a step toward Nifty. Instead of scampering like a rabbit, Nifty stayed put. He wagged a finger at Guts. "Not so fast, fat man. Daddy's talking. Where was I? Oh, yeah. So when a business associate approached me about taking down Ananias Goode, I signed on. Because wherever that motherfucker's involved, good-for-nothing Guts is bound to show his ass."

Guts leaped. He expected Nifty to run but he didn't, so Guts overshot his mark. He spun around, caught Nifty's arm and gave it a vicious twist, yanking it up and behind him. But there was no satisfying snap. Nifty popped his joints and wriggled loose, giving him just enough time to free his sword and catch Guts as he came at him again. He raised the sword and swung down with all his might. The blade entered cleanly, just where Guts's shoulder connected to his trunk. His eyes opened wide in wonder as he fell.

The whole room rattled when he landed against the ruined chifforobe. He slumped against it as dazed as a fighter caught between the ropes, sucking air while the referee counted him out. Guts's brain sent urgent messages through the nerves snaking along his damaged appendage, commanding it to rise, recover, revive. But his arm wasn't listening.

He was vaguely aware of Nifty crowing and strutting. "I told everybody," he boasted. "I told anybody who would listen that you'd gone soft. I told 'em you weren't as fast as you used to be. Guess I was right."

Guts struggled to stay alert. He shook off thoughts of his parents, Pearl, the ducks on the pond in Fairgrounds Park. He needed to be fully present with Nifty, to wait for the blustering freak to dance too close to his working hand.

"I bet you wonder where I got this sword," Nifty said. "Got it from Playfair. Naw, he didn't sell it to me. He wouldn't do that because he's too loyal to you. I stole it out of his Buick while he slept. You should see the things he has in that trunk. It's true what they say. He has everything a brother needs."

Guts scanned the room in search of something that could be turned into a weapon. His eyes landed on a framed photo that Nifty had knocked from Dr. Noel's nightstand. It was a picture of a couple in a nightclub, smiling against a backdrop of sequins and jazz. He saw that the couple was Dr. Noel and Ananias Goode.

Guts thought that he and Pearl should take a picture like that. He and Pearl.

Nifty held the sword like a bat. He moved it slowly through the air at a phantom target, like Rip Crenshaw warming up before the crowd. Guts slumped farther. He looked limp, sweaty, barely responsive. Watching Nifty, he thought of the Louisville Slugger in his trunk, the gift from Crenshaw. Why didn't he have the presence of mind to bring it with him? Nifty squatted beside him. "You should have killed me a long time ago, Guts. The North Side ain't big enough for the both of us. So I got to make some room. One of us has to go and it has to be y—"

In a quick, desperate move, Guts swatted the sword from Nifty's grip and grabbed his throat. He pulled him close and squeezed.

Nifty's eyes bulged, blood vessels straining against viscous yellow. Snot burst from his nostrils and his breath slowed to a whistle. Guts turned away. Nifty's struggles grew faint and finally still. Guts released him and he fell over, the sword lying flat under his body.

"Damn, never seen a nigger hugged to death before," Sharps exclaimed. He entered the room dragging a bundle behind him. The bundle was Artinces Noel.

"He got too greedy," he said. "I told him not to take you on, but he was smelling himself. I told him, 'Guts ain't too bright, but he's plenty strong. Maybe we should invite him to join our operation.' What a team we could have been, with my brains and your brawn. But you ain't much use with a broken wing. Look at you, bleeding all over the doctor's Persian rug." Sharps dropped the unconscious doctor near the door and got out a pearl-handled razor, the razor that once belonged to Rudolph Fisher. He crossed the room and leaned in close to Guts.

"Think of your reputation," he advised. "Go down strong, so your name will ring out. You don't want people saying you died crying like a bitch."

"Goode is on to you," Guts said.

"Ask me if I give a fuck," Sharps said, grinning.

"Grimes is on your trail. He has a badge. You should give a fuck about that."

Sharps grew serious. "Grimes? That spooky bastard's not in with Goode. He told me himself."

"Sounds like you fell for the okey-doke," Guts said, stretching his fingers under Nifty's corpse. "Didn't you say something about having brains?"

"I'm telling you they don't know each other," Sharps insisted. "That's bullshit!"

"Shh," Guts said. "I think I hear him now." He could feel the hilt of Nifty's sword at the edge of his fingertips.

"Stop!"

Sharps turned and saw Charlotte in the doorway, aiming a pistol at his head. Still on his back, Guts gripped the sword, raised it.

Sharps smiled again. To Charlotte, his leer looked reptilian. She could almost see the venom dripping off his fangs as he rose slowly to his feet.

"Say, Little Bit," he said. "Put that down before you hurt yourself."

Charlotte squeezed the trigger, just as Mr. Pippen had taught her. The gun's report was louder than she'd heard in the restrained confines of the Pippens' shed; it rang in her ears like a hammer dropped on a tin roof. Sharps ducked, and then slipped in Guts's blood. Losing his balance, he fell belly-first onto the sword. Calling forth all the vigor he had left, Guts ran him through, finishing the job. He exhaled. *Problem solved.*

He shoved Sharps away, then pushed him even farther with his 14 EEE.

Detective Grimes entered the front door. In the library he found bloodstained walls, overturned furniture, signs of a struggle. He squatted down and picked up an object with his black-gloved fingers, turned it in the lamp's faint glow. He saw that it was a tooth. PeeWee rose to a sitting position, moaning. Grimes punched him, putting him back under. He saw the bloody trail leading to the stairs. Following it to the second floor, he checked to see who was living and who was not. He scooped up any inconvenient evidence before using his radio to report a burglary gone terribly wrong. He waited for the lab techs and ambulances to cart away the broken and the dead.

But all that came after.

Before all that, Charlotte put the gun down. "Too much," she said. "Too much." She started to cry.

"Hush," Guts said, his breathing labored. "You did good. Gonna be fine."

Dizzy, she staggered over to Guts, lowered herself to the bloody floor and curled up against his torso. He wrapped her in his one good arm.

THE STRONG

ANANIAS GOODE SAT beside the bed of his unconscious wife. The machines beeped and whirred.

Mr. Logan sat on his front porch in his favorite chair. His lawn was freshly mowed. Crickets were singing and the sun felt good on his skin.

A few blocks away, Playfair loaded his deuce-and-a-quarter in preparation for the day's action. Gladys helped him.

Dr. Artinces Noel, bearing the scars of her recent struggle, sat at the kitchen table in her new house. She sipped tea while Charlotte talked. And talked.

At Fairgrounds Park, Mrs. Tichenor and Mrs. Means, co-founders of the Gateway City Horticultural Study Club, tended the Abram Higgins Memorial Garden.

Across the vast expanse of green, near the edge of the pond, Pearl Tolliver used one hand to toss breadcrumbs to the ducks. With the other, she held on to her husband, Lorenzo. He looked slimmer than he'd been in years and his arm was in a sling and encased in plaster. But he was feeling no pain.

The men of the Black Swan sat in bleachers alongside Softball Diamond No. 2. They drank from cold cans of Stag and Pepsi while Reuben Jones's youngest boy occupied his usual spot at the end of the bench.

The Little League infielders buzzed with chatter. The pitcher tossed warm-ups to the plate.

Lucius Monday, formerly hooked on cheap rotgut whiskey, had learned to get high on lemon meringue. He touched Reuben's shoulder to get his attention. Both men watched as Rip Crenshaw moved toward the dugout, riding a roar of recognition. Sunlight reflected off his World Series ring.

The All-Star spoke briefly with the coach, who gestured to Reuben's son. In the on-deck circle, Crenshaw helped him don his batting helmet, whispering in his ear all the while.

To a chorus of murmurs, 10-year-old Crispus Jones entered the batter's box. He relaxed as he'd been taught, his fingers cradling the bat. He watched the ball as it floated toward him in slow motion, big as the world.

The End

ACKNOWLEDGMENTS

I WOULD FIRST LIKE TO THANK MY ANCESTORS. In addition, many friends and relatives helped me complete this book, including my parents, Joyce and Irving Smith; my dear friend Fred McKissack, Jr.; my cousin Sal Martinez; and Doug Seibold of Agate; Joy Harris and Adam Reed of the Joy Harris Literary Agency; Linda Reisman, Paula Penn-Nabrit, and the late, dearly missed Charles Nabrit; and my colleagues at Emerson College.

Most of all, I am indebted to my wife, Liana, and our wonderful brood: Joseph & Sysseden, G'Ra, Indigo, Jelani, Gyasi, Genzya, and Amandla.